Two women, two worlds, hun
collision of their twin destinu

It's 1996.

Television journalist Morgan Reed is suddenly unemployed after a humiliating and very public divorce. Her estranged son Chad won't return calls. Escaping Philadelphia for the obscurity of a remote country village, she impulsively moves into the old Rectory. Soon unsettling paranormal events lead Morgan to believe that the house is haunted. When her charming but enigmatic neighbor, Victor Cenzo, invites her to collaborate on a documentary for the Milltown Historic Society, the two are drawn into a passionate but unsettling affair. As their research uncovers a long-buried village secret, smoldering karmic embers ignite, demanding retribution for sins of the past.

And in a parallel universe...

It's 1895

Evangeline Laury, wife of the village preacher and mother to three-year-old Willie, secretly yearns to be a great artist, but her domineering husband frowns upon such frivolity. When an opportunity arises, Evangeline gains his permission to attend classes with the renowned local Impressionist painter Daniel Duvall. A passionate affair results, climaxing in unspeakable tragedy. Mute with grief and shunned by her unforgiving husband, Evangeline ultimately summons the strength to seize her destiny and become one of the world's great female Impressionist painters.

THE ANGEL
Connection

JUDITH ANNE BARTON

ISBN: 0615687423
ISBN 13: 9780615687421

Blue Heron Press

To my mother who gave me the words and my father who gave me the will. And to my own Irish godmother, Lizzie

The Village of Milltown Bucks County circa 1895

Bucks County, Pennsylvania 1999

"Mom, wake up!"

I was dozing in the backyard, lulled by the dizzying perfume of my ancient lilac bush, now swollen with plump lavender blooms. The familiar fragrance hovered in the air, intensified by the warmth of the early afternoon sun.

I admit that I sleep more than I should. I am seduced by sleep. Sleep is my secret addiction, my hidden agenda. Little sips of catnaps, longer draughts of siestas, drunken all-night orgies of deep slumber.

You see, it's only in sleep that I'm truly awake, alive. And blissfully, so is he.

Just now, as I dozed, we'd been joyfully flesh to flesh, spirit to spirit, meshing and mingling through time and space. I tighten my embrace in a last lingering moment, then reluctantly open my eyes.

My son stands over me, his tall silhouette black and dazzlingly backlit.

I shift in the lawn chair, shading my eyes. "What?"

"Bad news," he says without preamble.

I sit up now, fully alert, bracing myself for whatever it is. "What?" I say, warily.

He pauses.

"Tell me," I say. *Don't tell me.*

"It's Madame."

Not totally unexpected, but still, a body blow. "Oh, no. Is she…?"

He nods. "Last night. In her sleep."

Guilt washes over me. "I should have been there," I say, thinking of her dying alone, wishing I'd visited more often.

Tears blur the cell phone that Chad passes to me. "It's her lawyer from Paris," he says.

I hesitate. This is happening too soon, too soon.

The lawyer's voice, though heavily accented, is assertive and to the point. After the briefest exchange of condolences, he asks the one hundred million dollar question:

"And so the time has come. What do you propose to do about *The Angel Collection?*"

The Rectory

ONE
CHAPTER

1996 Three Years Earlier

April in Paris.

The Musée d'Orsay sweeps up and up. Inside you can feel the ghostly space of the old train terminus, but now it's high-tech, and I'm disappointed to learn that the exhibit is way up on the top level, because I've been known to cry over heights.

But that's where the Impressionists are, so up we go, skipping past the Manets, Degases, and Matisses. My legs are wobbling, and I do not look down. Heights always remind me of my mother.

"Just because I'm afraid of heights, I don't want you to be," she used to say. This as I watched the sweat beads pop out on her ashen face whenever we crossed the Benjamin Franklin Bridge.

"I'm okay as long as I don't look down," she'd say, keeping a distance from the windows when we visited Daddy at his sixteenth- floor office on Broad Street. Through osmosis, I grew up leery of floor to ceiling windows, balconies, cliffs, tall buildings, fire escapes, and climbing to the tops of places like the Statue of Liberty or the lookout tower in Valley Forge Park. My mother, also claustrophobic and agoraphobic, refused to set foot on an airplane, never traveling farther than Florida, a three-day drive in the Cadillac.

When I was fifteen, my father cheerfully and determinedly booked me a plane ticket for the short hop from Philadelphia to Washington, DC. His wife's fears may have cheated her out of a full life, but he was damned if it was going to happen to his daughter. He wanted me to experience the thrill and adventure of flying. That first plane trip inspired me to travel the world, even if it meant risking the inevitable high place.

So here I am, climbing the steps of the Musée d'Orsay, rubber-legged and sweating, but determined to get to the top.

Initially I hadn't wanted to come. Hadn't felt like getting out of bed, really. And it wasn't jet lag. It was more like life lag.

After Kate and I had cut a deal that I would get up and get showered while she went out for pains au chocolat, I'd pulled the scratchy wool blanket up over my shoulders, trying to deep-breathe bad thoughts away. It's funny, because that reminded me of my mother, too. Here you are in Paris, I said to myself, *and you don't even want to get out of bed*. My mother never got out of bed before one in the afternoon. She'd stay up late every night drinking highballs and then Schmidt's beer until Jack Paar ended, then the late movie ended, then they played "The Star-Spangled Banner," and the TV screen went to snow.

In the mornings, my dad woke me up before he left for work. Mom never got out of bed to make me breakfast. I'd go into her room to bring her a glass of milk and kiss her good-bye. Her breath was sour-sweet, and she'd look at me through half-opened lids, say she loved me, and tell me I looked nice. Later, sometimes at school, I'd realize my slip showed or my socks didn't match.

But mostly it was a growling stomach I had to deal with. By ten o'clock I was famished, and even if we had early lunch, it was still an hour and a half away.

I told my first lie in fifth grade, when my stomach was growling. We were studying nutrition, and everyone in the room was supposed to tell what they had eaten for breakfast. One by one, kids stood at their desks and said, "Oatmeal with raisins and brown sugar!" or "Pancakes and sausages." As the teacher got closer to me, my heart thudded, and my brain raced. What would I say? I hadn't eaten breakfast, I never ate breakfast, my stomach was painfully, roilingly empty, and I was about to be humiliated in front of the whole fifth grade!

I decided to lie. For me, this was an original concept. When Miss Bury said, "What about you, Morgan?" I said, "Two pieces of French toast with maple syrup, and four slices of bacon, and a glass of orange juice." It was the best breakfast I could think of. French toast.

Now here I was in *France* and so depressed I didn't want to get out of bed. Maybe I should go on an antidepressant. I thought about my mother again. Back in the fifties, shock treatments were the antidepressants of the day. She endured them, dozens of them. One day, home from school with a cold, I rode in the backseat of our neighbor's Plymouth, while she drove Mom to the hospital for her shock treatment. I waited in the car for about an hour. When my mother reappeared, walking slowly toward the car in her gray gabardine coat, she looked bleached. White skin, white hair, even her coat looked white to me as I pressed my face against the window, willing her to feel better, to be happy, to be like other mothers.

Earlier this morning, gazing up through the casement window, I could just make out a slice of pale lemon Parisian sky. I heard the swish-swish of the street cleaners and pictured them sweeping the pavement across the square of Rue Vavin, the grass green of their overalls like thick flower stems bending this way and that. It occurred to me that in Paris even the street cleaners are chicly attired.

Then the downstairs double door rattled and slammed shut; Kate's feet thumped up the steps. I threw back the covers, and headed into the shower as her key turned in the latch.

Within a half an hour, we were on the Metro and heading to the Museé d'Orsay to see an art exhibition called *The Angel Collection*.

3

And now I've made it up to the top floor, where dozens of other ticket holders are slowly making their way into the gallery.

My mouth feels dry as I scan the artists' biographies carefully mounted on the wall at the main entrance to the exhibit. I'm thinking it's the vertigo that's caused the cotton tongue and scratchy throat. I wish I'd thought to bring a bottle of water.

As I focus on the biographies, my heart inexplicably begins to race.

Daniel Duvall, born Paterson, New Jersey 1859. Died, Giverny, 1936.

Angel, born Philadelphia, Pennsylvania 1872. Died, Giverny, 1952.

Daniel Duvall was a painter and teacher, whose style has been described as "American Impressionism." Inspired by the French Impressionists, Duvall developed his own naturalistic technique, building a reputation in both Europe and in America, where he taught in Philadelphia at the Pennsylvania Academy of the Fine Arts and at his Pennsylvania studio. Duvall soon became known as one of the finest of the New Hope Impressionists, dividing his time between Paris and his Bucks County farm, "Aquatong," where he worked and taught six months out of the year, focusing on the lush river landscapes and colorful portraits of his neighboring villagers.

Kate had ultimately lured me out from under my cocoon of self-pitying bedcovers by cheerfully announcing that this exhibition had its roots in Bucks County, Pennsylvania, where I'd recently, impulsively, decided to settle after the second marriage that left me with a bruised heart and a depleted bank account.

The erstwhile husband had been a well-known chef around town, even had his own local cooking show. We met when I was a television reporter assigned to do a feature story on him for the early news. His name was Pete Antraeus. He was charming, successful, sexy as all get out, and he and my son, Chad, became great pals. Chad started busing tables at Pete's restaurant while he was in film school at Temple and later, when he turned twenty-one, became a waiter. When Pete and I married, Chad took Pete's name, becoming Chad Antraeus. My son finally, gratefully believed that he was part of a real family.

Pete's restaurant, Antraeus, had been *the* place to wine and dine for most of the eighties, but then came the Philadelphia Restaurant

Renaissance, as it was called. Dozens of trendy new spots with hot young chefs began to draw clientele away from Antraeus.

We'd only been married for a few months when Pete asked me for thirty thousand dollars to invest in some renovations, plus hiring a new chef and a publicist.

He said he was burned out from the years of being on his feet in the kitchen and wanted to us to finally be able to spend our evenings together, snuggling in front of the fireplace in our recently purchased farmhouse in the suburbs. That sounded great to me. I had long ago grown disenchanted with hanging out at the bar at Antraeus after work, waiting for my husband to finish up in the kitchen. I was only half joking when I told him that I was afraid I'd turn into an alcoholic like my mother.

In addition to my substantial salary as a reporter, I had a moderate inheritance from my father, so money wasn't an issue. I handed over a check for thirty thousand dollars.

The search for a new chef and a new publicist didn't take long. Still, Pete continued spending long hours at the restaurant training his replacement, overseeing the construction, and meeting with the publicist.

Several weeks elapsed. When I asked Pete when the transition phase would be over, he was vague, said the renovations weren't going as well as he'd hoped and that some contractors had screwed him over. Then he asked for ten thousand dollars more. I balked, and he flew into a rage, shouting that all he wanted to do was ensure our financial security so that we could grow old together comfortably. A new image for Antraeus would guarantee that. How could I deny him this commitment to our future?

I relented, gave him the money, and continued spending my after work hours watching reruns of *Seinfeld* with a tray of takeout Chinese or Italian on my lap.

It was a Thursday night when Pete phoned from his cell to say he'd be later than usual. He claimed he had evidence that his bartender was stealing from the register and needed to go through piles of receipts. Don't wait up, he said.

Around four in the morning, the call came from the Atlantic City police. My husband, Peter Antraeus, had been involved in an automobile accident near the Aladdin Casino. He and his (female) companion had been taken to Sibley Memorial Hospital where he was being treated for a dislocated shoulder and broken ribs. The lady had been discharged earlier, but Mr. Antraeus needed a ride home. I told the officer to tell Mr. Antraeus to go fuck himself.

"I can't do that, Ma'am," he said.

Pete had gambled away my forty thousand dollars in the high-roller back rooms of Atlantic City. His "female companion" had been the new publicist *that I'd paid for.*

After the embarrassment and recriminations, my contract at the television station wasn't renewed. "Budget cutbacks," they told me. But I maintain to this day that the scandal of my embezzling husband cost me my career as a reporter. It was delectable fodder for gossip columns in all the Philadelphia papers. It was even picked up by the infamous Page Six in New York. My son was mortified. My own humiliation was complete.

So, after endless legalities, when the divorce was finally final, I'd followed the foggy whim of a broken heart and meandered to a place nobody ever heard of at what seemed like the end of the world. I, who had always sought the spotlight, now only wanted anonymity. Especially after that rag, *Center City Philly*, had published a *serialized* article about Pete and me. People whose loyalty I had never questioned offered up the most mundane and mortifying details of my relationship with my husband. As Judy Holliday said, "With fronds like these, who needs anemones?" I didn't know who my friends were anymore.

Some inner compass led me down a sloping country road into a sleepy little country village in Bucks County, Pennsylvania. The first house I looked at was a registered historic landmark. It had been the rectory for the Milltown Christian Church. For two hundred years it had housed the ministers of the church and their families. As I stepped across the threshold, the house just spoke to me, and it was as if I had no choice. I was pulled through the front door as if an invisible hand reached out and grabbed me. And then, wandering through those rooms, it was like my blood turned carbonated. I felt fizzy and light-headed. It didn't matter that there was only one full bathroom upstairs, with little more than a WC next to the little room off the kitchen. It didn't matter that there was no dishwasher, no pool for swimming my laps, or that there was a cemetery just on the other side of the church next door. It didn't matter that the barn was practically falling down or that the asking price was fifty thousand more than I'd planned on spending. I offered full price on the spot, and six weeks later, my mother's Seth Thomas clock was on the mantel over the fireplace, my books were on the shelves, my Villeroy & Boch china was in the cabinets, and I had my own post office box at the quaint General Store.

Within days of unpacking, I was struck by a crippling case of buyer's remorse, wondering what the hell I was going to do with myself: out in the country, miles from nowhere, clanking around in a creaky old house next door to a creepy cemetery.

I booked a flight, packed a suitcase, and bolted. Leaving town has always been my antidote to crisis. This time it was to Paris and my old TV cohort, Kate, an expat now living on the Left Bank.

But these post-divorce blues have been hard to shake. I'm scared to go home to a place that doesn't really *feel* that homey. And I'm still caught between heartbreak and humiliation, which is a kind of homelessness in itself. At least here in Paris nobody knows my pathetic story.

With a sigh, I return to reading the artists' biographies:

The painter known only as "Angel" was brought to Paris from Ireland in 1897 by the French art patron and manager, Paul Durand-Ruel. Introduced to her early work by Daniel Duvall, Durand-Ruel ultimately arranged Angel's first exhibition. That series of paintings, "Irish Country life," established Angel as an artist in her own right.

Suddenly, inexplicably, something lifts in me, and I feel a glimmer of hope, a kind of artistic communion. I make a silent pledge: I will recover. I will return to the house in Bucks County and really settle in. I'll write a novel, maybe, or buy some oils and canvases and paint the mysterious images that swirl and dive behind my eyes—maybe even get funding for a documentary! I'll take long walks along the Delaware River, and poke around in flea markets, and maybe even meet the real love of my life instead of another poseur.

I look up to see that Kate has hooked her purse over her shoulder and is heading into the gallery.

I hesitate, momentarily feeling a slight loss of balance and a sudden urge to go to the ladies' room. *Too much thinking*, I tell myself. Or maybe I'm still clammy from the dizzying climb. But there's no way I'm retracing my steps and subjecting myself so soon again to the heart-stopping heights. My thighs still feel as if they could faint on their own.

I breathe deeply and move toward the gallery. But as I pass under the arched entrance and into the room, my feet feel weighted, like I'm slogging through mud. Once more, I hesitate, momentarily surrounded by a group of boisterous students. They disperse, and suddenly I'm in a pulsing kaleidoscope of color: vibrant, lush, living. I pause, taking in the sweep of paintings by "Angel." There must be thirty of them, many life-size. The first grouping depicts various scenes from rural Ireland at the end of the nineteenth century. Robust men and black-eyed women, tousle-haired laughing children, rolling in the lush green grass, coaxing a cow into the barn, splashing one another with water from the pump. There's one painting of a gentle-looking woman hanging the wash, while a baby sleeps in a basket at her feet. Looking at them, a clot forms in my throat. I am stirred by some unspecified yearning, a kind of home-sickness. Then suddenly it's as if twin bees sting my eyes. Tears spring out, hot and fresh.

I circle the room slowly, dabbing my eyes, feeling silly. I force myself to pause for a long time in front of each painting, measuring my response and realizing that I have an odd, intense desire to climb into each frame, to touch the people. To say, *"I'm here! I'm here!"*

After some time, and with a kind of confused reluctance, I move into the next room and am galvanized by the paintings of Daniel Duvall that he called "The Angel Collection."

The light and radiance of the first paintings that I see create a new burning in my eyes. At the same time, I have the sinking sensation that I am crossing a threshold into a scary place. And then, yes, out of my peripheral vision, I sense paintings that are dark, very dark. Warily, and with a drumbeat in my chest, I begin to circle the room, daring to raise my eyes to the paintings. As I connect with the images, small explosions of emotion ricochet from my throat to my groin.

A luminescent portrait of the woman called Angel, painted by Duvall. Her long arms are outstretched, as if in benediction. There is a dazzling radiance about her, an aura. He painted her as if she truly were an angel.

Gazing at her, something warm and viscous floods my insides, pool-ing and thickening between my legs. I feel the blood rise to my cheeks and am somehow vulnerable, exposed. I squeeze my thighs together, self-consciously reworking the knot of my scarf. I cast a surreptitious look around to see if anyone is looking askance at me.

The next painting is of a mother and child resting in a meadow near a manger where lambs nuzzle and play. At first I am charmed by the idyllic scene, then a shadow, like some lowering, fast-moving cloud settles over me. My fists clench involuntarily, and oddly, so do my teeth. It's as if I am girding myself. And then my heart picks up its racing, and the clot in my throat thickens, blocking the oxygen. The scarf is strangling me, and I yank it off.

Mother. Child. This is a reminder that I do not need.

Another reason for my recent depression: my own son, my Chad, is lost to me.

Hello, little man.
How are you today?
You are my darling boy.
And I love you so.
Our own silly little song.

Gazing at the painting of the mother and child, thoughts I've barricaded come flooding in.

You stole my childhood, Mom!

Chad, no.

You destroyed our family! Twice! I don't even have a fucking name anymore!

You know I could never have stayed with Pete after what he did! And your real father hit me back then! You remember it. I had to leave to protect you!

Yeah, you have real talent for picking men! And me always in the middle. All that "you're the man of the house" crap.

I never meant to burden you.

You forced me to be your surrogate spouse! I'm always running around, trying to pick up the pieces of your life.

Oh! The pain of those accusations! I've stubbornly told myself it's the damn therapist who put these ideas in his head. The therapist that *I'm* paying for. Am I too defensive? Really, though, where else would he come up with a term like "surrogate spouse"?

We'd been inordinately close. For so long it was just the two of us. He always sensed when I was upset about something. He'd cuddle me and tell me everything would be all right. "I love you, Mommy. Don't worry, *I'll always love you.*" Single mother and her only child, we were each other's world. How was that wrong? Okay, maybe I made mistakes, but doesn't every parent?

I make a conscious effort to stop the monkey mind, staunch the panic. Resolve to take up meditation. Or shock treatments. *Only kidding.*

I turn from the mother and child scene in the meadow. It's too much. I look around and find myself confronting a painting that utterly resonates with darkness. Gone the idyllic meadow, the gamboling lambs; gone the lovely young mother caressing her golden-haired toddler.

I see:

The thunderclouds. The waterwheel. The pond. The inky water, just deep enough.

My insides begin to scatter. I am biting my tongue to keep from shrieking. The room topples sideways, and dazzling points of light strobe my eyes. I stagger toward the exit sign, fighting nausea. Out on the landing, I brace myself, leaning into the wall, not looking down. Under my feet the floor seems to give way; my body is spinning out, disintegrating. I feel myself falling down, down. Then everything goes black.

Daniel Duvall's Studio at Aquatong Farm

TWO
CHAPTER

Bucks County, Pennsylvania—1895

I have escaped!

Morning sunlight is casting a giant's handful of dancing diamonds on the surface of the river, and my heart is dancing too, because I am out of the house and on my merry way to buy new colors. My enquiries in the village regarding where I might replenish my artists' supplies have led me to the Lumberville Emporium, and I am giddy with visions of smooth, plump tubes of paint and multitudes of sable brushes.

As the wagon bumpity-bumps along Old Milltown Road, I gaze down at the bobbing halo of coppery curls on the bench beside me, and I gently lay my hand on the silken softness of my son's head.

I begin to sing to him, "To market, to market to buy a fat pig! Home again, home again, jiggity–jig." He laughs and sings along with me.

The road follows the graceful bend of the Paunacussing Creek through the woods and past several mills. There is a bit of traffic, with mule-drawn wagons loaded down with logs and barrels of linseed oil, and an agitated flock of sheep bleating in consternation as they are herded toward the Fretz wool mill. Willie giggles and tries to imitate the sound.

"Look, Willie!" Skittering across the road in front of us is a group of rather large, comical-looking fowl—wild turkeys, I surmise. To our left, rising from the creek with a spread of his heavy yet graceful wings, a silvery blue heron glides downstream toward the river. The woods are thick. There are hemlock, oak, and maple, sycamore, ash dogwood, and fir trees, too. All commingling and pressed close together—impenetrable, mysterious, reassuring somehow.

Turning off Old Milltown Road onto River Road, I am unprepared for the sight of the river. Here it is, the Delaware—the same river that hugs the shores of Philadelphia, so far away now. As I gaze at the barges and ferries that float smoothly upon its waters, I have a sudden yearning to be on board one of them. To be a passenger, or an animal, or a log, or sack of grain, to float down, down, not stopping until I am home again, until all that I have left behind in Philadelphia is mine to embrace and cherish once again.

The Delaware Canal runs parallel to the river, and workers are loading crates onto a mule-drawn barge that is poised at the lock just adjacent to a rambling stucco building housing a tavern and hotel. The swinging wooden painted sign over the entrance says, "Black Bass Inn; est. 1720." Across from the inn I see the Lumberville Emporium.

"Look, Willie! That's where Mama is going to buy her paints."

He smiles up at me. "Are you happy, Mama?"

"Yes! Yes, Willie, darling. Mama is so happy!"

Being careful to keep my distance from an enormous jet-black stallion restlessly pawing the mud, I fasten Jeremiah's reins to the hitching post and lift Willie down from the wagon.

"Come along, mama's big boy," I say, squeezing him tightly and setting him down on the ground. I feel the moist softness of his hand in mine.

"Mind the puddles," I say, leading him around several deep ruts filled with brackish water.

Just as we step onto the little porch that leads into the store, the door flies open, almost whacking us, and a man comes bounding out. I shrink back, instinctively tightening my grip on Willie's hand. Seeing us, the man stops quite suddenly, catching the door with his arm before it slams shut.

"How rude of me," he says softly. His voice seems to quicken the air around me; his gaze is so intense that I can't speak.

"Did I hurt you?" he says. "Or the child?"

Still tongue-tied, I shake my head, self-consciously pushing a stray tendril of hair behind my ear. I feel a queer uneasiness.

His face is arresting in an oddly good-looking way, but his overall appearance, unkempt, as if he had not slept for days. His hair is an unruly dark mass falling almost to his shoulders. His eyes are feral, but the irises almost cerulean and piercing. As he looms over me, holding the door open, it is obvious that he hasn't bathed in days. Yet I'm somehow compelled by him.

"Ow, Mama!"

Without realizing, I am crushing Willie's hand in mine. Red-faced, I quickly let go.

Still holding the door and arching an amused eyebrow, the man bows ever so slightly.

"Madam?"

"Thank you," I finally manage, but it comes out like a starched hanky that has been on the clothesline too long. He steps aside for me to pass. Then I realize that Willie is no longer at my side.

The man lifts his chin toward the road: "Your little one seems to be exploring the depth of that puddle."

I turn quickly, bounding down the steps, voice shrill as a harridan.

"Willie, look at you!" I lift him up by the arms and set him firmly down on dry ground. "I told you to stay away from the puddles. Look, your boots are soaked through! You'll catch your death!"

He begins to cry, and I feel guilty. I kneel down to him and pet him. The stranger watches with amusement, and I wonder if he judges me too strict a mother, or too soft.

Over my son's wails, I say, "Well, Mama told you not to go near the puddles." I take his hand and start toward the steps again, feeling like a ninny, as if it were I who had dirtied myself in the mud.

As I lead Willie into the store, the stranger mounts his horse, the black stallion. He looks back at me, almost mockingly, then flips the reins, kicks his heels, and takes off at a cantor down River Road, splattering mud in his wake.

"What can I do for you today?"

The proprietor of the emporium is a round little man with a big belly, bushy eyebrows, and a full, fluffy gray beard. He reminds me of Saint Nicholas.

"I'm Mrs. Laury, from over in Milltown. My husband, Reverend Laury, is the new minister at the Milltown Christian Church."

"Oh, yes, Mrs. Laury, I hear tell that your husband is doing admirable work over there in Milltown. Permit me to welcome you to the community. I hope to come to a Sunday service soon."

"You'll be most welcome, I'm sure," I reply. I then state my purpose for the visit. "Mr. Presto at the Milltown General Store said that you carry art supplies? Oil paints and such?"

"Indeed I do," he says, gesturing expansively toward the back of the store. "A whole selection over there by the dry goods." I turn in the direction he is pointing. "May I ask, is it yourself you're shopping for?"

"Yes, it is."

"Well, well, an artist and a preacher's wife, too. Did you see Mr. Duvall on your way in?"

"Mr. Duvall?" I say, turning back to him.

"Daniel Duvall. The painter."

"That man was Daniel Duvall?" I try to summon my composure as I realize that the discomfiting scene with my son was witnessed by one of the most important artists of the Impressionist movement. Why, Daniel Duvall is well known even in Europe! The familiar flush creeps up my neck, leaving telltale blotches in its path.

"He lives just down the road at Aquatong Farm. Back there in the woods past the quarry. Beautiful spot, like something out of a picture book."

"You don't say?" I reply, imagining how my classmates at the Academy of the Fine Arts in Philadelphia would squeal in envy upon hearing of my encounter. Of course I would leave out the embarrassing details. I move eagerly toward the rear of the store, dragging Willie behind me.

"My feet are cold!" he whines.

"Well, that's what you get for playing in the puddle. Mama told you."

"Carry me!"

Trying to ignore his importunings, I focus on the wall of goods in front of me. What joy! A shelf lined with dozens of thick, shiny tubes of every color I could desire, and a display of brushes, every size and shape, and sketchbooks, rolls of canvas. Maybe the proprietor really is Saint Nicholas, because the sight of all these beautiful supplies seems like Christmas to me. I stand there, looking, loving the sight of it, savoring the possibilities, the decisions I might make, feeling quite the artist. After all, hadn't I just met Mr. Daniel Duvall, and wasn't he, in effect, practically a neighbor?

Willie pulls on my arm, still sniffling. "Mama, carry me," he whines, clinging to my skirts.

"Oh, Willie! You try Mama's patience," I say, sweeping him up into my arms. He immediately wraps his legs and muddy boots around my waist, lays his silky head on my shoulder, and commences to suck his thumb.

Tenderness overcomes my vexation. "First you get mud all over yourself, and now it's all over me, and you won't even let me look at the paints," I say, rubbing his back in a circular motion and kissing his hair.

"I should have left you home with Lizzie," I say absently, scanning the tubes of oils, wishing I could hold each one in my hand just to feel the cool, smooth weight of it, but I need both arms to hold Willie, and if I put him down, he will start to cry again, creating a scene. I move back and forth in front of the shelf, longing to linger there, to draw out the decision making, but my back is beginning to ache, the bones of my corset pressing into my ribs where Willie's knees encircle me. I choose a fresh tube of zinc white and one each of viridian hue, cerulean blue, and Indian yellow. And a tiny round brush for detail work.

I set the brush and paints on the counter. That's when I see the handwritten poster.

Commencing the third week in April, Mr. Duvall will
hold classes in oil painting.
Thursday afternoons at Aquatong Farm.
All levels. Tuition two dollars.
Those interested may leave word at the
Lumberville Emporium.

❧ ❧ ❧

"William?"

I have tucked Willie into bed, and I am summoning the courage to speak to William. He sits stiffly at the dining room table, deeply engrossed in a pile of papers and a black leather-bound accounting book. He doesn't look up.

I perch on the chair opposite him, feeling as if my nerve endings are unraveling. I am exhausted from the dozens of conversations I have already conducted with him in my brain. I am afraid. Afraid to broach the subject. As long as the words remain unspoken, the art lessons are a possibility. The starched white collar of my husband's ministry encircles his neck like a benign noose. I realize that it binds me as well.

I take a deep breath. It comes out as a sigh.

"Is Willie down, then?" he says absentmindedly, still studying the figures in the book.

"Yes." A pause. "What are you doing?" I ask.

"The accounts from the church. They haven't been tended to in months. I don't know how I'll ever get it all straightened out. The Lord has given me an awesome task. Awesome."

"Maybe I can help you," I venture. You know I'm good with figures."

His nose remains buried in the book. "Oh, that's kind of you, my dear, but I fear I'll have to work this out on my own." He pulls off his spectacles and rubs his eyes.

"William?"

"Mmm-hmm?" Replacing the spectacles, he writes some numbers on a piece of paper.

"May we speak for a moment?"

"Can it wait, Evangeline? You can see how much work I have to do."

"I'm sorry, but I'd like to speak to you about something that holds importance. For me, that is."

"What's important is this ledger."

He returns to his figures. I fiddle with the ruffle on my sleeve.

"Fix me my cup of chamomile, will you, my dear?"

As I wait for the kettle to boil, I notice a pale ray of light seeping from under Lizzie's door. She is writing a letter home tonight, to Ireland.

I return to the study, bearing the steaming teacup like an offering. I've set a lemon cookie on the saucer.

William sips, his lips pursing. "Ah, just the way I like it. And a sweet. My good girl."

I wait as he sips and swallows again, watching the bob of his Adam's apple. He replaces the cup on the saucer and lifts his pen. I clear my throat delicately. "May we speak now?"

He sighs, puts down the pen, and leans back in his chair. "Very well, what is it that can't wait?"

Choose your words carefully!

"I learned today that the artist Daniel Duvall, a fine artist, quite respected—not just here in America, but in France, too…Well, he lives nearby, at a place called Aquatong Farm—can you imagine? A person of such eminence?"

"Probably a reprobate."

"I think not. I heard from two ladies at the General Store that he is quite admired hereabouts." *A little lie.* "In particular for the painting classes that he offers."

"I know what's coming, and the answer is 'no.'"

"Oh, William, don't. Please don't refuse me out of hand. You know how I've missed my classes in Philadelphia and how much I've missed being able to paint, what with Papa's illness and our move here to Milltown and all the responsibilities that come with settling in."

"Evangeline, our mission in coming here six weeks ago was to resurrect the church and to serve the community in the name of our Lord."

"I know," I say in earnest, "I know. But I can be a good minister's wife and have my painting too! I always have, haven't I? In the five years that we've been married?"

"This is not Philadelphia society. We must build from the ground up. These people are farmers, mill workers; they need guidance."

"William, I give you my sacred word. I will organize the Ladies' Bible Study, and choir rehearsals, and Sunday school, and perhaps even a youth fellowship group—"

"In addition, you will be expected to be involved in charitable works, Evangeline. Not frivolity. Your father, rest his soul, indulged it, but you were younger then. It's time to put away such childish notions. If for nothing else, then for appearances' sake. You're the minister's wife and Willie's mother; you must be a model of propriety."

"It would only be a few hours a week."

Ignoring me, he says, "Quite frankly, if you require a pastime, it would be much more useful to me if you joined the Milltown Ladies' Quilting Bee. Find out what people are gossiping about; I can't be everywhere at once. You have to be my eyes and ears."

A sharp throbbing has begun in my right temple.

Despising the quiver in my voice, I say, "William, I give you my word that I will fulfill my responsibilities. I'll be better at them if you will only grant me this."

His sober brown eyes assess me.

"Please, William. This has been such a difficult change for me. Papa's death, leaving the life I knew in Philadelphia, my friends, the house on Locust Street—"

"Evangeline," he says with exaggerated patience, "remember Esther: 'Whither thou goest, I shall go, and where thou lodgest, I shall lodge, and my people shall be thy people!'"

"But she was speaking to her mother-in-law!"

"Your impertinence is unbecoming."

"Forgive me. I just…I need—"

"Wife, what you need are some lessons in selflessness. We have come here to serve the flock."

My eyes burn with tears of shame and frustration. "I'm sorry, William, I am. I just…I beg you to understand—" The tears spill over, and I quickly brush them away.

"Oh, now, not tears. You're trying to manipulate me, Evangeline, and I won't have it."

"I'm sorry."

A pause as the clock strikes nine. William nibbles on the cookie.

"What about Willie?" he says finally.

An opening!

"Lizzie will gladly look after him. And he naps in the afternoon. He'll hardly know I'm gone."

"Lizzie's primary role is to help you with household responsibilities. That's why I agreed that she could accompany us to Milltown. Not to have her take on your role of mother while you go prancing all over the countryside, pretending to be an *artiste.*"

"It would only be on Thursdays. Just one afternoon."

He looks at me sharply.

The clock ticks the seconds away, mimicking the pulse in my throat. He rubs his hand back and forth across his brow as he does when he is agitated. Finally, he sighs.

"I admit that you've had many changes this past year."

I withdraw my hankie from my sleeve, and blow my nose as delicately as possible. He places his hands on the table then, and sighing heavily, pushes back his chair, and turns away from me, toward the window.

I wait.

"I won't have you painting all hours of the day and night. I'll allow Thursday afternoon. *Thursday* afternoon, and that's the end of it. Any shirking of your responsibilities here will not be tolerated. Have I made myself clear?"

My heart does a jig as I leap out of my chair and go to him. I take his hand and cover it with kisses.

He lifts my chin, forcing me to meet his gaze.

"'Who can find a virtuous woman?'" he intones. "'For her price is far above rubies.'"

I finish the quote for him. "'The heart of her husband doth safely trust in her.' Proverbs, thirty-one."

His face relaxes into a smile.

"You give me your word then?" he says, raising his eyebrows, as if addressing a child.

Swallowing back the joy that now rises to my throat, I face him solemnly. "I give you my word."

THREE
C H A P T E R

1996

Cruising north along the canal on River Road, I spot several flocks of Canadian geese nesting between the canal and the river. Family groupings of goslings, some tiny and fuzzy, some sporting the beginnings of feathers, huddle together on the grassy banks or float on the surface of the water under the watchful eyes of protective parents.

I'm on my way back from yoga class in Lambertville, and as I maneuver the Subaru wagon smoothly around the bends and curves of the winding road, I realize with no small measure of satisfaction that I have made the right choice in moving to Bucks County. There's this sense of *familiarity*, of being *rooted* here. The curling country back roads bordered by hand-laid stone walls, the lichen- and moss-covered cliffs that weep rivulets of rock tears in the morning sunlight, the covered bridges leading to one funky village after another—villages with names like Devil's Half Acre, Point Pleasant, Center Bridge, Upper Black Eddy, Riegelsville—each village steeped in its own unique history.

Finally the beauty and constancy of the ever-changing river: now blushing and shimmering in the pink gold light of late afternoon.

Just past the quarry, two deer leap out from the woods in front of the car. I jam on my brakes and watch them clamber across the road toward the canal. This is one hazard of the area that takes some getting used to. Development is driving the deer out of their habitat, and they are everywhere. I shudder, thinking how close I came to totaling the deer and the car.

Then I see the sign: Aquatong Road.

In short order, Paris, The Angel Collection, and passing out on the top floor of the Museé d'Orsay flash through my mind.

Without even checking the rearview mirror, I swing left, onto a narrow, winding road that follows a rushing creek into the woods. The sun is hidden here, lost behind the towering hemlocks and the neighboring cliffs of the quarry. Like a tunnel carved out of a forest, the road leads deeper and deeper into the woods.

About two hundred yards in, another sign: Aquatong Farm.

And suddenly the claustrophobic closeness of the woods gives way, opens up, expands into a picture postcard that might have been sent from Brigadoon. So this is Aquatong Farm, where the artist Daniel Duvall once lived! On my right, a grand stone manor house stands sentry on a grassy rise. Next to it a grape arbor. About twenty yards from that is a small barn-like building with a geranium-decked balcony that overlooks a fence-enclosed yard where an old rope swing droops from the thick branch of a towering oak tree.

Across the lane, on my left, are two small ponds and a large meadow, all enclosed by a split-rail fence. On the side of a fieldstone barn, a huge moss-covered waterwheel groans its way round and round, pouring cascades of water back into the pond. Two cottages flank the stone barn. Nestled at the edge of the forest as they are, with riots of colorful flowers tumbling from their window boxes, they look like a scene from

Grimm's Fairy Tales. A jangling of bells draws my attention to a wobbly legged lamb leaning into his mother's underbelly. The way that he yanks at her teats makes me wince. Dozens of other sheep and lambs graze nearby. Chickens cluck and peck at the dirt while roosters strut and scratch. Several geese parade past my car, heading for the pond.

I pull off the road and stop the engine. Then I get out of the car and walk to the fence. There doesn't seem to be anybody around, and somehow it doesn't feel like trespassing.

To the rear of the meadow, as isolated and reclusive as a hermit, sits a weathered, somewhat dilapidated manger. Crouching in a glade of giant sycamores, it casts a deep shadow in the late afternoon sun. Its roof is verdant with moss; its gate hangs on rusted hinges. Behind the sagging gate, the darkness of the interior glows blue black. A shroud of mystery and promise encircles the manger. Standing there in the silence of late afternoon, it seems to me that I can hear it breathe in and out.

Another memory of the Paris exhibit leaps to mind, and I recall the painting of the mother and her golden-haired child. This was where it was painted! For a moment I see them there, as they were on that day, laughing and surrounded by daffodils and lambs. A golden feeling of well-being melts my limbs, and I allow myself to fall into the illusion that I'm seeing myself with my own little son, where seer and seen are the same.

I don't know how long I remain there, but eventually I become aware of the sound of spilling water, and then I am walking toward the pond, toward the groaning waterwheel. I approach the fence and lean into it, letting my gaze fall to the center of the pond, where tiny ripples of water swirl and bubble and disappear under the silvery blue surface.

Mama! Mommy!

How dare you accuse me of such things!

Mom, it happened.

It didn't happen!

Stay here, sweetheart, just for a few minutes. Mama will be right back.

Just don't call me for a while, Mom.

How long?

I don't know.

But what if I need you?

I'm sorry about that.
Chad, I love you.
I'm drowning, Mom.
You're drowning! You're drowning! What about me?
I can't worry about you right now.
You ungrateful brat!
Then, fuck you, Mom.
Play with the ball, sweetheart, light of my life. Mama will be right back.
Mama!
Chad!
Mama!
Son!

Beaahhhhhh! The wet snout of a sheep nuzzling my leg through the fence jolts me upright. How long have I been standing here? The sky has darkened from blush to deepening dusk. A chill wind sucks small waves toward the edge of the pond. The water looks ominous and black and bottomless.

I smell danger around me, feel my breath coming shallowly.

I run to the car and yank the door open, turning the key before I've even settled into the seat. I shift hard into reverse and make a U-turn, then, sweat-soaked, as if I've fallen fully clothed into the pond, I press the gas pedal and high-tail it away from Aquatong Farm.

🌀 🌀 🌀

Balancing coffee, a bagel, my mail, the *New York Times*, car keys, and wallet, I approach the battered wooden counter of the General Store and set everything down while I dig around in my wallet for two dollars.

"So how are you settling in?"

It's the woman behind the counter, who serves double duty as the postmistress and proprietor. She's about sixty, tall, painfully thin, and stooped, with sun-leathered skin and a helmet of tight dark curls that cling to her skull like a bathing cap.

"Oh, little by little," I say, handing her the money.

"You've been here, what, a couple months now?"

"Yes."

"One of the oldest houses in the village, The Rectory. Housed all the ministers over the years."

"Yes. I understand it was built in 1720."

"There was a big scandal there about a hundred years ago. The minister's wife ran off."

My reporters ears perk up. "Really? There's a story!"

"Oh, you bet. If you're interested in local history, you should join the Historic Society."

She reaches under the counter and pulls out a pamphlet. "It's only fifteen dollars a year, but you get to participate in all the village activities, and it helps support the research and preservation of the village."

She thrusts the application into my hand.

"I'm the President. Of the society. Dorothy Ivey."

I extend my hand. "I'm Morgan Reed."

"I know. I sort the mail every day." She hands me my change.

I laugh. "Oh, that's right. I forgot."

"Looks like you got a couple of checks today."

"I...uh...yeah." *So much for privacy.*

"That's always a good mail day, when I can put a check in your box."

"Well, thanks," I say, scooping up the mail, wondering if she steamed it open and read it before depositing it in the boxes. I grab the paper, coffee, bagel, wallet, and keys, too.

"Hey, don't forget the application."

I turn back, jamming the form into the pile of mail. "Oh, yeah, thanks."

Anxious to escape, I push open the screen door and step out into the sunlight.

I make my way between two cars, tearing open one of the envelopes that holds a check for a voice-over. Suddenly a movement in my peripheral vision causes me to look up and to the right. I see a flash of white fender coming toward me.

My God! This truck is actually going to hit me, and there's nothing I can do about it!

Then I am up in the air. The mail scatters like a cloud of doves, the mug is flung out of my hand, and I can see the coffee splashing out and hear the shatter of pottery and the jangle of keys before I slam down hard on the pavement.

Kaleidoscopic colors pulse and shift and silently explode. A pleasant shimmer of sound, like a choir of crickets chiming tiny bells. A series of zaps in my brain.

"Oh, good god, are you all right?"

I reluctantly open my eyes. A dark-haired, robustly handsome man is bending to help me, concern furrowing his eyebrows into a V.

"I'm so sorry," he says. "I didn't see you coming. Are you hurt?"

I scan my body. My right shoulder throbs.

"I don't know."

"I think I just grazed you. I am so sorry."

I try to sit up.

"No, no, just lie there for a minute until you're sure you're okay."

A small crowd is gathering. I am embarrassed. I sit up.

"Shall I call an ambulance?" someone says.

"No, no," I say, "I think I'm okay."

"Well," says the cute guy, "you must let me drive you to the hospital for a check."

Except for the shoulder, I feel remarkably clearheaded and healthy.

"Do you think you can stand up?" he asks.

Gently he puts his arms around me and helps me to my feet.

"God, I'm such an idiot," he says. "I thought I looked both ways."

"Me too."

I brush myself off and take a good look at the face that's attached to the arms that are holding me up. *Interesting!* He looks to be about fifty. Nice smile. A surreptitious inspection of his person reveals khaki shorts, moccasins, and a T-shirt that says, AARP. Nice legs. No wedding band. Although experience has taught me that that doesn't necessarily mean anything.

"Are you dizzy? Does anything hurt?"

"I think I landed on my shoulder. It's a little sore."

"Your knee is bleeding."

I look down and see the kind of skinned knee you get when you fall off your bike hard.

He gingerly takes my good arm and leads me over to a bench situated against the front of the store. "Here. You sit down here for a minute. I have a first aid kit in my truck."

"That really isn't—" I say. But it's a weak protest, which is how I intend it.

It doesn't matter, because he is already opening the door to the white truck—a battered pick-up that looks like it has about two hundred thousand miles on it.

I am not so preoccupied with my injuries that I don't manage to sneak a peek at his butt as he leans into the cab of the truck.

He returns with a metal kit, which he places next to me on the seat of the bench. Opening it, he fishes around and comes up with gauze, iodine, and Band-Aids.

Then, kneeling in front of me, he dabs at the scrape.

"Ow," I say.

"I really think you should let me run you to the hospital."

"No. I'm okay, really."

"I almost killed you. I think that makes me karmically indebted to you for the rest of my life."

"I think that's when you save a life," I say.

He looks up. "Either way. You know, you do look a little pale. You're sure no hospital?"

I shake my head.

"Is there somebody you want me to call?"

My son, but he probably wouldn't care.

"No, nobody."

"At least let me drive you home."

I let him lead me to the truck. While I wait, he gathers up the scattered mail, the newspaper, the wallet, and the keys and hands them to me through the window. Then he picks up the shards of coffee mug and smooshed bagel and disappears into the store.

Reappearing a few minutes later, he gets into the driver's seat and places a brown bag on my lap.

"There's a fresh bagel and cream cheese."

"Thanks."

He turns the ignition and twists his neck to look behind.

"Observe me backing out very, very carefully."

"I only live right up the road," I say.

"I know where you live."

I raise an eyebrow. "Everybody seems to know where I live."

"It comes with village life. Actually kind of charming. You'll get used to it."

In less than a minute, we are in my driveway.

"One last chance to let me drive you to the hospital or a doctor or something."

"No, really."

He comes around and opens the door, gathering up my paraphernalia and helping me out.

"By the way, I'm Victor Cenzo. I live down the road."

"I'm Morgan Reed."

"I know. I used to see you on TV."

Does he know about my scandalous past?

I give him the standard line for people who say they remember me from my on-air days. "You have quite a memory."

"It wasn't that long ago. What are you doing with yourself these days?"

I sense that he's aware of the mess with Pete but has the breeding not to mention it. I'm so grateful.

"Producing documentaries," I say. "Freelancing."

Should I tell him I haven't had an assignment for eight months?

"I used to shoot," he says casually.

"Really?" For a moment I forget about my knee and shoulder.

"I ran around the country for years shooting for network sports. That got old after awhile. I should say, I got old after awhile. So I started my own production company—which went very well until I ruptured a disc on a white-water rafting shoot. And that was that. I sold the company, moved up here, and started making furniture."

"I guess this is where people come to start a new life."

"Well, you know, the rat race. What does it all mean in the end?"

We are on my porch.

"Do you miss it? I ask.

"I got over the belief that I was an artistic genius a long time ago," he said. "What about you?"

"I miss the power of knowing that I can get almost anybody to take my calls," I say.

"An honest admission. How's the documentary business, anyway?"

"It's hard to get funding for the kind of work I like to do."

"Which is?"

"Oh, something meaningful, having to do with the arts, about the human condition."

"So underneath that tough reporter's façade lies the spongy heart of an idealist." Before I respond, his gaze turns to the house. "I love old houses. This one's a beauty. Any ghosts yet?"

"God, I hope not!" I say.

"Hey, it comes with the territory."

"Stop. I'll never sleep again."

"Plus you are right next door to a cemetery."

"You had to remind me."

"I'm only teasing."

I wonder if he really is teasing.

"Have you ever seen one?" I say. "I'm almost afraid to ask."

He demurs. "That's a story for around a campfire."

"You have seen one, haven't you?"

He pulls open my screen door. "I think you've had enough excitement for one day."

I let out a dramatic groan and hesitate at the threshold.

"Do you want me to go ahead and check for you, just in case?"

"I'm glad it's light out. Otherwise the answer would be yes."

"Oh, don't worry, they won't hurt you."

He's playing with me.

"Gee, now I'm thoroughly reassured," I retort. "And me with a bum knee, so I can't run."

He turns serious. "Listen, you should put some ice on it."

"I will."

"I really apologize for what happened. Seriously. If there's anything you need—"

"I'm fine, thanks."

He places the bagel, mail, newspaper, and wallet in my hands, saying, "Quite an auspicious meeting. Or should I say inauspicious?"

We both laugh, and I balance all the things I'm holding to shake his hand. His grip is firm and warm. I watch him descend the steps, cross the lawn, and climb into his rusty truck. He waves and beeps as he backs down the driveway and onto the road.

I'm thinking about him a few hours later as I sit watching *Oprah* with a plastic bag of ice propped on my knee. He said to call him if I needed anything but didn't offer his phone number. He didn't ask for mine, either. He probably is married after all. The ice stings as it settles on my knee, and my shoulder aches despite the two painkillers I swallowed. I feel ridiculous that I let myself imagine even for a second that he might be available. Or interested if he is available. Did he send out any signals? Well, not really, but flirting would have been highly inappropriate after he almost ran over me. Although he was being kind of playful and flirty about the ghosts.

God, let's not go anywhere near there.

I remind myself how long it's been since anybody has flirted with me. I am forced to admit that I'm as rusty as his battered truck when it comes to flirting. It used to be so easy, so dependable. You meet a man, you're attracted to him, you flirt with him, he flirts back, and you decide whether or not you want him. Here in post-divorce-perimenopause-land, I can't even *recognize* flirting, let alone get it right.

As the ice starts to melt, I think about the irony of having been hit by a truck in the middle of Milltown Square. It's no bigger than a parking lot, really. The heart of the village is the General Store, which houses the post office and, opposite that, the Milltown Inn, a long-ago hotel and stagecoach stop that is now a cozy local watering hole, with apartments on the second and third floors. The reporter in me has done a little reading on the history of the village. Once upon a time, it was exactly what its name implies: a thriving mill town. At the height of activity, in the mid-nineteenth century, there were eighteen operating mills between the village and the river two miles downstream from the Paunacussing Creek. The success of the mills was dependent upon the rushing waters of the creek, whose three tributaries converge here in the center of town. I read somewhere that this spot was once a Lenni Lenape Indian village. The possibility makes me smile, because my grandmother always insisted that we were descendants of a Lenni Lenape Indian princess.

Maybe my ancestors have called me to this place.

I try to imagine what daily life must have been like in this house a hundred years ago, the human drama that has played out within these walls. Births, deaths, arguments, lovemaking. Some preacher thinking up sermons.

If walls could talk.

The conversations that took place right here in this room. What were they about? The fireplace is cold now, but I imagine orange flames rising toward the flue while a blizzard swirls outside. And how many Christmas trees stood decorated in this room, in that corner? What about mistletoe? Was it there, under the arch that leads to the dining room? What kisses, what whispered promises? How many children have hung stockings from that mantel, aglow with excitement and expectation? My mind drifts through the seasons of the years that this house has sheltered people. How long, I wonder, has the lilac bush been growing in the backyard? Everything is so lush and vibrant now. Was it the same way then? I picture ladies in long dresses and wide-brimmed hats drinking lemonade on the front porch. I imagine a horse-drawn wagon in the driveway.

I am standing on the front lawn, looking at the house. It is dusk, and a soft rain is falling. There is a horse and wagon in the driveway. A young woman stands on the porch, her hands covering her mouth in horror. Two men are arguing violently near the porch steps. There is a sudden shift in my perspective, and I am in the wagon. I can feel the hard bench beneath my sitting bones. My clothes are soaked through, and my arms ache from the weight of the thing that I hold in my arms. I look down to see what it is, but my eyes are so blurred by tears that I am unable to make it out. The sagging weight grows heavier and heavier, threatening to pull me down into a fathomless vortex. I open my throat to scream. I am voiceless.

My own shriek jolts me back to the now. The theme of the five o'clock news blares from the television. I blink and check my watch.

How long was I asleep?

My throat is dry, and my shoulder aches. I feel disoriented and alone, sorry for myself, and longing to talk to Chad.

Hey, guess what? You'll never believe it, but I was hit by a truck in the village square today.

Mom! Are you okay? I can be there in an hour. Do you need anything?

I'm fine. I just wanted to hear your voice.
I love you, Mom.
I love you too, honey.

I limp into the kitchen and put the kettle on, letting myself sink deeper into self-pity. While I wait for the water to boil, I gaze out the window at the cemetery across the way.

Some of the gravestones date back to the Revolution. I have always been fascinated by old graveyards, and particularly the gravestones of children. The brevity of their little lives, the sorrow and tenderness expressed in the inscriptions carved into the cold stone, never fail to stir my imagination. What were the circumstances of this child's death? Why was he taken so young? How did the bereaved mother continue the daily rounds of her existence with a gaping hole where her heart once was? The thought of losing a child is unfathomable to me. I do not see how one survives such a loss. It's bad enough when your child stops speaking to you. That's the equivalent of a little death every day.

࿇ ࿇ ࿇

The Sunday after the accident, I awaken to a glorious spring morning and a sinking heart. The day stretches out before me, but I have no one with whom to spend it. My shoulder and knee are healing, but I'm growing restless with my loneliness, with the silence of my telephone. True, my now-distant friends call to check in, but the one call I'm waiting for, the one I also dread, is the one from Chad. The one that does not come. It's been more than two months since our horrible conversation. The shock of his accusations and the explosion of his anger have so stupefied me that I feel paralyzed to address it, let alone pursue it. And so it crouches there between us. A frightening monster that I recoil from, all the while knowing that as the parent I should be the one to slay the monster before it destroys both of us. I almost wish the truck had really run over me. That I was in a coma. Then he would have to come to me. To forgive me. I allow myself to play out a dramatic scene of reconciliation.

Do I dare call him? Even though he warned me not to? How long do I wait? What if I never call him and he never calls me, and it just goes on this way? What then?

I putter around in the kitchen making an omelet with some leftover broccoli and feta cheese, then settle down with a third cup of coffee and the *New York Times*. That kills about an hour and a half. I put the dishes in the newly installed dishwasher, rinse out the coffee pot, wipe the counter clean, and stand there with the sponge in my hand, staring out the window. Across my backyard I can just make out a corner of the cemetery. I decide that a sojourn among the dead is the perfect ironic match for my morbid mood.

Letting the screen door slam behind me, I inhale the earthy aromas of early May and instantly feel my sprits lift. Mature lush plantings crowd each other out, vying for center stage in the annual spring spectacle of color. Near the barn, dogwood trees blaze bubblegum pink and deer-belly white. The enormous lilac bush, lush with mounds of mauve blossoms, floats its sweet once-a-year fragrance right up to the back door. I walk over to it, gently press my face into the blossoms, and breathe deeply.

I will bring armfuls of lilacs into the house. I will fill the rooms with this intoxicating fragrance.

I note that almost overnight the front yard is dotted with dandelions. The azaleas near the porch are ready to pop, and a few days' worth of scattered showers have polished the world to a crisp apple green.

I meander toward the graves closest to the church. They are the oldest, and the engravings so timeworn that even as I bend to my knees and run my fingers over the cold carved stone, I am barely able to read the dates. I manage to decipher 1746 on one, but it's impossible to make out any names at all. Some of the markers are lopsided, having sunken so far into the earth, as if from grief, that no engraving is visible at all.

As I wander from stone to stone, a tall marble obelisk near the back of the cemetery draws my attention. It towers above the other graves. I slowly make my way toward it, wondering if it represents the final resting place of some wealthy town personage or landowner.

The obelisk rises from a small mound overlooking the entire graveyard and the village beyond. It is crowned with a cross and bears engraving on two sides. I move closer. The first side reads, "Rev. William

Xavier Laury. Pastor of Milltown Christian Church. Born December 22, 1855, died June 13, 1899. Rest in the Lord."

Moving around to the other side, I find a carving, a lamb in bas-relief. Beneath it the words, "Suffer the little children to come unto me." Under that inscription is a cross and more engraving: "William DeVore Laury. Born October 15, 1891. Died September 8, 1895. Our Willie, Beloved Lamb of God. Out of our arms, into His."

Three years old!

Something contracts in my chest, and despite the dampness of the grass, I sink to my knees. A picture of my own son Chad at age three flashes into my mind. With the clarity of crystal, I recall the tenderness and joy of those toddler years, long gone now. Whether it is my own loss I am mourning or the loss of the child buried under the obelisk, I don't know. The feelings mingle and churn, their combined force slamming into my solar plexus.

A distant lawnmower drones, sending the sweet sour fragrance of freshly cut grass my way. A hawk circles overhead. A pickup truck accelerates, heading up the hill out of the village. Even as life goes on around me, a sense of hopelessness sets in, and in an instant, I am weeping. I permit myself to cry with abandon for a good five minutes. It's only when I spot an animated young couple being yanked in my direction by a determined Dalmatian that I pull myself together and scurry across the cemetery toward home.

The explosion of tears has brought on a killer headache, and I rummage in the medicine chest for three aspirins. I lie down on my bed, pull up the comforter, and close my eyes, waiting for the pills to take effect.

It's dark when I open my eyes. The headache is gone, and my stomach is growling. I lie there for a few minutes, listening to the music of the wind chimes down on the porch. The discordant melody soothes me, and I feel a calm resolve. Without giving myself a chance to chicken out, I reach for the phone and dial my son's number. Three rings. Then the machine. His voice. "This is Chad. You know the drill."

My calm resolve deteriorates into raw emotion, and my voice wobbles.

"Chad? It's Mom. I know I'm not supposed to call, but…

it's just that I was thinking about you, and I wanted to…hear your voice. And, really, I guess I just did on the machine. So, I hope you're okay, honey. I hope everything is going okay with your job at the production house—hope you're learning a lot. And I love you. I love you, son. Bye. Oh, and really, whenever you feel like you want to talk, I would really welcome that conversation. I'd love you to come up to Bucks County and see the new house. Old house, I should say. Okay. Bye."

I hate myself for the emotion and weakness revealed in that quivering voice. I pray that he doesn't replay his messages in front of anyone. Especially not in front of a girlfriend. Does he have a girlfriend? Does he hate women because of me? Is that what this is all about? I wonder how he's doing with the production assistant's job I managed to wheedle for him through my old contacts in Philadelphia. Not that he couldn't have gotten it himself, but those jobs are hard to come by, and it helps to have pull. Too bad I don't have enough pull to wheedle a producer's job for myself. I realize it's my damaged pride at being out of the business that keeps me from picking up the phone and asking old colleagues for help. Better and easier to ask for help for Chad. His talent will see him through the rest of the way. I think about how I used to take him with me on stories when he was home sick from school, how I used to sit him up at the anchor desk when the studio was quiet, how he used to play reporter using a wooden spoon for a microphone. I begin to cry again. Big, sucking sobs.

The phone rings.

My God! He's calling back!

"Hello?" My heart is hammering as I snatch up the phone.

"Hello!"

"Who…who is this?" I clear my throat and force some energy into my voice.

"This is the person who slammed you into oblivion. How's that knee?"

Oh, my God. It's not him. It's him! Disappointment, pleasure, embarrassment, and confusion war with each other as I sit bolt upright and will my nose to unclog.

I stammer. "Oh, it's, um, it's fine, Thank you. I mean, a little sore, but…"

"Am I catching you at bad time?"

"No, oh, no, I was just…"

"You sound like you have a cold."

"Allergies," I lie.

"Oh, yes, it's that time of year, isn't it?"

"Uh-huh."

"Well, I just wanted to check in to see how you're doing."

I'm ready to take the pipe. That's how I'm doing.

"I think I'm going to live."

"Well, that's a relief. I've really felt embarrassed to call. I feel so awful about what happened."

"Oh, don't."

"And then when I didn't see you in the village—"

"It wasn't your fault. Really. I'm fine."

There is a pause. "So what have you been up to?"

"Oh, just trying to get organized around here. Settling in. Finding places for stuff."

"What a beautiful day, huh?"

"Yes, it was."

"Except for those allergies."

"Except for the allergies."

"Okay. Well, take care."

"Okay."

"Bye."

"Bye."

"Oh, by the way, if there's anything I can do for you—you know, something that's needs doing around the house—I hope you'll call me. I'm pretty good with a hammer. And finding places for stuff."

"Thanks, I appreciate that. I'm not good with a hammer."

"Got a pencil?"

"What?"

"A pencil. That thing you write with. To jot down my number."

I scramble in the drawer of the night table for a pen that isn't dried up. "Okay. Yes. Got one."

"It's 397-0470."

I write it on the side of the tissue box. "397-0470."

"So promise you'll call if you need anything. It would ease my conscience to help a damsel in distress. Preferably if I'm not the cause of the distress."

"Okay. Thanks."

A quick "catch you later," and he's gone.

I sit up fully and swing my legs over the side of the bed, doing a cursory examination of the knee I have just declared almost recovered. The scab is fully formed. I just have to keep my hands away from it.

I pad downstairs in the dusk and make my way into the kitchen. There are some portobello mushrooms and sun-dried tomatoes in the refrigerator, and after opening a bottle of sauvignon blanc, I set out to chopping garlic and soaking the tomatoes for a quick pasta dinner. As I sip the wine, I fantasize about calling him back to invite him to join me for dinner. Then I check out my red eyes and slept-on hair. Besides, it would be too forward anyway.

But he did call, I offer myself as a kind of consolation prize. That's something.

The air is still warm enough to eat outside, so I carry my usual place setting for one out to the back porch and arrange it on the glass-topped table.

By the time I sit down to eat, the sky is blush pink, and the soft palette of the sunset spills over onto everything. Even the grass is tinged with pink-gold. The wine has mellowed me, and the ache in my heart is beginning to recede. Chad has not returned my call, but *he* has called. Somehow that's enough to lift my spirits for today, for right now, although the memory of the little dead boy called Willie threatens to pull me down again.

After dinner, three glasses of wine notwithstanding, I decide I need an activity for the evening other than sitting in front of the TV. The new shelf paper for the upstairs linen closet has been sitting on my bedroom floor for three weeks. Probably the least exciting activity imaginable, but the mundaneness of it might be good therapy tonight.

I clean up the dishes and climb the stairs with scissors and ruler in tow.

Heading down the hall toward the closet, I look down at the floor, marveling at the grain of the random-width pumpkin pine floorboards, worn and sagging in some places but still supple and orange gold beneath my feet.

The closet sits between what I refer to as my office, and the guest bedroom, although I haven't entertained any guests there yet. Like most old closets, it is quite shallow, but it has been fitted with narrow shelves from top to bottom, and it is these that I want to cover before stuffing them with bed linens, towels, and bathroom supplies.

I begin at the top shelf, carefully measuring and cutting. By the time I get to the bottom shelf, I'm pretty pleased with myself. The CD player switches to Andrea Bocelli, and I begin to hum along to "Time to Say Goodbye." For the bottom shelf, I have to squat to lay the shelf paper. But I lose my balance (so much for yoga) and plop down hard on my butt. I feel a floorboard shift and give. As I lift up to rub my aching ass, one end of the floorboard flies up like a seesaw, and the other end sinks into the opening in the floor. I look down and notice that there is another loose floorboard adjacent to the first one. I lift it, and it comes up easily. Then I lift the other board and lay them both aside. This reveals an opening about two feet long and eight inches wide. I peer in and see a very large, dark-colored envelope resting under the floor. It's coated with dust. I shrink back at the thought of what crawling things might also be under there but reach in anyway and carefully withdraw the envelope.

It's a portfolio.

Tied at the top with faded ribbon, and sticky with cobwebs, its dimensions I estimate to be about thirty by sixteen inches. I back out of the closet and lay it down on the floor, making a feeble attempt to brush away the gook. Then I untie the ribbon and fold back the cover.

There are at least twenty tissue-thin pages of charcoal drawings. Studies and figure drawings; mostly of nudes, several of an angelic-looking child, all beautifully rendered, but many of them muted in spots with what appear to be faded blotches, as if something was flung on them. Slowly I page through them, carefully laying each one out on the floor. Soon the entire upstairs hall is a carpet of stained white rectangles with black etchings. I search in vain for a signature on the drawings, a clue to their origins.

Nothing.

Gazing at a study of the child, the lightness and excitement I feel at the discovery is suddenly overridden by some unnamed grief. Like a cloying shroud, it wraps me, weighs me down, sucks my breath. The Andrea Bocelli CD begins to jump and stutter, then ends abruptly. The suddenness of the silence paralyzes me. There is a buzzing around me, like dozens of baby bees are swarming around my head. Or are they *in my head?* I listen, but I can't distinguish the external atmosphere from my body, from what's happening inside me. I feel hot, so hot, yet trapped in something icy cold. At the same time, electrons seem to be bouncing from wall to wall. I can almost hear them. Almost *see them.* The buzzing grows louder until there is nothing but a bouncing buzz all around me. In a flash I remember Victor's joking about ghosts, and I squeeze my eyes shut. The idea is too powerful, too paralyzing.

I am afraid to move and more afraid to stay where I am. And yet the journalist part of me is recording everything with equal amounts of skepticism and fascination.

Suddenly the pipes along the floorboards begin to ping, and although I am familiar with the sound of the heat coming on, I let out a little shriek. I didn't touch the thermostat, so why the hell is the heat coming on? I push myself upright, relieved that I am not paralyzed, grateful that my legs work, overwhelmed that I can stumble, and trip over myself to my bedroom. There I turn on the light, slam the door, and huddle on my bed, panting like a woman in the final stages of labor. For a few minutes, I lay on the covers, squeezing my eyes shut and focusing on taking deep breaths. I don't like having my eyes shut, though, so I open them, and the first thing I see is the phone number on the tissue box.

One ring. Two rings. Three. He answers on the fourth.

"Mmmph." I have obviously woken him up. I look at the clock radio and realize it's almost eleven.

"Oh, I'm sorry," I say.

"Who is it?" he mumbles.

"I didn't realize it was so late." *Feeble excuse.*

"Who is this?"

I try to make my voice light. "It's a damsel in distress."

He is instantly alert. "What's the matter?"

"I'm sorry. I just…I feel silly calling, but…You're going to think I'm a nut case. I had no idea it was so late, but you said, if I needed anything…"

"I meant it. What's the problem?" He's all business.

How should I put this?

"It's not a problem exactly. It's…I kind of scared myself. I'm a little afraid here. The ghost thing…"

"Boy, you're impressionable."

"I'm serious."

"Do you want me to come over?"

"I'm sorry, I…it's probably nothing—"

"Well, then why did you call me?"

"I found something, and this weird thing happened, these noises— and I got scared being alone."

"Is somebody trying to get into the house?"

"No, no, not that…I'm sure I'm okay and everything, but—"

"Do you want me to come over or not?" Impatience.

I take a deep breath. "I'm sorry. But I am kind of freaking out. I didn't know who else to call."

"I'll be right over."

The Milltown Hotel

FOUR
C H A P T E R

1895

There are ladies of ill repute in the Milltown Hotel!

I overhear William discussing this with the church elders in the par-lor. One of his first missions, he says, is to purge the village of evildo-ing. He says that God has instructed him to appeal to the prostitutes directly, to bring them under the wing of the church and convince them to "go and sin no more." William vows to bring them all into the arms of God or drive them out of town. The meeting ends quite late, I imagine, because I am fast asleep when I feel William's hand on me. Afterward, I lie awake a long time, wondering how those women can perform such acts with total strangers. It's quite embarrassing enough doing it with one's own husband.

As I guide the wagon past the quarry toward Aquatong Farm, I am feeling as giddy and nervous as a young girl. My paint box and easel are on the bench beside me. I have put on a fresh shirtwaist and brushed my hair one hundred times before pinning it up again under my broad-brimmed straw bonnet with the black grosgrain ribbon that hangs down the back.

William left for Frenchtown early this morning and will not return until tonight. I am glad, for I could not have hidden my excitement from him. Lizzie told me that if I looked at myself in the mirror one more time, I would turn into a pillar of salt. She has her biblical references all mixed up, but that is because she is Catholic. I admit that I have bitten down on my lips and pinched my cheeks raw, but I do want to look pretty today for Mr. Duvall.

"All this fussin' ya'd think ya' was goin' ta meet the queen," Lizzie grumbled. But I can tell she is happy for me, and I am grateful every day that William let her come with us to Milltown. She has always been more mother to me than housekeeper, and Papa would have turned over in his grave had William sent Lizzie back to Ireland after all her years of faithful service to our family. William is a good man, as Lizzie reminds me every day, though it has taken years for her to accept the fact that as his wife, I am, in her eyes, a "fallen Catholic." After my beautiful French-born mother died along with my stillborn brother, Father renounced his promise to raise me in Mother's faith. He was so grief-stricken that he renounced God, too, and it wasn't until years later, upon meeting William, who was the chaplain at Pennsylvania Hospital, where father practiced medicine, that he and I began to attend church again. This time, as Protestants. Lizzie was horror-stricken—even more so when, at Father's urging, I accepted William's proposal of marriage. But her love and loyalty superseded her disapproval, and over the years we have developed a tacit understanding not to discuss religion, though it is, by virtue of William's work, woven into the fabric of our daily lives. Lizzie attends Mass regularly at Saint Monica's in Doylestown, and William learned long ago that she is not a candidate for conversion.

A bubble of love and gratitude rose in my heart as I called good-bye to my helpmate and companion. She and Willie waved to me from the porch, then she lifted him into her capable arms, and they disappeared into the house.

Now, as I ride down the road, humming to myself, the music of the creek accompanies me, and I feel us both tumbling joyfully toward the river, toward release, toward something greater than the sum of our parts.

About a mile past Lumberville, I turn the wagon onto Aquatong Road. The woods are thick here, shading the meandering lane. To my left, beyond the creek, massive granite cliffs mark the natural wall of the quarry, where dozens of men labor daily, carving rocks out of the face of the earth. The lane undulates through the dark verdant tunnel of giant trees and masses of rhododendrons until suddenly I come upon a clearing. The trees begin to recede, and a segment of sky appears, fanning out like an overhead canvas of palest blue. I hear the tinkle of bells and the comically guttural bleating of sheep. And then, there they are in a small meadow to my left. At least a dozen newborn lambs are frolicking on wobbly woolly legs and suckling their mothers. At the far edge of the clearing, three or four clusters of soaring dapple-barked sycamore trees rise up, up toward the heavens, their elongated shadows spanning the little meadow with dramatic patterns of dark and light. Involuntarily, I hold my breath. There is something so exquisitely melancholy about the trees—something almost human and breathing. They are like giant ballerinas, frozen en pointe, arms stretching gracefully toward the sky. Beneath the sycamores, almost starkly centered in the meadow, is a small deserted shed of weathered ash-colored wood. Its worn gate droops half off its hinges; its roof is blanketed with velvety green moss. It stands alone, half in sun, half in shadow, a broken down little hut of austere beauty.

Chickens and geese crowd the lane as my wagon draws closer to the farm buildings. To my left, a large pond feeds a creaking moss-covered waterwheel, which hugs the side of a tiny caretaker's cottage. Pansies spill out of window boxes, and a rocking chair sits on the sagging porch, overlooking the pond, where mallards and their mates skim the water two by two. Opposite the pond, on a sloping green rise, sits a stately stone house with brick-red shutters and a large veranda. To the rear of the house I can see a grape arbor, and beyond, several levels of gardens bordered by stone walls. Not far from the house, on a slightly higher rise, is a fat red barn, and just next to it, a smaller building, fronted by French doors leading out to a balcony that overlooks the entire panorama. *I wonder if that is his studio*, I say to myself. The landscape that stretches out before me shimmers with a mystical radiance; it is a natural paradise carved out of the forest. I feel myself to be in the setting of a fairy tale, and I half expect Hansel and Gretel to step out of the woods and make their way down a path of crumbs to the little cottage with the waterwheel. While gazing over that panorama of heart-stopping beauty, something shifts in me, and my artist's soul knows that it has come home.

In another grassy enclosure, down the slope from the big house, about a dozen people are setting up easels. I recognize the tall, dark figure of Daniel Duvall wandering among them.

I pass through the gate and hesitate, searching for a spot to set up my easel. The others are chatting and laughing. They seem to be well acquainted, and I feel enormously self-conscious.

"It's the lady from the Lumberville Emporium!"

Duvall approaches me, and in an attempt to smile, I feel the corners of my mouth quiver. As he draws closer, he says, "Have you forgiven me for nearly knocking you over a few weeks ago on the steps of the emporium?"

Thankful that he can't see the trembling of my knees, I reply, "Of course."

"Daniel Duvall," he says, extending his hand as if I didn't know. I'm embarrassed at my own cold palm, damp with nerves. His grasp is warm, firm, and dry.

"Mr. Duvall," I say, "it's an honor to meet you—to have this opportunity—"

"And you are Mrs. Laury."

The eyes are no longer bloodshot, but they are still that startling blue, turned up at the corners like some feral creature. The face, despite prominent cheekbones, shows signs of dissipation, and the nose looks as though it has survived a brawl or two. Deep laugh lines shelter a mouth that is slow to smile. The activity is all in his eyes, and right now as they bore into me, I have the sensation that they see everything. Silently they compel me to return the directness of their gaze, and as I do so, not without shyness, I have the oddest sensation that this man can read my most intimate thoughts. The idea frightens and comforts me. I am awed in his presence and overcome by a schoolgirl's desire to please him.

Having broken through my initial trepidation about making the first stroke on the canvas, I feel myself being drawn deep, deep into the familiar, private cocoon of creation. My eye takes in the old waterwheel, slowly turning, making silvery ripples on the pond. Adjacent to it, with the woods as a backdrop, the caretaker's cottage with the riot of purple and orange pansies spilling out of the window boxes. And in the foreground, a swing, its thick ropes and sturdy wooden seat suspended from somewhere high up in the rustling leaves of a mighty oak tree.

I choose the silent swing as my focal point, with the waterwheel and the cottage in the background. I adjust my easel to achieve the right angle. Soon I am absorbed in that point of convergence, that condensation of awareness, that connection between subject and canvas, with my eye as the link to pull it all through my arm, to my hand, to the brush, to the stroke, to the vision.

Standing here on the grass, in the sweet-smelling open air, I feel a freedom that I haven't felt in so long. I belong to myself again. Only to myself.

Near the end of the class, we all line our paintings up against the fence, and Mr. Duvall approaches the canvases one by one, asking the class to give a critique and adding his own comments. I silently assess my work, comparing it with the others, and my heart begins to hammer when it comes my turn to be judged.

"I don't see any depth in the perspective of the swing to the waterwheel." It is a woman's voice. I dare not turn to look at her, lest I reveal the sharp blade of defensiveness rising in my chest. She prattles on, and try as I might to see my painting through her eyes, I believe her comments to be unjustified and downright spiteful.

Then I hear Mr. Duvall speaking on my behalf.

"I disagree," he says. "There's absolutely nothing wrong with that perspective. It has drama, originality. Mrs. Laury has painted from the heart. She has a style that is uniquely hers."

He turns to me. "Good work."

How can I help but smile, and blush, and bow my head, not wanting to show how quickly shame can turn to pride.

$$\text{\textbf{\textit{ω}} \quad \textbf{\textit{ω}} \quad \textbf{\textit{ω}}}$$

The days of my week drag as if to deliberately taunt me. I feel I only come fully alive on Thursday afternoons between the hours of one and four. To be painting again! In between classes I am like a passenger on a long train ride, thinking only about my destination. I move through my ordinary days with a brisk efficiency, making sure the household runs smoothly, paying calls to church members who are ill or shut-in, planning the agenda for the Ladies Bible Study, coordinating the altar flowers and the after-church socials, and appearing punctually at the weekly quilting bee, trading the sting of needle pricks for an earful of village gossip for William. But painting is all I really think about. Even at night, as I tuck Willie into his little bed and listen to him say his prayers, I am watching the way the candlelight flickers and dances across his angel face, and I am thinking about how I would paint it.

$$\text{\textbf{\textit{ω}} \quad \textbf{\textit{ω}} \quad \textbf{\textit{ω}}}$$

"We are fortunate today to have a live model."

As Daniel Duvall speaks, a young woman, wearing a white kimono, situates herself on a lawn chair. She has very white skin and silky black hair drawn up into a knot. Several long tendrils curl at the base of her neck. Her eyes are outlined in kohl, and her lips are painted scarlet. Under the robe, she appears to be quite thin, nearly skeletal.

I commence to mix the palest of flesh colors on my palette, excited at the prospect of painting this live model in the glorious outdoors. Glancing up from my palette, I am shocked to see Daniel slip the kimono off the shoulders of the model, arranging it so that her bosoms and the entire front of her body are exposed. I have never painted a nude before, and I quickly avert my gaze and busy myself with my palette, feeling a hot prickle of shame creep from my shoulders to my hairline.

By and by, I steal a glance at the others, who are studiously absorbed in their work, with a nonchalance that suggests the painting of a naked woman is an ordinary occurrence. I chastise myself for my lack of sophistication.

Biting my lip, I force myself to look at her, pretending she is a piece of fruit. I concentrate on the lines of her body, trying not to think of it as a body at all. I lightly paint an outline of her figure, stretched out on the lawn chair, her thin legs delicately crossed at the ankles. I draw the folds of the fallen robe and sketch in the background. Then, hastily, I begin to add color.

Suddenly Mr. Duvall is at my shoulder, and I feel myself go crimson.

"Take a look at your proportions," he says. "Look at the relationship of the head to the shoulders to the breast to the elbows. See here." He takes a piece of paper from my sketchbook on the ground and quickly makes an outline of the reclining figure. Then he places dots on the points of the body that relate to proportion, from the eyes down to the ankles.

"Leave the painting for a minute. Take your sketchbook, and let's do some studies first."

I follow his instructions, replacing the canvas with a sheaf of paper.

"Now take a few minutes and just look at the model. Look at the lines of the body. See how the light and shadow fall on the folds of the robe. The dark shadow under here." He indicates the right breast.

There is perspiration on my upper lip. To be discussing this naked woman with a man! To be looking at her as he stands alongside me!

"What's the matter, Evangeline?" His use of my Christian name increases the awkwardness of the moment.

"Nothing," I reply.

"You've never painted a nude before, have you?"

"No. Women weren't allowed to at the Pennsylvania Academy of the Arts."

"You studied there?"

"Briefly, yes."

"I often teach there."

"I know," I say, feeling my cheeks grow warm.

"Well, first of all, you must forget that she's a live naked woman and simply see her as a subject. You see you've avoided her breasts entirely."

I want the earth to swallow me.

"Take the charcoal," he says, speaking to me gently as if I am a child, "and just sketch the defining light and shadow. Like so." He leans over my shoulder, so close that I can smell the man smell of him and feel his breath on my face. I am reminded of tobacco and coffee and something sour-sweet that is vaguely appealing. He makes a few lines on the page. Breasts appear.

"Now you do the shading," he says, stepping away.

Taking a breath, I begin to shade in where he has sketched.

"Good," he declares. "We want to see the muscle and tissue beneath the skin, sense its presence, its roundness." I look at the model, then at my sketch, then back at the model. I make a few lines and feel my hand relaxing.

"Better," he says. "Make a couple of sketches before you return to the canvas."

With each sketch I feel more inspired. I begin to fall in love with the human form, the hills and valleys of it, the hollow shadowy places, the harsh angles and graceful curves.

I draw parts of the body separately, then only the head, then the upper torso, then only a foot, then the entire reclining form. By the end of the afternoon, I am excited and seized with a craving to begin putting color on the canvas. But it is time for the critique. My afternoon has vanished, and I must wait the endless week until next Thursday.

Daniel approaches me as the others are lining their paintings against the fence. He studies my drawings one by one. His silence unnerves me. When he looks up, the blue eyes meet mine.

"You're an artist," he says simply.

My heart soars.

☙ ☙ ☙

I tiptoe into Willie's room and quietly settle myself in the rocking chair, sketchbook and charcoals in hand. The afternoon sun casts a golden glow over his sleeping form. He rests on his side, with his head on his arm, his thumb barely grazing his lips. His chubby cheeks are lightly flushed, his bow-shaped mouth pursed as if it has settled into a kiss. The mass of coppery curls frames his dear face, and beneath his delicate eyelids a sliver of ocean blue peeks out, bordered by incredibly long lashes. His perfection always amazes me, but in this moment of absolute stillness, I am struck once again by the miracle of Willie, and my throat tightens at the sight of my precious gift, my little son.

I begin to sketch the outline of his small body, always in motion, now in repose, marveling at how utterly relaxed he is—enveloped in that deep and heavy slumber that is the entitlement of the very young. His limbs are sturdy, but he has not yet outgrown the chubby roundness of babyhood. He looks so much like a sleeping angel that I decide to draw feathery wings on his shoulders and give him a bed of clouds for a resting place. Keeping in mind what Daniel has taught me, I imagine the muscle and tissue and bone beneath the roundness. Rocking back and forth, I make several sketches, contentedly drawing and dreaming of the man my son might someday become. I know that he is smart, and I pray that he will also be a compassionate and kind human being. I wonder if he will follow his father into the ministry, or perhaps become a physician like my own dear departed Papa. Maybe he will develop an interest in the arts—perhaps take up painting and someday become a great artist. *Oh, but it's a hard life*, I think to myself. But I would encourage him if he chose it. And if he did have a gift, perhaps I could convince William to let him study abroad in Paris or in Italy! Whatever his calling, he will attend a great university. Perhaps Harvard, or Princeton, or the University of Pennsylvania in Philadelphia. Perhaps he will become a lawyer or a professor of philosophy. And then, one day, he will marry. It is hard for me to imagine surrendering my place in Willie's heart to another woman. What if she and I don't get along? Oh, that will be impossible. Willie will never choose the wrong person to be his wife. He will choose someone gentle and wise and lovely, and we'll all get on famously and have wonderful holidays together. And I will never lose my place in my son's heart. And he'll always come to me when he has a problem to discuss. We'll remain close as close can be. Just as we are now.

I set down my charcoals and sit there rocking, watching Willie, with my thoughts and my dreams making lovely lazy pictures in my head, inhaling the familiar fragrance of talcum powder and baby sweat and rumpled bedclothes. Suddenly his eyes pop open, and he peeks out at me from behind the bars of the crib. The rosy mouth curves into the dearest of smiles. He pulls himself to his feet and reaches out his arms. "Mama," he says.

FIVE

C H A P T E R

1996

I have been a good mother.

This is what I tell myself at 11:10 p.m. as I lift my trembling hand to run a comb through my hair and put on a fresh coat of lipstick. Even though I'm scared out of my wits at the prospect of a ghost, God forbid, I am expecting a gentleman caller, and old habits die hard. But it occurs to me as I rummage through my makeup bag for the Mocha Mauve, that it's been hours since I left that message on Chad's machine, and he hasn't called back. *Did you really expect him to?*

I think of our last conversation. His accusations caught me so off guard that I couldn't respond. I couldn't defend myself. Yes, there had been some poor choices in men. And maybe there had been too many men coming in and out of our lives. I was single and hungry for excitement, for validation, for comfort. For sex. It was the late seventies, and we were all heady with the freedom of feminism and the pill and the supposed eradication of the double standard. I thought I was discreet, but how many times did I pour my heart out to Chad when a love affair went wrong, when the married ones went back to their wives?

And then there was always the irrational fear about his safety. The need to keep him close to me, attached to me, especially after the violence of his father. We were a team, weren't we? It was like that song, "You and me Against the World," the one that Helen Reddy sang. "I love you, Baby," she says at the end of the song. "I love you too, Mommy."

That was us.

And now he doesn't want to have anything to do with me.

"Anybody home?"

I'm startled—rattled really—when Victor's voice calls from downstairs. I take a final look in the mirror and clamber down the steps. He's standing just inside the foyer.

"The first thing you should do is lock your door," he says.

"I thought it was locked."

"Well, it wasn't."

"God."

"Not that it isn't perfectly safe around here, but a lady living alone should take precautions."

"I was so distracted. I guess I forgot."

"So what's up?"

"I…uh, would you like something? A glass of wine, or…?"

"A glass of wine? A few minutes ago you sounded as though you were at the brink of disaster. I didn't even stop to put on my shoes."

I look down at his bare feet.

"I'm sorry. It was just really weird."

"Don't tell me you saw a ghost."

I look at him. "Do you think that's possible?"

"You mean you did?"

"I don't know. It's not like I saw anything, it's…what I felt around me." I paused. "Listen, I don't know about you, but I'm having a glass of wine."

"You twisted my arm."

He follows me into the kitchen, and I hand him the corkscrew and a bottle of merlot. I get two glasses out of the cabinet.

"So tell me what happened," he says, pouring the wine.

I relate the story of the closet and the shelf paper and the loose boards and the sketches.

"That's wild. Are they any good?"

"I haven't even thought about that, but yeah, they're good. They're really good."

"Maybe they're worth something."

"Oh, right."

"Hey, you never know. This area is known for its painters. So, where are they? Upstairs?"

"Yeah, but wait." I put my hand on his arm.

"You don't want to show them to me."

"No, it's not that, it's—" *How do I put this?* "—the reason I called you was because all this weird stuff started to happen when I was looking at them. The atmosphere went kind of funny-like, static-y. I thought I heard—well, not heard really, but felt—some kind of buzzing thing. It scared me. That's why I called you."

"Aha, a ghost experience?"

"Stop it. I don't want to even think it. Really, it's too scary. I couldn't live here if that happened."

He starts to speak but apparently thinks better of it. "Just show me the sketches."

We leave the kitchen. He takes on a falsetto voice and makes that mocking noise that indicates something otherworldly: "Ooh-whee-ooh!" I give him a playful slap on the shoulder. That's when the phone rings. I jump. It's late. Who would be calling me?

Chad?

"You go ahead," I say, retreating back into the kitchen and grabbing the phone. I punch the talk button.

"Hello?"

"It's me." Quiet. And do I detect a note of sullenness?

53

My heart is pulsing in my throat. *Don't screw this up!*

"Chad?" I fight for a big inhale, but the breath comes shallow. "I'm so glad you called back."

"What did you want?" A challenge: unyielding, suspicious. I try the breath again, and thankfully, it comes.

"Well, I just was hoping that we could reestablish some kind of communication. At least begin some sort of dialogue. You know, I've moved to a new place. In Bucks County. I left you a couple of messages about that. I'd love you to come up and see it."

The voice from midway up the stairs calls out: loud, and unmistakably male.

"Are you coming upstairs?"

I freeze. And through the phone, Chad's voice turns icy.

"Oh. You have company. Late-night company."

"No, no, it's not—my neighbor—"

"Don't explain, Mom." The voice is tired now and bitter. "Why did you even bother? Nothing has changed. Or is this your way of getting back at me?"

"Chad. Please. Just—"

"Bye, Mom."

I stand with the phone in my hand. Victor appears at the kitchen door.

"What's up?"

I don't answer.

"Bad news?"

I replace the phone in its cradle.

"My son."

"Short conversation. I hope I didn't interrupt—"

I just sigh. "No, it wasn't you."

We are sitting in the living room, sipping wine. Having checked under every bed and opened every closet door, Victor has pronounced the house ghost-, intruder-, and monster-free, at least temporarily. The sketches are spread out on the floor.

He looks at his watch.

"Jesus, it's almost one o'clock." He gets up. "Are you going to be okay?"

I follow him into the foyer. "I'll sleep with the lights on."

"It's really a fascinating discovery. You should do some research, try to find out who did them."

"I know."

We both look back into the living room at the patchwork quilt of white squares resting silently on the carpet.

Suddenly the segment of carpet nearest to us begins to rise, creating a kind of tunnel effect. As the first tunnel dissolves back into the floor, a second one ripples and rises, then a third, and a fourth, until the entire carpet of sketches is undulating like miniature ripples upon a lake, a subtle low-rise ballet of pale parchments breathing up and down, astonishingly alive.

I cannot speak. Instinctively I grab Victor's arm and hold onto it for dear life as the seconds pass. Ten, twenty, thirty.

"Maybe now's the time to call Ghostbusters," he whispers. I whip my head around to look at him, and his face is drained of color. I'm not reassured. When I turn back to the carpet, the sketches are relaxing back into place, as if recovering from a jostle of gentle wind. Then they lay lifeless against the blues and rubies and greens of the motionless Oriental rug.

"What. Was. That." I can barely get the words out.

"Beats me, lady. Do you have a heating vent under the rug?"

"No, it's baseboard."

We stand silently for a few moments, staring at the paper-covered carpet.

"Probably some trapped air formed a pocket under there," he says dubiously.

"Do you think?"

He scratches his head. "I really don't know what to think, but I've got a long day tomorrow. Are you going to be all right?"

"Tell me this isn't some version of the Amityville Horror."

"Oh, come on, lighten up. I'm sure there's some perfectly reasonable explanation having to do with aerodynamics or physics or something."

"Or something."

"I can sleep on the couch if you want me to."

Bingo! "Oh, would you mind? I'm...I'm really kind of freaked out."

"No problem. Just give me a blanket to hide under in case that carpet starts rocking and rolling again."

55

After settling Victor downstairs, I climb self-consciously into my own bed. His reassuring presence hasn't taken the edge off this evening's bizarre events. If anything, I'm even more anxious, more keyed up. A sensual awareness of him pervades the space between us, expanding in my groin like a balloon filled to capacity, about to burst. I wonder, *Is he feeling it too?* I fantasize his footsteps on the stairs, his silhouette in the doorway, his body sliding wordlessly into my bed. I wait and I listen, finally sinking into sleep as if descending into a thick, inky vortex of weighted nothingness. It is cool and safe here; there is no beginning and no end, no need for breath, no desire for escape.

The dream image rises out of the void like a familiar face. I am simultaneously watching and participating. My senses are fully alive, and the sweet smell of earth and grass assaults my nostrils. The sun is hot like a blanket. I am on my back, naked, making love with—who? Strong arms enfold me, as I feel myself arch to meet the powerful thrusting of this man, this man, this nameless, beloved man. In the dream I open my eyes and am blinded by the sun. I close my eyes, and behind my lids a kaleidoscope of reds—blood red, scarlet red, vermilion red, ruby red—all swirl and circle and advance and recede. I inhale the fragrance of my lover, believing that, like an animal, I can intuit his identity by smell alone. One certainty exists: I love this man. He is the other half of me. We begin to roll on the grass, tumbling over and over, our bodies still locked. He throws back his head and laughs, and I laugh with him, opening my eyes. And when he rolls to the top of me, I realize that the face is Victor's. I say his name: "Victor." And then I roll on top of him, and his face becomes another face, one that is familiar, yet unknown. And we roll over and over on the grass, and the man is Victor, then he isn't Victor, and we're rolling faster and faster down a grassy slope toward water, toward deep water, and I try to stop us, but it's no use; we gather speed as we roll, tightly enmeshed, a tangle of arms and legs, and I reach out to try to stop us, but we plunge into the water, spiraling down, down, down into the inky depths, melded whiteness cocooned in black, climaxing in an awesome and awful shudder as we drift silently toward a bottomless eternity.

I awaken to the sound of someone fussing around in the kitchen. It's barely light out, and I'm groggy, but I fling myself out of bed, throw on jeans and a T-shirt, splash water on my face, brush my teeth, comb my hair, carefully apply subtle dabs of blusher and lipstick, and in a final bold move, spritz one brief spray of cologne in a vague area between my left ear and right shoulder. The eight minutes of hasty ablutions are filled with imaginings of shared coffee and conversation on the back porch; a new intimacy; an official beginning to something.

As I scamper downstairs, the aroma of fresh-brewed coffee makes me want to burst into song. In the living room, the blanket and pillow are neatly folded on the sofa.

"Victor?"

The only sound in the kitchen is the gurgle of the coffee maker. Suddenly that's drowned out by the revving of an engine. I hurry outside in time to see his truck backing out of the driveway and roaring up Holicong Road.

The Milltown Christian Church

SIX

CHAPTER

1895

I have taken a supper tray to William, who is working late on his Sunday sermon. Willie is safely tucked in, and I have an evening all to myself.

As Lizzie finishes tidying up the kitchen, I approach her. "Lizzie," I say cajolingly, "I have a proposition for you!"

"And what might that be, I wonder," she says, raising a suspicious eyebrow.

I clasp her hand in mine. "I want you to let me sketch you."

"Oh, mercy, you don't want to be makin' no pictures of me," she says, drawing her hand away.

"Yes, I do. I want you to pose for me. I need practice drawing the human form."

"Go on with you," she says, shooing me with her apron.

"Please. It's just the two of us, please say 'yes.'"

"What did you have in mind, may I ask?"

I attempt to make it sound very businesslike. "I want to draw you in your skivvies."

"Sweet Jesus, have mercy. I never!"

"Oh, please, Lizzie, please. I'll never show it to anyone, I promise."

"And what if the Reverend walks in on us?"

"He won't. He's barely begun his sermon. Even so, we can do it in your room. We'll close the door."

Her lips are pursed, but I can see that she is relenting. "Don't you dare be puttin' my face on it," she warns. "I don't want anybody, especially the Lord, recognizing me in that book of naked bodies you got there."

I throw my arms around her. "Oh, Lizzie! You're an angel. I'll get my sketchbook and meet you in your room."

She wipes her hands with the drying cloth and folds it over the sink. "Sure an' we'll both be goin' straight to the devil," she mutters, making the sign of the cross.

After coaxing Lizzie onto the settee at the foot of her bed, I turn the lamp low and arrange it so that half of Lizzie's heart-shaped face is in shadow, the other half illuminated in an eerie glow. After some more grumbling on her part, I convince her to unpin her hair, and the coarse black ringlets fall becomingly on her plump shoulders. She has a full bosom and fleshy, rounded arms with dimpled elbows. How luminous she looks, sitting there in the cozy glow of the single lamp! Her plain visage, tending toward sadness, seems transformed, her jet eyes are shining, and it strikes me as I arrange her hands in her lap how lonely she must be, living all these years without a husband or a family of her own. Ireland is so far away. As my hand races back and forth across the paper, we sit in companionable silence, lost in our own thoughts.

"Lizzie," I hear myself asking, "Were you ever in love?"

"O' course I was. Every young girl falls in love."

"Who was he? Was it back in Ireland?"

"Who wants to know, Miss Curiosity?"

"I do. I wonder about it."

"Well, you can stop your wonderin'. It was a long time ago."

"What happened?"

"I came to America to work for the Doctor and his wife, your sainted mother, may the Lord God rest both their souls. That's what happened."

"Didn't he want you to stay?"

For a moment her eyes take a faraway gaze. Her face softens. Then she clears her throat, huffing.

"If you'll just pay attention to your drawin' and stop nosin' around in things that aren't your business, we can get through this before the Reverend walks in and sends us both into hellfire and brimstone!" She shifts impatiently, ruining the pose.

"Oh! You moved!" I say.

She opens her mouth to respond, when there is a sharp knocking at the front door. We both freeze. Lizzie's arms fly up to cover her exposed breasts.

"Oh, my Lord, Jesus, Mary, and Joseph!" she whimpers, frantically jamming her arms into the blouse.

"Who in the world can that be?" I whisper, springing up from my chair. I close my sketchbook and hug it to me as I hurry out of the little room, through the kitchen, and out to the parlor. Peeking around the corner to the entrance hall, I can just make out the faces of Sarah Webster and Mrs. Presto. Behind them, two or three other women, all of them clutching Bibles.

The Ladies' Bible Study Class!

How could I have forgotten that this is Wednesday night! I race back into the parlor, hastily shoving the loose pages of drawings into the sketchbook. I drop it onto the secretary desk. Then I yank down my rolled-up sleeves, trying to fasten them and button the top buttons of my shirtwaist at the same time. I race through the kitchen into Lizzie's room, licking my fingers and trying to smooth my disheveled hair. My heart is thudding in my ears as I berate myself for being so stupid, so selfish. How could I have forgotten that this is Wednesday night! How could I have allowed myself to be so caught up in my own petty pursuits that I have completely overlooked my obligations? My panic increases as I realize that I have no lesson plan for this evening's class.

I fling myself into Lizzie's room. "It's the Bible study group! Why didn't you remind me?"

She is confounded. "Me? How can I keep track?"

"Put the kettle on!" I check my hair in the dim light of her mirror. "Is there any of that pound cake left?"

"I don't think there's but a smidgen," she says.

"Slice it thin," I hiss over my shoulder and hurry to answer the door.

The ladies are none the wiser as I graciously welcome them into the parlor. I think Miss Sarah Bernhardt could not have given a more convincing performance than I. First, I quote a verse from the New Testament: "God so loved the world that he gave his only begotten son, that whosoever believeth in him shall not perish but have everlasting life, John Three:Sixteen." I then ask each of the ladies to recite her own favorite verse from the New Testament and to share with the group why she has chosen that verse and how one can apply it to daily life. The hour passes quickly, and Lizzie is soon setting out coffee and tea on the silver service, and she has managed to find some oatmeal cookies to compensate for the meager servings of pound cake.

William arrives, and as the ladies gather around him, chirping out their greetings, he beams at me. "So, Evangeline, the ladies have been telling me that this evening has been a particularly stimulating one."

Sarah Webster edges next to him. "Reverend, your wife is an angel."

I smile. "May I refill your cup, Sarah? William, dear, how about you? Would you like a cup of coffee?"

"By all means, my dear," he says.

Reaching for the silver coffee pot, I spy the sketchbook on the secretary under Sarah's half-filled cup. I move quickly. I set down the pot, and with one hand I reach for the sketchbook, and with the other I lift Sarah's saucer. But in my haste, I knock over the pot, which topples onto the sketchbook, then rolls onto the floor with a clank, splashing Sarah with hot coffee. Sarah yelps and bumps into the secretary desk, knocking the sketchbook to the floor next to the felled silver pot. The loose pages scatter onto the rug, quickly absorbing the rust-colored brown stains of leaking coffee. All eyes fall to the drawings on the floor: the unfinished charcoal of a half-dressed Lizzie, the sketches of a sleeping Willie, and the dozens of studies of breasts and bellies and thighs and reclining naked women.

In an instant I am on my knees, gathering the telltale pages with trembling fingers. Lizzie's voice trills somewhere above me. She is ushering Sarah toward the kitchen.

"Oh, let's be takin' take care of that lovely dress before it stains," she says. A shuffle of footsteps. Then a heavy silence.

I am trying to cover the remaining pages with my body as I scoop them up. The awkwardness of it, the humiliation, the dread surge through me, and I am afraid I will be sick on the floor. Or on the sheen of William's polished black shoes, which are rooted to the Persian rug just inches from the hem of my skirt.

William makes not a move to help me as I rise clumsily to my feet, clutching the drawings to my breast.

"I think I hear Willie stirring," he says. The words, coldly and precisely articulated, strike me like a series of greenfly bites in rapid succession. "Why don't you go up and check on him? I'll bid good night to our guests."

🖎 🖎 🖎

I am in disgrace. I could bare that, I suppose. But it is the sudden extinguishing of what I have held so precious that slackens my blood, strangles my breath. I wonder how I will get out of bed in the morning and all the mornings to come. My hope, my private source of joy and pride, has been turned to shame. William has forbade me from returning to Aquatong Farm. He has denounced Daniel Duvall as a reprobate and declared me a dishonor to him, to our family, and to his ministry.

I replay the disaster over and over in my mind, praying that the ladies were too distracted by Sarah's stained dress to perceive the essence of the drawings, praying that in time William will forgive me, praying that I will find the will to exist in a world bereft of Thursdays at Aquatong Farm. I fall asleep dreaming of a palette of flesh, of bleeding red wounds of color, of the smell of paint and blood and human tears. Of Daniel Duvall galloping away on his stallion, splattering me with mud.

SEVEN

CHAPTER

1996

"Let's come to order, please. You guys in the back, there are some seats up here."

It's the annual spring gathering of the Village Historic Society, a kind of neighborhood cocktail party cum board meeting held at the inn. It's noisy and friendly, and I'm trying in vain to keep up with the names that are being thrown out as Victor introduces me around.

When he called this morning to remind me of the meeting, my knees went rubbery with relief. It had been five days since he'd sped off into the sunrise, and I'd been circling my telephone for three of them, repeating the mantra: "Wait for him to call you, wait for him to call you." Thank God I listened.

He suggested that we meet at the inn, which we did, and now I'm on my second glass of wine as we squeeze into the last two chairs in a packed room. While the official board members make desultory conversation and pass papers back and forth, I inhale the Victor pheromones and feel the press of Victor flesh made possible by the proximity of the seating arrangements. Our bodies—from shoulder to thigh—are actually touching, and is the heat I feel from the contact emanating from me or from him?

The sound of applause interrupts my reverie. Apparently the Annual Village Road Rally was a great success, as was the Crafts Fair. As Dorothy Ivey runs down the year's itinerary for the Historic Society, I find myself really paying attention. I scan the volunteer form that's been passed out, trying to decide what to sign up for. One event that seems most intriguing is called Films in the Field. At dusk, on the last Monday of each summer month, villagers cart lawn chairs, bug spray, and beverages of choice to the parking lot next to the General Store, where hamburgers and hot dogs are served up straight from the grill. After the picnic, people settle into their chairs for the outdoor movie. They are usually old classics, like *Sweet Smell of Success or Sullivan's Travels,* projected onto the side of the General Store. The more I hear, the more I feel buoyed by the sense of community spirit and just plain fun. I permit myself to drift back into fantasy: sharing popcorn and bug spray with Victor, side by side under the summer stars. Me, a happy city mouse turned country mouse.

"And now to new business. This is pretty exciting." Dorothy Ivey pushes her glasses back up on her nose and clears her throat. "We're one of only six US villages to receive a grant from the National Historic Preservation Council to make a documentary about our own dear Milltown. The grant is for a hundred thousand dollars."

Whistles and applause explode through the crowd.

"Way to go!" shouts Victor, and he turns to me with a big smile.

Dorothy waits for the applause to die down.

"The subject matter can be about the general history of the village or about some specific aspect of the local history. We're going to be taking bids and proposals from production companies and see what we come up with. Any of you with film making experience are welcome to make a proposal."

Butterflies dip and flit in my solar plexus. I immediately begin to formulate a proposal in my head. God! What an opportunity! I would produce a documentary about Impressionist painters from the area. I have a flash about the Paris exhibit, the one where I fainted. Daniel Duvall and Angel. And Aquatong Farm, the site of Daniel's studio, just down the road. I feel the hand of fate in my move to Milltown. I've got to get this job.

After the close of the official meeting, there's more socializing around the bar of the inn. Victor excused himself to go to the men's room about ten minutes ago, and out of the corner of my eye, I see him in animated conversation with some horsey-looking woman at the other end of the bar. I'm dying to talk to him about the documentary.

"You look so familiar." This from one of the board members. I think her name is Adele, and she and her husband run an antique store in the village.

"Oh, I know now," she says with recognition. "You're the one who was on the *tee*-vee." She says TV with an emphasis on the *tee*. I think it's because she was brought up in the South.

"Right," I reply. "I used to be on the news."

"You're awfully pretty."

"Thank you."

"Are you here with Victor?"

I spot Victor hail-fellow-well-met-ting it at the end of the bar.

"Kind of. We're friends."

"Boy, he doesn't waste any time." She pauses, assessing me. "Listen, I don't know you from Adam, but I do know him. And I hope you won't be offended if I just offer a word of sisterly advice?"

I stare at her blankly, and she pulls me into a corner.

"Just protect your heart," she says kindly. "He's very charming and fun and can seem so romantic. But I've watched it happen time and time again. Women allow themselves to fall in love with Victor, and Victor disappears. Just be careful."

I feel a hand on my shoulder. "There you are! Hello, Adele."

"Hi, Victor," she replies benignly.

He turns to me, smiling. "What do you say? Are you ready to leave? Shall I walk you up the hill?"

The night air is heavy and sweet with the fragrance of honeysuckle and clematis and freshly turned earth. The documentary and Adele's warning are battling for my attention in my head. I'm confused: deflated, yet jazzed.

"So, what do you think? Are you going to make a proposal?"

"I want to. Do you think I should?"

"What do you mean, do I think you should? I saw how excited you got when Dorothy announced it. You elbowed me so hard you almost broke my ribs! Of course you should. No question."

"These people hardly know me. Would I have a shot?"

"Of course! Who has your level of experience? Besides, do I need to remind you: it's not what you know but who you know. And I, my dear, happen to know everybody on the board."

"I'd kill to do it, really. I'm already seeing it in my head."

"Well, get a proposal together."

"And you'd put in a word for me?"

"I'll be your personal lobbyist." A pause. "Do you have a reel?"

"Of course I have a reel."

"Let me take a look at it."

"Am I auditioning for you?"

"Well, I'd like to see what I'm selling."

The tape ends, and I click off the VCR. Although I'm confident about the quality of my work, the moment is awkward as I wait for Victor's reaction. And wait.

"Say something!" I blurt.

He turns to me, scratching behind his ear. "How would you like to do it together?"

"What?"

"I was just thinking: you can write it and produce it; I'll shoot and edit."

"Really?"

"I think it might be fun. And I think we have a great shot at getting it if we propose it together. I mean—two locals? How could they possibly resist us? And who could do a better job, seriously? Why don't you come to my house for dinner tomorrow night, and we'll talk about a proposal."

I'm elated. "I'll bring some wine that I brought back from France."

"It's a deal. See you at seven."

EIGHT
C H A P T E R

Spring burst through the village in a tangled profusion of fragrance and color. The earth relaxed and loosened, as tender green shoots appeared in the yard, in the lane, by the roadside. New vines clung to the old stone walls surrounding the churchyard. Pink and white dogwood blossoms, like enormous pastel bouquets, dotted the woods and fields. Daffodils by the hundreds seemed to spring up randomly in the most remote places. Birds began to twitter and fuss long before dawn, and the smell of freshly turned soil permeated the air. The Paunacussing was a lively combination of rushing waters, gurgling tributaries, and tranquil pools.

I observed all that beauty with a silent yearning, a dull acceptance that without my art, I could appreciate nature but never completely experience it. I could reach out for it but never fully embrace it.

Willie and I took long walks during those bittersweet May mornings. We wandered across the meadow, down the slope along the edge of the woods to the creek, stopping to pick wildflowers.

Jack-in-the-pulpits and skunk cabbages carpeted the damp earth leading to the creek, and families of fuzzy newborn ducklings, their feathered parents in the lead, glided atop the sparkling water.

One sunny morning, after checking to make sure we were well hidden from the road, I pulled off my shoes and stockings, then Willie's, and hitched my skirt up, tucking it in my waistband. I waded into the water, feeling a rush of numbness as the cold closed around my ankles. I liked the shock it sent through my legs; it jolted me out of my lethargy, and for a few tingling minutes I felt fully alive again. I lifted Willie into my arms and held him in front of me, rhythmically dipping his feet into the chilly waters, then raising him up in the air. He squealed and laughed and implored, "Do it more, Mama! Do it more!"

"You like the water, don't you?" I said, setting him down in the stream and taking his hand.

"It's cold," he said, grinning and reaching down to splash with his free hand.

"It is cold," I said, "but it feels good, doesn't it?"

"It feels good, and it feels cold," he agreed, swaying toward me and wrapping his arms around my legs. I scooped him back up into my arms.

"That's enough for you, young man," I said. "We don't want you catching a sniffle, now, do we?" I hugged him to me, feeling his cool damp hand around my neck. "Pretty soon Papa will be baptizing people right in this creek," I said.

"What's 'babtie'?" he asked.

"Baptize," I said. "That means bringing people to God. That's what your Papa does."

"Can I baptie with Papa?" he asked. I looked into those guileless ocean-colored eyes. "Maybe someday," I said, kissing his cheek and stepping out of the water onto the bank.

I stood there for a minute, just holding him against me. "Oh, Willie," I said sadly, rocking him back and forth. "Oh, Willie, Willie, Willie."

Although our lives seemed to go on as usual, William shunned me in subtle ways. We talked, but we no longer had conversations. He seemed to be absent from the house more, and when he was home, he appeared distracted. At bedtime, he dutifully dusted a dry kiss on my cheek before lowering the lamp, then placing a pillow between us, he turned his back— never touching me, never reaching for me. Oddly, I kept hoping that he would. However unpleasant the act itself, I reasoned that the union of our bodies in the dark might ease the way back to a union of our hearts. It didn't happen, and I silently wondered how long my chastisement would endure.

One day I was on my way to the millinery shop to look for a new spring bonnet for Lizzie. Her birthday was in a week's time, and I wanted to surprise her. As I crossed in front of the Milltown Hotel, I spied a young woman coming toward me whom I immediately recognized as Clara Shaw, one of the prostitutes who resided there. William had pointed her out to me on a prior occasion, and her wildly unkempt, frizzy brown hair was unmistakable. He had described her unique plight thusly: She was the sister of his childhood friend he had grown up with in Doylestown. She had run away from home years back, and, according to rumor, had joined a circus in some faraway exotic country. One day she suddenly turned up in Milltown, penniless and ill. But in her absence, the family farm had burned to the ground, her parents had died, and her brothers had headed west to seek their fortunes. In desperation, Clara took up residence and a life of iniquity at the hotel, which was a busy way station for travelers and a regular stop for the stagecoach.

William seemed almost obsessed with driving the prostitutes out of the hotel and out of town. But Clara, he had confided, was an exception. He hoped that through his ministry he could help her see the error of her ways. He would bring her into the church, into the loving arms of the Lord, and ultimately, through the act of baptism, Clara Shaw would be saved.

I held these Christian thoughts as I summoned a bright smile and greeted her. "Good Morning, Miss Shaw."

She stopped, slowly turned around, and looked upon me warily. I extended my hand, which she seemed to regard as a strange object. "I'm Evangeline Laury," I said. "The Reverend's wife. I know he was a great friend of your brother's. He speaks so fondly of him." She continued gazing at me with a mixture of curiosity and mistrust, saying nothing.

"I just want you to know that if...if you should need anything, I'd like you to call on me. We live just up the hill in the white house next to the church." I pointed toward Holicong Road.

"In fact," I said, "perhaps one day you would come and have tea with me. We could...we could talk."

"What would us two have in common to talk about?" she said with a haughty lift of her chin.

"I don't know," I said, faltering. "Perhaps...perhaps you could tell me what William was like when he was a boy living on his family's farm in Doylestown."

"I didn't truly know him then. I was too young."

"Well," I said, searching for the right words and not finding them, "Well, anyway, I hope we meet again."

For a moment I thought I detected a softening in her gaze. Then she turned and hurried away.

I felt a deep sense of disappointment. I had been given an opportunity to aid William in his mission to save this girl. By failing to reach her, I had once again failed him.

❧ ❧ ❧

As the choir voices filled the church with the strains of the "Jubilate Deo," I guided Willie down the center aisle and into the first pew. More than three weeks had elapsed since the disaster with my drawings. I had not touched a charcoal or picked up a brush since that night. Although I told myself repeatedly that it was only temporary, inwardly I nursed a feeling of dread that I would never paint again. How could I dare? For William, it was a closed issue. For me, it was a seeping, suppurating sore, a mourning with no end.

I thumbed through the hymn book, found number forty-seven, and settled back to wait for the service to begin. From time to time, I turned around, smiling and nodding, and searched the congregation for new faces.

Just as William stepped up to the pulpit, I glanced toward the balcony, and my heart seized.

Daniel Duvall was staring down at me.

I quickly turned back to the front of the church, frozen in my seat. My hands grew icy, and I began to perspire. What was he doing here? I stifled a wellspring of sheer joy that was quickly overshadowed by panic, as I frantically wondered whether anyone in the church recognized him. Would William recognize him? Did anyone here even know who he was? They must!

The service was an agony of suspense. I had to force myself not to turn around again. Waves of guilt swept through me. Would William think I had somehow lured Duvall here? Even as I sat in the pew, wringing my cold hands, I could feel Daniel's eyes on me, looking down from the balcony, and William in front of me, looking down from the pulpit. Wedged as it were between them, I felt like a butterfly pressed between two panes of glass.

When the service ended, I rose on trembling legs and, taking Willie's hand, stole a glance up at the balcony. He was gone. Then I craned my neck toward the back of the church where William was greeting the congregation. The tall dark figure of Daniel was nowhere to be seen. *Thank goodness*, I thought, as I made my way down to the basement for the reception.

Totally unnerved, I surveyed the table where coffee, tea, and cookies were laid out. I gave Willie a cookie and made myself busy pouring coffee. I heard the murmur of voices as people began to trickle into the room and over to the table. With trembling hands I passed coffee around, greeting people by name and looking anxiously toward the door. William finally came in, flanked by Thomas Webster and Jonathan Paist. He wore his usual after-service glow, and I relaxed a bit, even thinking that perhaps I had imagined Daniel Duvall's presence in church.

Then I saw him. He was standing on the other side of the room, speaking with a group of ladies that included Sarah Webster. Our eyes met briefly, but I quickly turned away, willing him not to approach me. Yet when I glanced up again, he was heading not in my direction, but toward William! He intercepted him and extended a handshake, which William ignored. Words were exchanged, and I saw William's features tighten imperceptibly. They talked for perhaps two minutes, then Daniel bowed slightly and turned away from William, just as Felix Presto and his wife approached. I clutched a plate of cookies and quickly moved toward a circle of people, greeting them and offering refreshments.

I felt a hand on my elbow.

"Excuse me, Mrs. Laury, may I have a word with you?"

I turned to face Daniel Duvall, an artificial smile pasted on my face. "Oh! Good morning!" I said, a little too brightly.

"Your husband thinks I'm a heathen," he said softly. "Forgive me if I've embarrassed you by coming here, but I've missed seeing you at class. I feared you'd suffered some mishap, an illness perhaps."

"Would you like a cookie?" I said, holding out an empty plate, still smiling the artificial smile. "Or a cup of coffee?" He frowned at my obvious discomfiture.

"No, thank you," he said gently. "Evangeline, I said this to your husband, and now I'll say it to you. I hope you don't stop painting. You have a special gift. I know your husband sees me as some kind of libertine and that he has forbidden you to come to class, but I hope that won't prevent you from continuing with your work in some fashion."

I was certain that William was watching our exchange. Though trembling lips threatened to give me away, I maintained a formal demeanor as I said, "I don't think that will be possible for a while." Tears edged, almost spilling. I fought for control, feeling William's cold, disapproving gaze from across the room.

"Look, if there's any chance you can come back to the farm, don't hesitate. It doesn't have to be on the lesson day. Any day. I'm usually there in the afternoon. I'd like to work with you because I think you're enormously gifted, and I would hate to see that gift wasted."

"Thank you," I managed.

"I'll leave now so that I don't embarrass you further. I hope we meet again."

After bowing slightly, he made his way through the crowd and disappeared through the door.

William and I sat at opposite ends of the table with Willie between us. Except for the steady rhythm of Willie's foot absently kicking against the leg of the high chair, the silence was deafening.

Finally William spoke. "Did you have knowledge that your Mr. Duvall was going to make an appearance this morning?"

"Of course not," I said quietly, feeling my jaw tighten. "And he's hardly 'my' Mr. Duvall." I reached over and held Willie's foot in my hand. "Stop it, Willie," I said. "Don't kick." He slid down low in his high chair, looking first at me, then at his father. "Have you finished? Do you want to get down?" I said.

He nodded. I stood up and lifted him out of the chair. "Go ask Lizzie for a cookie," I said, and he toddled off to the kitchen.

"He made quite a pretty speech about your purported gifts as an artiste," he said derisively.

I stared at a spot on the tablecloth.

"I told him that as far as I am concerned, his so-called classes are a travesty and a scourge and no fit place for any Christian man or woman, let alone my wife." My husband spoke with finality, fastidiously wiping his mouth with the linen napkin, then setting it down next to his plate. He folded his hands under his chin. "I also told him in no uncertain terms his appearance at a church service with true God-fearing people only to further his own vulgar agenda was at best spurious and at worst blasphemous. Then his audacity at speaking to you, the wife of the pastor, with my entire congregation to witness—the insolence! If I weren't a man of God, he'd have gotten a helping hand out the door, I tell you!" William slammed his fist on the table. He then inhaled deeply and ran his hand across his brow, smoothing his hair. "I trust he will not be making a return appearance."

He rose from his chair. "We won't speak of this again," he declared. Stopping at the door, he didn't turn around, but his tone softened as he said, "Despite this morning's outrage, I'm willing to forgive you the business with Duvall."

I remained silent. He did face me then, extending his hand.

"Come. Come now, and let us pray together."

Later, in bed, he pushed my nightgown up to my throat and rolled on top of me. He was heavy, so heavy. I suppose I should have felt grateful that he was taking me back, bucking and thrusting himself into me. But all I felt was empty and violated. I wished that I could float out of my body, like an angel.

NINE
CHAPTER

1996

I bump down the long driveway, more like a lane, raising clouds of dust and scattering gravel in my wake. Next to me on the seat is a bottle of Châteauneuf-du-Pape.

Victor's farm encompasses ten acres, several of which he leases to local farmers. The fields have recently been tilled, and the smell of fresh earth and new growth stirs something in me, makes me once again glad I moved to the country. The rambling two hundred-year-old farmhouse house at the top of the lane looks a little tired. The fieldstone needs repointing in spots, and the clapboard could do with a fresh coat of paint. Still it is a welcoming and comfortable-looking house, and I imagine that it shelters Victor very nicely, though surely he must rattle around, judging by the size of it.

There is a beautiful stone bank barn just west of the house and a couple of other outbuildings, probably a springhouse and a smokehouse. Just beyond the barn is a tranquil pond, now shimmering in the pale rose of the setting sun. Canadian geese glide peacefully, making tiny ripples on its surface.

I park my car in the turnaround behind his truck, check my face one last time in the rearview mirror, and make my way up the porch steps to the front door. It is unlocked. I call out. No answer. I tentatively step inside, still calling his name. Something smells good, like fresh-baked bread, but the house is silent. I follow the aroma to the kitchen, a big, airy, old-fashioned farm kitchen, with ancient appliances, except for a microwave and a bread-baking machine. There is a long harvest table in the center of the room set with placemats, cloth napkins, china, and crystal for two. A fat white candle set in a round brass tray surrounded by oranges is the centerpiece. Not bad.

I put the wine down on the table and wander to the back door and out onto a long stretch of slate patio shaded by a huge magnolia tree in full blossom. The patio overlooks another smaller pond, with a weeping willow and a sagging dock where a canoe is tied up. It is incredibly beautiful in a wild, unpretentious way. I hear the distant drone of a lawnmower and follow the sound with my eyes. A shirtless Victor careens around the side of the barn toward the house, waving. He cuts the motor as he approaches me.

"You're punctual, and I'm late," he says. He is sweaty and unshaven. "Let me put this away in the garage and get a shower. Help yourself to some wine in the fridge."

Off he drives to the barn.

Okay, I say to myself, feeling slightly less important than I did a few moments ago. *At least he set the table.* I go back into the kitchen and open the refrigerator. A bottle of Pinot Grigio is in the side door. I fumble through drawers for a corkscrew, telling myself to wait for him but feeling disconcerted enough by his casual welcome that I need a glass of wine.

Just as I have one poured, he comes in the back door, whistling.

"Good, you found it." He barely stops as he heads out of the kitchen and up the stairs. "Give me ten to clean up. There's a beautiful view of the sunset from the porch swing on the back patio."

I settle myself in the swing and am calmed by both the wine and the gold-tinged blush of the fading day.

"Okay!"

He's cleaned up, shaved, wearing khaki Bermudas and a soft blue polo shirt. He rubs his hands together. "I'm going to get cracking on the barbecue. Pour me a glass of that, will you? How do you like your steak?"

Now he seems to be fully present, fully attentive, and I relax.

I volunteer to make a salad with fresh mustard vinaigrette dressing, he throws a couple of potatoes in the microwave and slices the freshly baked bread on an old-fashioned wooden cutting board. I watch as he grills the steaks to perfection, feeling grateful to revisit the simple but lovely experience of spending a pleasant evening with an attractive man. It's been a long time. The wine I brought is a perfect complement to the meal. We polish off the bottle.

"Showtime," he says, standing up and dousing the candle. I volunteer to help with the dishes.

"Later," he says. I follow him through the living room into a kind of combination studio-den lined with built-in bookcases. Hundreds of videotapes and DVDs are crammed into one wall of shelves. The other wall is overflowing with books and CDs. A home editing console occupies an alcove near the entrance.

A big screen TV, DVD player, and VCR face a worn leather sofa and coffee table. In the corner there's an antique desk peeking out from under a mess of papers. I also spot three national Emmy Awards on the mantle of the stone fireplace. They are dust covered, and a NY Yankees baseball cap is irreverently slung over one of them.

Victor pulls a tape from the shelf and slides it into the VCR. "I want you to see this one. This is a documentary I did on Salem, Massachusetts. It's got that historical feel."

We watch the documentary and talk late into the night. We instantly agree that we want to propose a documentary about the early Impressionist artists of Bucks County, the ones who paved the way for all the writers and painters and performing artists who settled here after. I tell him about the exhibit I saw in Paris, about Daniel Duvall and the mysterious Angel. I begin to scribble notes so fast that my hand can't keep up with my brain. By 1:30 a.m., we have a proposal, a good one, to submit to the Historic Society. I haven't felt this alive, this juiced in years, and I drive home feeling drunk with ideas, splendidly inspired. I fall asleep instantly and wake up a few hours later to jot down more notes. Just like the old days.

The next afternoon, Victor and I meet at the General Store to hand deliver our proposal to Dorothy Ivey of the Historic Society.

Days pass, then a week, and I don't hear from Victor. Driving past his farm on the way into Doylestown, I peer down the lane, but the place looks deserted. I vaguely recall his mentioning something about being out of town for awhile, but at the time, I was too excited about the prospect of our working together to pay attention, and now I'm trying to recall his exact words.

Exactly three weeks after submitting our proposal, I'm collecting my mail at the General Store, when Victor walks in.

"How's my partner in crime?" he says with a grin, turning the key in his mailbox.

As I tear open a thick envelope with the Historic Society logo on it, there's an ear-shattering whoop from Victor, who waves his own congratulatory letter in the air.

We've simultaneously been notified by the Historic Society that our proposal has been selected, and we are awarded the grant to make the documentary! He lifts me up in the air and sets me down with a bear hug. Then he kisses me firmly on the lips right there in front of the mailboxes and everybody.

I don't ask him where he's been hiding.

Over the next ten days, I immerse myself in research, spending hours wandering through the American Impressionists in the Michener

Museum, The Philadelphia Museum of Art, and The Barnes Foundation
out on the Main Line. I discover a gem of a library—The Spruance
Library in Doylestown, a repository of local history, where I pore over
newspaper articles from more than a hundred years ago. There are stories
from the *Doylestown Gazette* about the comings and goings of local
painters of the day: Edward Redfield, Cecilia Beaux, and, especially,
Daniel Duvall. There's a photograph of Duvall standing among a group
of student painters in a setting that looks to be Aquatong Farm. I vaguely
recall seeing this same photo among a few others at the Paris exhibit of
The Angel Collection.

One afternoon, bleary–eyed from thumbing through cellophane-
covered pages of old *Gazettes*, I spot a headline: *"Minister's son dies
suddenly. Tragedy saddens community of Milltown."* It was dated
September 10, 1895.

*Condolences are being received by the Reverend William Laury,
pastor of the Milltown Christian Church, and Mrs. Laury, upon the
sudden death of their three-year-old-son, Willie. The circumstances of
his death were not immediately known, though he appears to have died
accidentally. Funeral services will be held at the Milltown Church on
Friday, after which the boy will be interred in the adjacent cemetery.*

My heart begins to pound, and I remember the obelisk at the crest
of the cemetery next to my house engraved with two names—that of
the Reverend William Laury on one side, and on the other, the name of
the three-year-old Willie. How I had wept to read the inscription: *"Our
Willie, Beloved Lamb of God. Out of our arms into His."*

This yellowing death notice wrapped in protective cellophane is a
galvanizing link to that weathered monument that I can see from my
bedroom window. There was a real event and a real little boy who died,
and the house I live in had been their house. Their grief had drawn the
shades and silenced the rooms.

The realization sickens me and excites me.

But that isn't all.

Three days later, I find another article that rivets me. It is dated
March 14, 1896:

Mrs. Laury of Milltown Gone Missing

Authorities have no clues as to the whereabouts of minister's wife.

Mrs. Evangeline Laury, charming wife and helpmate of the Reverend William Laury, pastor of the Milltown Christian Church, disappeared from her home at The Rectory some time between Wednesday and Friday of last week. The Reverend was away on church business in Frenchtown and came home to find his wife and some of her belongings missing. Also missing was an orphaned infant the couple had been caring for. According to Sheriff Harold Rickert, there was no sign of a struggle, and no clues have been discovered.

Mrs. Laury had been suffering from an undisclosed illness since the tragic death of her son, Willie, last year and had rarely been seen in public.

This was the scandal that Dorothy Ivey had mentioned! The minister's wife that had run away. I check the date of the first article about the little boy's death. Mrs. Laury left town about six months after that. I wonder what had made her go and where she went. Once again I find myself thinking about the human drama that had unfolded in my house.

I can't wait to talk to Victor.

❧ ❧ ❧

"What do you say we take a drive?"

Victor and I have just finished dinner on my back porch. I'd made pasta with asparagus and pancetta, a spinach salad with strawberries, almonds, and Roquefort cheese, and a loaf of crusty peasant bread, most of which still remained untouched on my plate. I am so keyed up about my discoveries at the library that I've jabbered nonstop through dinner and imbibed at least three glasses of wine. Finally I'm winding down, and we begin to talk about a script outline. The sky is turning blush, I feel a buzz from the events of the past few days, from the wine, and from the man, and harbor a secret satisfaction that this project requires so much together time. I sense that he feels the same, even though nothing overtly romantic has transpired between us. There's a mercurial aspect to him, a constant shifting. He never remains in the same place, physically or emotionally.

Yet sometimes there are such lovely moments. Like the time he rubbed my back with those great hands after I'd complained about being hunched over the computer for too long, tracking down link after link. And sometimes I look up to see him staring at me. But as strong as the attraction seems on both sides, there's this *uncertainty.* He makes me feel slightly *off-balance.* Am I a friend? A colleague? Or could there be something more between us? It scares me, this not knowing where I stand.

Yet when he suggests that we take a ride, I can't get the dishes in the kitchen sink fast enough.

As he makes his way around to the driver's side of the truck, I flip the mirror on the visor. My face is actually flushed. I quickly flip the mirror back and wonder if he'll detect a level of eagerness that might be deemed inappropriate, or worse, a turnoff. I toss my hair around so the telltale high color is partially concealed.

We drive about eight miles up River Road and across the narrow bridge to Frenchtown, then cruise south on the New Jersey side of the river to Stockton, where we pass back over the bridge to Pennsylvania. Along the way, Victor points out certain landmarks to me, saying things like, "They play great oldies music there on Saturday nights. You should check it out." Not "we should check it out." Should I infer definitively that no romance is on the horizon?

Now I realize, with a jolt, that we are heading into Aquatong Farm. The picturesque complex of buildings is even more magical at sunset with shimmering rivulets of pink light bouncing off the crest of cascading water on the waterwheel.

"I want to get B-roll of this place in all different kinds of light," he says. He stops the truck, and we get out. There's an eerie silence about the place. There are no animals in sight. Only the groan of the wheel and a whooshing sound of cascading water break the silence. We walk over to the split rail fence and stand watching the wheel and the pond, the sucking up of water, and the cascading down. I am so aware of the proximity of his body to my own. I can smell his male smell, feel his arm against mine.

I think it was Sean Penn who said, "You can't fall in love by yourself." I've often thought about that statement and hoped it was true. And now I'm thinking, *How can he not be feeling what I'm feeling?*

The very air around us seems to be vibrating, electrified.

I feel his eyes on me and turn to him. I don't know who makes the first move, but the next thing I know, I am in a kiss so sweet and deep that I think I might pass out.

We kiss for a full three minutes or so, with the pond and the water-wheel as a backdrop.

"Whoa, wait." He extricates himself. We're both panting. "Time out."

He wipes his mouth and runs his hands through his hair.

"Geez, woman, what kind of spell are you casting?"

I'm reeling from the kiss—stupefied, still tasting him.

"I apologize," he says abruptly. "I shouldn't have let that happen."

The sting of rejection suddenly clears my head. "What are you talking about? It was wonderful. It was bound to happen sooner or later."

"No, no, no, no. I want us to be friends."

"We can be friends and be attracted to each other. It's the best of both worlds."

"In the beginning, maybe. But then it gets very messy. It always gets messy."

"It doesn't have to," I say, wondering where he's going with this.

"With me it does, trust me." The warning words of that woman Adele leap into my head.

He puts his arms around me and hugs me tight. It feels like a kind of consolation prize. "You are a lovely woman. A man could get lost in you. But it's not going to be me. I don't want to do anything to mess up this documentary. Or this friendship."

One final squeeze, and he lets go.

Then he says, "Let's get out of here. This place is giving me the creeps."

We are silent on the ride home. I don't know what he's thinking, but what I'm thinking is, "*A man could get lost in you.*"

A man could get lost in you means that all is not lost.

That night I fall instantly and deeply into a dream, where I'm making passionate love to a faceless man. The eroticism of the act is so intense that I feel myself climaxing in my sleep. Down, down I sink into a prism of ecstatic shudders, floating and rocking in a suffusion of rapture and contentment. Then, in an instant, I am on my back, defenseless, panicked. Something heavy and dark presses against the length of my body, weighing me down, strangling my breath. I flail my limbs, lungs bursting. In that crucial moment between sleep and waking, I manage to choke out a scream. I frantically push against the suffocating mass and feel it lift and hover. I see it rise to the ceiling, a figure in black with a gleaming ring of white encircling its throat.

I open my eyes, straining in the darkness. The figure floats to the foot of the bed and disappears. My heart is thudding. I sit up and grapple for the lamp switch. A soft breeze drifts through the screen, billowing the sheer white curtains. In its wake, a hint of lilac.

Was it a dream or a ghost?

I sit there with the sheet pulled up to my chin, for a full five minutes, willing myself to breathe deeply.

Finally I scurry to the bathroom, run the water cold, and splash my face.

Back in my room, I reach for the pen and notebook I keep in a drawer next to the bed for middle-of-the-night brainstorming. I open the notebook, needing to journal the upsetting dream and the dark-of-night anxiety out of my psyche and onto the page. Strangely, words don't come, but I'm wide awake now, and the fear begins to dissipate. There's a strange vibration, a pleasant tingling inside my head.

I put down the pen and get out of bed. Switching on the hall light, I pad to the bedroom next door, which I've set up as my office. The charcoal sketches, carefully smoothed out on my worktable, shimmer like snow doused with moonlight. I gather them up and carry them back into my bedroom, gently laying them out on my bed.

The drawing on the top is of a sleeping cherub of a child, with a whisper of feathery angel wings spanning out from his tiny shoulders. I study the tender lines of his cheeks, his rosebud mouth. *Could this be Willie?*

An urge, a *craving* to write seizes me. I grab the pen and notebook. I begin to journal the erotic dream, then the phantom figure weighing me down, squeezing the breath out of me. A torrent of words cascades onto the page, and my hand can barely keep up. I am scribbling, but without thought, without formulation. I don't know what I'm writing, because it doesn't seem to be coming from me, but it goes on for two pages. My hand cramps, but the pen seems to be going on its own.

Suddenly it stops, midpage.

I pry the pen from my hand and massage my knuckles, staring at the jumble of words splattered across the paper.

First, my conscious writing about the dream:

It's 1:10 in the morning, and I'm freaked out about a dream I just had. For a minute as I was waking up from the dream, I thought I'd seen a ghost, which of course is the last thing I want to have happen, especially since Victor has teased me so much about ghosts, and then there's the incident of the carpet rising and falling, which is completely inexplicable.

It's there that the tone of the writing changes into something unrecognizable and mystifying:

My husband turned away from me onto his back, and presently I heard the familiar rumble of his snoring. I drew the folds of my nightgown down over my knees and tucked my feet inside. Within the fragile fortress of my batiste tent, I felt sheltered and comforted and soon succumbed to my own slumber where by and by I found myself adrift in dreams of such shocking and licentious nature that their mere recollection sends a fever of shame to my cheek. I saw myself engaged in carnal activity with a faceless man, committing unthinkable acts with lascivious abandon. We fed on each other's flesh, licking and tasting, biting and consuming, and though I feared the retribution of hell for breaking the Seventh Commandment, this certainty did not deter me from plunging more darkly and deeply into debauchery and unbridled lust. For as strange as it seems, as I sinned, as I ensured my eternal damnation with each exquisite thrust, my entire being began to pulse with light, expanding and illuminating into a blinding radiance. Shimmering feathered wings burst through the flesh of my shoulders. And thus, out of my darkest desires, in a shuddering explosion of a thousand glorious suns, I took flight. I was an angel.

I blink and stare at the words I've written.

The phone rings, jolting me out of a kind of mental paralysis. I glance at the clock—1:29. Too late for anything but bad news, but I punch the talk button as if it's my only link to the sane world.

"Hello," I whisper.

"Mom?"

It's my son.

TEN

1895

Lizzie covered her ears. "Don't be tellin' me such things. I won't hear it. You're set on gettin' us both into trouble again."

"No, I'm not," I said. "It's just for this afternoon. Just this one time. While I have the chance."

"Oh, yeah, and supposin' the Reverend should be comin' home early from his trip to Philadelphia, and you not here? Then where'll we be? In a dead potato patch and no help for it at all."

I was following her around the kitchen. "He won't come home early. I checked his desk agenda. He has meetings all afternoon. And he told me himself that he won't be back until late tonight." As I reassured her, I was reassuring myself.

She shook her head. "There's no good can come of it, sneakin' around," she said ominously.

"Oh, Lizzie, it isn't sneaking around."

She eyed me balefully. "Oh?" she said, putting her hands on her hips.

I looked away. "Well, not really. I mean, I don't want to go against William's will, but…Oh, Lizzie, I just have to paint! I have to. It's this… this need I have inside me. I've endured these last weeks just only by pretending that I would be able to take up my painting again tomorrow, or the next day, or next week. But then I remember that he doesn't want me to do it at all, not any time, and it makes me feel like I can't breathe, like I'm suffocating!"

I began to pace. "Last night, with William gone, I had the freedom to sketch, and everything felt so right again, so real and natural to me. And I felt happy and sad at the same time. Then I remembered Daniel Duvall's words to me—that I have a gift that shouldn't be wasted, and I thought, maybe God is sending me a message by having William travel to Philadelphia without me. Maybe there is a reason for my disappoint-ment. A godsend, even. Maybe I was meant to…to take this opportunity! I mean, he's gone, and I have the chance to go to Aquatong Farm for a lesson, and it won't hurt him! In fact, it will make me a better wife, because I'll be happier and not this melancholy person that he's had to live with." I stopped pacing to see if I was winning Lizzie over to my side. There was sympathy in her dark eyes. I grasped her shoulders. "I just have to go this one time! Just this one time. Don't be angry with me."

She put her arms around me. "Oh, darlin', I'm not angry with you."

"Don't think ill of me," I said into the warm cushion of her shoulder.

She caressed my hair. "I could never think ill of you," she crooned. "I just don't want you to get yourself into any more trouble, that's all." She pulled away from me, held me by the shoulders, and looked into my eyes. "I know this is important to you. I know it's a part of you that's screamin' and cryin' to get out. But be careful my Vangie girl. You're steppin' across the line here. It's a dark day when a woman defies the law of her husband, and him bein' a minister and all. If he finds out, there's nothin' but misery will come of it."

"I know," I replied gravely. "And I'm afraid, but there's something else that's stronger than my fear of what will happen if I go."

"What's that, darlin'?"

"What will happen if I don't."

Low-hanging clouds and a threatening sky shrouded the tree-lined lane leading to Aquatong Farm. My heart was skipping all over my chest in a frantic, nervous dance. As I drew into the clearing, I sensed an eerie stillness. The sheep, beige wooly lumps on the grass, were all sleeping and up against the fence. Even the chickens and ducks were quiet. There was no one in sight. I stopped the wagon and simply sat there, listening to the quiet.

Suddenly I was deathly afraid. Why did I come? What if someone had seen me turning into the lane? What if William cut his trip short? I was clutching the reins so tightly that my hands were numb. Guilt washed over me as I realized that I had made a horrible, terrible mistake. I was a bad wife, the worst kind of person. William trusted me, and I had broken that trust. I had disobeyed him, and I would be punished!

"Evangeline!"

I looked around and saw no one.

"Evangeline! Up here!"

I followed the voice until I saw Daniel Duvall standing on the balcony of the stone cottage up on the hill. He waved to me. "I'll be right down!" he called.

I felt so weak with relief that my body trembled as I slowly stepped down from the wagon and tied Jeremiah to the hitching post. Hearing his voice and seeing him, it was as if I'd arrived at a safe house, when in reality, I had arrived at the most dangerous place of all.

Daniel came hurrying toward me with a great, welcoming smile on his face.

"I can't believe it!" he said, coming up to me. "I'm so glad you came. I was just finishing lunch. Won't you join me?" He made a gesture toward the cottage.

"I've...I've had lunch, thank you. I...just thought that maybe—"

"Well, whatever," he said, taking my arm. "Come and have a cup of tea. Can you stay long? Can we have a lesson?" He seemed so pleased to see me that I blushed and couldn't help grinning back at him.

"I've been thinking about you," he said as he guided me up the rise to the cottage. "Thinking, 'Now what is that Evangeline doing today, and is she painting?' And today you appeared like some goddess I've conjured, rising up out of the mist! I believe you may be my muse!" He laughed as he opened the creaky door that led up the stairs and into his studio. "I must confess, after my exchange with your husband a few weeks ago, I never expected to see you here. I hope you've forgiven my boldness. I have a tendency to speak my piece without regard for the consequences." He paused at the door. "Have you forgiven me?" he asked.

"Of course," I said.

"And your husband?" He looked directly at me.

Averting my eyes, I said quickly, "He's in Philadelphia."

With no comment, Daniel stepped aside, and I crossed the threshold into his studio.

It was an enormous room, chaotic and vibrant with color. Two sets of French windows opened out to northern and eastern exposures. His canvases were everywhere: on the walls, leaning against the furniture. I gasped at the sight of them. Each one was a burst of color: strong, bold, turbulent strokes bespoke the artist's movement that was being called Impressionist. I had seen a few of Daniel Duvall's paintings at galleries, but the power of his talent, consolidated in this room, almost blinded me.

There were brushes and palette knives crammed into pots and jars, and tubes of paints scattered everywhere. There were rags and bits of brightly colored fabric draped over lamps. An enormous gilt mirror rested against one wall, reflecting the two of us as we stood in the doorway. I was fascinated by how small I looked standing next to Duvall.

A battered sofa, draped with several fringed, multicolored shawls, sat in the middle of the room. There was a wood stove nearby. On the far side of the studio, behind a red and gold lacquered Oriental screen, was a studio couch covered with several rumpled afghans. There was a cluttered workbench, with a roll of canvas on top of it. In the center of it all stood his easel, the work in progress concealed behind a drop cloth. A rickety table next to the easel held his palette. His palette! A beautiful oval of brilliant blotches.

And the smells! Turpentine, and linseed oil, and melted candle wax, and smoldering wood. And there was another smell, a not unpleasant combination of musk and sweat and tobacco.

A small dining table near the stove was set with a teapot, a cup, and the remains of his lunch.

"Do you live here?" I ventured, bombarded by all the sensations that the room evoked in me.

"Sometimes," he said, "when I'm immersed in a painting. Come, let me find you a chair. If you'll join me in a cup of tea, I think I can hunt up another cup around here somewhere."

He led me over to the table and pulled out a chair. I sat down, clutching my hands in my lap, while he carried another chair from someplace in the room and set it down across from me. There was an energy in his voice and his motions that made the air kinetic. Even in the act of sitting, he seemed to shift the balance of the room.

"How long can you stay?" he asked, tapping the teapot with his finger. "Still hot enough, I think," he said, smiling at me and beginning to pour. Then he suddenly jumped up again. "Oh! Another cup." He disappeared behind the screen, returning with a heavy mug. "Not fancy, I'm afraid, but it will have to do. Milk?"

I watched, fascinated, as he poured the steaming tea, first filling my mug, then his own. His hands were large, and his fingers seemed to go on forever. The nails were stained with paint, and the knuckles were covered with tiny whirls of fine black hairs. His wrists were hairy, too, and I couldn't help but let my eyes roam up to where the collar of his heavy linen shirt fell open, revealing a tangled mass of swirling chest hair.

I immediately dropped my eyes as a voice inside told me I should never have come.

"Is your tea all right?" he asked.

Though my mouth was dry, I feared that if I took one sip of the tea, I would be ill. My stomach was in knots.

"Yes," I said. "Yes, it's fine, thank you."

"So. How long can you stay?" he said eagerly. Do you have a few hours?"

"I don't know," I replied, deliberately vague. "I'm not sure, really. I was just passing by."

"Really?" he said, raising an eyebrow.

I realized how dithering I sounded but continued the pretense.

"Yes, I just thought I'd stop and see if you were…if you were here."

He looked puzzled. "So you didn't come for a lesson then?"

"Well, I don't know. I suppose, maybe. I mean, I don't want to take up your time. I'm sure you're very busy."

"Don't be silly. There's nothing that can't wait. I told you I'd be happy to give you private classes. I meant that."

"Thank you."

"But if you'd rather not today, that's fine, too."

Make up your mind, Evangeline! I chided myself.

Standing, I said, "I'm sorry. I really must be going. I apologize if I've interrupted your lunch. I'll see myself out."

He quickly rose, concern shadowing his face. "What is it? Have I said something? Have I made you uncomfortable?"

Flushing, I shook my head. "No. I just…it's just that I should get home. My son…he'll be waking from his nap, and I—"

"Then you can't have a lesson?" he said. "I thought—"

"What time is it?" I interrupted, looking around.

He reached into his pocket and pulled out a watch. "It's half past one," he said. Still I stood there, not wanting to go, but certain I mustn't stay.

"Is that too early or too late?" he asked, slightly teasing.

I remembered how brave I had felt the night before, how good it was to be with my art again, how confident I had been that I should return to this place.

"Well?" he said. His smile was contagious, and it soothed me some-how. I felt my resolve loosen like an unlaced corset.

"Well, I suppose I can linger for a while longer. Since I came all this way." I permitted myself a smile, a genuine one.

"Excellent!" he said, rubbing his hands together. "Then we must get you started immediately. We'll have tea another time." He began to move around the room in a burst of activity. He produced another easel from somewhere and set it up near the big mirror. "I want you to try a self-portrait today. Did you bring your paint box?" His eyes twinkled. "By any chance?"

"Yes. Down by the wagon." I said it sheepishly, knowing he had seen through my ruse about "stopping by."

"I'll get it," he said, starting toward the door. "In the meantime, I want you to go to the mirror and start thinking about how you want to paint yourself. Start really looking at yourself."

I laughed, excited at the prospect of having his undivided attention for a lesson. "Just look at myself in the mirror?"

"I can think of worse assignments," he called as he thundered down the stairs.

I walked over to the mirror. It was perhaps eight feet by four feet, with a heavy, elaborately gilded frame. I studied the young woman who stared back at me. She had Willie's eyes, round, yet more green than blue, under dark, finely arched brows. Her cheeks were flushed, and I held my palms up to them, feeling the heat in my face. I peered at my nose. It was mostly straight, without a hint of freckles, thank goodness! My skin was clear, and I had a good strong chin, my father's chin. In fact, as I stared at myself, I saw only the component parts of my parents and my son: Maman's high cheekbones and dark wavy hair, and the shape and color of the eyes were also her. Willie had inherited those eyes. How luminous their reflection now!

"What do you see?" His voice boomed from behind me as he came through the door, carrying my paints. He approached briskly, seeking my image in the mirror, squinting in concentration.

"Shall you paint yourself with the bonnet on or off?" he said.

"I don't know. What do you think?" I so wanted to please him.

"It's up to you. On? Off? Off? On?" he repeated playfully, making a funny gesture with his hands, as if he were balancing the two ideas. "Which shall it be?" How charming and boyish he was!

I laughed. "On, I think."

"On?" he said. "On it shall be."

"No," I said, suddenly changing my mind. "Off." I reached for my hatpin and removed the straw bonnet.

"Off it shall be," he said, taking it from me and setting it down on a chair. He came back to study me once again in the mirror, his eyes moving over my reflection. "That's good," he said, "because of the cloud cover, the diffused light is very nice on the waves of your hair." One clap of his hands and he said, "Very well! Let's get started. Why don't you mix up some flesh tones. Start with three shades of flesh. Remember, a dot of red or yellow in the white goes a long way."

I began. While I worked, Daniel opened a sketchbook and sat on a stool nearby. "Do you mind if I sketch you while you paint?" he said.

"All right," I said. It pleased me immensely that I interested him as a subject. Inwardly I chastised myself for being so vain.

"When you've mixed the flesh tones, make another mixture and add a touch of blue for some shadowing. Did you bring a smock?"

Without waiting for my answer, he reached for a blue shirt that hung on his easel and helped me into it. It was enormous on me, and he laughed and helped me roll up the sleeves.

"You look as if you were playing dress up with your father's night-shirt!" he said. I didn't reply that the shirt smelled of him and that as the worn fabric settled on me, I felt a comfort in it.

Thus attired, I began to paint.

Every several minutes he would put down his sketchbook and quietly approach, sometimes saying nothing, sometimes offering a suggestion. When I had stroked in the outline and some of the background and begun to apply the flesh hues, he stood behind me, offering direction and encouragement.

"Now I want you to really look at yourself. Not as you envision yourself, but as you really are." We both stared at me in the mirror. "You have fabulous cheekbones," he said, "but there are tiny shadows, almost like dents, right here and here." He barely touched under my cheekbones, and I saw that he was right. There were indentations.

"Your eyes are marvelous," he said. "Green shot with slate, and flecks of hazel, aren't they? Now, remember, they're different sizes. They're not exactly alike. No one's are. That goes for your mouth. It isn't symmetrical. And be careful coloring in the lips. You see how the lower lip is quite full and actually a shade lighter than the upper lip, which is rather narrow."

Then, very delicately, he traced his finger along my jaw. The gesture was intimate and impersonal at the same time. "And you see here, how your jaw comes around to your chin, but it isn't perfectly symmetrical. One side is ever so slightly higher than the other." He paused. "You look rather French," he said appraisingly.

"My mother was French," I said. "From Paris."

"Really?" he said. "Est-ce que vous parlez français?"

"Il y a longtemps que j'ai parlé français," I said shyly, pulling the words from a long-ago memory. "Depuis la morte de ma mère."

"C'est dommage," he said. "Vous parlez bien. Have you been to Paris?"

"No," I said, stepping back to look at my work, then referring again to the mirror. "I always wanted to go, but…" Thoughts of marriage and motherhood and obligations made me sigh.

"I live in Paris part of the year," he said, matter-of-factly.

"You do?" I said, knowing full well that I had heard such gossip at the General Store.

"Yes. I spend the warmer months here. From April through September or so. Then I go back abroad for the shows."

"Who lives here while you're gone?" I asked, thinking of how desolate this place would be without his presence.

"I have a couple that lives here. A caretaker and his wife. They keep the place running in my absence."

Time seemed to hover and was kind that day. There was no urgency, just the steady, relaxed focus on the work interspersed with snatches of conversation.

"When I was a girl," I said, mixing a touch of cerulean blue into the white, "I used to dream that I would follow in Mary Cassatt's footsteps. Run off to Paris and be a great artist!"

"What happened?" he said.

"I beg your pardon?"

"To your dreams?"

A sweet sadness overtook me. I shrugged. "Oh, I don't know. I guess I grew up."

He didn't reply, and I looked at him. I thought I saw pity in those crystalline blue eyes.

"I know Mary," he said. "She once visited me here. Before her first one-woman show in New York at the Durand-Ruel galleries on Fifth Avenue."

"Mary Cassatt!" I said. "Here?"

"In this very room," he said. "I have two of her paintings up at the house. You admire her work?"

"Oh! Yes! She's one of my favorites! Her portraits of mothers and children. They, somehow, they touch my heart. I think I appreciate her work even more now that I'm a mother."

"You like being a mother?" he asked.

"Oh, of course," I said. "Willie is my life. But I suppose every mother adores her child!"

"Not mine," he replied, a measure of regret in his voice.

I stopped painting and looked at him. "Why do you say that?"

He continued to sketch. "Because it's true. She abandoned me."

"How horrible," I said. "How old were you?"

"Seven," he said.

"But…but why? Why would she do that?"

"That's a question I've asked myself many times." He stopped sketching and looked off into space. "I suppose she was looking for a better life. My father was killed in the war—at Gettysburg—and after he died, she had to go to work in the silk mills. We lived in Paterson, New Jersey. It was a hard life, I guess, especially with a child to support. My grandparents helped out—we lived with them. But one day, she up and ran off with a traveling salesman."

"Did your grandparents raise you?"

"For a few years. But then they died, and I was shipped off to the orphanage." He returned to his sketching. "At the orphanage they saw I had talent, and a fund was set up to raise money to send me to Europe to study. I left for Paris when I was seventeen."

"Were you successful right away?"

He laughed. "It took me six years to get my first show. Then I began to sell a few paintings, and I got in with the Impressionist crowd. We started making a name for ourselves. I won a few prizes. It went on from there."

"I've always admired your work," I said, feeling the color rise to my face.

"Have you?" he said, looking genuinely pleased.

His pleasure emboldened me. "When I heard that you lived here and gave lessons, I couldn't believe my good fortune."

"And so you signed up at the Lumberville Emporium."

"Yes."

"I remember seeing you that day. Almost trampling you as I came out the door. And then your boy splashing around in the mud! It was really quite amusing watching your reaction when you discovered that he had escaped from you and jumped into a mud puddle!" He chuckled at the memory.

I blushed even more, recalling how embarrassed I had been that morning. "Sometimes motherhood can be very exasperating," I admitted.

"I must have jumped into one too many mud puddles," he replied.

We laughed together then, but in truth I felt sorrow for his pitiable childhood.

"You really love your child, don't you?" he asked.

"More than anything in the world," I said. Then I quickly added, "Well, except for my husband. But it's different with a child. There's a special bond." I paused. "Do you have any children?"

"Me? God, no! At least none that I know of."

How scandalous, I thought.

Duvall continued, "I'd be a horrendous father!"

"Why do you say that?"

"Because I'm too egocentric."

"Are you...are you married?" It was a bold question, but I felt I could ask it.

"I'm not good at that, either, I'm afraid."

"You've been married?" I asked.

"Once. A long time ago."

"Oh."

"How long have you been married?" he asked. "If you don't mind my asking."

Suddenly I thought of William. "What time is it?" I said, a feeling of panic rising in my throat.

He pulled out his watch. "Five past four. Is that bad?"

I threw down my brush and tore at the buttons of the smock. "I have to get back," I said. "I didn't realize the time."

He rose quickly and came over to me. "Here, let me help you clean up."

"The brushes," I said, feeling a bit frantic. "I have to clean the brushes, and my hands are covered with paint!"

"Here, here," he said soothingly. "Don't worry about any of it. I'll get you some turpentine for your hands, and leave the brushes to me."

"Thank you," I said, hurriedly replacing the caps on the paint tubes and throwing them into the box. Daniel appeared with a rag soaked in turpentine. "Here. Use this. There's some soap and water on the washstand behind the screen."

I rubbed at my hands and fingers, trying not to miss any paint spots. I paid particular attention to my fingernails. There couldn't be any traces that William might see. Then I ran to the washstand and scrubbed my fingers with soap in an attempt to eradicate the clinging odor of turpentine. Back in the studio I pinned on my bonnet with trembling fingers.

"I'll just be a minute with the brushes," said Daniel. He saw the panic on my face. "You really are in a hurry, aren't you?"

"Yes," I said, feeling breathless.

"Well, you want to take the canvas and paints home with you, don't you?" he said.

"I don't know," I said.

"Well, will you have a chance to work on the piece at home?"

"No. No, not at home."

"You aren't painting at home?"

"No," I said, feeling shame.

"Evangeline, doesn't he let you paint anymore?" Daniel said softly. I shook my head.

"I'm sorry," he said. "I feel responsible somehow."

"No, it's all right," I said wanly.

There was an awkward silence, the first of the afternoon.

"Well," he said finally. "Do you want to leave the canvas and paints here for when you come back?"

I nodded, not trusting myself to speak.

"You will come back, won't you?" he said.

The catch in my throat was painful. "I don't know," I whispered. "But...but, thank you for today."

Then I ran out the door and down the steps.

As the wagon creaked along the lane, I turned around once. Daniel Duvall stood on his balcony, watching me.

All the way home I tortured myself with the thought that William might have come back early. I stopped at a fishmonger's by the river and bought some fish, thinking that if William was home, I would pretend that I had just driven to Lumberville to purchase fresh fish for dinner. William didn't like fish, but it was the best idea I could come up with, and perhaps the smell would mask the evidence of my forbidden afternoon.

Blessedly, he wasn't there when I arrived, and in fact, I didn't hear his carriage pull up to the house until after eleven. I was in bed, and when he finally slipped under the covers beside me, I feigned sleep.

In truth, I lay awake all night, tormented by the conflicting emotions that waged a war inside my head. I relived every moment of the afternoon, remembering how welcoming Daniel Duvall had been—how he had put me at my ease and even made me laugh. I thought about the beautiful clutter of his studio, the way he stood next to me in front of the mirror, guiding my work, helping me to see myself as I really was. I remembered the way his smock hung on me and how comfortable and safe I felt inside it. Then I remembered the fear when I realized what time it was, and waves of guilt flooded me. How could I have gone there? What could have possessed me to defy William? How could I lie in bed next to him, knowing that I had deliberately disobeyed him, gone behind his back in the most flagrant way? If I were a good wife, I would never return to Aquatong Farm.

Then the guilt was temporarily washed away in a torrent of despair. If I didn't go back to Aquatong Farm, how could I continue to paint? Did the development of my skills as an artist depend on the development of my skills as a liar and a conniver? Were the two inextricably entwined? In order to be a good painter, did I have to be a bad person? If I listened to the voice in my heart, could I ignore the one in my head? And what made me even think that I had any real talent? Maybe Daniel Duvall said those things to me because he was trying to be nice. It was my false pride that was the problem, I decided. I had delusions of grandeur. My foolish dreaming must cease at once. I must be attentive to my real life's work, which was being a good wife to William and a good mother to Willie. They needed me, and I needed them. We were a family, and family is the most important consideration.

I watched the first pale rose tendrils of light spread across the floor, then over the ivory crocheted coverlet, to the bedpost, and beyond to the washstand. My dry eyes throbbed in tandem with my head. I heard Willie babbling happily to himself in the next room, and wearily I swung my legs over the side of the bed, reaching for my dressing gown. Then I tiptoed to the nursery and peeked around the door. He was sitting in his crib, singing to his teddy bear:

I love Mama; Mama loves me.

I love Papa; Papa loves me.

I love Lizzie; Lizzie loves me.

"Peek-a-boo!" I said softly. "Good morning, sunshine!"

He greeted me with a beatific smile. "Good morning, Mama," he said, standing up and holding out his arms. I lifted him out of the crib and covered him with kisses.

ᘒ ᘒ ᘒ

"Come out on the porch," said William, setting his cup down in the saucer. "You too, Lizzie. I have a surprise for Evangeline."

"Mama! A surprise!" said Willie, clapping his hands and kicking his heels against the highchair.

"A surprise? For me?" I said. "What is it?"

William stood, an immensely pleased smile wreathing his face. "You'll see. Come along." He pulled my arm through his. I exchanged glances with Lizzie, who seemed just as curious as I was. She quickly lifted Willie down from his chair, and the four of us hurried out to the front porch, with Willie leading the way.

"It's a bicycle!" I exclaimed, running over to the shiny two-wheeler that leaned against the porch railing.

"Oh, Lord, will ya' look at that," said Lizzie.

"I got it at John Wanamaker's," said William, beaming.

"What's a bicycle?" asked Willie.

"It can take us places," I said.

"Now I won't have you riding it on the Sabbath," warned William. "And it's not to be used for conspicuous enjoyment. But I thought it might be a pleasant way for you to do your errands and pay your visits around the village. It's much more practical than having to hitch up the wagon every time you've somewhere to go."

"Oh, and there's even a little basket on the front for Willie to ride in!" I said.

"Can I go too, Papa? Can I go too?" said Willie, pulling on William's waistcoat beseechingly.

"*May* I go too," corrected William, sweeping Willie up into his arms. "Yes! Just as soon as Mama learns how to drive it."

"Oh, William, I don't know what to say! This is wonderful. Thank you."

"Well, I know how disappointed you were that I couldn't take you with me to Philadelphia. I wanted to make it up to you."

"You did," I said. "Oh, you did!"

"They're supposed to be very good for touring in the country," said William. "They're growing quite popular."

"Lizzie, you can ride it, too!"

Lizzie held up her hands. "Oh, you won't be findin' me on that contraption. I'd surely topple over into a ditch and bust my head open."

"Oh, don't be a ninny," I said. "It can't be that hard to ride!" I turned to William. "May I try it now?" I asked, as excited as Willie.

"By all means. Why don't you just start out here on the lane that runs between the house and the church. Don't go down to the road yet. My understanding is that it's a matter of balance."

For half and hour I pedaled and wobbled and giggled, while William, Lizzie, and Willie cheered me on. When I finally felt confident, I rode down the lane to Holicong Road and gingerly coasted down the rise to the square. Heads turned as I called "hello" to passersby, not confident enough to take my hands off the front bars to wave. When I reached the square, I turned the bicycle around and walked it back up the hill, flushed, slightly out of breath, and triumphant.

"Did you see me?" I called to my smiling audience of three who awaited me in the front yard. "How did I do?"

"Oh, you looked grand," said Lizzie, "flyin' down the hill like a bird."

"Hooray for Mama!" cried Willie. "Me next!"

William ruffled his hair. "I think she needs a little more practice, son, but she's getting it. She's getting it." A smile of great satisfaction lit his face as I approached him, leading the bicycle. "So you like your present?" he said, his eyebrows lifting.

"Yes!" I said, bracing the bicycle against the porch. I had a sudden urge to embrace him, but the dictates of the church regarding displays of affection prevented me from doing so. Instead, I spread my arms wide and exclaimed, "It's grand!"

"Good," he said. "Now I've got to get over to that church and down to business before the heathens take over the world."

"I'll walk you over," I said, putting my arm through his in wifely fashion. "I want to hear about your trip."

"It was productive," he said as we strolled across the green toward the church. "Quite so, in fact. Good reports about the work we're doing here are filtering back to the Christian Conference." He patted my hand that was tucked through his arm.

"As a result, I'm afraid I'm going to be busier than ever. But I'm pleased."

"What are your plans?" I asked.

"Well, to start, of course, we have the baptizing here on the last Sunday of this month. I want you and the ladies of the Quilting Bee to make the baptismal robes. Twelve of them. Actually, perhaps you should make an even sixteen, in case we bring some last-minute converts into the flock. I want you to arrange a church supper for the day of the baptisms. And a special program of sacred music. Voices joyfully raised in song. You can speak to Jonathan Paist about that."

"Of course. Perhaps, 'A Mighty Fortress is Our God' and 'Onward Christian Soldiers'?"

"Excellent choices. Once the baptism here in Milltown has been completed, I'll be conducting baptisms all over the county: Locktown, Johnsonburg, Hope. Those will be on Mondays. And I'm going to set up an attendant congregation at Frenchtown. I'm going to carry on the Lord's work until not a vestige of corruption shall remain."

We had come to the church. "You seem very contented," I said.

"I am," he agreed, smiling.

"And Clara Shaw?" I asked. "She'll be converting, definitely?"

"She's my prize pupil," he said. "But such a challenge. I had to call on all the powers that the Lord has given me. At times I felt I was struggling with Satan himself. I've spent many hours on my knees over that poor, wretched girl."

"I'm proud of you," I said, touching his cool fingertips. "And the bicycle. It was a wonderful surprise. Thank you."

"Remember," he said, "No conspicuous enjoyment."

"No conspicuous enjoyment," I repeated. "I promise."

ELEVEN

C H A P T E R

1996

I am staring across the table at my son. He is here, in my house, in my kitchen, and he is speaking to me, sort of. I am raw in my state of alert. Aware that a misconstrued gesture, an ill-timed lift of an eyebrow, an inadvertent sigh, will drive him away.

His DUI arrest may be the best thing that's ever happened to me.

It shows how screwed up I am that I was grateful—no, even thrilled—to drive more than an hour in the middle of the night to bail him out of the Radnor police station.

He smelled like a brewery, filling my car with his stench and his sullenness, but it was a blessing to have him safely strapped in the passenger seat. I was taking my boy home with me, and he was too drunk and too scared to protest. Best of all, he'd called me! He called *me*!

I led him up the stairs to the guest room, laid out fresh towels, and turned down the bed. Within minutes, he was stretched out between the clean sheets. I turned out the light, pulled the door shut, and stood in the hall, listening to the pre-dawn stillness, breathing gratitude for my son's presence.

Now it's past noon of the following day. I've been awake since nine thirty, drinking coffee, smoking, anticipating, dreading, and rehearsing for this conversation. The sound of the toilet flushing upstairs sets my heart racing. The faint thud of his slow steps on the stairs, then in the living room, sends me scurrying to the sink, looking busy, acting nonchalant.

Wordlessly he slouches into a chair and plants his elbows on the kitchen table. I pour coffee into the mug I've had waiting for him on the counter and set it down in front of him.

"Did you sleep okay?"

He nods. "Do you have any milk?"

Oh, my God, do I? I yank the refrigerator door open, pull out a carton that, thankfully, seems to have about two inches of milk in it. Skim milk. Behind his back, I sniff it. Still fresh.

"Oh, right, I forgot you take milk. This is two percent. I'll pick up some whole today." I set the carton down.

He pours the milk into his coffee and looks around for a spoon. I throw open a drawer and, grabbing one, hand it to him, then sink into the chair opposite him. Now we're face-to-face.

Silence as he stirs his coffee. I watch his incredibly long fingers making little circles with the spoon.

Finally he sips. Then says, without looking at me, "Sorry you had to drive all the way down there."

"No, I'm glad you called me. Really."

"It's fucked up." He presses the heels of his hands against his eyes.

I hesitate, feeling my way. "Do you want to talk about what happened?"

"What happened? I got busted for drunk driving, that's what happened."

I let the sarcasm pass, and wait.

He sips again, taking his time. He sets the mug down.

"Okay. So I got in a fight with a producer because I messed up an interview tape that I was logging. I left it in my car with the window open, and it got rained on. We've had some other, shall I say, run-ins. So the bitch got my ass fired. And it was downhill from there."

"What are you going to do?" It's not a challenge, simply a question.

"Like I know."

"It's a given you're going to lose your license."

"No shit."

It takes effort not to react to his surliness. But as he rubs his red-rimmed eyes again, I make a quick decision, reasoning that I'll consult with Victor about it later.

"I can offer you a job. With me. Working on a documentary. I'll pay you. You can stay here. It's a good project."

"What is it? Some wimpy PBS thing about the mating habits of butterflies?" He smirks, and now I really want to smack him.

"Do you want to hear about it or not?" I ask.

He leans back, crossing his arms. "It's not like I have other options. I'm listening."

I begin by telling him how the project came about through the Milltown Historic Society.

"This area is really considered the birthplace of American Impressionism." I continue, "Just down the road is the home of one of the most famous American Impressionists—his name was Daniel Duvall. We're focusing on him and one of his students, a woman called Angel. I saw an art exhibit of their work last month in Paris. It's really kind of an amazing coincidence—"

"Who's 'we'?" His expression hardens. I realize that his hostility regarding me is hair-trigger. I may have hauled him out of the pokey, but he still sees me as the enemy. He smells fresh meat, and he's ready to pounce.

"My partner," I reply equably. "My collaborator. Naturally I needed a shooter and editor, and he used to work for the network. He's got a great demo reel. And he's right here in the village, a neighbor, so it's so convenient."

"I can shoot, Mom."

"Well, that's true, but first of all, you and I haven't been in touch, unfortunately, so it wouldn't have occurred to me that you would partner with me on this. And secondly, my co-producer and I won the grant jointly. It's our project together. And, Chad, realistically, you don't have that much hard field experience, do you? You're tremendously talented, but—"

"Don't patronize me."

"I don't mean to patronize you. But, let's face it, you're barely out of school a year."

"You sound like that bitch that fired me. She never let me shoot one frame. Half the stuff she came back from the field with was green because her asshole cameraman couldn't even white balance."

"That must have been frustrating for you." I'm trying to keep this conversation from deteriorating further.

"Yeah, so I think my own mother should give me chance to shoot. And edit. Why do you need this other guy?"

"I told you. The project is as much Victor's as it is mine."

He smirks. "Ohhh, *Victor*," he says leeringly. "*I see.*"

He pushes back his chair and gets up. "I wouldn't want to come between you and *Victor*."

"Chad, can we just for a minute, set aside the bitterness and the subtext? Please?"

He rolls his eyes, recrosses his arms, standing his ground.

I say, "You've been refusing to even speak to me for months. In spite of that, I rushed out to the Main Line to bail you out, and now I'm offering you a job—a good job, under *any* circumstances—on an exciting project. It'll be great experience for you, great for your resume. It's not fair of you to resent that I'm working with someone else. You've essentially cut me out of your life."

"Oh, you want to get into issues now?"

"I just said, no, not right now. At some point, hopefully, yes, but right now—look, fate, or what happened last night, or whatever, got you here, got us at least talking again, and I think this project could be a good thing in so many ways."

"Yeah, well, it seems like you still have a knack for triangles, Mom."

A thud to my solar plexus.

I shake my head, get up, and dump my cold coffee into the sink, turning my back to him so he can't see me blinking back tears. As I carefully rinse the cup, I watch brown-tinged water ooze down the drain like my hopes.

"How much?"

"How much what?"

"How much will you pay me?"

I feel my shoulder blades slide down my back, and I pause with the cup still in my hands. "I'll pay you five hundred a week for eight weeks." I almost tell him he can live here for free and I'll feed him, but my hurt prevails: "You can give me back fifty dollars a week for room and board."

He walks to the sideboard and pours himself another cup of coffee. He empties the last of the milk into his mug, reaches for a spoon. The only sound is the clink of metal against ceramic as he stirs, stalling for time. He sips.

I grab a dishtowel, drying my own cup to a fare-thee-well.

Finally, he says, "So when do I meet Victor?"

ƒ ƒ ƒ

I let him wallow in his hangover for the remainder of the afternoon. Around five o'clock, though, I've had enough. The sight of him splayed like a sloth on the sofa, munching potato chips and clicking back and forth between ESPN and CNN has me grinding my teeth.

I take the remote from him, turn off the television, and say, "Come on, we're going for a walk."

A groan from the sofa. "Mom, I have a killer headache. I don't want to walk anywhere."

"You need to get out of the house, move around. There's a beautiful walk down Milltown Road to the river. Consider it research. This is the area that inspired so many American Impressionist artists. If you're really going to work on the documentary, I want you to get to know it."

With a sigh, he sits up, running his hands through his hair. "Let me get my shoes," he says dully.

The walk from the village to the river is about two miles of winding country road, with the rushing creek on one side and rising granite cliffs on the other. Spring colors dot the landscape: forsythia, daffodils, columbine, and lilies.

We're silent as we stroll, Chad with his hands stuffed in his pockets, probably sulking, me quietly happy just to have my son, bratty as he is, beside me on this beautiful walk that I'd enjoyed in solitude dozens of times. I feel somehow comforted by nature, secure in the pastoral beauty of these surroundings, confident that even Chad's resentful heart might soften in the face of such simple, intrinsic loveliness.

By the time we arrive at the river, some of the tension seems to have dissolved. As the mighty Delaware stretches out before us in a giant undulating ribbon of silver, I tell him a little bit about the canals that run parallel to it—how they were built by Irish immigrants. I describe how mules used to tow the barges and how the locks used to operate. He actually seems interested.

We chat fairly amiably on the way back as I tell him the story of my impulsively buying the house in Milltown, my sojourn in Paris, and deciding to apply for the grant from the Historic Society.

As we approach the Rectory, I say, "I want to show you one more thing before we go in the house."

I lead him across the yard, past the church, to the shallow rise dotted with weathered gravestones.

"Gee, this is a real upper," he says, eyeing the cemetery. "You didn't tell me you lived next door to a graveyard."

I lead him to the obelisk marking the graves of the minister, William Laury, and the little boy, Willie.

"These people lived in our house more than a hundred years ago. Look, the little boy was only three when he died. Isn't it sad?"

Chad seems more focused, suddenly, than he has all day, and he kneels down and runs his finger over the engraved name, *William DeVore Laury. Our Willie.*

"I found a newspaper clipping about Willie's death," I say. "At the Spruance Museum Library in Doylestown. And there was another article about his mother, the minister's wife. About six months after Willie died, she just disappeared. Ran away or something."

Chad has sat back on his haunches and is staring at the words carved into the stone. He repeats them: "'Beloved Lamb of God. *Out of our arms into his.*'"

He rubs the back of his neck with his hand, then runs it across his brow. "Whew. I don't feel so good."

He does look a little green.

"I've got to get out of here." With that, he lurches over to the side and vomits on the grass. Great, heaving spasms shake his body. I stop myself from reaching out to put a hand on his head.

When it's over, he's trembling. I lower myself down onto the grass next to him.

"Are you okay?"

He spits a few times, then wipes his mouth on his shirt.

"I told you I was hung over."

When we arrive back at the house, Chad immediately flings himself back down on the sofa and falls asleep. I telephone Victor and leave a message inviting him to dinner the following night. Then I plow through the bookcase in my office, searching for the hardcover curator's book I'd purchased from *The Angel Collection* exhibit in Paris. I page through the book, daydreaming about how wonderful it would be to actually shoot the original paintings and not have to settle for the photographic representations here in the book. Though, even to include photographs of the paintings in the documentary, I'll undoubtedly have to get releases from the current owners, which could be a major pain in the butt, depending on where they are. That can be Chad's first assignment, though he'll probably be insulted by it, considering it beneath him. Still perusing the book, I now note that many of the paintings by Angel and Duvall— in fact, most of them—are from a private collection of one Anne-Claire Goudonov Sancerre in Giverny, France. Kate and I had made a day trip to Giverny on my recent trip to Paris. A series of happy recollections drifts through my mind: Monet's bright pink house, his enormous studio, the colorful kitchen, and of course, the lush surrounding gardens and ponds, clusters of plump water lilies floating on its surface, just like in the paintings I'd admired. There was something magical about the tiny village of Giverny, the gently undulating River Epte nearby. I had imagined the artists of long ago, setting up their easels under the trees, catching shadow and light as it played through the leaves and bounced off the gliding surface of the water. I saw picnics on the grass or something more daring—perhaps an artist painting a beautiful woman as she reclined seductively on a blanket, naked except for a tumble of wild-flowers woven into her hair. I had *felt connected* that day in Giverny, somehow sad on our return to Paris. It wasn't until several days later that I saw *The Angel Collection* at the Musée d'Orsay and became so overwhelmed by the paintings that I flat out fainted.

How strange to learn that the permanent home of most of those paintings is Giverny.

At dinner, Chad is bleary-eyed and still a bit hungover, but he duti-fully jots down the website from the curator's book and promises to start searching out the Sancerre woman first thing in the morning. While I load the dishwasher, he watches a Phillies game, then heads back up to bed. I turn in early too, suddenly exhausted by the past twenty-four hours. Before getting into bed, I pause outside Chad's room, listening. There is only silence, but it's a comforting silence, because I know that my son is sleeping in that room. I lean my head against the doorjamb as a rush of gratitude once again suffuses me.

As I pad back down the hall, it occurs to me that Chad is sleeping in the room that probably belonged to little Willie. Without even thinking, the words tumble out in a prayerful whisper: *Bless my son.*

Just past midnight I'm jolted out of a thick sleep. A cry or a moan is coming from the next room. It sounds, unbelievably, like, "Mommy!" I sit up in bed and listen. It is. It is "Mommy," and it's coming from Chad. I make my way down the hall, flipping the switch, and hesitate outside his room.

"Mommy! Mommy! Help, help me, Mommy!" The cry of a child. The voice of a grown man.

I open the door, and the hall light spills over the tangled bedcovers, where he's thrashing and gasping out my name. The anguish in his voice is heartrending.

"Chad? Chad!"

I lean over him, press my hand on his shoulder.

"Honey, wake up!"

"Whuh?" He sits up with such a start that I draw back. He's drenched with sweat. "What are you doing?" He shakes his head to clear it.

"You were dreaming. A nightmare." I decide to spare him the embarrassment of the "Mommy" thing. "Do you remember what it was about?"

He runs his hand through his hair. "I don't know. I felt like I was drowning. I couldn't get air."

"Can I get you some water or some aspirin or something?"

"No." He coughs, clears his throat.

I linger by the bed. "Are you sure?"

"I'm sure. No big deal. Go back to bed." He flops down on his back, his arm crossed over his face.

And just like that, "Mommy" is dismissed.

I pad back to my room and lie down on my back, thinking that it didn't seem so long ago that he would wake up crying from a bad dream, or worse, night terrors, and I would rush to his room and pull him out of his bad dreams and into my arms, smoothing his hair, whispering words of comfort, kissing his tears. How he would beg me to lie down with him then until he fell back to sleep. And of course I would. I'd go through my repertoire of lullabies: "All Through the Night," "Over the Rainbow," "Count Your Blessings," "Stay Awake." I recall the blissful melding of our two hearts as his little body gradually relaxed in my embrace. His trust in the safety of my arms reinforced my own sense of being safe. I would stop singing then and listen, with my eyes closed, as his breathing became slow and deep.

He's not your little boy anymore. He's a man.

I sigh, turn over, and close my eyes.

In the dream I am sleeping in this room, in this bed. I sense a change in the atmosphere around me, as if it's suddenly carbonated. I sense, more than hear, a buzzing very close to me. Then I see a form standing at the foot of the bed. The same one I saw a few nights ago. He's dressed all in black with a round white collar. Without taking his eyes from me, he carefully removes the collar and sets it down on the bureau. Then he dips his hands into a basin of water and washes them. In the dream I can hear the gentle sloshing of the water in the basin as he rubs his hands together back and forth, back and forth. While I watch the man standing at the bureau, I am aware that this is a dream. From a higher state of consciousness, I am observing myself dreaming. As the man is drying his hands, I awaken.

My mouth is so dry that my tongue feels like it's glued to my palate. I quickly turn on the light and reach for the glass of water that

I keep on the night table. My hand trembles slightly as I drink it all in greedy, quenching gulps. I tell myself that it was only a dream, probably brought on by my research, by the articles about the minister, by Chad's upset at the cemetery. But still, there's a sense of foreboding. Is this dream going to haunt me? Or is it the house itself that is haunted?

I lie awake with the light on, until the black sky dissolves into a welcome lavender blue, *dilly dilly.*

I've fallen back to sleep, deep REM sleep, just past dawn, when there's a knock on my bedroom door. I look at the clock: 6:50 a.m.

"Mom?"

"What? What's the matter?" I sit up wide-eyed, clutching the sheet as Chad opens the door and pokes his head in. He's dressed in sweatpants, waving papers at me.

"I found her!"

"Who?"

"Madame Sancerre!"

"What are you doing? It's barely seven a.m."

"I couldn't sleep. I kept thinking about that little kid who died. Like maybe in the room where I'm staying. It freaked me out, so I got up and decided to go online, check out the curator's website. It took a while, but finally one of the links led me to the rep for *The Angel Collection*, then to the mysterious Madame herself. Check this out."

He hands me his stash of papers, saying, "Can I kick ass or what?"

He has already exchanged two e-mails with Anne-Claire Goudonov Sancerre, in which he described our project, requested and received her phone number, and asked when it would be convenient for me to telephone her.

"So you can call her at six o'clock her time. And it's okay. She speaks English," he says.

"You did good," I manage, staring at the telephone number he's handed me.

Three cups of coffee and a long shower clear my mind, and at precisely noon, I make the call.

"Madame Sancerre? Anne-Claire Goudonov Sancerre?"

"Qui parle?"

"My name is Morgan Reed. I'm a filmmaker, calling from Pennsylvania, in the United States. My assistant said that this would be a convenient time to speak with you."

"Ah, yes, Ms. Reed. I was expecting your call. You are very prompt. How may I help you?"

Fortunately I've made notes to myself in preparation for this conversation.

"First of all, I'd like to thank you for taking the time to speak with me."

"Not at all. Your assistant describes a project that appeals to me. Telling the story of Angel and Duvall. It is a quite remarkable story, and really, no person has yet attempted it. Or, shall I say, no person has told it from the American perspective. You say you are in Pennsylvania?"

"Yes. Bucks County, Pennsylvania. In fact, I live not far from where Daniel Duvall had his farm. Aquatong Farm."

"Oh my. You are near to Daniel's farm?"

"Yes, are you familiar with it? It's quite unique and beautiful."

Her voice suddenly turns frosty. "No. No one in the family has ever returned to that place."

What does she mean, "no one in the family"?

"Well, I'm so pleased that you approve of having the story told from an American perspective."

"Yes, I do approve of the idea itself, however it is difficult for me to give my approval to you since we've not met."

"Well, all I really need, Madame, would be your consent, your written consent, to use photographs of the paintings in our documentary. Would that be a problem?"

"Well, yes, of course it would be a problem, because if someone is going to make a film about my grandparents, I must certainly have approval of the finished product."

For a moment, I can't find my voice. "Your 'grandparents?'"

"Mais oui. Yes."

"To whom do you refer?"

"To Duvall and Angel, of course. You did not know?"

I swallow. "No, I did not."

"Oh, I assumed that you did, and that is why you contacted me. Angel was my grandmother—my step-grandmother, really. And Duvall, of course, then, by common law, was my step-grandfather."

My heart is hammering. I struggle to keep my voice calm, professional. "I'm sorry. I had no idea. That certainly casts a whole new light on this conversation and on your desire to protect the legacy of Daniel and Angel. I respect that. And I appreciate what an incredibly valuable resource you are, Madame. You must have a treasure trove of information about both of them."

"Bien sûr."

"And, of course, this is why you have so many of the paintings. Now I understand."

"I've kept them here in the family house in Giverny. I feel they belong here. This is where my grandparents had happy times, painting and raising my mother. I also have marvelous memories of summers and holidays here. It is, you might say, my own little shrine to Angel and Duvall."

I'm remembering how much importance the French place on decorum and manners, and I'm trying to summon every ounce of breeding I possess.

"Madame, I can certainly understand your hesitation about placing the story of these great artists, who were your family—placing their story in the hands of a complete stranger. May I ask you, if you please, what references would you need—what credentials would be necessary to put you at ease—at least so that we might have your permission to use the photographs of the paintings and, perhaps, even do an extended interview with you by telephone or via e-mail. I could send you the questions, and, you could answer them at your leisure."

There is no hesitation at the other end.

"Well, I would have to meet you, of course. You would have to come to Giverny."

My first thought is, *There goes the project.* My second thought is, *We have to go!* My third thought is, *What if we go all the way over there, and she doesn't like the way I knot my scarf?* Then I'm doing wild budget calculations in my head. *If only I hadn't committed to hiring Chad, we could swing it.* I toss that thought out before it starts to take root.

"I see. Well, I would certainly love that. Perhaps it's a possibility. May I discuss it with my business partner and call you back in the next day or so?"

Chad pokes his head in as I'm punching in Victor's number.

"How'd it go?" he asks.

"Unbelievable! Angel and Duvall—" Before I can finish the sentence, Victor picks up. "Victor? You're not going to believe this!"

Chad watches as I breathlessly relate to Victor the details of my conversation with Madame Sancerre. His interest quickens even more when he hears me tell Victor that she wants us to come to Giverny.

On the phone, Victor says, "How did you find this woman?"

I look over at Chad and smile. "My son tracked her down."

"Your son?"

"Yes, he's here. I want you two to meet. That's why I invited you for dinner. We've got so much to talk about."

"Well, you're certainly full of surprises. All right. See you later, then. In the meantime I'll go over some numbers, get an estimate of how much a trip like that would cost. I can tell you it would be a hefty slice of the budget."

"But think what we'd get out of it! Can you imagine having the opportunity to actually sit down with Angel and Duvall's granddaughter! That is, if she approves of us."

"How could she not? One of us has class, and it isn't me."

"Stop, you do so. I'm so psyched!"

"No doubt about it. You've struck gold."

"Victor!"

"What?"

I shout into the phone, "I want to go to Giverny!"

He laughs and hangs up.

I turn to Chad, so jazzed I feel like running around the block. Instead I impulsively throw my arms around his neck. He lets me.

"Oh my God, I cannot believe how great this could be!" I beam at him. "I feel an Emmy coming on!"

"*Très* cool and *mais oui*," says Chad. "Can you drive me down to Manayunk so I can dig up my passport?"

TWELVE
C H A P T E R

1895

Lizzie was in the backyard hanging out the wash, when I came riding up the lane on the bicycle, Willie in the basket in front of me. I stopped the bike, balancing it while I helped Willie down.

"Lizzie!" I called. "You have a letter from Ireland!"

"Lizzie," echoed Willie, "you have a letter fromarlin."

I bent over and placed the letter in his hand. "Here, you take it to her," I whispered.

Willie ran to Lizzie, holding the letter out in front of him. Lizzie turned quickly, standing stock still, her face as white as the wash. Then she wiped her hands on her apron and blessed herself, saying, "Jesus, Mary, and Joseph, I hope nobody's dead."

I sat next to her on the porch as she carefully opened the letter and began to read. Willie leaned into her lap, watching her face.

"What is it?" I couldn't help asking. "Is it bad news?"

She didn't answer me. She slowly read through the first page, then turned to the second page. There were several pages, and it took her a long time to read it. I sat rocking, watching her lips move across the words, watching her face for some reaction. From time to time she stopped reading, let the letter fall in her lap and stared off into space, as if remembering something. When she finally finished, she took out her hankie and wiped her eyes, sniffling and sighing.

"Lizzie?" I said tentatively. "Are you all right?"

She nodded slowly without looking at me.

Finally she folded the pages, replaced them carefully in the envelope, and put the letter in her pocket. She rose from the rocker and said, "I think I'll be takin' a little walk by myself."

I watched her back as she stepped off the porch, caressing Willie's head as she passed him. She walked around the lilac bush toward the back of the house, where she wandered in the meadow for a half hour or more. I stared at her from the kitchen window, wondering what had been in the letter that troubled her so.

When I finally saw her walking slowly back to the house, she looked weary, as if she were returning from a long, difficult journey.

I greeted her at the back door. Her expression was solemn, her eyes glazed from weeping.

"Lizzie?" I said. "What is it? Can you talk about it?"

"Let's go out to the porch," she said.

I followed her obediently, afraid to say anything.

Once again we settled ourselves in the rocking chairs. I pulled Willie onto my lap, rocking him, while he looked at a book, leaned against me, and sucked his thumb.

"When I was a girl," she began, "I had a sweetheart." Her voice took on a dreamlike cadence. "Oh, he was a fine, handsome creature of a man, my Seamus was. Every girl in the village wanted him, but he had eyes only for me. And for me, there was no other lad in the world. When I saw him coming down the lane, or kneelin' in the church at Mass, or drivin' his father's cows out to pasture, his shoulders burstin' through the shirt on his back, my heart would stop where it was. I was seventeen, and he was nineteen, and we were in love like the storybooks, laughin' and teasin', and speakin' low as lovers do. There was a magic between us that pulled us t'ward each other, grabbin' and touchin' and breathin' heavy, and filled with such a longin' to be close as close. And we would both be tremblin' till our teeth rattled, and then we would tear apart, vowin' again and again to wait until our wedding day to belong to each other completely. He wanted me to be pure, and I wanted to be pure and perfect for him, and so we waited, with the fire burnin' in our loins, while the banns were posted, and the plans for our wedding were laid. And my mother and me sewed on my wedding dress, a beautiful gown of the whitest Irish lace. Oh, such a bride I was goin' to be!

"And on the mornin' before the day of the wedding, very early it was, Seamus came to the door and said he needed to speak to me. There was a look on his face the like of which I've never seen. When I saw him I thought sure somebody died. He asked me to go walkin', and when I reached to take his hand, like we always did, he put his hand in his pocket and kept on trudging ahead, lookin' at the ground, not speakin'. I felt a chill in my heart, for never, in all our days together, had he not held my hand when we went walkin'. We walked a mile or more like that, him not speakin', and me afraid to ask. Finally he stopped and turned to me, and he had tears streamin' out his eyes, and his face all crumpled up like a an empty sack, and he seized me in his arms so's I couldn't breathe, and then this young boy, my beautiful young husband-to-be, breaks down cryin' in my arms like a babe. Great, heavin' sobs, and oh, then, I felt such a fear, my blood turned to ice, and I felt I would faint with him there holdin' me. 'I can't marry you!' He just said it out. 'I got Bridget Foy in the family way, and Father Reilly is marryin' us as soon as the banns are posted.' And after he said that, we both fell on the ground, holdin' each other and cryin' with the tears and the dust smearin' all over our faces. And he kissed me and swore to me that I was his only love, his only true wife, but we both knew that his deeds had showed otherwise. And finally there was nothin' else to say, and we broke away from each other, and got up from the ground, and brushed the dirt off ourselves. And he walked one way, and I walked the other, and I never looked back, even when he called my name. And the followin' week, I went to the agency and booked a passage to America, where I found a place with your mother and father, God rest their souls."

"And you never heard from him again?" I asked. Lizzie, dear, sad Lizzie.

Her tear-swollen eyes met mine. "Not till today."

I swallowed. "What did he say?"

"He said—" Her voice trembled and broke. "He said that Bridget has died, and he wants me to come back home and marry him and help him take care of those poor motherless children." Her chin wobbled as tears seeped down her cheeks.

The air closed in on me, and I put my hand to my throat because I couldn't catch my breath. I was back in my nursery in Philadelphia, hearing them carry my mother's lifeless body down the stairs. My heart cried out, *Lizzie! Don't leave me! Don't leave me!* I leaned toward her and put my hand on her shoulder as Willie looked from me to her and back again. He started to whimper. I pressed him to me and said in a small voice, "What will you do?"

"Oh," she moaned, "oh, dear Lord, you know I love you. I love you and my little Willie like you were me own, but I love him, too, with a love that's still burnin' in me, even after all these years. I long ago gave up any hope of havin' a husband and babes of me own, but now it seems like the Lord has handed me a gift, a miracle, and at the same time, it means that he'll be takin' me away from you. My heart feels as torn in two as it did that mornin' when Seamus told me he couldn't marry me. Oh, help me, Vangie, help me. I want to go to him. I have to go to him, even if it means leavin' you. I want a husband of my own, a babe of my own if 'tisn't too late. I want to see my family again—my brothers and my sisters, and my mother and father while they still have some years left to them."

She came to me then and knelt down beside me, enveloping Willie and me in her arms. Willie was crying by now, and so was I. The three of us huddled there, holding each other.

Finally I pulled away. I studied that dear face, so twisted with emotion. I smoothed her hair and wiped the tears from her cheeks. "Dearest Lizzie," I said. "Of course you must go to him." She looked at me with such gratitude that a light seemed to shine from beneath her skin, and the tears shimmered in her dark eyes, and the most beautiful smile I had ever seen wreathed her face.

She took my hand and pressed it to her lips. "God Bless you, my darlin' Vangie. God bless you and keep you forever and all time."

⁊ ⁊ ⁊

Lizzie's departure was scheduled for the week before the baptisms.

I was grateful for the activity that occupied our final days together. The distraction kept me from dwelling on the misery I felt at the prospect of losing her forever. I didn't know how to prepare myself, let alone Willie, and so I carried on with him as if nothing were amiss.

In addition to the usual obligations that dictated my life, I was engaged in a continual round of sewing circles, choir meetings, and baking for the baptismal supper. When there was a rare free moment, I helped Lizzie fashion a modest wedding trousseau. As her trunk gradually filled with towels and linens and lace-trimmed petticoats, my heart filled with tender memories of all our years together. I reflected on her incalculable gift for kindliness, which had brought me so much solace when my mother died. I didn't dare let myself contemplate what I would do when she was gone.

On the day before her departure, we were in her little room off the kitchen, putting the final touches on her trousseau. She was to leave the following morning on the train from Bull's Island. That train would take her to Trenton, then on to New York, from whence her ship would sail.

We worked quietly side by side, each with our own thoughts.

From time to time I stole a glance at her and marveled at the transformation that had come over her since the arrival of Seamus's letter.

She glowed with the radiance of a young bride, her skin creamy with a hint of blush, her black eyes sparkling with newfound dreams. She went about her chores humming softly to herself, and her rounded body seemed to melt into soft curves. Yet sometimes I would watch her as she tended Willie, or catch her studying me, and then her expression turned wistful, sorrowful even, and she would reach for her handkerchief, dabbing her eyes.

"Darlin'," she said finally, "I think that trunk'll be splittin' its sides if we put so much as another doily in it."

"Oh, I almost forgot the most important thing," I said. "Something old!"

I dashed upstairs to my room, where my special gift for Lizzie lay waiting, wrapped in tissue paper. I carefully lifted it from the drawer and carried it back downstairs.

I stood in the door of her room and said, "I want you to have this. For your wedding day." Her mouth fell open, and she gasped as I unwrapped the layers of tissue and held up my wedding veil, a panel of Alençon lace, crowned with a circlet of seed pearls and crystals.

She attempted to speak, then paused, shaking her head. "Oh, dear Lord, No, Vangie, no, I can't," she whispered.

"Of course you can," I said, placing the crown of pearls on her head and arranging the lace down her back. "See how beautiful you look." I turned her to the mirror over the washstand.

She stared at herself. "Oh, 'tis becomin', isn't it?" she whispered, smiling at her reflection. Then she turned back to me. "But are ya' sure? This was your mother's before you, God rest her soul. Maybe you'll have yourself a little girl someday. It should stay in the family."

I laid my hands firmly on her shoulders and looked into her eyes. "You are family," I said.

She looked at me with a world of tenderness.

"And you're my family, darlin' girl," she said, putting her arms around me. "Don't you ever, ever forget that."

"I won't," I said, hugging her tightly. After a moment I pulled back. "You'll be a beautiful bride!" I said. And I meant it. "Wait till Seamus sees you!" We both began to giggle.

Then Lizzie grew solemn. "Come and sit with me for a minute, darlin'. I've a few words I been wantin' to say to you, and now's as good a time as any."

Still wearing the veil, Lizzie sat down on the bed and patted the spot next to her. I sat down, and she took my hand in hers. "You're a good girl, Vangie. A good girl." She squeezed my hand. "And some small credit, I think, goes to myself. I tried to raise you right." Then she sighed. "But there's a place in you I never could reach. A spirit in you I could see but never understand. You've a flame burnin' in you somewhere, and I'm afeared it's gonna burn a hole if you're not guardin' against it. I worry that without me here to pull in on your reins, you'll go gallopin' off into God knows where, doin' God knows what. I know it's been hard for you here, and I know the Reverend forbiddin' you to paint like he did near broke your heart. But he's your husband, Vangie, and he's a man of the cloth, a good man, and you took your vows before God and all creation to be a good and faithful wife to him. And you have to make the best of it. You have a beautiful child, God bless the ground that baby walks on, and you have to think of him. Always of him. He deserves the best of you, as does his father. This business of sneakin' off to be paintin', that's going to come to no good."

I started to speak in my own defense, but she hushed me.

"No, darlin', listen. I know how much it means to you. But it's the wrong thing to do. It's betrayin' your husband's word, and you can't do that. It's against God's law. A woman's place is in the home and at her husband's side, and not runnin' off to paint pictures with some strange man. If you hold your patience, I'm sure that after awhile, the Reverend won't be mindin' if you take out your paints now and then. Draw the pretty flowers and the fields and the forest creatures, maybe even paint a picture of Willie and surprise the Reverend with it one day. Do it like that, and I feel in my heart that he won't say no to lettin' you do what makes you happy. But it can't rule your life. Because this is your life. Not the other. You can't have the other. And if you think you can have both together, you're sorely mistaken. You married the wrong man for it."

I sat with my head bowed, not knowing how to respond.

Finally I said, "When you told me about Seamus, about how he made you feel, I tried to imagine what that was like, but I couldn't, and it troubled me. I love William. I want to be a good wife to him. But sometimes it seems that I should be feeling something that isn't there. You said that when you saw Seamus, whether it was in church or coming toward you down the lane, you said—I remember your words: that your heart stopped where it was." I looked at her, suddenly overtaken by a longing, a need to have her explain it all to me. "I've never felt that, Lizzie! I don't know what that feels like."

She sighed. "Vangie, some marriages are based on passion, and some are based on respect, and some, maybe a little combination of the both. Don't look for somethin' that isn't there. Try hard to make the most of what is."

125

I sighed. "I do love William. But I wish I felt…something…something like what you talked about when you described your feelings for Seamus."

She put her arm around me. "It's never to late," she said. "Such feelings can grow."

But somehow I didn't believe her.

✍ ✍ ✍

As much as I dreaded the sound of the train whistle, I longed for it. Lizzie, Willie, and I had been standing on the platform at Bull's Island for ten minutes, making small talk and trying to rise above the oppressive shroud of melancholy that hung over us. William had wished Lizzie a safe journey earlier that morning, before leaving for Frenchtown.

"Lizzie, you shall indeed be missed," he had said, shaking her hand.

"Look after my girl, Reverend, sir. We've been together since she was six years old, and with the ocean separatin' us, she'll be in sore need of patience and kindness."

"You have my word," he assured her, glancing at me and smiling beneficently.

Lizzie's eyes shimmered as she said, "I know that your precious boy will grow to be a fine man, Reverend, just like his father."

William beamed.

Willie and I had driven Lizzie in the wagon to the train stop on the river.

Now we stood next to the tracks, all the important words having been spoken, facing the final, terrible hurdle of the last embrace, the last blessing, the last look.

Lizzie held Willie in her arms, rocking him back and forth, back and forth. "Oh, and you're goin' to be a good boy for your Mama, aren't you, love?" she crooned. "And grow up a strong, fine young lad, just like I promised your father you would?"

Willie nodded, then touched her face. "Why are you crying, Lizzie?" he asked.

"Because I'm goin' home to Ireland, son," she said.

"You can come back tomorrow," he said, patting her cheek.

"Oh it's a far distance away," she murmured, struggling to keep some measure of composure. "I shan't be back for a long time. But I'm happy, really I am."

"Are you crying for happy then?" asked Willie.

A train whistle cut through the morning haze.

"Yes, cryin' for happy, love," said Lizzie. And she hugged him to her breast, squeezing her eyes shut and cooing into his ear, "Oh, my darlin' baby boy, God bless. God Bless." She gently set him down and turned to me. We faced each other solemnly, stoically.

"I love you," I said, trying to speak over the rock in my throat. "I'll always love you."

"And I love you, my darlin' Vangie. C'mere, my girl." We held each other fiercely. I clutched the comforting roundness of her back and her shoulders, and buried my face in her neck, and inhaled the sweet, familiar fragrance of her.

"Oh, Lizzie," I cried. "Oh, Lizzie!"

She pulled back, her face a study in anguish.

"Tell me I'm not makin' a mistake, leaving ya' here to fend for yerself!" she cried.

"I'll be all right," I lied, pulling her to me once more. "Write to me," I cried.

"This your baggage, ma'am?" asked the porter.

"Yes, the trunk and these bags," said Lizzie, drawing away from me. She withdrew a hankie from her sleeve and wiped her eyes.

"Well, then," she said.

"Be happy, my darling Lizzie," I said. Then I added, "Tell Seamus he'd better take good care of you!"

She smiled through her tears—such a smile that I knew this leave-taking was harder for me than it was for her. She was on her way to a new life with the man she loved.

We walked with her the few steps to the train. The porter put out his hand to her. One quick kiss for each of us, then she boarded the train and disappeared. I pulled Willie with me along the outside of the car, searching for her. Finally she appeared at a window, and we waved to each other as the train started to move out of the station. The whistle blew, and through a blur I saw Lizzie grow smaller and smaller, until she and the train were a black dot on the horizon. Then I stumbled back to the wagon, clutching Willie's hand, almost oblivious to his cries of, "Wait, Mama. I can't go so fast."

Across the bridge, then north on River Road, I tried not to cry, for Willie's sake. But the tears pooled up in my eyes and spilled over, until I could barely see the road in front of me. The thought of returning to that empty house depressed me even more, and I had a vague longing to just continue on River Road, past Lumberville, past Milltown, and on up into the quiet oblivion of the deep pine forests of the north.

How would I manage without her? She had been mother, sister, and ally to me—a sympathetic ear and a voice of wisdom. No one understood me the way Lizzie did, certainly not William. He loved me—that much was true—but he was too immersed in his work to be interested in what I was thinking or feeling. I was there to serve his needs, not the other way around. And I silently acknowledged that that was as it should be in a marriage. But without Lizzie, who would I talk to about the things that really mattered to me? Who else understood my need to recreate the things I saw, the things I dreamed? No one else in the world. No one else, it came to me in a flash, but Daniel Duvall.

That thought jolted me, and I was suddenly aware of my surroundings. I realized that I was approaching the turn into Aquatong Farm. Without making a conscious decision, I pulled on the reins and felt the wagon veer left across River Road and onto the familiar lane through the woods.

"Where are we going, Mama?" asked Willie.

"I'm taking you to see the animals," I said.

"Where's the sky, Mama?" he asked, craning his neck to look up at the hemlocks and sycamores and giant blooming rhododendron that loomed, casting deep shadows across the narrow road.

When we broke through to the clearing, Willie cried out happily, "There's the sky, Mama! There it is!"

I lifted him down from the wagon, at the same time searching for a sign of Daniel Duvall.

"You go say hello to the baby lambs. I'll be right back." I guided him over to the fence that enclosed the sheep, then hurried up the hill to Daniel's studio. I rapped on the door and called his name.

"Mr. Duvall? Daniel, are you there?"

There was no answer.

"Can I help you, Miss?"

I turned quickly to my right and saw a man coming toward me, up the rise. He had a wizened face and a bulbous red nose, and he was dressed in farm clothes. I realized that it must be the caretaker.

"I…I was looking for Mr. Duvall," I said awkwardly.

"He ain't here," said the man. He stared at me.

"Do you know when he's expected?" I asked.

"Can't say as I do."

"Thank you," I said. As I hurried past him, I couldn't help but notice that his person emitted the sweet, stale smell of alcohol.

"Willie," I called, "come here to Mama. We're going home."

"But, Mama, look at the duckies on the water. Look, Mama, at the little duckies."

I clasped his hand. "I see, darling, but we have to go now."

"No, Mama, I want to see the duckies swim in the water!"

"No, Willie, we have to go now." I pulled him along toward the wagon and lifted him onto the seat.

"I want to see the duckies," he wailed.

"I'm sorry," I said, "we'll come back another time."

"No! Now!" he cried, trying to stand up in the seat.

"Willie! Sit down! Sit down now, or you'll fall!" I reached for his arm and forced him down into the seat. He continued to cry as I turned the wagon around and headed back down the lane. When I had rounded the gentle curve that hugged the banks of the creek, I stopped the wagon and let the tears fall. I took Willie onto my lap and hugged him to me as we both cried. But he cried because he'd been taken away from the ducks; I cried because I felt I hadn't a friend in the world.

Then I heard the clip-clop of horse hooves. I looked up and saw Daniel Duvall riding toward me from the direction of River Road.

Watching him approach, I wiped my eyes and hushed Willie.

He dismounted and threw his reins over a tree branch. He drew near, wearing a puzzled expression on his face.

"Evangeline? Are you all right?"

"Yes," I said, "yes, I'm all right."

"I'm just returning from the village. Are you here for a lesson?" His eyes took in Willie, and he looked confused.

"Oh! Oh, no, I've come from the train stop at Bull's Island, and I—" I hesitated, not certain that I could explain what had brought me to Aquatong Farm.

"Why don't you step down so we can talk," said Daniel, extending his hand. I turned back for Willie.

"Come, my big boy," I said. "We'll have a short visit."

Willie obeyed silently, his tears temporarily forgotten by the appearance of the strange man on the horse.

"Shake hands with the gentleman, Willie."

Willie obliged but was more interested in Daniel's horse. "Can I ride the horse, Mama?"

"Would you like to climb up?" asked Daniel.

"Yes," said Willie. Daniel swept him up and deposited him on the saddle, then took the reins from the tree for Willie to hold in his hand.

"Look, Mama! I'm riding the horse!"

"Be careful," I said.

Daniel turned to me and studied my face. "So you were at Bull's Island this morning? Taking your husband to the train?"

"No, my friend. My companion and helper. She's been with me for years, and today she left to go back to Ireland."

"And you're very sad."

"No, I'm...I'm happy for her. She went back to marry her old sweetheart." I looked up at him and attempted a smile. "So I'm happy for her."

"Then why are your eyes swollen from crying?" he said. I felt something in me give way. Pretensions were of no use with this man. He seemed to pull the truth out of me before I knew what it was myself. I lowered my head as I felt new tears sting and spill over.

"So you were driving by after your emotional farewell, and you needed to talk to a friend."

I nodded. He drew a handkerchief from his pocket.

"I'm glad that you think of me as your friend. And I also wish that I could continue on as your teacher."

"I wish you could too," I said. I glanced briefly into the crystalline blue of his eyes.

"Is there any chance of that happening again?" he said.

I shook my head. "No, I don't think so. I'm very busy getting ready for a baptism that we're having in a few days' time. And now that Lizzie's gone, I have no help at home until I can find someone new. I've put an advertisement in the *Doylestown Intelligencer*, but it won't appear until next week. And whomever I do find, it won't be the same. No one will ever take Lizzie's place. For Willie or for me."

"Perhaps you could bring him here with you. My housekeeper could look after him for a few hours."

"That's very kind of you, but I can't involve my son in my...my deceitful acts."

"That's how you see it?" he said gently.

"There's no other way to see it. My place is at home, keeping house for my husband and helping him with his work."

"What about your work?" he said.

"One can hardly call painting fanciful pictures my 'work.' You're a renowned artist. I'm just a silly woman."

"Stop it. Stop being self-deprecating. Gender has nothing to do with it!" His cheeks puffed out in frustration, and he jammed his hands in his pockets.

"I apologize—"

He interrupted. "And don't apologize. Acknowledge that you possess a rare talent—a God-given talent. At least grant me that."

I nodded thoughtfully, pressing my lips together. "Perhaps some time in the future I'll be able to take up painting again, but not now—not without my husband's permission."

As we stood awkwardly, he said, "Well, if you ever change your mind..."

I nodded. "Thank you."

"Evangeline?" His eyes probed my face, searching for an answer. But I didn't know the question. He then shook his head, as if to clear it, and placed his hand under my elbow to help me into the wagon. I set my boot on the step, but it skidded off. I lost my balance and fell back against him. He arm came around my waist to steady me, and I leaned into him. I turned my head slightly, and our faces were inches apart. I could feel his hot breath on my brow, and it conjured the thick sensations of that afternoon in his studio. I felt the size and power of his arms through his shirt, and it was as if my own strength drained from me. I looked into his eyes then, a long deep look that pulled me in and down and around into some swirling, whirling pool where I had neither the need nor the desire to breathe. For some seconds I let myself be there. Then, with all my might, I drew myself back, back up through the dizzying, spinning swirls, back to the surface, and back to the heat of the late-morning sun, and the rush of the creek, and the birdsong, and Willie, still on the horse, calling, "I want to get down!"

Daniel released me and went to Willie. He lifted him off the horse and carried him over to the wagon, setting him on the seat. Then he came back to me. I kept my eyes averted as he gently helped me climb up. Light-headed and slightly giddy, I clutched the reins, snapped them hard, and headed down the cloistered, shadowed lane toward River Road.

That night I dreamed I was standing in the murky silence of that lane. The trees loomed over me on both sides, their branches extending down like bony fingers. I was afraid because there seemed to be no air or light in that place. Suddenly I turned to my left and saw Daniel riding toward me on his massive stallion, a little girl on the saddle in front of him. As they passed by, they both looked at me without smiling. At the clearing I could see the sun washing over them so brilliantly that it absorbed them into its radiance, while I stood cloistered in the dark. I awoke with a start. The back of my neck and the roots of my hair were damp, my nightgown was sticking to my body, and my hand was pressed between my thighs.

Evangeline Laury, "ANGEL"

Daniel Duvall

Reverend William X. Laury

Willie

Lizzie

Seamus O' Connell

Clara Shaw

Elizabeth

THIRTEEN

CHAPTER

1996

I'd just finished setting the table on the patio, when Chad emerged from the house, the screen door whacking shut behind him. He was freshly showered and, to my secret satisfaction, had shaved off the scruffy stubble that I thought had gone out in the eighties, but seems, more than a decade later, to still be some male symbol of hip rebellion or something. His natural elegance catches me off guard and touches my motherly pride. We'd made a quick round-trip to Manayunk to collect his belongings from the dump of an apartment he'd been sharing with three other guys.

"Anything I can do?" he says now.

"Maybe start the grill in a few minutes," I reply.

Just then Victor calls out, "Hello!" and rounds the side of the house, bearing a bottle of wine and a bouquet of peonies from his garden, just like a real gentleman caller. He presents the gifts with a flourish and kisses me on the cheek. I feel secretly girlish and flattered, yet self-conscious in front of Chad. Is Victor pouring on the charm out of a sense of rivalry, or is it sincere? I feel teased, toyed with—once again off-balance—especially after his puzzling retreat from our wild kiss at Aquatong Farm.

I needed to be in control tonight. The prospect of finessing this evening between my son and my would-be lover/partner had kept me edgy and hyper all day. I just want everybody to like everybody. Add the prospect of going to Giverny to meet Madame Sancerre, and I feel like I'm on speed.

"So, the prodigal son!" says Victor as he and Chad shake hands.

"Uh, I don't think so. Doesn't prodigal mean wasteful and extravagant?" shoots back Chad.

"Oh? Does it?" says Victor. "I'll have to check my *Webster's*. I thought it meant gifted. No insult intended. Great work, tracking down the lady in France."

"No problem."

I jump in. "Chad, why don't you open the wine? I'll just, uh, put these flowers in water." I scamper inside for a vase, anxious about leaving the two of them out there alone for more than thirty seconds. As it turns out, I have to hunt around for the right size vase, and when I get back outside, Victor says pointedly, "So your son tells me that he's joining us on the documentary."

"Yes! That's why I initially invited you over—so the three of us could talk about it. It all happened so fast. And then the way he tracked down Madame Sancerre! How awesome is that!"

Chad pours the wine, and I notice that his hand trembles. Hangover residue?

"Since we have the budget for an assistant, and Chad's available, experienced, and obviously knows how to kick ass, it just seemed perfect." I accept a glass of wine from Chad. He hands one to Victor, then pours a hefty one for himself. I shoot him a withering look, but he ignores it.

"Hair of the dog," he murmurs, lifting his glass.

"Well, cheers everyone," I say. "To Madame Sancerre!"

"Vive la France," salutes Chad.

We clink glasses, and I take a big gulp, steeling myself for whatever is to come.

"I checked into flights to Paris," says Chad.

Victor's eyebrows shoot up, and he aims a puzzled look at me.

"Is that what you were doing on the computer all afternoon?" I ask.

"We'd have to go soon, and that's going to cost us. With meals, hotels, travel time, work days, I guess we're talking five or six days—" says Chad.

"Assuming she likes us, and we don't have to turn around and come home," I say.

"She'll like us," says Chad confidently.

Now Victor turns to me, speaking as if Chad weren't even there. "We can't afford to take three people," he says. "We're risking everything with you and I going—especially with no guarantees that she'll give us the story. I think it's worth the risk, but there's no way—I mean, Morgan, get real. If we get to shoot over there, it's going to be strictly a one-man band."

The three of us stand there in a thick, uncomfortable silence. I feel my face grow hot. In my excitement, I hadn't really thought about whether or not all of us would be going. How stupid! And of course, Chad—I steal a glance at him—Chad feels that he owns the story already, or at least part of it, because he scored Madame Sancerre. I realize that I'm clutching my wineglass so hard it could shatter in my hand.

Chad is staring into his. Then he swirls it, lifts it toward Victor with a slight flourish, and says, "Whatever." Then he raises it to his lips and downs its entire contents in two swallows.

Victor clears his throat. "Well, this looks festive," he says lamely, indicating the table. I'd carefully laid it with a pretty blue and yellow Provençal cloth and napkins I'd picked up at an outdoor market in Paris. The print was a perfect background for my blue and white dishes. Three fat white candles await the click of a lighter. The peonies are a perfect addition.

"What can I do?" offers Victor. My level of discomfort is so great, I can only think of escaping to the kitchen.

"Maybe you and Chad could get the grill started. I have to check on a couple of things inside."

This suggestion is followed by a few stilted, manly exchanges about charcoal and lighter fluid, so I refill my wine glass and, in my own version of a Hail Mary pass, beat it through the screen door into the house.

I've just mixed vinaigrette for the salad, when the screen door slams. I drop the jar, spilling its contents all over the counter, and look up to see a somber Victor approaching.

"Oh! You startled me!" I say, reaching for a sponge and wondering if I have enough balsamic vinegar to start all over again.

"Sorry. But *you* startled *me*," he says. "First you spring this assistant thing on me, and before I've even had a chance to talk to you about it, he's got himself on a plane to France. Give me a break."

"I'm sorry. It all happened so fast. And I never told him he'd be coming to France—*if we went.* I think he was really excited about tracking this great source, and I was excited too, and it just snowballed."

"I don't like being made out to be the bad guy here. And I don't like being manipulated. I mean, who got you this job, anyway?"

I let that pass. "First of all, did we or did we not agree that we had a budget for an assistant?"

"Did. But with this France trip, who knows."

"Well, he is qualified, he needs a job, and he's already shown his stripes. Why not him?"

"The nepotism thing never goes over well."

"Victor, he's my son—"

"Precisely—"

"What's the point in putting out an ad and interviewing, when he's right here and he's available?"

"I don't like the idea of your going behind my back. We're partners. I mean, is this how you do business?"

"I wasn't going behind your back. It just all happened so fast."

"You keep saying that."

"It did."

"I thought you and he weren't on good terms."

"That's part of why I offered him the job," I confess. "To try to get him back—get him back on track with his life." I pause, making a hasty decision for full disclosure. "He got arrested for drunk driving the other night."

"Oh, great."

"He called me to come and get him down on the Main Line. It meant a lot to me that he reached out. We haven't been on speaking terms for months." I put my hand on Victor's arm. "Victor, I just want my son back, and this seems like a perfect opportunity. He's talented; he really is. He just needs a chance."

"I don't want to be embroiled in your family drama."

I'm taken aback. I don't know how to respond.

"I mean it," he continues. "It is not my problem to save your son."

"I'm not asking you to *save him.* Give me a break." I turn away, run the tap water in the sink, and take my time rinsing the sponge.

"He's got a major chip on his shoulder," says Victor, "bigger now, with this France thing. And for a kid who's just been arrested on a DUI, he's sloshing down the wine pretty good. The bottle's almost empty."

The screen door opens again, slams again, and Chad steps into the kitchen, empty wine bottle in hand.

"Hey, Mom, any more wine?" He looks from Victor to me, sensing the tension. "Hope I'm not interrupting anything."

"There's another bottle in the refrigerator," I say tightly. He walks past us, opens the refrigerator door, and pulls out a bottle of Chardonnay.

"Corkscrew?"

"It's outside, isn't it?" I feel Victor watching. Judging.

"Oh, right," says Chad, heading for the door.

"Don't you think you should slow down? Considering?" I say.

"Oh, I'm cool. I just thought, for you guys."

He pushes the door open.

"Don't let the door slam!" I call after him.

THWACK! The warning comes a little too late, as warnings often do.

We finally sit down to dinner. The grilled salmon is way overcooked, but far be it from me to say anything. I'm suffering my own humiliation at the hard, sticky rice and the overdressed salad, a result of a tense and hasty remix of the vinaigrette. At least the asparagus is bright green and tender. And the bread crusty and warm. But the tension has settled itself around the table like another overcooked side dish, and my stomach roils at the sight of a tipsy Chad and a sulking Victor—both chewing morosely, eyes firmly fixed on their plates.

Chad picks up the wine bottle and reaches across Victor to refill my glass. He misses, splashing Chardonnay into my lap.

"Whoops. Sorry." It comes out, "Shorry."

"I'll do that," says Victor. "I'm closer." And for a moment, while I blot my sodden linen pants with my napkin, I think they're going to fight over the wine bottle. But Chad relents. Victor pours.

Chad clears his throat.

"So, you guys want me to book your flights, make your travel arrangements 'n' stuff?" His speech is definitely slurred.

He looks at me, then at Victor. Neither one of us answers.

"I mean, thass what an assistant *does,* right?"

"I think Victor and I need to discuss the plans a little more before we actually book it. But thanks."

"No problem. So, Victor, my mom tells me you used to shoot for ABC Sports. *Monday Night Football.*" It came out, "moneynighfooball."

"Is that what she told you?" Cold. Guarded. Giving me a look.

"Yeah, she said sidelines for, like, seven years or something. That must have been shum gig."

"It was when I was twenty years younger."

"My mom used to date a football player. Didn't you, Mom?"

Two pairs of eyes are on me. I shift in my seat.

"Years ago," I say, brushing it off.

"Quarterback for the Eagles," continues Chad. "Chuck Hagman. Remember him?"

"Great player," says Victor.

"Good old 'Uncle Chuck,'" says Chad. "He even took me to the locker room for my twelfth birthday. Innraduced me to all the players."

"That must've been cool."

"Yeah, my mom had a cool job. She got to meet all these famous people, rock stars and stuff, and lossa times I got to go along."

"I remember your mother from TV."

"Yeah, she was pretty famoush."

"Will you two stop talking about me as if I weren't here?"

"Well, you were famous, Mom."

"Locally and fleetingly," I say dismissively. "Listen, I have to go to the ladies' room. Maybe the two of you can start to clear, if you don't mind. Then we'll have dessert."

Upstairs, I pee and put on fresh lipstick. It occurs to me as I inspect myself in the mirror that Chad wasn't the only one who had drunk too much wine. I had anesthetized myself half into the bag. I run the tap cold and glug down two full glasses of water before making my way down the hall to the stairs. Clutching the banister, I very deliberately place one foot in front of the other until I reach the bottom. Then I step out onto the front porch, breathing deeply, willing myself sober. I inhale the fragrances of grass and earth and growing things, then gaze up. Out here, far from city lights, the stars seem closer—more brilliant, like diamonds dipped in ammonia. I track the Big Dipper, then follow the tiny blinking lights of an overhead plane as it silently soars toward its destination. Where? New York? Maybe Paris! Maybe I would be on such a plane in a few days' time. Flying off to Giverny with Victor, assuming we can get past the awfulness of tonight. I watch the lights of the plane until they fade into the night sky, then return to the house.

In the kitchen Victor is brewing coffee.

"Good idea," I say. I get out coffee mugs, dessert plates, and forks.

The coffee helps, and so does my homemade Key lime pie, which turns out to be Victor's favorite dessert. Like almost every man I know, with a full stomach he seems to mellow a bit, and Chad appears to pay attention when Victor and I take turns telling him more about the rich history of the area and the artists who have painted here—Daniel Duvall in particular. Gradually the tension tiptoes away, and I began to think that the three of us might make it as a team after all.

Then Victor relates the story of the night I'd found the charcoal drawings, my midnight phone call to him, how he'd come racing over here so fast he forgot his shoes, only to witness the carpet rising and falling and rippling off the floor. Chad's jaw drops.

"No way," he says, looking at me.

"It happened," I say. "I know it sounds crazy."

"Your mother was so freaked out—"says Victor.

"*I* was freaked out! You were ready to call Ghostbusters!" I say. I turn to Chad. "You had to see it to believe it."

"It kept going like this," says Victor, using his hand to demonstrate the rising and dipping of the carpet. "As I said, your mother was so freaked out, I ended up sleeping on the couch just to run interference in case there were any uh, otherworldly beings on the premises."

I see Chad's mood suddenly change, see the challenge in his eyes. "So you slept on the couch, huh? Right in the room with the levitating carpet?"

Victor has no idea what he's triggered. Laughing, he turns to me. "What I didn't tell you is that I was awake all night because I was scared shitless! And with God as my witness, I swear the rug moved again after you went upstairs. It got to a point where I had to just close my eyes and pray!"

"No wonder you flew out of here so early the next morning," I say, trying to underscore that he had slept on the couch, really. *Really, Chad.*

Victor says, "Well, I made you coffee before I left, didn't I?"

"Yes, you did, thank you."

"Boy, I was never so glad to see the light of day," says Victor. "That was weird stuff."

Chad looks from me to Victor, watchful and inscrutable. His face seems pale and hard in the candlelight. Then he says, "Now I'm the one that's freaked out!"

"Well," says Victor, "as I told your mother, when you live in an old house, you have to expect the unexpected."

"What do you think it was?" asks Chad.

"I have no idea," says Victor.

"So don't tell me there's some ghost thing going on. You don't believe in that stuff, do you?"

"I don't discount it," says Victor.

"Mom?"

I hesitate, not knowing how to respond. "I don't know what to think. That whole night, from the moment I found the drawings, there was some other level of energy kind of buzzing around me." I shiver involuntarily. "Let's not talk about this."

"My room in Manayunk is starting to look really good about now," says Chad.

"Don't you dare chicken out and leave me here alone!" I say half jokingly. "Why do you think I was so happy to drag you back here with me?" I make a cross of my index fingers as if to ward off evil.

"Well, on that note," says Chad, getting up, "I think I'll head into the kitchen to prepare a garlic necklace before going up to my room to check under the bed and in the closet. You don't have any holy water laying around, do you?"

"Just remember, there's a church next door," says Victor.

"Yeah," says Chad, "there's a cemetery too." He extends his hand. "Nice meeting you, Victor, ghost stories notwithstanding."

Victor stands up. As they shake, he says, "Hey, great hustling on the French connection. Sorry the budget's so tight. Maybe there'll be some other road trip in the future."

"Yeah, righto." Chad brushes his lips against my forehead. "Night, Mother. If you see a ghost, call Victor, not me."

He disappears into the house.

Victor helps me clean up, and then I walk him out to the driveway. The night tucks itself around us, soft and sweetly fragrant. We linger at the truck.

"So," he says.

"So," I say.

"I'm still not happy that you sprang him on me."

"He's a good kid, Victor, when you give him a chance."

"He has an attitude."

"That's just the stuff between him and me. Which I hope can be resolved by my having him here. And it's understandable that he'd be disappointed about being left behind when—notice I said *when*—we go to France."

"I heard you."

"I just want my son back."

"Well, it's not going to be at my expense or the outcome of this documentary. It's nothing against you, but this is business."

"I know. And I apologize again for not discussing it with you first, but…" I shrug. "I just acted on impulse."

"Just so we're clear."

"We're clear. So what do you think? Giverny or bust?"

"Let's do it, kid. Call the lady back, and find out when she'll see us."

"Okay."

"Okay."

"Thank you for a lovely evening."

"Oh, so now it was a lovely evening?"

"It verged on lovely, from time to time."

"Well, thank you for coming. For the flowers and wine. Sorry about the overcooked…whatever."

"Yeah, your son and I didn't earn any medals with the salmon."

A kiss is lingering in the space between us. I wait for him to make the move.

He does.

As we come up for air, I see through the dreamy haze of my half-closed eyes, a silhouette in the upstairs window.

Chad. Watching.

There's a light under his door, so I knock. The response is sharp, challenging. "What?"

I push the door open a crack. "Need anything?"

"An exorcist might help."

I take a few steps into the room and, once again, make the sign of the cross with my index fingers.

"I'm sleeping with the light on," he says.

"You know what? That's a good idea. Why not sleep with it on, if it makes you feel better."

I take another step closer, testing the water. "I'm sorry that we can't take you to France. I know you were revved up for the trip."

"Hey, you're the boss. Or, he's the boss. Whatever."

My grown-up self that knows I should say good night and close the door is elbowed aside by my inner child who's still seeking approval. Especially from her son. "What did you think of him?" I ask.

"What do you care?"

"I'm curious. Since we're going to be working together, hopefully."

"You mean if he gives me his stamp of approval?"

"I'm hoping that we can all behave like professionals and not let personal issues spill over into our work."

"Don't you think I'm sort of a third wheel now? I mean, what do you need me for, if the two of you are going off to maybe shoot this whole thing over there?"

"Well, there's going to be stuff for you to do while we're gone and a ton of B roll and postproduction when we get back."

"Nice little romantic interlude for the two of you, huh?"

"What?"

"A little getaway? Hey, maybe you can save money sharing a room."

I feel my face tighten. "What's that supposed to mean?"

"How long have you known this guy anyway?"

"A while. And it's not what you think."

"How do you know what I think? I know what I *saw. And you knew I was watching.* It was for my benefit."

"What? It was not. And I didn't know you were watching." I feel so cornered. "I'm sorry if you saw anything that embarrassed you."

"It wouldn't be the first time."

"I beg your pardon?" My face grows hot.

He turns away. "You don't want to know," he says wearily.

He's right. I don't want to know because the prospect of knowing weighs on my shoulders like a cloak of shame. I shake it off.

"Chad," I begin, sitting tentatively on the edge of his bed. "I know we have issues to work on. Could we just—I'm tired, and I know you are too. Can we just save it, call a truce?" I lay my hand on his shoulder. He shrugs it away.

"Stop it. You always do that."

"Always do what?"

"Try to pull me in."

"I was just—"

"You always used to come into my room after your loser guys left. Come into my room in the dark, and hug me, and lie down next to me. I could smell it on you."

He might as well have slapped me. For a second or two I'm speechless. Finally I sputter, "That is not true!" But the heaviness of guilt settles in my gut as I realize that perhaps it is true. I try to remember, try to look at what he's just told me. Yes, I did long to be with him when the door closed behind my lovers, leaving me bereft. Bereft except for my beloved son, my constant. "I just wanted to be close to you," I stammer, "to reinforce that you came first, that I loved you, that—"

"Do you know how sick that was?"

How can I speak? What defense can I offer?

"Making me compete with your men, trying to make me jealous—do you know how powerful that is for a young kid! How could I compete?"

"It wasn't about competing! You're my son!"

"Yeah, right," he says.

"Your therapist has put stuff into your head about me. I've always loved you! I did my best!" I hear my voice becoming shrill.

"My therapist didn't put anything in my head, because it was already there! I didn't make it up, Mom, it happened! There were men—so many men—coming and going and coming and going. I'd get my hopes up, and then they'd be gone. I just wanted a dad like the other kids. For as long as I can remember, I just wanted my own dad."

"Your 'dad' was a violent, abusive man. He hit me! You saw it. The second time it happened, I had the good sense to get us both out of there. You know all this, Chad. How I literally escaped with you and some clothes stuffed in garbage bags. How we found the shelter."

"Okay, so you're some hero, but after that, all those years, I wanted a father, a real father, not that parade of guys you dated and dumped."

"I wanted it for you too! Don't you think that's what I wanted? What I was searching for all those years? It's what I hoped we'd finally have with Pete."

"Yeah, that turned out great," he says, lighting a cigarette.

I stop myself from telling him not to smoke in the house.

"Every time there was a breakup, I tried to make things okay, tried so hard to be your own little man, wanting to protect you to take care of you, to make sure nobody ever hurt you again. I was so scared by the responsibility of you. You were always so much bigger than life, and I always felt so small. But all I ever really wanted was a family. Every time I'd get my hopes up. Every time I'd end up picking up the pieces and handing you tissues."

A rock of regret is lodged in my throat.

He draws hard on the cigarette. "And then there was Pete."

We have never talked about what happened, not really.

Chad continues. "That last night, after you kicked him out and called me, crying. I couldn't get there fast enough. But I was so scared.

"We watched a video of Against All Odds. And when that song, 'Take a Look at Me Now' came on, you were crying, and you said, 'Dance with me,' and I did. I slow danced with you, and it meant so much to me, because I thought I was saving you again, protecting you, *healing you* from what that bastard had done, that I could be the man in your life, the one that never let you down, that was always there for you—and you let me believe it! You fostered it! *You slow danced with me like I was your lover! Do you know how sick that was?* It's classic Oedipus, Mom! And you're Jocasta, and I've been wondering for a while now if I'm going to have to put my eyes out or something so I don't have to see you with other men and be scared and hopeful, and basically maybe so I don't have to look at you at all ever again."

His hand shakes as he holds the cigarette.

In a low voice, he says, "Do you know how much guilt I have that I didn't protect you from what Pete did?"

"Chad, it had nothing to do with you."

It's as if he doesn't hear me.

"And then the minute I think, maybe, maybe there's a way that we can have some kind of relationship, something healthy, on a different level—what happens? I look out the window, and there you are. Again. And there I am again. On the outside, waiting for my turn to be back on the inside. Back with just the two of us together. Me protecting you. Then I remind myself: I've worked through all that. I'm over all that. But you come in here, just like all the other times, come into my room and sit down on my bed, all coy and glowey from your make-out session, planning a trip to France with your new boyfriend—that *doesn't* include me—and you reach for me like all the other times..." He is crying now. "And, Mom," his chin wobbles with the effort to say the words. "It has to stop! It has to stop, or I'll have to go away again. And this time I won't come back. I'll never come back."

The guilt has lowered into my chest, where it settles like strong indigestion, burning and heavy—an attack on my heart.

I lie back on the pillow, leaving the light on. I remember the horror of that night when Chad's father punched me in the face for the second time and left a necklace of bruises on my throat. How I'd thrown those clothes in the plastic trash bags, grabbed Chad from his crib, and driven around like a mad woman, finally parking the car in a remote area of Valley Forge Park, too ashamed to go to my father. At dawn, a park ranger had tapped on the window and ultimately guided me to a shelter, where Chad and I stayed for a week. Finally I told my dad everything. We moved in with him until I got on my feet, starting as a singing waitress, and gradually making a career in television.

Lying here, I honestly try to recall the relationships, realizing that it was beyond me to compile a list of names. Almost twenty years of dating. There were many that Chad knew nothing about, had never met. Others, whom I deemed "special," I had brought home, introduced to my son, in the hope that we all might have a future together. Then there would come the inevitable breakup, my feeble attempt to explain to Chad why Bob, or Dick, or Harry didn't come around anymore. The look of disappointment on his young face. Then his bravado, the concerted effort to cheer me up, make me happy.

"There's nobody good enough for you but me, Mom!" he'd say. I'd agree with him.

And that time we danced together after the disaster of Pete? It was Chad that initiated it, wasn't it? I didn't want to hurt his feelings; he seemed so sweet and earnest. And to my recollection, there was an innocence, a purity, a mutual pledge in that brief slow dance: We've survived so much. We'll get past this too.

And I didn't intentionally lie down next to him after being with a man, did I? I tried to face the question squarely: Did I? The probable answer had me rummaging in my night table for a sleeping pill and oblivion.

Instead, there are nightmares. The minister hovering spread-eagled above me, holding Chad in his arms, weeping. His tears dropping down on me, flooding me, choking me. This time, my own shrieking wakes me, and it's Chad who comes flying into my room.

"Mom! Mom, wake up!" He doesn't touch me, just stands next to the bed.

I open my eyes to see his face over me, pale and frightened. I begin to sob. "Oh! Oh!"

"What? What, Mom?"

"I thought you were dead!" I cry. "I thought I killed you!"

FOURTEEN

C H A P T E R

1895

The preparations for the baptism were almost complete. The white-as-snow baptismal garments hung in the church vestry, starched and pressed and ready to be donned. The choir had been rehearsing extra hours all week, and a special selection of songs was planned for the procession down to the creek and the recessional after the ceremony. The ladies of the village had been cooking all week in preparation for the celebratory supper.

To that end, Willie and I had gone out early in the morning to pick strawberries and blueberries. I had baked two strawberry rhubarb pies and two blueberry pies, using Lizzie's old recipes.

Her absence was painfully apparent. Not only was my workload doubled, but I missed the sound of her voice, her sturdy reassuring presence, crooning to Willie, or blessing herself, or muttering a curse under her breath when she burned herself lifting the frying pan off the stove.

When Willie asked when she was coming back, which he did often, I told him that I didn't know but that she loved us and would come back if she could. That seemed to satisfy him. I couldn't bring myself to tell him the truth. It hurt too much to think about. Instead I made myself think happy thoughts about Lizzie: trying to imagine where she was on the Atlantic Ocean and picturing her joyous reunion with Seamus in Dublin.

These thoughts of Lizzie served to blur the daydreams I was having about Daniel Duvall. It shocked and frightened me to realize that I missed him in almost the way I missed Lizzie. It was absurd, I told myself. I hardly knew him, but somehow, every time I saw him, it was as if I were reaching a place where my thoughts and feelings were not only understood but protected. In floating images, I saw the clear, water-pool blue of his eyes and relived the confounding moment when I fell back into his arms. These thoughts disturbed me, and I tried to push them away, but they were stronger than my will.

William was in a state of jubilant anticipation in the days preceding the baptism. With a bounce in his step, he moved between the house and the church and around the village, taking immense pleasure in the smallest details of the upcoming ceremony.

The day of the baptism dawned blue skied and balmy, a perfect June morning. By noon the congregation and the candidates, decked out in their holy robes, were gathered at the rear of the church. With William leading the way, followed by the choir singing a capella, we all marched en masse across the meadow. Children and ladies stopped to gather wild-flowers for impromptu bouquets as we followed the procession down the hill, past the patch of woods that hugged the ridge, and into the field adjacent to Webster's Mill. At last to a grassy clearing that bordered that part of the Paunacussing Creek that emptied into a tranquil pond before spilling over into a waterfall and finally into the mill-run that fed the moss-covered wheel that drove Webster's Mill.

There we all gathered in a circle around the edge of the pond, while the choir sang, "A Mighty Fortress is Our God." William delivered the invocation, then called upon the candidates to come forward. They moved in a group to the edge of the water, the brilliant sun bouncing off their robes in silvery radiance.

"Jacob Wilder!" called William. Jacob Wilder, a husky boy of not much more than sixteen, shyly stepped into the water next to William. They walked to the middle of the pond, where the water came up to their waists. William put one hand on Jacob's head and one on his shoulder, and his booming voice rang out to the tops of the trees, "I baptize thee in the name of the Father, and the Son, and the Holy Ghost." Then he plunged Jacob backward into the water, almost staggering under the weight of him. Jacob came up gasping and blinking his eyes, the perfectly pressed and starched white gown clinging to his bulky body. Jacob knelt down, his eyes closed, his hands folded in prayer.

"Mildred Presto!" boomed William. "Are you ready to meet the Lord?"

Felix Presto's wife stepped forward. "Yes, Reverend," she said in a tremulous voice.

William took her hand and gently guided her into the water. When they reached the middle of the pond, he put one hand on her gray head and one on her shoulder. "I baptize thee in the name of the Father, and the Son, and the Holy Ghost!" he cried, and Mildred squeezed her eyes shut and held her nose as William plunged her backward into the water.

She came up coughing and rubbing her eyes. When she opened them and looked around, a beatific smile appeared on her face, and it stayed there as she slowly made her way back to the pond's edge.

Willie watched, fascinated. "I want to baptie with Papa," he said. "I want to baptie in the water."

"Shhh," I whispered. "Someday when you get bigger."

One by one, they gave themselves over to William and to God. I had counted thirteen, when William called out, "Clara Shaw!"

I had been too preoccupied to notice Clara in the group, and now I craned my neck, waiting to see her step forward to be baptized. This was William's crowning moment, as well as Clara's, and I didn't want to miss it.

"Clara Shaw!" boomed William, his chest puffing out. "Come forward to meet the Lord!" A murmur rippled through the crowd as everyone looked around.

Clara didn't appear.

Standing at the pond's edge, drenched with water, William boomed, "Clara Shaw?"

A hush fell over the proceedings.

"Where is Clara?" said William, holding his hand up to shield his eyes as he searched the congregation. "Is she not among us?"

Nobody spoke. For a split second I saw a wild look take hold of William, then he said, "Has Clara not joined us today?"

I watched him struggling to maintain a semblance of dignity as his robe clung to him and droplets of water dripped off his nose and chin.

"No Clara Shaw?" He stepped out of the water, skidding on the muddy bank. Someone reached out to take his arm. He shook it off. He ran his hand through his soaking hair and flicked the droplets off his fingers. Then he cleared his throat, and said, "Let's all join in a hymn of thanksgiving for the blessings of this day. Jonathan?"

Jonathan Paist and the choir burst into song, and the rest of the congregation joined in. William's voice rose above them all as he made his way through the gathering, smiling and shaking hands, but I knew that in his heart he was raging, that his perfect day had been ruined, and that he believed himself to be a failure because Clara Shaw was the symbol of his victory over corruption, and she was nowhere to be seen.

℘ ℘ ℘

"Deceitful Jezebel! Lying whore! Fork-tongued daughter of Satan!"

William paced the room, his face livid with rage. I had never seen him so angry.

"Oh! The false tears of repentance! How she led me on, how she made a mockery of all that is held sacred!"

"William," I said. "Please, you'll wake Willie!"

"To humiliate me so! In the face of God and the entire congregation!"

"William," I begged, "you'll make yourself ill!"

"It was a mockery! A sacrilege!"

"But you don't know that it was intentional! Maybe something happened to her! Has anyone seen her?"

"Seen her! Hah! She's run away! Back into the arms of Satan! She represents all that I detest!"

"But you don't know that," I insisted. "Don't be so quick to judge her until you know the circumstances."

"Evangeline, you are naive. You don't understand the nature of betrayal. She planned it all along! Played me for a fool. And I…I was so gullible. So blind in my desire to save her that I ignored the warning signs. Oh!" he groaned. "I have failed! Failed miserably and completely! I'm a sinner, too! Pride cometh before a fall! My pride, my own loathsome pride blinded me!"

"William, you're being too hard on yourself. There must be an explanation."

"She can explain on Judgment Day. She can look into the face of the Lord with her explanation and see if he offers salvation! "And as for me…as for me—" He stopped his pacing and leaned on a chair, breathing heavily. Then he put his hand up to his eye and pinched the bridge of his nose, and I realized that he was fighting tears.

I went to him, putting my arm around him and speaking low. "William, it's all right. You did the best you could. It's not your fault. Some things are beyond all of us, even you. You're a great and good man. You must not blame yourself. Let it go. You've done so much here that's good. The people respect you. Don't let this one disappointment deter you from your work. Please, dearest."

His body shook. "I tried so hard," he said, his voice breaking.

"I know you did," I said soothingly. "Come, sit down with me."

He let me lead him to the sofa, where he sat down heavily and put his head in his hands.

"Would you like some chamomile tea?" I asked. "Maybe it will comfort you."

"Brandy. A small glass."

"I hastened to the cabinet, reaching for my mother's crystal decanter. I poured a few inches of the thick amber liquid into a tumbler and gave it to my husband. He drank it swiftly, in three gulps, and wiped his lips as he set the glass down.

"Sit with me for a few moments," he said. "Pray with me. Help me to ask God for forgiveness." He clutched my hand, squeezing it until I almost cried out.

"Dear Lord," he intoned, and now there were tears on his cheeks, "bless this miserable sinner. For I have failed you utterly in the name of pride. Teach me humility, oh Lord. From all blindness of heart, from pride, vainglory, and hypocrisy; from envy, hatred, and malice, and all uncharitableness, good Lord, deliver me."

Later in bed, he took me roughly, leaving me feeling bruised and sore. In the middle of the night, I awoke to find him pushing into me again, muttering and whispering words that shocked me. The next morning I wondered if I had dreamed it all, but my aching body told me otherwise.

⁔ ⁔ ⁔

Some days later, Willie was down for his nap, and I was in the kitchen setting out two loaves of bread to rise, when there was a knock on the front door.

I wiped my hands on my apron, thinking that there were never enough hours in the day since Lizzie had gone. Although my outside obligations had returned to normal since the baptism, I could barely meet the challenge of church activities, domestic chores, and keeping an eye on Willie. I hoped that the knock on the door didn't signal the arrival of one of the townswomen paying a social call. I had far too much to do.

I pulled off my apron and hung it on a hook, then, briefly checking my appearance in the mirror over the sideboard, I went to answer the door.

Standing on the front porch, almost cowering, was Clara Shaw.

The sight of her rendered me speechless.

"Please, ma'am," she said in a tremulous voice, "Don't send me away. I've come about the position you advertised in the paper."

"Miss Shaw, I…I," I faltered.

"Please. I remembered what you said to me that day in the village. About if I ever needed anything." The poor girl looked terrified.

The memory gave me pause. "Yes, yes, of course," I said, relieved that William was in Frenchtown for the day. "Please come in." I opened the door wide and stood back as she stepped into the hall and stood there timidly, her narrow shoulders sagging.

"Why don't we go into the parlor," I said, directing her to a chair and sitting opposite her. I noted that her face looked pale and pinched, and there were purple shadows under her eyes, as if she hadn't slept in days.

"I know you must think it's brazen of me to come here," she said haltingly, "especially after…after…" She looked down at her hands folded in her lap. "But I didn't know where else to go. My cousin's family took me in for a while, but now they don't want to have anything to do with me. I tried to find work in the mills, but I was told that they had no place for my kind. Then I saw your advertisement in the paper, and it seemed like it was the answer to my prayers, and I was hoping that you would find it in your heart to show me mercy." Her plea came out in a breathless jumble.

I remained silent, too confused to venture a response of any kind.

"I'm a hard worker," she said. "I'm strong. I'll work from sunup to sundown and beyond. And you won't never have to give me a day off. And I'd be a big help to you with your little boy. He's sweet. I seen you with him in the village."

Finally I found my voice. "But why…why did you come to me? Surely there must be other places that are looking for hired girls."

She bowed her head. "I'd be on the street again as soon as they found out."

"Found out what?" I asked.

There was an uncomfortable silence. I waited.

"I'm in the family way," she whispered. I could barely hear her as she continued. "It's why I couldn't come to be baptized."

"I see," I said stiffly.

"I was too ashamed to tell the Reverend after all he done for me."

I nodded, listening intently.

"And it's why I have nowhere else to go. And you being a Christian woman and saying you wanted to help me, I just thought you might be sympathetic to my situation. And take me in."

She continued before I could reply.

"You wouldn't even have to give me wages. I'll work for room and board. And right up until the baby comes, too."

A dull throbbing began behind my eyes. How could I turn this poor girl away? I had stood there in front of the millinery shop and told her that if she ever needed anything, she could come to me. And now she was in dire straits. As a true Christian, I was obliged to take her in. I knew at that moment that God was testing us, William and me—testing our faith and commitment. William couldn't possibly object. And it would certainly solve my immediate problem of finding a hired girl. I made the decision on the spot.

"When is your baby coming?" I asked.

"Most likely January or February, I figure," she said.

"Very well," I said. "It's settled. You can stay."

"Oh, thank you, ma'am, thank you! I knew you was a good Christian woman!"

I stood up. "Do you want to go fetch your things?" I said.

She smiled sheepishly. "They're on the porch," she said.

"Well, why don't you get them, and I'll show you your room."

"Yes. Yes, thank you," she said and hurried out the door to the porch.

Within seconds she reappeared, carrying two worn suitcases and a hatbox.

I led her back past the dining room, through the kitchen, to Lizzie's room. It was the first time I had visited that room since Lizzie's departure. When I opened the door, the sweet familiar fragrance of my absent friend enveloped me, and I felt a pang of remorse at bringing a stranger into the space that was hers.

"This will be your room," I said.

She set her bags down on the bed and turned to me. "I don't know how to thank you," she said solemnly. "But I promise you won't regret helping me out like this."

I ran out to meet William as his carriage pulled up shortly after six o'clock.

"William, I have to speak to you," I said.

"Come with me into the barn while I unhitch the horse," he said.

When Obediah was unbridled and safely tucked in his stall next to Jeremiah, William said, "What is it?"

I blurted it out. "Clara Shaw is staying with us. I've taken her in as a hired girl."

"What?!" His eyebrows rose, and his eyes bulged. "What are you saying? How dare she? Have you taken leave of your senses?"

I put my hand on his arm, and in a low, urgent voice, said, "William, she came to me today, begging for a position. She's been turned out by her cousins and turned away everywhere else. William, she didn't come to the baptism because she's going to have a *child*! She has nowhere else to go! And as Christians, it's our duty to take her in! God sent her to us, I know he did."

"Good God," said William with awe. "She's with child?"

"Yes, it will be coming some time after Christmas."

"But why did she...why come here of all places?" he sputtered, his voice rising with irritation once again.

"She saw my advertisement in the *Intelligencer* for a hired girl. Besides, where else could she go?" I said. "And I so much as told her she could come to us if she were ever in need. I met her on the street one day. Some weeks ago. I wanted to reach out to her then because I thought it might help you. She rejected me, ignored me really, and I felt so badly that I hadn't been able to get through to her, but now! Now in her hour of need, she has come to us, and now we all have a second chance."

William's hand swept across his brow in the familiar gesture of consternation.

"You do agree with me, don't you?" I asked. "I mean, it's all right if she stays?"

"Evangeline! You test me!" he said.

"I test you? No, William, it is God who is testing all of us."

After a lengthy pause, he said, "Perhaps. Perhaps."

"Then it is all right?" I said.

"I suppose it will have to be," he said, "since it seems you've already made the decision." Then he looked directly into my eyes and caught my arm. "But, Evangeline, I give you warning. This girl has demonstrated by her actions that she is unstable, unreliable without rectitude or good judgment. Such creatures will try to deceive for their own purposes.

Spread falsehoods. You must bear that in mind in your dealings with her. She is a proven liar!"

"Perhaps the security of a loving Christian home will help," I said.

※ ※ ※

True to her word, Clara was a hard worker. Each morning, when I awakened, I could hear her stirring downstairs in the kitchen. Then the mingled aromas of coffee and frying bacon and biscuits would waft up the stairs. She worked quietly, barely speaking unless spoken to. Around William she was particularly shy and withdrawn.

When she was with Willie, she came out of herself somewhat. She would have long conversations with him, and he made her laugh often. A few days after her arrival, Willie asked me where she came from and why she was staying in Lizzie's room. I responded by telling him that she was our "new Lizzie." For several days he addressed her as "new Lizzie," despite my efforts to correct him.

"Her name is Clara, Willie. When you speak to her, call her Clara."

"But you said she was our new Lizzie."

"She's like Lizzie, but her name is Clara."

Willie put his thumb in his mouth. "I want her to be new Lizzie," he grumbled.

They played silly little games together, and with each passing day, I began to feel more comfortable about leaving Clara in charge of Willie when I had an errand to do or a call to make.

One day Clara was dusting in the parlor, when she commented on my still life paintings.

"These are pretty paintings you got on the walls," she said, moving the feather duster carefully over the frames. "They make me sort of happy and sad at the same time when I look at them."

"Thank you, Clara," I said. "I painted them."

"You painted them," she said, her eyes growing wide. "Oh, ma'am, I didn't know you had such a talent."

"I don't know about that," I said modestly.

"Oh, yes, you do," she said. "I can tell by looking. You're quite the artist. Do you have any others I could see?"

I thought of my sketchbook with the coffee-splattered nude studies hidden under the floorboards upstairs. I thought of my paints gathering dust in Daniel Duvall's studio. It was as if a fist gripped my heart.

"Not really," I said. "I haven't been painting much recently."

"Oh, that's a sin," she said. "You really should keep up with it. A talented artist like yourself." A flush of color enlivened her pale face as she said shyly, "Maybe you could draw me someday. If you need a model or anything, I'd be good at that."

In my mind's eye, I saw dear Lizzie self-consciously posing in the lamplight.

"Maybe some day," I said.

"I always dreamed of being an actress on the stage," said Clara wistfully. "That's why I ran away from the farm. To New York. But it didn't work out." She brightened. "I did get a job with Mr. Barnum, though! To be a Circassian beauty in his museum sideshow. With my hair being frizzy and all, I looked the part." Clara's eyes grew dreamy. "I was going to be called Zoledad. I don't know what it means, but isn't it pretty?"

I nodded, spellbound by what she'd told me. Clara! In a circus sideshow!

"But then, somebody found out that I wasn't a real Circassian girl from Constantinople, and I was let go." Clara shrugged her shoulders. "I guess you might say I fell in with a bad crowd. And I met this man, Bertie, and he made himself out to be this impresario. He said he wanted to help me. But really he was just taking advantage of me. And one thing led to another, and then I came back here all down on my luck and found out that my brother Charlie had died in a fire out West, and the rest of my family was nowhere to be found. And I felt so bad about everything, I just went to work in the hotel."

Stunned by the entire account, I remembered William's warning about not believing everything Clara said. Still, I felt compassion for her.

"That's a sad story," I said.

"Ain't it? Well," she sighed, "I'll never be no actress." She patted her stomach. "Especially now." Then she brightened. "But you can still be a painter, and I could model for you, and that would be kind of like being on the stage. Maybe some afternoon when the little one is sleeping! I am kind of exotic looking, don't you think?" she said, fluffing her wild hair.

"Yes, you are," I said. "But as for my painting you, I'm afraid not." I absentmindedly straightened one of the paintings she had dusted. "Reverend Laury doesn't approve of my painting."

"Why not? It's not against the Bible, is it?"

"No," I said. "Not that I'm aware of."

"I should think he'd be proud to have a wife with such talents."

"Well," I said, choosing my words carefully, trying to decide how much to tell this strange creature. "It's a bit complicated. I was attending art classes at Aquatong Farm. With William's approval, of course. But then he discovered that there had been a…a nude model at one of the classes, and he—well, he felt it was unsuitable for me to attend anymore. After all, I am the minister's wife."

"But can't you paint on your own? In your spare time?" she asked.

I sighed, feeling the familiar sadness seep back. "No. He really prefers that I not paint at all."

"Well, if you'll excuse me for putting my two cents in, I don't think that's fair," said Clara. "I don't see how it can hurt anybody if you bring some beauty into the world."

I laughed at her outspokenness. "William doesn't think like you," I said.

"You must miss it though," she said. "Doing the thing that you love."

"I do," I said. "I had this wonderful teacher. Daniel Duvall."

"Oh, sure, everybody around here's heard of him," she said reverently. Then added, "He used to come to the hotel. The girls would fight over him."

I felt the blood drain from my face and I sank onto the settee. "Oh, excuse me, ma'am! I meant no disrespect, discussing such things!"

"No, no, I just felt a bit…It's so hot today, isn't it? Could you fetch me a glass of water?" I said. As Clara hurried to the kitchen, I attempted to compose myself, pushing away images of Daniel cavorting with women.

Clara returned with the water. "So Mr. Duvall was your teacher?" she said, handing me the glass.

I took a few sips and nodded, not yet trusting myself to speak.

"Imagine that," she said. "Why, he's famous even in France, they say."

"Yes," I said finally. "He encouraged me. He even offered to give me private lessons."

"That would be like Eleanora Duse offering to teach me acting. I'd give anything for an opportunity like that," she said wistfully. "Excuse me for saying I envy you. I know that's a sin."

"You shouldn't envy me, and not because it's sinful," I said. "Circumstances are such that I'm not able to accept Mr. Duvall's offer." I stood and moved to the window, gazing across the lawn to the road. "In a way it would be better if I'd never met him," I said. "Then I wouldn't have this…this longing for something I can't have." I surprised myself with my own candor. Why was I revealing so much to Clara?

"Well, why can't you take the lessons? I mean, it's really none of my business, but that never stopped me before. And the Reverend is gone so much of the time, he'd never be the wiser. And it's not like you'd be doing anything really wrong. How can it be wrong to try to better yourself? To develop a God-given talent? And I could watch Willie for you, and it would be just between you and me. You been so nice to me, Mrs. Laury, taking me in and everything, that I'd like to do something for you. Return the favor, so to speak."

I was taken aback. Was this girl tempting me, trying to lure me into doing wrong? Was she a "daughter of Satan" as William had called her, or was she simply trying to be a friend? For a liberating moment, I envisioned myself riding my bicycle down that road, arriving at Aquatong Farm, and seeing Daniel waving to me from the balcony. I saw him rushing down the steps and out of the studio to greet me. I saw us both smiling and chatting as we walked back up the steps to the studio.

"That's very kind of you, Clara, but I couldn't go against my husband's word."

"Well, surely, he wouldn't mind if you painted at home from time to time."

"I don't know," I said.

"What if you painted something special, just to please him? Like a picture of Willie? How could he be angry at you for making a painting of your own little son?"

I remembered my angel-like sketches of the sleeping Willie.

"You could give it to him as a present," Clara said.

I mulled over what she had said. "Do you think so?" I asked.

"I think it's a grand idea, even if it's my own," she said. "What have you got to lose?"

"My paints are at Aquatong Farm. In the studio there. I thought I would be going back."

"Well, go over and get them. I'll watch Willie."

Why not? I thought. William would be gone until supper, in fact he was gone so much these days, baptizing and preaching in neighboring towns, that I hardly ever saw him. I could easily do the portrait during his absence and surprise him with it for his birthday. It was silly to have my paint box at Aquatong farm, when I knew I wouldn't be returning for lessons.

"Yes," I said to Clara, as well as to myself. "Yes, I think I will."

As I pedaled my bicycle up the lane and into the clearing, my knees were wobbly, and I was out of breath, not so much from exertion but from a deep excitement mixed with foreboding. I could barely hear the bleating of the sheep and the welcoming tinkle of their bells over the pounding of my heart. My eyes felt dry in the harsh sunlight as I searched the premises for a sign of Daniel. I felt ashamed at how happy I was to be in the space that contained him, almost forgetting the purpose of my visit.

I leaned the bicycle against the fence and tried to steady my breathing as I walked up the slope to the studio. The heat was oppressive, and trickles of perspiration ran down the back of my neck and under my arms, where my stays dug into my flesh.

I knocked on the door. No answer.

Then I knocked again.

"Who is it?" The voice from within was harsh, and I barely recognized it.

"It's me," I called back, feeling frightened. "Evangeline."

I heard the pounding of his feet on the stairs. Then the door was flung open. "Evangeline!" he said.

His eyes were so bloodshot that it hurt me to look at them, and there were specks of paint on his face. He hadn't shaved in days, and his dark hair was in wild disarray. He looked like a madman. He looked like the man I had first seen on the steps of the Lumberville Emporium.

"I…I'm sorry," I said, "if I've interrupted something."

As if he were awakening from a deep sleep, he rubbed his eyes and said, "No! No, come in. Please, come in." He stepped back and held open the door, letting me precede him up the stairs.

I could smell the studio before I saw it, the comforting mixture of paint and candle wax and turpentine. And I could smell Daniel as he stood behind me, the musky combination of sweat, and tobacco, and something else I couldn't define. The heat made me lightheaded.

"You surprised me, he said, smiling and pushing his hair back out of his eyes. "You always surprise me."

"I came to get my paints," I said.

"Oh," he said. He studied my face, and his expression was one of curiosity and tenderness. I felt awkward and moved away from him.

"I'm sorry if I've disturbed you," I said.

"No," he said. "I told you. You haven't disturbed me. I've been working on a painting, and I've been holed up in here for days. Haven't slept much." Once again, he brushed back his hair. "I must look like a caged beast. I feel like one." He wiped his hands on his trousers.

"What are you working on?" I asked. "May I see it?" I cocked my head toward the easel, but it was facing away from me.

He paused, as if debating. "Well, I don't usually let anyone see my work before it's finished."

"Oh," I said, "I understand." I tried not to reveal my disappointment.

"You might not understand completely," he said with amusement, and his weary eyes seemed to caress my face. I looked at him quizzically, my feelings on the verge of being wounded.

"What do you mean?" I said.

He paused again, chewing on his lip. "It's a portrait of you," he said.

"Of me?" I whispered, incredulous.

He nodded, almost imperceptibly, his gaze fixed on me.

"May I see it?" I said.

He stepped back and gestured toward the easel. "It's not quite finished," he said, "but I'll make an exception in this case."

I moved gingerly toward the easel, slightly giddy with anticipation.

He stood behind me. "I call it 'Angel,'" he said.

My breath caught. It was a nearly life-size canvas of me standing in front of the mirror, painting my self-portrait. My figure was framed against the enormous French doors, and a shaft of diffused light shone down and all around, enveloping me in a shimmering radiance. The mirrored reflection was a masterpiece of chiaroscuro and implied form that suggested a luminous celestial being, an angel.

I felt a thrill that started somewhere in the core of me and radiated down through my fingertips until they began to ache. Tears sprang from some closed-up place in my being that seemed to gush open, flooding me with oceans of released liquid longing that seemed to have been dammed up inside me since the beginning of time.

He put his hands on my shoulders, barely touching them, but I could feel each one, separately, branding me as if they would drive me to my knees, which is where I wanted to be. I wanted to worship at the altar of his genius, his raw power, and his rapturous and transcendent vision of me.

"It's how I see you," he said in a low voice. "How I've seen you since that first day."

My mouth felt dry, and my heart thudded. It seemed that the studio was shrouded in a blanket of trapped heat. My limbs were weighted, and I didn't trust myself to move or stir. Although he stood directly behind me, I didn't have the strength or the courage to turn around and face him. I closed my eyes and tried to inhale, but my breath came shallow.

"Do you like it?" he whispered. Very gently, he turned me around until we were standing face-to-face. He searched my eyes. "Do you like it?" he said again.

His face blurred as stinging tears spilled over, forming rivulets on my cheeks. With the lightest touch, he wiped them away. His fingers were warm.

"Why do you cry?" he whispered. He lifted my chin. "Why do you cry, my Angel?"

"Oh!" I said. "Oh!" And I tried to look away from him, away from those all-seeing eyes, but he held my face in his hands, and I could smell the paint on them and the tobacco, and his breath was on my face, and I wanted to taste it all, and drink it all, and then he was kissing me, and it was as if everything mingled, and what was me was him, and what was him was me, and I held onto him to keep from falling, and there was heat everywhere—heat and energy and colors swirling, and a need to be as close as close could be—and as I fainted, I thought of Lizzie and Seamus cleaving together as they fell down, down, down into the darkness.

Strong arms scooped me up and carried me across the room. I felt my cheek rest against the matted hair of his chest. I was weightless and floating, and somewhere inside I knew that as long as I didn't open my eyes, I could remain in this lovely place, where my body tingled, and my head was empty, and nothing was real but the strength of his arms as he cradled me, before gently laying me down on a bed of clouds. If I opened my eyes, I would have to acknowledge what had just happened and, in doing so, confront it.

"My Angel," he whispered, and the sound of his voice drew me back.

I looked at him.

His face was taut and ashen, concern etched in every line and crease. The blue eyes burned with a feverish intensity.

"Are you all right?" he asked, smoothing my hair.

I closed my eyes once more, turning away from him. I felt empty space as he moved away, heard retreating footsteps. Within moments he returned, and there was the sound of sloshing water. Then a cool wet cloth moved gently across my forehead, my throat, and my wrists and fingers.

Reluctantly I opened my eyes once more.

He smiled. "Better?" he asked with tender concern.

I stared at him, watching as he dipped the cloth in a pan of water, then wrung it out, and gently pressed it against my forehead.

"I don't know who I am anymore!" I whispered. Burning tears of shame welled up, and I turned my head to the wall.

After a long time, I heard him sigh. "It's my fault," he said finally.

I turned back to him, covering my eyes with my arm and shaking my head in misery. "No!" I cried. "No! It's me. I'm turning into someone that I don't recognize." I sat up so suddenly that I knocked over the pan of water, I pushed my way past Daniel and set my feet on the floor. The top buttons of my dress were undone, and I hastily fastened them with shaking fingers, feeling my shame mount. Finally I stood.

"Evangeline," he said, reaching for me.

"No," I said. "I have to go. I came for my paints. I want my paints, and then I have to go." My voice was pitched high, and it trembled. "Where are they?" I said, looking around the studio wildly. But the painting called "Angel" so dominated the room that it blinded me to everything else. For a panicky moment, I feared I would never be able to move past it, to find my way to the door. I was trapped between the painting and him, between the woman I knew and the shameless creature that tarried in this room.

He came up behind me, grasping my shoulders. "I'm sorry," he whispered into my hair. "I'm sorry. I didn't mean to upset you."

I fought the longing to lean back into him, to swoon into his arms again, to return to that floating place where there was no before and no after. Instead I stiffened, repeating, "I have to go now. My paints, please."

I heard him sigh as he reluctantly released me. Then he walked across the room to the workbench. He lifted the box with one hand, and with the other he reached under the bench and brought out my half-finished self-portrait. Coming back toward me, he held it out. "Do you want the canvas too?" he asked in a barely audible voice. His face was a dark storm now, anguished and bewildered.

I gazed at the painting, remembering that afternoon, and my resolve was momentarily displaced by an exquisite longing. Then I looked at him. The energy that swirled around him was dormant now. The power that radiated from him seemed to be sucking him inward. He looked defenseless and utterly, utterly sad.

"The canvas?" he repeated.

"No, you keep it," I said. "I've no place to put it."

"Very well," he said. Then he cleared his throat. "This means…Does this mean, then, that I won't see you again?"

I shook my head, not trusting myself to speak.

He handed me the paint box. "I want you to know," he said, and I thought I saw moisture in his eyes, "that this wasn't—that I'm not—" He looked away, then shook his head. Finally he looked back at me. "You mean something to me," he said. Then he looked down at his feet. "I suppose I've no right to say that to another man's wife. But there it is. Seeing you today, after spending these weeks painting you, feeling you right here in the room with me—well, when I saw you in the flesh, it was as if all the passion that I'd poured into the painting filled the room. It overflowed onto you. I forgot myself. Forgive me."

I stood there, lost in him, letting his words settle over me. "I forgive you," I whispered, wishing that he didn't look as sad as I felt, inexplicably glad that he did.

"It's good-bye, then?"

I nodded.

"Be the artist I know you can be," he whispered fiercely. "Don't let him take that away from you! Promise me!" He gripped my arms. "Promise me!" he commanded.

"I don't know if I can promise," I said.

He released me. "Then you will be wasting your life." The certainty of his prediction frightened me.

"No, that's not true!" I said sharply. "I'm a wife and a mother, and I help my husband in his work. That's more than enough for any woman."

His jaw clenched. "You're not any woman!" he shouted. "How long will it take before you realize that?"

"What can I do?" I cried. "What can I do? I'm in it now! I'm in my life, and I have to make my peace with it!" I quaked at the truth of my words and the shrillness of my voice as they bounced off the walls and settled over us like a shroud. We stood facing each other. A minute passed.

"Make your peace with it, then," he said wearily. "Make your peace, but for God's sake, at least try to carve out some corner that's your own."

Every inch of me drooped, and the box of paints was suddenly like an anvil pulling down on my arm. I felt exhausted, as if I were sloughing through salt water as I slowly walked to the door.

He didn't move to stop me.

As I put my hand on the doorknob, he said quietly, "I only say these things to you because I believe that we're kindred souls."

Barely pausing, I opened the door, stepped through it onto the landing, and softly closed it behind me. I felt disembodied as I descended the stairs, as if I were leaving my vital organs— my heart, my mind, and all my innards—in that studio. The hand that opened the downstairs door wasn't mine; the heavy legs that made their weary way down the slope weren't mine.

The heat of the sun, reflecting off my bicycle, nearly blinded me, and I groped for the basket in front of the handlebars as I hefted my paint box into it. Then I stood there for a moment, gathering my strength for the ride home. I heard the tinkle of bells as a lamb approached the fence and stuck its wet nose through the opening and nuzzled my skirt. I looked across the pond at the moss-covered waterwheel, turning and creaking against the side of the old mill cottage, with its profusion of red and yellow and purple flowers spilling over the window boxes. I shaded my eyes as I gazed across the grassy meadow to the little wooden shed, serene and perfect in its austerity. The giant sycamores cast deep shadows across the emerald green of its moss-covered roof, and a flock of lambs frolicked nearby. Was it any wonder I had been drawn back to this place again and again? It had awakened some primordial yearning in me—opened me to possibilities in myself that had lain dormant. In this place, above all others, I had felt the freedom to experience myself apart from my ordinary world. I had been permitted—no, *encouraged* to believe in myself as a singular, unique, gifted human being.

An artist.

Only then did his final words filter into my awareness. "I only say these things to you because I believe that we're kindred souls."

The thunderclap of comprehension nearly staggered me. Amazed, I looked back up toward the studio as if it were a holy shrine.

Daniel stood on the balcony watching me.

Kindred souls.

My heart thundered.

Suddenly I was running, scrambling back up the slope, pulling on the door, tripping up the stairs.

He met me on the landing, and our bodies collided as he crushed me in his arms with a groan. Frantically he searched for my mouth, which opened to receive him as if I required his breath for my own survival. I offered him my hunger, my thirst, my emptiness, my longing. He gave me his fire, his lightning, his passion, his purpose. I craved him in every pore; there were too many seconds to endure before we were skin to skin, flesh to flesh. I became a vessel of liquid nerve endings, crying out as he filled me with the feast of himself: lips, tongue, fingers, and, ultimately, the crowning thrust of his manhood. He plunged deeply into that part of myself that seemed to have been waiting only for him. With each exquisite thrust I came more alive, soaring higher and higher and still higher, until that moment when I knew that heaven was in sight and, with it, the moment of my death.

And so I died and was reborn in Daniel's arms.

☙ ☙ ☙

"Tell me what you're thinking," said Daniel, wrapping me tightly in his arms.

All pretense had vanished, and I felt my most authentic self revealed for the first time in memory.

"I'm thinking that if I could paint and make love to you at the same time, that would be the closest thing to heaven," I said.

"Painting someone is like making love to them," he said. "That's why, when you first arrived here this afternoon, I felt so close to you. I'd been making love to you on the canvas for weeks!" We laughed as he covered my face with kisses. "I'd been having a lovely time of it," he said, "but this is much better." He squeezed me tightly and sighed. "Lying here close to the flesh and blood of you and looking at your image in the painting. I never dreamed you'd come to me. My Angel." He kissed my forehead.

"Why do you call me that?" I asked.

"It's your name," he said. "Angel. From Evangeline."

"No one has called me that since my mother died. Not even Lizzie."

"Well, you are an angel," he said into my hair. "I was so afraid I'd lost you forever when you walked out the door. I cursed myself for being so selfish, so impetuous! To sacrifice ever seeing you again for one kiss." He grinned. "One staggering kiss. Come to think of it, I do believe you're the first woman to ever faint from a kiss of mine."

I felt flattered and threatened.

"Have there been many other women, many other kisses?" I ventured.

"None like you, my darling," he said.

"I was afraid, too," I said reflectively. "So afraid."

"And now?"

"I'm still afraid. But now I'm more afraid of being without you than I am of being with you. I've lost my will for doing what's right. If it weren't for Willie, I—"

He put his finger up to my lips. "Shhhh," he said. "Don't speak like that. It serves no purpose. Instead, let's plan when I'm going to see you again. And how we can figure out a way to have you paint fabulous pictures while I make passionate love to you. We can't waste a moment of our afternoons together." He rolled on top of me, grasping my wrists. The weight of his body excited me, and I could feel his hardness against my thigh. "I want to be your teacher and your lover," he said. "I want to show you everything! Everything there is to know about painting, and everything there is to know about how a man and woman can please each other. Will you let me?"

"I have neither the strength nor desire to resist," I said. "Nothing else seems real anymore."

He kissed me then, and as his lips touched my breast, I opened myself to him joyfully and naturally for the second time that afternoon. It was as if we had been together forever.

On the ride home, I could barely sit on the bicycle without wincing. The dark, moist place between my legs was a delicious wound, tender and raw, and full of him yet still craving him. My womb felt heavy and swollen, as if it had absorbed his essence and was holding it like a sponge. I wondered if my bruised lips were noticeable. Even my tongue was sore at its root.

Giddily, I pedaled down the lane and onto River Road. Even the thought of facing William didn't frighten me. I was immured in a bubble of happiness as I glided into the village square and spied Sarah Webster coming out of the milliner's shop.

She waved and called to me, "Hello, Evangeline! See you at Bible study tomorrow!"

The words hit me like a bucket of icy well water. I lost my balance, and the bicycle wobbled beneath me. Clutching the handlebars to steady myself, I pressed down on the pedals with all my strength and made my way up the hill, head down, heart hammering. *What have I done? I* thought. *What in the name of God have I done?* I looked up at the darkening sky, half expecting to be struck by lightning.

I climbed the steps to the front porch, smoothing my skirts, attempting to compose myself. Willie cried out when he saw me, and I swept him up into my arms, holding him fiercely and burying my flushed face in the folds of his neck. He wriggled away, saying, "Mama, you smell funny."

Clara's gaze met mine for a moment before she said, "Let's let Mama go upstairs to freshen herself before Papa gets home, shall we? And we'll finish mixing the biscuit batter." She took his hand, then looked back at me. "I put on a pot roast for dinner."

"That's fine. Thank you, Clara. William likes pot roast."

Upstairs I poured fresh water into the washbowl and hastily set about removing all traces of my forbidden afternoon. I changed into a fresh shirtwaist and redid my hair. The blood pounded in my ears as I stared into the mirror. Who was this new woman? My eyes glittered in their sockets with the exhaustion of too much happiness. My skin was translucent, my lips ripe with carnal pleasures. As I combed and twisted my hair into a tidy knot, there was an aching in my fingers: the ache of longing.

When William arrived home a short while later, he found me sitting in the parlor, reading a story to Willie. I greeted him with warmth and inquired about his day. He settled down beside me, took Willie onto his lap, and began to speak. As he droned on, I nodded and cocked my ear, all the while keeping my eyes focused on him. But inside my head, newly inspired thoughts roamed freely. I stifled a yawn, secretly yearning to close my eyes, and lie down, and squeeze my thighs together in dreams of Daniel.

Instead I smiled at William and touched his hand, amazed at how easy it was to play the role of faithful wife.

FIFTEEN
C H A P T E R

1996

The morning following Chad's horrible accusations, I shower and dress quickly, practically slinking past his door—willing him to stay asleep until I'm out of the house.

I start the car, intending to head to the river for a long walk along the canal. The events of the previous night crowd my head. I need to think.

But at the foot of the hill, I turn left instead of right, and a mile down the road, I turn into Victor's drive and bump my way up the lane, coming to a stop in front of his house.

I slide out of the car and crunch across the gravel to the front door. I knock.

"Victor?" I call. I hear footsteps, and the door opens.

"I was just thinking about you," he says. "Did you talk to Madame Goudonov Sancerre?"

"I haven't even thought about that. I need a cup of coffee," I say.

He steps aside, beckoning me in. "What's the matter?"

"Rough night," I say.

I follow him into the kitchen and stand next to him while he pours me a cup of coffee.

"Let me guess. You and your son had words."

I nod. "How did you know?"

"I told you. He has an attitude." He sips from his own mug of coffee. "What happened?"

"I should have been more discreet last night. He saw us kissing, and it brought up all this…stuff!"

Victor shakes his head, setting his mug down on the counter. "I knew this arrangement wasn't going to work."

"No! No, it's not that. The work part will be fine, I just—" The words come tumbling out, like a pent-up confession. "I feel like I was such a horrible mother! I always thought I was protecting him, and he claims he felt he had to protect me—and maybe he's right, but all I remember is loving him, trying to raise him in the best way I knew how, and now it seems everything I did was wrong."

Victor looks uncomfortable. "Why are you telling me this?"

"I just feel like such a screwup." With no thought, I lean into him, wanting…What? Comfort, absolution, or just the feel of his arms around me. There's an awkward beat before he responds, and the response itself is awkward. He half holds me, lightly patting my back. I slide my arms around his neck. "Please, just hold me."

"Morgan—"

"Just for a minute." *You sound whiny.*

I hear a sigh of resignation and then gratefully feel the full strength of his arms around me. I burrow in, turning my face to his neck, holding on for dear life. My lips graze his ear, and he utters something I can't really hear, then it feels as though he seizes me—almost cutting off my breath. He grabs a handful of my hair and with a gentle tug, draws my face back and stares at me with the oddest expression, almost fearful, like somebody who's about to plunge off a cliff. Then we're kissing. It feels desperate on both sides, and it occurs to me that I might be lost and found at the same time.

Then he groans, pulling away. "Oh, no. No." Then, just as quickly, he's back to kissing me, kissing me like crazy, reaching under my shirt. We lose our balance, and the next thing I know, we're on the floor, pulling at each other's clothes. The smell of him and of us together mingles with the acrid aroma of the coffee above us and the dry, dusty smell of the floorboards beneath us, and it all feels breathless and familiar and rough and tender—totally safe, yet terrifying. My ancient silent longing is suddenly a raw and noisy craving, and with it comes a tiny warning that I will never be able to get enough of him. In the urgent jumble of zippers and buttons and kicked-off underwear, I half remember my dream, of the man with two faces— how we tumbled down, down, slipping together as one into inky depths of the water, our shimmering bodies brilliant in the murky abyss, embracing each other, and the fathomless darkness that drew us further and further into an unknown place that had no beginning and no end.

And before I can edit, the words just pop out as if they're three little people with minds of their own.

"I love you," I whisper dreamily, "I'm so in love with you."

And everything stops. He stops. I feel the crushing weight of him on top of me for a full thirty seconds before he rolls off, onto his back, away from me, until not even the sides of our arms are touching.

Outside, I hear the discordant caw of a low-flying crow.

In here, on the pinewood floor, are scattered clothes and silence.

I take a deep breath and dial Anne-Claire Goudonov Sancerre's number. Our conversation is brief. I tell her that we would like to meet with her as soon as possible, and she suggests a date for the following week. We agree to finalize details via e-mail.

I try to summon the courage to phone Victor with the news that the trip is a "go," but I chicken out and shoot him an e-mail instead, telling myself that I just need a little more time to get over my hurt and humiliation before snapping into professional mode. And that's what it would have to be from now on. If Victor and I are going to make a success of this marvelous opportunity, we're both going to have to put aside any personal considerations and focus on getting the job done. I make a silent commitment to myself to do just that. I concentrate on composing the e-mail, diplomatically asking if he would like to make the travel arrangements himself, or if I should give that assignment to Chad. After pushing "send," I lean back in my chair, wondering what it would be like sitting next to Victor for a seven-hour flight. The prospect of the trip that had seemed a wonderful adventure now seems fraught with tension and awkwardness. How would it be traveling together, working together, eating meals together after what happened this morning?

In the moments following the debacle on the kitchen floor, neither of us knew what to say. I had dressed quickly, blinking back tears of shame, and silently left the house. I sought refuge at the river, where I walked the towpath for an hour or more. I felt like I'd been punched in the stomach and believed it was my just punishment. There I was, doing exactly what Chad accused me of: pulling a man into our troubled relationship, creating a triangle. And that wasn't all. Whatever had possessed me to blurt out those forbidden words?

I love you.

The man's supposed to say it first, you jerk! You scared him away!

I'll make it right, I tell myself as I stare at the computer screen. *With Victor and with Chad.*

Now I try to put it all out of my mind by ruminating on the kinds of questions that I'll ask Madame Sancerre in the interview. What an opportunity! Within minutes, my mind is fully engaged as one idea flows quickly to another, then another.

I begin to page through the curator's book of paintings from the Paris exhibit of *The Angel Collection*. In the book, I come upon a very dark painting of Duvall's. My insides begin to quiver. I recognize the painting that led to my passing out in the Musée d'Orsay. It depicts thunderclouds over an inky pond, a shadowy waterwheel churning in the background. I realize now, of course, that this is the pond at Aquatong Farm.

My hands tremble as I type the question, "How do you account for the contrast in Duvall's style—for example: between the brilliant, joyous, and light-infused paintings and the dark, brooding, almost tragic ones?" It occurs to me—not for the first time—that since Madame Sancerre is actually the *granddaughter* of Angel and Duvall, she should have a much richer knowledge of the inspiration for their works. So I shall ask her: "Do you know the stories behind the paintings?"

No sooner have I finished typing the question, than my fingers begin to move across the keys at an accelerated pace, and words pop up on the screen too fast for me to be able to read them. I feel a humming in my head and an electrifying energy in my fingertips. I type without thought or formulation.

As suddenly as the strange moment has begun, it ends. I lean into the screen to read what's there.

I was drowning; drowning in the feel of him, and the taste of him, and the smell of him.

I was drowning in the love of him.

We lay there together, trembling, sweating and breathless. Eventually I gently drew away, saying, "I have to check on Willie."

He playfully pulled me back down. "But I want more," he said.

I laughed, disentangling myself. "We have a lifetime of mores," I said, kissing his brow.

I stood up and walked naked to the French doors and looked out.

There's nothing after that. I scroll to the top of the writing and read it again. My mouth is dry. *What the hell is this?*

I turn on the printer and punch the buttons to print the words on the screen. I know I need to *hold the hard copy* in my hands, to really *see it.* And I need to be able to share it with somebody. The printer begins to click and hum as it whizzes across paper. I wait, breathless.

Then I hear Chad's footsteps thudding up the stairs.

"Chad!" I call. "Come here! The oddest thing just happened." Last night's painful exchange and this morning's humiliating rejection are momentarily forgotten.

He appears at the door.

"What?" Sullen, withdrawn.

I snatch the paper from the printer and thrust it at him.

"Look at this. Read it. It just…practically typed itself. Am I going nuts?"

He takes the paper and glances at it.

"There's nothing here," he says. "The page is blank."

I snatch the paper from him, and my jaw drops. "That's not—" I return to the computer and scroll up and down the screen.

From his position at the door, Chad says to my back, "If this is your way of just trying to pretend last night didn't happen, it's pretty lame."

"No, I'm telling you…"

I keep scrolling. The last text on the screen is the question I'd written for Madame Sancerre. After that, there's nothing.

"This is bizarre," I mutter. I'm staring so hard at the blank screen, my eyes feel like they're bugging out of my head. "There was a whole—an entire page of—my fingers were going so fast on the keyboard, I didn't know what I was writing! It was like a part of a story or something—about Willie…" I turn back to him. "Don't look at me that way!"

"What way am I looking at you?"

"You know, like you're going to call the men in the white jackets."

He laughs abruptly and shakes his head. "Mom, you have to admit—"

"I know. It's sounds nuts, but—" Then I remember. "Oh my God!" I jump up from the desk and slide past Chad, hurrying down the hall to my bedroom, calling, "My journal!"

Chad stands warily at the entrance to my bedroom as I rummage in the nightstand to retrieve my journal.

"The other night—just before I got the call from the police station to come and get you—this other thing happened. I had just laid some of the sketches across the bed…"

He folds his arms, signaling his refusal to cross the threshold into my bedroom. I sit on the bed, paging rapidly through the journal. "It freaked me out, but then I got the call from you to come and get you, and—so much has happened." I locate the pages. "Here!" I hold the journal out to him. *As if offering up proof of my sanity.*

"That came out of me—like automatic writing, I think they call it. It was as if the pen was moving on its own. It's dream-like…and, a little embarrassing I know, but…Just look at it."

With an exaggerated sigh, he comes into the room and takes the journal, scours the pages.

"The top paragraph is me writing." I say. "Then the writing becomes very old-fashioned."

He reads. Then looks up at me.

"Are you putting me on? After our conversation?"

"Of course not!" I say.

He hands the journal back to me. "It's a little too hot and heavy for me," he says. Then, pointedly, "Why don't you show it to *Victor.*"

"Please don't misunderstand. It's the way it came out. I was writing in my journal, and the pen just went on its own. It's called automatic writing."

"I know what it's called," he says drily.

"Well, if you're going to be part of this project, and I hope you are, then I'm going to share things with you as I would any colleague. So kindly leave the personal issues out of it for now."

He looks chastised, so I continue.

"When this writing happened, I'd been looking at a sketch of a little boy—I'll show you." I run past Chad, down the hall to my office, and grab the portfolio of sketches, returning with it to my room. "Remember when Victor told the story of the sketches on the carpet and the carpet going up and down?"

"Yeaahhhh." Now I feel like some asylum inmate that he's trying to mollify.

I lay the portfolio on my bed and carefully open it. The sketch of the little boy is on top. "I was looking at this sketch, wondering if it was the little boy, Willie, the one who died—it's his grave we went to over at the cemetery. Remember you threw up?" I'm talking too fast. I'm like a standup comic trying to hold an audience.

"Thanks for reminding me," he says. He walks over to the bed and looks at the sketch.

"So I was thinking about that, and I had this urge to write, and what came out was what you just read."

Chad gently pages through the sketches, studying them. He turns to the nudes.

He raises his eyebrows. "Pretty risqué for the olden days," he says. "No wonder these were hidden under the floorboards. The minister would hardly have approved."

"The point is, I guess I was thinking about the little boy in the cemetery and wondering if this was him in the drawings, and I don't know, that writing just poured out of me…and then on the computer…the name 'Willie' came up." I sighed, rubbing my aching forehead. "There's so much weird stuff going on."

"You think?" said Chad sarcastically. "I feel like I'm in an episode of *Murder, She Wrote*. Or *The Twilight Zone*. I don't know which. It's all just giving me the willies." He pauses. "Get it? The 'willies.'"

"Ha-ha." I wait a beat. "So I talked to Madame Sancerre. Victor and I are going over next week."

"Oh, great. So now I'm going to be alone in the house with the rising carpet."

"Maybe it'll cure your skepticism," I say.

"Can't wait," he says.

"In the meantime, I want to go over the elements of the documentary. Get you up to speed."

"Let's do it."

I reach for the curator's book from *The Angel Collection*.

"This curator's book is a good place to start. And—hey! I've got an idea. Let's take a drive. I want to show you Aquatong Farm. It's where Daniel Duvall lived and painted when he was in Bucks County. In fact, while I'm in France, I want you to shoot stills over at the farm. You can ride my bike over. I want you to shoot at different times of day to evoke different moods. You'll see what I mean when we get there. It's an amazing place."

Hemlocks, soaring sycamores, and giant rhododendrons cast their shadows over us as we wind our way down the narrow road leading into Aquatong Farm. I pull to a stop next to the fence, and we get out of the car.

"You were right," concedes Chad. "This is amazing."

"Duvall's studio was up there," I say, pointing. "And look, look at that sweet manger in the field there. There are paintings of that. You can check them out in the curator's book from *The Angel Collection*."

We stroll over to where several ewes and lambs nuzzle against the fence. Chad reaches through to pet one of them.

"Hey, baby," he says, then to me, "How'd you find this place?"

I remind him of the story of the Paris exhibit, about my seeing the paintings, how I passed out. Then I explain how I discovered Aquatong Farm one day on my way home from yoga and realized it was the very place that Daniel Duvall had painted his masterpieces.

For several minutes afterward, we're silent, gazing at the manger, watching the animals, listening to the occasional bleating of the lambs, the clucking of chickens, the distant sound of the rushing creek. I imagine the lovely young woman in the long dress and the sweet little boy playing on the grass near the manger. A deep tranquility settles over me. As the breeze rifles the yearning sycamores, a wisp of certainty and a glimmer of hope give me the courage to speak my heart.

"Chad," I begin, "I want to tell you that I am deeply, deeply sorry for any mistakes I made while you were growing up."

"Mom—"

"No, please, let me say it." My voice quivers, but I press on. "I know all parents say this, but I did the best I could. When we left your father, I think I went a little crazy. The hurt and fear, then the responsibility of you—having to take care of you all by myself—I was just, kind of in shock, I guess. And I was young and so lonely, too. Sometimes, on Sundays, just the two of us, I thought I'd go crazy with loneliness. I wanted a family, too, so much. A father for you, a husband to take care of us. I hoped to have more children. And as the years went by, I just kept thinking that Mr. Right was just around the corner."

"You shouldn't have laid that all on me—!"

"I know I shouldn't have. I see now how wrong it was."

He rests his elbows on the top rail of the fence, hunching his shoulders like a turtle about to pull into his shell. "Why did you keep picking the same loser guys? You could have had anybody."

"It's no excuse, but it probably has a lot to do with my mother. You know she was alcoholic and depressed. I kept trying to make her happy as a kid, and I guess that set the pattern for me to always fall in love with wounded birds. Always believing I could change them."

He shakes his head condescendingly. "Mom—"

"I'm just trying to be honest with you! We need honesty now. I realize I did rely on you too much. Too much and too soon. Made you grow up too fast. Confided things that I just should have kept to myself."

"When you used to tell me all your stuff, I pretended to understand because I knew that's what you wanted. But it scared the shit out of me. I didn't know how to fix it."

Instinctively I tense my diaphragm, trying unsuccessfully to repel the queasiness of guilt.

"I'm so sorry for that," I say, meaning it. *Meaning it, Chad!*

It comes out hoarse, and I clear my throat, gathering myself, choosing the words carefully.

"And I'm sorry for all you went through when Pete and I split up. I know how much he meant to you and what a loss that was. I just—I screwed up! So many times! I hurt you and disappointed you, probably embarrassed you too, but—Chad." I pause, not wanting to blow it by bawling. "I love you. I love you unconditionally. I want only your happiness, and I'll do anything to make things okay between us. I'll listen when you want me to listen, and try not to flinch when you say stuff that's hard to hear, and just—whatever I can do to make things better, I will do. Can you please, just, maybe, begin to forgive me?" I'm a noodle, waiting for his response.

There's a long silence, during which I fear I've ruined everything by broaching the horrible subject.

A beat, then two.

I stand unmoving next to him.

I hold my breath as he lightly lays his arm across my shoulders.

"Thanks," he says, finally. "Thanks for saying that. It means something to me." Relief barely registers before he takes his arm away.

"Can we call a truce?" I ask, daring to look at him.

"Yeah," he says, "we can call a truce. It's better than calling the men in the white jackets."

He turns away from the fence. "Let's get out of here. This place gives me the creeps."

We begin to stroll back along the fence until we come to the pond and the waterwheel. It flashes through my mind that the last time I was here was when Victor and I first kissed. I pause, watching the mossy waterwheel squeaking and groaning as it sucks the water up one side and deposits it back down on the other.

"Mom, come on," Chad says, walking backward toward the car.

The sun has descended behind the granite cliffs of the adjacent quarry, casting a heavy purple shadow over the pond.

Suddenly Chad is beside me. "Mom, what are you doing? What are you looking at? Let's go."

I'm startled, momentarily disoriented. "Hmmm?"

"Let's go back."

I gaze once more at the reflection of the waterwheel on the rippling pond waters. It's hard to pull myself away.

"Okay," I say, following him back across the lane.

As we slowly walk back to the car in the deepening sunset, a rooster crows.

Chad opens the car door, pauses. "One thing," he says.

I pull my keys from my pocket. "What?"

"Just take it slow with Victor. For everybody's sake."

The Manger

SIXTEEN
C H A P T E R

We began meeting on Mondays and Fridays, when William was certain to be gone all day.

Sometimes I was able to steal away in time for lunch, and we would take our paints and a picnic basket to a shady, secluded patch of grass next to the creek. There we would munch on bread and cheese while working on our canvases, always saving a part of the afternoon for glorious lovemaking on Daniel's battered studio couch, or if we couldn't wait, on a blanket in the open air under the trees.

Our time together was so precious that we constantly grappled with ways that we could make the most of it. Our passion for painting was often in conflict with our passion for each other, and often the latter won.

But as much as I craved Daniel physically, I also craved him intellectually. I wanted to learn everything that he could teach me. I was consumed with appetite: driven by gluttony for Daniel's body, Daniel's mind, and everything there was around me to paint—all the colors and sights of this world and the world inside my head. The restrictions of crowding it all into three or four hours was simultaneously exhausting and exhilarating.

Clara was my ally. I swore her to secrecy, and despite Williams's stern admonishments regarding her character, I admitted to her that I had decided to resume my lessons, that I would be going to Aquatong Farm two afternoons a week. I believed that she was trustworthy for no reason other than she was dependent upon my charity. But there was a more guileless kind of loyalty at work with Clara. A kind of sisterly allegiance; an unspoken countenance that whatever I was doing with my afternoons, she understood, and she would never betray me.

On those sun-drenched afternoons, languid and at peace from beautiful lovemaking, we would once again return to our easels side-by-side on the banks of the Aquatong Creek. I teased out stories from Daniel about his life in Paris and his friendships with other artists in the Impressionist movement. I particularly loved to hear about the American women artists: Mary Cassatt, Cecilia Beaux, Lilla Cabot Perry—all of whom had made names for themselves painting in the Impressionist style and moving in the artistic circles generally reserved for men.

One of my favorite subjects was Giverny, the artists' colony outside of Paris, where Claude Monet lived. Daniel had been a guest at Monet's home on several occasions. There he had met, among other artists, Lilla Cabot Perry, who lived next door to Monet, and the three had spent many a glorious afternoon painting on the banks of the River Epte and many a stimulating evening drinking wine and smoking cigarettes in Monet's salle à manger or playing billiards at the nearby Hotel Baudy.

"Are the gardens truly beautiful?" I asked.

"Magnificent. And he's never satisfied. Always planning, expanding." He squinted as he pushed a glob of citrus green onto the canvas with a palette knife.

"In a way, this is my Giverny," he said. "I was so inspired by Monet's house and gardens, the people that it attracted, and the techniques that I developed there, that I decided I needed my own plein air paradise. One that would serve as a backdrop for my painting and as a source of inspiration for other artists. So five years ago, I bought Aquatong and began offering classes. Of all my local students, only you have a true gift, real potential for greatness."

"You needn't flatter me, darling. I've already been seduced."

"You know it's true…I've told you that from the first moment I saw your work."

I smiled, remembering how secretly pleased I'd felt on my first day of class, when we students had been called on to judge each other's work. How Daniel had stood up for me when I'd been criticized.

"When were you last at Giverny?" I asked.

Without taking his eyes from his canvas, he said, "I refuse to tell you unless you come over here and give me a kiss."

I happily obliged.

He growled with pleasure. "Not too juicy a kiss, though, or I'll have to put down my brush and ravish you on the grass. Then we'll miss this exquisite light."

I laughed and hugged him. "I'm so happy," I whispered. Then resuming my own painting, I said, "Now, tell me about the last time you were at Giverny."

"The last time was two, no, three years ago for the wedding of Monet's stepdaughter Suzanne to Theodore Butler. It was quite an event, because Monet and Alice, his common law wife, were finally married just a few days before that. Everyone came out for it: the peasants, and the townspeople, and all of Monet's and Alice's friends. It was a charming country wedding, with everyone marching first to the town hall, then to the church. The party lasted all afternoon and well into the evening. Monet was on edge all day, though."

"Why was that?" I asked, loving every detail of the gossip.

"He never was keen on Butler somehow. Even threatened to sell the house when it looked like the romance was serious. But Alice got him to come around."

"Are they happy? Butler and Suzanne?"

"Oh, the last I heard, very much so. They've already got two children. Butler's quite the family man. Even his painting reflects that.

Although it seems that someone told me that Suzanne hasn't been well since the birth of the little girl this past winter."

"Do you have plans to go back? To Giverny?" I made an attempt at nonchalance, but the answer mattered very much to me.

"I don't think so. I hear it's changed. There isn't that spirit of discovery and individuality that made it so special. Many of the original colonists have become residents there, marrying and setting up households, retreating more or less from the group to spend time at home. Having babies and withdrawing into family life." His tone showed a trace of scorn.

"What's wrong with family life?" I asked.

"Nothing. For some. But I can't imagine trying to work with a bunch of squalling children about." He put down his brush. "Let's see how you're doing," he said. He walked over to me and put his arms around me from behind while he inspected my canvas.

"I think your strokes here," and he indicated an area I'd been working on where the waters of the creek cascaded over a grouping of rocks, "can be looser, freer. Think of the freedom of the water as it flows along. Remember that each object you paint is surrounded by atmosphere. I want to feel that when I look at the painting. I want you to feel it. Paint with your eye, but don't be afraid to paint with your heart." He kissed the back of my neck, and I felt goose bumps rise. "You have such a wonderful heart," he said.

I was painting like a madwoman and making love like a wanton. The outpouring of energy on those afternoons should have consumed me, but the reverse was true. The more I painted, the more I wanted to paint. The more Daniel and I made love, the more I craved him. I was ravenous all the time, but not for food. I became quite thin and wondered if William saw what I saw when I looked in the mirror. The feverish burning in the eyes, the sharper planes of the cheekbones, the love-swollen lips.

The realities of my existence were reversed. The village of Milltown, my home, my obligations as William's wife, my day-to-day activities, all seemed to be a dull pageant play that I was forced to sit through.

Only at Aquatong Farm, painting in plein air or lying in Daniel's arms, did I feel that I was in the real world.

The exception to this new reality was Willie. He became more real, more precious to me. Perhaps it was because my emotions had been laid bare, feelings stored up for years were just under the surface of my skin, all churning and inflamed and ready to rupture at any moment. Sometimes, in Daniel's presence, I would burst into tears for no reason.

And then I was late.

For five days, I silently prayed every time I went to the privy or undressed at night. On the morning of the sixth day, when at last the familiar crimson stain appeared, I shook with relief, then spent the day picturing the child that I might have conceived with Daniel.

It never occurred to me that I might become pregnant by William.

When my relief subsided and the familiar, but now welcomed cramps set in, I felt infinitely sad and had a desperate need to rock Willie in my arms. Looking at him, tears sprang to my eyes, and I pulled his sturdy little body close to me. I embraced him with such a crushing intensity that he pulled his thumb out of his mouth and said, "Ow, Mama, you're hurting me!"

Later I delicately broached the subject of pregnancy with Clara, working my way around to how a woman might prevent an unwanted birth, or worse, interrupt it.

She went to her little room off the kitchen and returned, clutching her Bible. She withdrew a well-worn piece of paper that was folded within its pages. Then she pressed it flat, carefully copied it onto another piece of paper, and wordlessly passed it to me. It was a recipe that listed a combination of herbs and tonics that a woman could ingest to induce miscarriage. Before I was able to summon the courage to ask her why she herself hadn't taken the mixture, she said simply, "It didn't work on me."

I put the recipe away, concealing it, literally, in my recipe box.

Guilt was always welling up in me during those days. I spent less time with Willie and tried to make up for it by taking him with me on my bicycle whenever I could or by reading to him in the afternoon instead of just before bedtime. Often we went wading in the creek or picking raspberries on the other side of Webster's meadow. He was getting to the age where he needed playmates, and sometimes I invited village children to play in the backyard.

Awakening one Monday morning, I immediately sensed that something was wrong. As William slept peacefully next to me, I listened for the familiar sound of Clara moving about in the kitchen downstairs.

The house was eerily silent.

I inhaled deeply, testing the air for the fragrant aroma of brewing coffee. I smelled nothing.

I crept out of bed and put on my dressing gown. Passing Willie's room, I peeked in to see if he was awake yet. He was not.

I went downstairs, through the parlor, and the dining room to the kitchen. Clara was nowhere to be seen, and the door to her room was closed. I knocked. "Clara?"

There was a muffled response, so I opened the door. Clara was lying in bed with the sheet pulled up to her chin.

"What is it?" I asked. "Are you ill?"

"Oh, ma'am," she said in a teary voice. "I'm scared. I started bleeding last night."

"You didn't take the... You didn't use the recipe?" I asked.

"Oh, no, I would never do that now that I'm feeling life."

My own heart began to thud as I approached her and laid a hand on her forehead. It was cool. "You stay right where you are. I'll get the doctor."

"I'm not going to lose the baby, am I?" she said, starting to whimper.

"No, of course not," I said, attempting a calm I did not feel. "You just need to rest, that's all. Stay off your feet. Would you like a cup of tea?"

She sniffled. "That would be nice, if it isn't too much trouble."

"It's no trouble. I'll be back in a few minutes."

I closed the door after me and went outside to pump water for the kettle. The heat was already beginning to burn the mist off the meadow. It was going to be another hot day. I thought of the way the sweat poured off our bodies when Daniel and I made love in the steaming heat—how all of our juices dripped and mingled and flowed together and how I loved to taste myself on his lips.

As water gushed from the pump into the pail, it suddenly struck me that if Clara was confined to bed, she couldn't look after Willie in my absence. The thought of not seeing Daniel made me physically ill.

I put the kettle on and went back upstairs. William was at the washstand shaving.

"Clara's not well," I said.

"What's the matter?"

"She started bleeding last night."

He stopped shaving. "Is she going to lose the child, then?" he asked.

"I don't know!" I retorted, with a degree of impatience that surprised me, causing William to raise his eyebrows. "But I think you should stop at Dr. Mardigian's on your way out of the village and ask him to come over this morning."

William wiped his face and hands with the towel. "Of course." He reached for his shirt. "I knew it was a mistake to take her in. Now instead of her helping you, it'll be the other way around."

It was exactly what I had been thinking, but I didn't want him to know that. "It may be just temporary," I said, brushing off his jacket.

"Mama! Papa!" Willie stood in the door grinning.

I put my hands on my hips and stared at him open mouthed. "Did you climb out of your crib?" I asked, exchanging a meaningful look with William.

Willie continued to grin and ran to me, hugging my legs.

I caressed his hair. "You are such a monkey!" I said. "Isn't he a monkey, Papa?"

William swept Willie up and lifted him high in the air. Willie shrieked. "He most certainly is! Is it time for a real bed for this young fella? Is it?"

Willie laughed. "I want to sleep with you," he cried. "With you and Mama."

"Oh, no you don't," said William, setting him down. "That's against the rules. But maybe your own real bed soon. Maybe when you're four."

"When am I four?" Willie became instantly absorbed in his fingers, struggling to calculate how many were three and how many were four.

"In October," I said. "October fifteenth."

"When is that?"

"When fall comes, sweetheart," I said. I knelt down beside him. "Willie, Clara isn't feeling well today, so I want you to be very quiet, and don't be a bother to her."

"Can't she play with me while you go away?" he said.

"What do you mean, silly?" I said quickly. "I'm not going away." I grabbed his hand, hustling him out of the room and down the stairs.

The doctor came and went, saying that there was nothing to do but wait and see. "Nature has a way of taking care of these things," he said, and prescribed total bed rest until either the bleeding stopped or Clara miscarried the child.

Clara was weepy and in need of reassurance, which I found difficult to offer. Not only did I dread the prospect of her having a miscarriage before my eyes, I dreaded the prospect of her being confined to bed. I considered asking a neighbor to look after Willie for the afternoon, quickly dismissing the idea as too risky. I didn't want anyone in the village to know my business. But the prospect of sacrificing my time with Daniel was unendurable.

I decided to take Willie with me.

"Where are we going, Mama?"

Willie was happily ensconced in the bicycle basket as I pedaled down River Road, feeling the beads of sweat gather on my forehead under the brim of my wide straw bonnet. The sun was at its zenith, and clouds of dust rose from the road as we passed through Lumberville, where the smell of fish from the river and the clamor of activity from the canal did nothing to dispel my turmoil. I had left chores undone, and I had no idea what I would serve for dinner that evening. I made a mental note to remind myself to stop at the market on the way back home.

"We're going to see the animals at the pretty farm. Remember I told you I'd bring you back?"

He clapped his hands together. "Are we, Mama? Are we going to see the animals?"

"Yes, we are," I said, smiling at him, "if I can just get past all this wagon traffic"

"I love you, Mama," he said happily.

"I love you, too, Willie-Silly."

As we arrived in the clearing and coasted over to the fence, I spotted a shirtless Daniel already set up to paint, some yards from the moss-covered manger, at the foot of a giant sycamore. Lambs frolicked around him, but he was so engrossed in mixing his paints that he paid them no heed and, in fact, didn't even see us approaching. I let go of Willie's hand and told him he could play with the animals. He immediately began to follow one of the lambs toward the manger. He passed into

Daniel's line of sight before I could say "hello," and Daniel looked up and around with a start.

"What in the world?" he said, looking from me to Willie. "What are you thinking?"

"I know," I said, wanting only to put my arms around him. Instead I lightly rested my hand on his forearm. "But I had no choice. Clara's not well. She may be losing the baby. The doctor has ordered complete bed rest." I looked into his eyes. "I just couldn't bear the thought of not seeing you today," I whispered.

"My darling, I want to be with you, too, but isn't this a bit risky?"

"All I'm doing is bringing him to see some animals. That's what he thinks."

"But what about painting? Can you work with him here? I wanted to show you some new strokes today." He leaned into me, whispering in my ear. "And what about making love? How can I fondle you with your little boy looking on? Just looking at you right now—" He pulled my hand toward his groin.

I yanked it away, "Stop it!" I mumbled with a half giggle. I turned to look for Willie, who was some yards away, squealing and laughing as he chased a befuddled rooster.

"I'm sorry if we can't make love today," I said, leaning to him, "but at least we can be together. Isn't that better than nothing?"

"We'll see," he said dubiously. "I brought your easel and paints out. The 'Rushing Waters' canvas is looking wonderful. I'd hoped you'd be able to finish it today. I want us to get on with some figure painting." I bent over to remove my shoes, and he pinched my bottom. "Ouch!" I said, playfully slapping his hand away.

I stood up, brushing my skirt. "On second thought, I don't think I'll paint today. I'll just watch you and play with Willie."

"Angel, darling, what a waste of time and talent."

"No, it's all right. I'm just happy to be near you."

"I've an idea, then," he said. "Why don't you and Willie arrange yourselves near the manger. I'll do a picture of the two of you."

"Oh! How lovely!" I said. "I'll fetch him." I made my way across the cushion of grass, calling, "Willie, darling, come to Mama. Come and take my hand." Willie came running over. "How do you want us?" I called to Daniel.

"Why don't the two of you recline on the grass, just to the left of the little gate?"

"All right. Come, Willie, let's sit down here on the grass." I took his hand.

He pulled away. "I don't want to sit down."

"Come on, darling, just for a minute. For Mama. Please?"

"I want to play with the lamb."

"You can, in a minute. In fact, if you sit down with me now, I'll bet the lamb will come over to see you."

"He will?" said Willie, permitting himself to be pulled down onto the grass in front of the little shed.

"I'll bet he will. Let's just sit here as still as still can be and watch to see if he comes over."

"Perfect!" called Daniel. "Gorgeous. Don't move."

"Is he coming Mama?"

"Shhh. Not yet."

Willie sat absolutely still for a minute. Then he whispered, "Is he coming, Mama?"

"Not yet, but soon, I think," I said.

He wriggled next to me. "I want to go see where he is."

I pressed on his leg. "No," I said as gently as I could. "If you look for him, he won't come. Just sit very quietly."

He sat for ten seconds. "Now?" he whispered. "Is he coming?"

"Pretty soon," I said. "Just stay sitting as you are, and he'll come."

He twisted his head around, trying to see the lambs, which had wandered in a flock to the edge of the fence and were all settling against their mothers for an afternoon nap.

"They're over there!" he said, pointing. He looked at me as if I had betrayed him. Then he stood up abruptly and, before I could restrain him, ran off toward the lambs.

I stole a glance at Daniel, who stood with his hands on his hips, shaking his head.

"Willie!" I called. "Willie, come back here!"

He ignored me. "Willie! You come back here!" I stood up and started after him. Daniel by now had his back to me, his arms folded, his head down.

I reached Willie and swept him up in my arms, carrying him back to our place in front of the manger. He began to kick. "I want to see the lambs!"

"You're coming back here with me until I say you can get up," I said firmly. He began to shriek. "I want to see the lambs! I want to see the lambs! You said I could see the animals!" Sweat poured off me as I lugged him back to the manger.

"For God's sake, put him down!" shouted Daniel. "It's not worth it. He's scaring the birds out of the trees."

I stood holding the wailing, twisting Willie, looking at Daniel, and wondering what to do. Finally I released Willie, and he ran back to the sleeping lambs.

I went to the fuming Daniel, out of breath and sticky with exertion. "I'm sorry," I said. "He's only three and a half. It's hard to make him do something if he's got his mind set on something else."

Daniel stood scowling as he clutched a handful of drawing pencils.

"How about just me, in front of the manger?" I ventured.

"Fine," he replied testily.

"Don't be angry," I said.

I slowly walked back to the manger, resuming my place on the grass.

After about five minutes, Willie wandered over to me and plopped himself down in my lap. "I'm tired," he whined, putting his thumb in his mouth and leaning against me.

Daniel peered around from the easel glowering at me. Then he walked in a circle, head down, shoulders sloping. He bent over to pick up a stick and hurled it across the field.

I sat there watching him, feeling the weight of Willie in my arms and the weight of my heart in my breast. I didn't know whether to try to get up or stay where I was.

I pressed my cheek against Willie's damp curls. "Do you want to take a nap now, or do you want to play? It's too hot for me to hold you."

He snuggled in closer. "Nap now. Like the lambs."

"Well, how about if I put down a blanket, and you can sleep on the grass?"

He nodded against me.

"All right, you wait here, and I'll get you a nice blanket to rest on." I attempted to extricate myself from him, but he clung to me.

"Carry me," he whined.

"Willie, sweetheart, you're getting too big for me to carry you everywhere. You wait here, and I'll bring you a nice blanket." I finally managed to stand, and he began to whimper.

"I'll be right back."

The whimpering rose in volume to full-out crying.

"Willie, hush now. Mama will be right back. You don't want to wake up the lambs with your crying, do you? Shhhh."

He snuffled and put his thumb back in his mouth. I walked over to Daniel, who had his back to me and was gazing into the distance, smoking a cigarette.

"Could you get the blanket?" I asked tentatively. "I think he'll go to sleep if he can lie down."

Wordlessly, Daniel headed for the studio. He returned a few minutes later with the blanket that we used for our picnics and our lovemaking. He handed it to me without meeting my imploring gaze.

"Please," I whispered, feeling my throat tighten. "Don't be angry." I walked back to Willie and spread the blanket out on the grass. "There," I said, trying to sound soothing, "now you have a nice bed, and you can take your nap like the lambies. Lie down now, and go sleepy-bye." I rubbed his back, feeling the ridge of small ribs beneath my hand.

Miraculously, without resistance, he stretched out on the blanket and closed his eyes. His thumb slipped out of his mouth, and his breathing grew settled and rhythmic. With great relief, I felt my own shoulders release. I eased my way off the blanket.

Reaching Daniel, I slipped my arm through his, leaning my head against him. "I'm sorry. I'm sorry our afternoon isn't what we wanted it to be."

He rumpled my hair. "I'm sorry too, my Angel, but this will never work."

A stone dropped in my chest. "What do you mean?"

He ambled toward the creek with me following. "You just can't bring him with you. My housekeeper is gone most afternoons looking after her ill sister, otherwise, as I suggested once before, she could look after him. But if there's no one else, then until Clara recovers, we shan't be able to meet."

"But I have to see you!" I clutched his arm.

"Angel, darling girl, what good is it to be together if we can't make love, or do our work, or even have a conversation? We accomplish nothing, we're both frustrated, and here's an entire afternoon wasted." He stopped walking and turned to me, his blue eyes looking directly into mine. "And, Angel, it isn't right, bringing your child into this, into our private world. Not only do you place yourself in jeopardy if he should reveal where he's been, but it simply is wrong. We're adults. We've made a choice to carry on this illicit affair—but he's a complete innocent. To make him party to our secret meetings, to rely on a three-year-old keeping a conspiracy of silence is ludicrous and places you at risk. It's something that I can't live with. And neither can you."

His words tapped into my shame. I couldn't look at him.

Then, gazing over my shoulder, he said unhappily, "And now he seems to be awake, and he's coming toward us, and I think the best thing to do is to take him home, and don't come back again until you can come alone."

I turned. There came little Willie, toddling our way. Speaking quickly over the thickness knotting my throat, I implored, "I can't be without you."

"Nor I you, my love, but these are the circumstances that we've been dealt, and we have to make the best of them."

"But what will I do?" I whispered as Willie approached.

"Mama?" Willie looked from me to Daniel. "Is the man going to let us go home now?" he said.

I glanced at Daniel. Was his pained expression a result of regret or anger?

"Yes," I said, taking Willie's hand. "Yes, we're going home now."

I walked quickly to the bicycle, pulling Willie along with me, wanting to look back, but not daring to for fear I would cry out with longing and frustration. I lifted Willie into the basket and stepped onto the bicycle. Gripping the handlebars I pedaled fiercely down Aquatong Lane, my cheeks aflame as Willie opened his chubby arms to the cooling breeze, his cry of delight echoing across the nearby quarry.

When we finally arrived at the Rectory, I led Willie up to the front porch and pulled him onto my lap. As the rocking chair creaked on the floorboards, I said, "Willie, look at Mama. Do you know what a secret is?"

"Yes," he solemnly replied.

"Well, you and I have a secret."

"We do?"

"Yes, we do. A big secret, one that belongs only to you and me, and nobody else in the world. Not Papa, not anybody."

"Not Papa?" he said, eyes round with amazement.

"No. And our secret is that we went to the special place to see the animals today. And if we don't keep the secret, then we can never go back to see the animals again."

"Not ever?"

"Not ever, unless we keep our secret just between you and me. Can you do that?"

He nodded.

"Do you promise me? Promise, promise?"

He nodded again.

"And you won't tell anyone, because you want to go back to see the animals again someday, don't you?"

"Yes, because I want to see the lambs and the rooster."

"Okay, then. That's our secret. And it's very special. And you're a big boy, and Mama loves you so much!" I hugged him tightly. "So much!" I repeated.

We went into the house, and I tiptoed to Clara's door, peeking in. She was sleeping. I put my bundles in the kitchen, having stopped at the store for a ham and some potatoes. I decided I would bake the ham and make potato salad for dinner, along with some juicy red tomatoes from the garden. I put Willie down for the rest of his nap and went out to the garden to pick the tomatoes.

The air was still thick with heat, and stepping back out into it, I could feel myself drooping and wilting, as if all strength and all hope had been sucked out of me.

I could smell the warm, slightly acrid fragrance of ripening tomatoes as I knelt by the garden. I thought of Daniel, and my fingers ached as they pulled down on the thickening vines in search of the ripest tomatoes, and the core of me felt cheated and hollow at not having held my lover inside me that day. My hand closed around smooth, firm, warm red flesh, and I yanked gently. The tomato popped off. I held it up to my nose and breathed deeply. The skin was slightly split, and a seam of orange-pink pulp oozed out. *Like me*, I thought. *Like me*. Growing and ripening in the sultry summer sun, until one day something split apart in me, and the juicy pulp oozed out, and everything that had been held inside of me was released.

And now what? What? I suddenly felt a pang of longing for Lizzie. I yearned to feel the comfort of her arms around me, hear the soft lilt of her voice crooning a lullaby. I tried to imagine what she might be doing, at that very moment, so far across the sea. It was night in Ireland. Was she in Seamus's arms? Was it the same between them as it had been all those years ago? Did her heart still stop at the sight of him? Now that I finally understood what she had tried to explain to me about love, I wondered if she would understand why I was risking everything to have it for myself, if only for a little while. And if she understood, would she forgive?

I pulled off two more tomatoes and slowly rose to my feet. As I walked back to the house, I felt heavy limbed and old.

"How was your day?" asked William.

"Fine," I said. "Hot."

"And how did you occupy yourself?" he asked, helping himself to another serving of potato salad.

"Oh, this and that," I said, hoping I didn't sound evasive.

"We went riding on the bicycle!" said Willie proudly.

I stiffened.

"Oh, now did you?" said William. "Where did you and your mama ride to?"

"We went—" Willie looked to me, confused.

I jumped in. "We went riding—just around. Down Milltown Road and back. For the breeze."

Willie watched, looking from me to William.

"Yes, it was brutal," said William. "On the way back from Frenchtown, I stopped twice to water Obediah." He chuckled. "I must say that I was delighted to be standing up to my waist in water today! There's much to be said for total immersion baptism." We both laughed, and I breathed more easily at the change in subject.

"How many did you baptize today?" I asked.

"Seven. And on Friday in Tullytown, there will be eight."

"Wonderful," I said.

"Papa, I have a secret!" declared Willie, as if he would burst to tell it.

I slid a sharp glance his way. My heart skittered like a flat stone on a calm lake.

"What's that?" asked William, smiling at our son. He raised his eyebrows in exaggerated curiosity.

"Would you like a cookie now?" I said quickly, rising to lift Willie out of his chair. "You can have a cookie and take one in to Clara. I'll bet she's finished her tray and would like a cookie."

I took his hand to lead him into the kitchen. "It's my secret!" he said proudly, looking back at William.

"Well?" said William. "Tell Papa."

"Come, sweetheart, let's get a cookie," I said, trying to keep the tension out of my voice.

Willie tore his hand from mine and ran back to William, climbing onto his lap. He leaned into William, cupping his little hand around William's ear for a whisper.

I felt myself go weak.

And then the whisper erupted, filling the room, simultaneously swelling and deflating in my brain: "When I'm big, I want to baptie like you!"

"Oh, well!" said William, with a hearty voice, "that's a wonderful secret. We'll see what we can do about that!"

SEVENTEEN

CHAPTER

1996

Sunlight glints off the wing of the plane as we make our descent through the lavender-hued dawn into the aeroport Charles de Gaulle. Victor fastens his seatbelt, having just returned from the lavatory, where he'd obviously shaved and freshened up. I can smell toothpaste on his breath, and the fragrance is so early-morning intimate, so personal, that it makes me want to lean into him, to lay my head on his chest, and inhale.

We hadn't spoken much during the flight. He plugged in his iPod the minute we left Philadelphia. I watched a dumb movie, then took a couple of Tylenol PMs and drifted off to sleep, awakening only once to shift positions and surreptitiously wipe drool off my chin. I took a bleary peek at Victor, relieved that he was snoring away and probably hadn't seen the spittle oozing out of my slack mouth. *At least I don't snore*, I thought smugly as his rhythmic drones dissolved into the hum of the engines.

Before drifting back to sleep, I remember thinking, *Here we are, sleeping together, but we're really not* sleeping together. Then everything went dark until about a half an hour ago, when the announcement about our approach into Paris—*Mesdames et Messieurs, nous commencons notre descente*—penetrated the grogginess of induced sleep, and I awakened.

It seemed to take forever to clear the camera gear through customs, but finally here we are in a rented car, traveling northwest on A13 toward Giverny.

We had booked reservations in a nondescript hotel in Vernon, a few kilometers across the Seine from our final destination. The plan was to check in, sleep for a few hours, and hopefully be clearheaded and professional for our four o'clock appointment with the august and mysterious Madame Sancerre.

I was too keyed up to close my eyes and fearful that if the jetlag kicked in, I'd sink into that thick, heavy sleep like anesthesia you can't wake from. Instead I unpack, soak in the tub, wash my hair, and spend an inordinate amount of time making myself presentable. The six hundred dollars I'd blown on a simple, elegant little black suit was worth every penny. I pull my hair into a passable chignon, add silver hoop earrings, and I am, as they say, good to go.

Victor is waiting for me in the lobby. As I approach, he whistles, then says with a thick accent, "*Formidable.*"

"Not bad yourself," I say. He's wearing well-cut gabardine slacks, a beautiful cream linen shirt, and a navy blazer. I always like to see a man in a navy blazer.

"Shall we?" he says, offering his arm.

On the way to Giverny, we kibitz about how we'll handle the meeting, doing silly role-playing, joking around to ease the tension.

We have no trouble finding the house, which sits just back on the main road in the village, not too far from Monet's famed residence. I feel a shiver of pure delight, a thrill, actually, when we pull into the gravel drive. My tension dissolves into a kind of sweet happiness, a comfort level. It's almost as if I'm *coming home.*

"Oh, it's beautiful, isn't it, Victor?"

"Like a postcard. Let's get this show on the road."

We approach the front door of the house. It is more like a chateau, really, lemon colored, with a façade of shiny black-shuttered French windows. Trellised laurel vines, carefully tended, stretch and wind their way up toward the mansard roof. A slate path leads us to the enormous front door, also painted shiny black. In the center of it is a polished brass lion's head knocker.

Victor and I exchange glances. He winks. I take a deep breath and smooth back my hair. Then I lift the lion's head and let it drop.

A bright-faced young woman in maid's attire opens the door. She says, "Bonjour" in that chirpy lyrical French way and stands back to let us enter, saying, "Bienvenue. Entrez, s'il vous plait. Madame vous attend dans le jardin. Oh! Je m'apelle Suzette. Suivez-moi." Before I can translate, Suzette is leading us down an airy corridor toward the back of the house. I sense paintings, one after the other on either side of me, but we're moving so fast to keep up that I can't really look at them.

Then a rush of bright light and riotous color as we find ourselves on the back terrace, where Madame Sancerre sits at a linen-covered table in the shade of a blooming tulip tree. There is a silver tea service on the table and a tray of little sandwiches and cakes.

The terrace overlooks extensive gardens, which are just coming into full bloom. There's a fragrance in the air, of grass and rosemary, jasmine, roses. The setting is splendid.

"Voici, Madame!" Suzette calls out cheerfully to our hostess.

Her hair is white, and she wears it in braids wrapped around her head like a crown. She is still handsome, even in her seventies, with good bone structure, erect posture, and a sense of her own style. The aubergine suit she wears looks like classic Chanel. I also observe the three strand set of pink-tinged pearls, the matching earrings, the sizable diamonds flashing on her fingers and think, *I should be scared of you, but somehow, I'm not.* I have a strange sense that everything I say and do from this moment on will be exactly right.

I approach first and extend my hand.

"Madame Sancerre, how good of you to let us come. I'm Morgan Reed, and this is my partner, Victor Cenzo."

She takes my hand and holds it, ignoring Victor.

"You are very pretty," she says, considering me. "You remind me of someone."

"Oh. Thank you for the compliment. And this is Victor Cenzo." I repeat the introduction.

She turns to him then and really looks him over. She slowly extends her hand with the palm down, and darned if he doesn't bend over and kiss it, saying, "Madame Sancerre, a pleasure." He manages it with such aplomb that my mouth almost drops open.

"What a magnificent setting this is," I say, looking around. "Your gardens are exquisite."

"Yes, this is a good year for the perennials. If you like, we can take a walk through later. Please sit down. I've had Suzette prepare tea for us. Tell me how you like it, and I shall pour. And please help yourselves to some sandwiches. Don't be shy." It's an order.

She pours a cup. "Morgan?"

"Lemon will be fine, thank you," I say. I hesitate to ask for sugar, too, not wanting her to think me fussy. But she says, "Wouldn't you like *un petit peu du sucre?*"

So I say, "Yes, thank you, that would be lovely."

She passes me the tea and says, "Please," indicating the sandwiches and cakes. Eating is the last thing I want to do, but I realize that she might be testing out our table manners, looking to see how civilized we are. I reach for the starched white linen napkin in front of me and slip it into my lap. Victor follows suit.

"And you, Monsieur? I'm sorry…"

"Victor," he says.

"Ah, yes. Victor. How do you take your tea?"

"Just milk, thank you." She adds milk and passes the cup and saucer to him.

"Ah, that's very kind of you. Thank you," he says smoothly.

"Now don't be shy. You must be hungry after your flight," she says, pouring tea for herself. "Airline food is inedible."

I take a plate and say to her, "May I serve you?"

"Yes, thank you, I'll have the watercress sandwich and one of those little meringues." I feel her watching me as I lift a tiny sandwich with the silver server and place it on her plate. I do the same with the meringue.

"Victor?" I say, lifting a plate for him.

"Thank you," he says, so properly that I really feel like laughing. He's like a kid in school, having lunch with the principal. "I'd like a few sandwiches, thank you."

I serve him, with no spills, then serve myself, feeling an enormous sense of relief when the food is finally safely delivered onto the plates. Now all we have to do is eat, drink, and speak at the same time, without spilling, spitting, choking, or otherwise embarrassing ourselves. I glance at Victor. He picks up a sandwich and nibbles at it.

"This is so lovely of you," I say, sipping my tea. "Thank you." I wait for her to broach the subject of the documentary, being aware that it would be impolite to bring up business during tea.

Instead we chat about Bucks County and the Pennsylvania countryside. Though she has made countless trips to New York and other parts of the United States, including Philadelphia, she has never visited Bucks County. She intimates, as she had in our phone conversation, that it holds dark memories for her family.

After tea we stroll the lush gardens, stopping periodically to admire her prize dahlias or to fret with her over the black gladioli that are late in blooming.

I'm drawn to a large cluster of mature lilac bushes. Their fragrance is intoxicating. I walk to one of them and press my face into the pale lavender blossoms.

"Angel planted these," she explains. "Almost a hundred years ago. She said they reminded her of Pennsylvania."

"They're my favorite flower," I say. "I have a beautiful lilac bush like this one in my backyard. It's so big, I think it must have been there forever."

"It was her favorite flower too."

Suddenly I register what she's just said. "I had forgotten that Angel was born in Philadelphia. I knew Daniel lived in Pennsylvania of course, but…There's little information about Angel's life prior to her work with Duvall in France."

"Yes, she grew up in Philadelphia," answers Madame Sancerre. "And then, later, of course, there was Bucks County and all of that terrible business. She never went back. No one in the family has ever gone back."

"May I ask what you refer to?"

Madame Sancerre sighs. "There was a tragedy," she offers.

I wait for her to reveal more.

"The child. Her little boy."

"Little boy?" I venture.

"Yes. He died there under mysterious circumstances."

I steal a quick glance at Victor. Some atavistic sense triggers a steady thrum in my heart. I feel lightheaded. There's a buzz in the heat of the late afternoon, which suddenly feels like a smothering blanket. I'm afraid I might vomit. I clutch Victor's arm for support.

"What was her little boy's name, Madame?" asks Victor.

"Willie. He was three years old when it happened. She never spoke about it."

I manage to say, "Madame Sancerre, what was Angel's real name?"

"Her given name was Evangeline. When she married the minister, she became Evangeline Laury."

"Did she live in a town called Milltown?" I ask. "Milltown, in Bucks County, Pennsylvania?"

"Yes, Milltown, Pennsylvania. That was the place."

My breath is shallow, catching in my throat. I feel a reassuring press of Victor's hand on my back, bracing me, bracing both of us.

"Madame Sancerre," I say, "I live in Angel's house! The former rectory! I found her drawings hidden in the floorboards! And I've visited her son's grave! It's in the cemetery next door."

For a moment there is a vast silence, broken only by the hum of insects, the whisper of a breeze. The elderly woman's hazel eyes blink rapidly. Slowly she brings her hand to her throat.

"My God," she whispers. "What are you telling me? How can this be?"

I shake my head. "I don't know. I don't know, but it's true."

We stare at each other as if our eyes are meeting from across the ages. A primal recognition requiring no language.

She gathers both of my hands into hers. We're the same height, and her gaze is so direct, so penetrating.

"How strange this is," she murmurs. "I had a sense about you from the moment we met. As if I'd known you before." Her eyes never leave mine as she says with wonder, "Where did you come from?"

"From far away, I think," I say in a daze.

"Perhaps not so far," she replies. "Perhaps not." She squeezes my hands, and something gives way inside me. I bow my head, stifling a sob.

"I'm sorry," I say finally. She releases my hands, and I sweep tears from my cheeks. "This is quite unprofessional of me. It's just, there's so much…so much—" I'm unable to complete the thought.

"Apologies are not necessary between kindred spirits," she says kindly, turning her gaze to include Victor. "I'm certain that you're both consummate professionals. Of course you know that you have my blessing to proceed with the documentary. Our meeting is much more than mere coincidence. And naturally I shall do everything I can to help."

I am in bed by nine that night. Emotionally exhausted and jet-lagged, all I want is sleep and oblivion. I'd even turned Victor down when he suggested a celebratory dinner, toasting the craziness and serendipity and triumph of the afternoon. I seek only quiet, the cool of the sheets, the inky darkness, and relief from the fusillade of thoughts ransacking my tired brain. Sleep doesn't come right away. Just as I feel myself drifting off, an arm or a leg jerks, pulling me back from the edge. I once read that when your limbs spasm like that, right at the threshold of sleep, it's because you're slipping into the astral world, the world of flying and time travel, and your gross body is restraining your astral body before it slips its earthly bonds and hurls itself into galaxies past, present, and future.

Finally, though, I dream deeply. In my dream, I am in Ireland, of all places. It seems to me that it's during Victorian times. Though I've never been to Ireland, all of it seems familiar to me. I'm staying with a family in a whitewashed house somewhere in the emerald countryside. There are several children, including a baby girl, who seems undernourished and sad, and it's because I haven't been taking proper care of her. And there's a woman, a motherly, sweet woman, who looks after me so dearly. I'm sick in bed, and she brings me trays of food, and sits with me, and strokes my hands, and tells me everything will be all right. Then I'm standing in front of a mirror, crying and smearing black paint all over my face with an artist's brush, and the sweet woman comes into my room and takes the brush from my hand and pulls me to her and holds me and rocks me like a baby until I stop crying.

  

We set up for our on camera interview in the studio where for years Angel and Duvall had painted side-by-side. Madame Sancerre has kept it exactly the way it was at Angel's death more than fifty years ago. It's a bright, airy, high-ceilinged room overlooking the gardens. And though no one has painted here for half a century, I believe I can smell the faint sweetness of the oils, inhale a trace of paint thinner, a whiff of tobacco. Madame motions to a striking portrait resting on one of two easels. It's of an elderly woman. "This is what Angel was working on when she died. Her self-portrait."

I approach the painting. The strokes are harsh, almost punishing. The lined face seems simultaneously beautiful and ravaged. But it is the eyes that draw me in. They stare out at me. I can't turn away.

"Morgan? Morgan?" Victor's voice interrupts the spell. "What do you think about having Madame seated here, with the portrait in the distant background?"

Just then Suzette comes into the studio, carrying a vase filled with lilacs.

"Merci, Suzette," says Madame Sancerre. She turns to Victor and me. "The lilacs are in such perfect bloom."

"Yes, yes, that's lovely," I say, glad to be drawn away from the portrait's haunting eyes. "The lilacs just over Madame's shoulder, Victor, with the portrait in the background. Good."

Victor begins to move two chairs into place for the interview, then checks his framing through the camera lens.

"Morgan, can you move the vase over a few inches to your right?" he says. "It's blocking the portrait. Madame, could I please see you in your chair?" Madame Sancerre settles into the chair.

"Here," Victor says to me, "come see what you think."

I peer through the lens. The framing is perfect. Within a few minutes, Victor has us both miked, and we're ready. I remind Madame Sancerre to speak in complete sentences for our editing purposes.

"Madame Sancerre," I begin, "Tell me about your connection to the artists Angel and Daniel Duvall."

"Angel and Duvall were my grandparents. Well, step-grandparents, really. They raised my mother, although she was not their biological child. The circumstances of my mother's birth were never discussed. It's always been rather a mystery. I know that Angel brought my mother, who was just a baby, with her when she left Pennsylvania, where she had been living."

"Can you describe how Angel and Duvall met?" I ask.

"I do know that she took some painting lessons from him. He used to give lessons in plein air painting on his farm, and she was one of his students. But they never spoke much about that time, and as a child I understood not to ask. They preferred to talk about their time together in Paris and, of course, the happy memories of their life here at Giverny. My mother, Elizabeth Duvall, was raised here. Here, and in Ireland."

The mention of Ireland startles me. I recall my dream of the previous night.

"How does Ireland fit into the picture?" I ask.

"Oh, Angel had…sort of a family there. A kind of godmother. Her name was Lizzie. She lived in the country with her husband and children, and my mother often spent summers there or stayed there when Angel and Duvall had to travel for their work. Angel adored Lizzie. My mother said that Angel was inconsolable when she died. It was only when I was born, so my mother told me, that Angel's cloak of despair lifted."

The interview continues for two hours, until I see Madame begin to wilt. We break for lunch.

Suzette has set a lovely table on the terrace, with pâtés and tapenades, a gazpacho, green bean salad, crusty bread, and a selection of cheeses. We wash it all down with a crisp white Burgundy.

After lunch, Madame Sancerre excuses herself for her customary afternoon rest. She invites us to film in the garden, or the house, or the main gallery, where most of the paintings are housed. After promising to rejoin us in a few hours, she disappears into the house on Suzette's arm. Victor and I agree instantly that we'll use the time to begin to shoot the paintings.

While Victor retrieves the camera gear from the studio, I walk across the lawn to what Madame has referred to as the Main Gallery, a wing of the house opposite the studio. I hesitate at the door, feeling a rush of excitement, a feeling of *momentousness*, if there is such a word. I turn the weathered antique latch and push the door open. A suffusion of color and light assaults me, and several seconds pass before I'm able to focus. The first painting to capture me is the life-size portrait of Angel. I had seen it at the Musée d'Orsay in Paris and been weak-kneed at its radiance—at the masterful play of shadings of white, cream, gold, blue, silver. Once again, it seems to vibrate with life. Angel's long arms are outstretched, as if in benediction. There's an aura about her. Duvall had painted her as if she truly were an angel on earth. I feel everything go still around me. My heart is whooshing like a bellows of angel wings in my ears.

"Bless me!" I whisper. "Bless me, Angel." I don't know what makes me say that. It just comes out.

Suddenly I need air, and I pull the door open and step outside. I see Victor coming across the lawn with his gear, and I hurry toward him.

"Here, let me carry something," I say, grabbing a bag of tapes.

"You look like you've seen a ghost," he says, giving me the once over.

"Jet lag," I shoot back.

I let him go first across the threshold into the gallery. He stops and slowly sets his gear down as his eyes scan the walls. For a few seconds he's speechless. Then he says, "My God, I feel like I've walked into the core of the sun."

He moves slowly from painting to painting. I stay close to him, grateful for the comfort of his presence, knowing that I couldn't be alone in that space, but not understanding why.

We don't speak. We just slowly circle the vast room, looking. We approach the painting of the woman and the little boy in the meadow by the manger. Aquatong Farm. I know it for certain now. And Angel and Willie. I know that, too.

"It's them," I whisper.

"I know," he replies.

"When I look at it—I know this seems crazy, but I have this longing to…to *climb into it…to be there, where they are.*"

"You have been where they are," he says softly, his eyes not leaving the painting.

Suddenly I'm scared. "What do you mean?" I ask.

"We've both been there." His voice sounds weird.

"Oh," I say, "you mean, we've both been to Aquatong Farm."

For several seconds he doesn't respond. Then, as if he were returning from some far-off place, he says, "Right, right." Then he nervously jingles some change in his pocket. "This is a trip, huh? Kind of a déjà vu thing."

The next painting, in contrast to the idyllic scene in the meadow, is a study in darkness. The waterwheel and the pond, the hovering storm clouds. We stare. My insides begin to shake, just as they did when I first saw this painting in Paris. I swallow the scream that starts to build in my throat and turn to Victor for some kind of reassurance. He is sweating profusely. I can smell his fear.

"Victor."

He faces me. Our eyes meet. There is no reassurance.

"I'm sorry," he blurts out. "I'm so sorry."

Before I can ask "for what?" his arms are around me. We cling together, like lost children, and I'm astonished at the intensity, the need that's expressed in his embrace.

"I love you," he blurts. I can't believe my ears, but then he's kissing me, and I don't know if I'm dizzy from the kiss or the paintings or the jet lag, but I literally swoon in his arms, and the next thing I know, we're both on the floor. When I open my eyes, all I see is his face. His dear, familiar face. At first etched with concern, then softening into relief, then at last, opening into the happiest smile I have ever seen.

My cell phone rings. I fumble in my pocket.

"Hello?"

"Mom!"

"Chad! Hi!" I prop myself up on my elbow. "How are you?"

"Okay, I guess."

"What do you mean, you guess?"

"I took a bunch of pictures at Aquatong Farm yesterday."

"That's great! How do they look?"

"Well, that's the thing. I'm kind of freaked out."

"What's the matter?"

"The pictures. I just picked them up. They have like these shadows on them."

"You mean they didn't turn out?"

"It's not that. The focus is clear as a bell. The scenes look great, but these shadows...well, they're not really like shadows, they're more like...Mom, they're like ghosts."

EIGHTEEN
CHAPTER

1895

"Why so quiet, my Angel?"

Daniel lay sprawled naked on the studio couch, while I sketched in silence. He had been posing for me for the better part of the afternoon. It was the last of several studies I had drawn in preparation for painting a nude portrait of him.

Despite the turbulence that roiled my insides, I was captivated and fascinated by the lines of his body. The long, lean tautness of it. The powerful shoulders sliding easily into rounded, muscular upper arms. The graceful forearms covered with dark hair, the delicate wrists, and long, tapering fingers stained and callused. The broad, hairy chest, and flat belly. The thrust of the pelvic bone as it seemed to cradle the smoky dark thatch leading downward to the brownish-pink lumpy mass of his manhood, now in repose. His long, well-formed thighs and solid, muscular calves. I lovingly sketched in the ridges of his tendons, the swollen rivulets of his veins, the harsh angles of his bones, the rounded bulk of his muscles and tissues. His head was large, made even larger by the mane of dark hair that fell almost to his shoulders. His generous brow, the coal-black eyebrows, and those incredible, all-seeing eyes. The slightly crooked nose, the full lips—all of it conspired to undo me as I worshipped him from my perch on a stool and struggled with the unanswered questions that tormented me until I thought I would shriek.

"Angel? Darling, where are you? Speak to me," he said almost playfully.

I didn't reply. He started to get up.

"Don't!" I said sharply. "Don't move when I'm sketching you!"

"My, my," he said. "The artiste at work." He lay back, resuming his pose. "Come, I know when something's wrong. You haven't even let me make love to you today."

"Well, we agreed that it's important that I get more work done for you to show to Mr. Durand-Ruel," I said.

"Of course it is. But you're being cold to me. Something's wrong. Now what is it? Come on, out with it. You can't hide anything from me."

Still I didn't respond. I could feel trickles of sweat in my armpits and at the back of my neck. Finally I said in a low voice, "Who else comes here besides me?"

"What do you mean?"

"Who else comes here besides me? When I'm not here?"

He looked at me speculatively. "Do you want a list?"

I returned his gaze, not answering.

"Students come here. Friends come here. Other painters, artists come here. Models come here."

"And other women?" I said, feeling relief that I had said it and fear at his answer.

"What are you getting at?" His gaze turned harder as he reached for a cigarette.

Sarah Webster's nattering at the quilting bee had dominated my thoughts, smoldered in my mind for the better part of two days. I told myself it was only idle gossip, but she had seemed gleeful as she recounted several anecdotes about Daniel and his supposed escapades with women. Red-faced, I'd imagined that it was for my benefit alone that she described him as "dashing" and "such a ladies' man." Then there was a darker story. Upon hearing it, I deliberately poked my finger with the needle twice, then left the table on the pretext that I needed a breath of air. Surely those women had no way of knowing about my affair with Daniel! Surely it was only coincidence that Sarah had brought up his name! And surely the things she said about him were not true!

I braced myself to confront Daniel. "I'm asking if there are other women, besides me." I hoped he couldn't see that my chin was trembling. "It's my right to know."

"Evangeline, you do know. I have women students and women friends that come here that I socialize with occasionally. I'm not a cloistered monk." He sat up on the couch and drew hard on his cigarette.

"I want to know if other women come here—to be alone with you." My voice was a low monotone, sinking even lower as I uttered the last four words.

"Do you mean, do I have other lovers? Is that what you mean? If that's what you mean, why don't you come out and say it?" He crossed his legs, letting the cigarette smoke flare from his nostrils. Then he folded his arms and stared at me. His eyes were icy, and his gaze froze my insides. My hands felt suddenly stiff, and I desperately wished I hadn't initiated this confrontation. I wanted to close my eyes and cover my ears.

"I thought we'd settled this," he said, getting up and coming toward me. "You want to know if I sleep with other women besides you? I've told you before that I'm faithful to you." He said these last words with a clenched jaw.

"Well, what about the women you were with at the Black Bass Inn last Saturday night?"

"What?" He started to laugh, then stopped, looking incredulous. "Where did you hear about that?"

I attempted to summon some dignity as I said, "I heard about it at my quilting bee. That you were with women, painted women—like gypsies—and that they threw themselves all over you—"

"Oh, stop! This is ridiculous!" He reached for his pants, pulled them on, and began to pace. "The gossip mill at the village quilting bee! A bunch of thin-lipped, dried-up old ninnies sitting around speculating on the sex life of the rest of the world because they have none of their own! And you listened to it!"

"Well," I said defensively, "I know it's true. My neighbor knows someone who saw you! You can understand that I was upset to hear it."

He sighed and snuffed out his cigarette. "Evangeline—"

I shuddered at hearing him call me by my Christian name.

"I have a life other than you, just as you have a life other than me."

"I don't have a life outside of here! Not a real one! My real life is with you!"

"And mine with you, but as we are both so painfully aware, that life exists for only a few hours a week. We can't just sit in a vacuum and stop breathing for all the hours and days of the week except Mondays and Fridays between noon and four! When I'm not with you, I continue with my life. And that includes seeing my friends and teaching my classes and dining out and whatever other activities are productive and enjoyable and help me to pass the time, the huge gaps of time between our meetings."

I was trembling. "I want to know who the women were that you were with at the Black Bass Inn."

"The women that I was with," he said, sarcasm coating every word, "are lesbians."

"What?"

"They're lesbians. They make love with other women," he said matter-of-factly. "Are you satisfied?"

"What…what do they do with each other?"

"The same things that men and women do with each other, only in a somewhat more limited fashion."

This startling information sidetracked me, and for a few moments I contemplated what he had just said. The images that floated through my mind both fascinated and repelled me.

"They are lovers with each other—not with me, as your small-town gossips would have you believe—and they pose no threat to you. Really, Angel, you have to stop being so jealous and insecure."

"How can I help but be insecure? I only see you for a few hours a week. I don't know what you do when I'm not here!"

With exasperation he said, "There are boundaries to this relationship. We're both adults, and we have to accept that."

"I don't accept it!" I despised myself for being so petulant.

"Well, what are you going to do about it?" he said softly, his eyes meeting mine.

I stood there, unable to respond. He came to me then and put his arms around me, resting his chin on my forehead.

"Angel, can't you be grateful for the moments that we have together? Can't we just live in the present and not be concerned about the time that we don't spend together as long as the time that we do spend together is true and honest?" He drew back and looked into my eyes. "When I'm with you, there's nowhere else I want to be. When I'm away from you—" He paused. "When I'm away from you, it's difficult. And so I try to fill the hours with work and amusement. But this is what we have now. This and nothing more."

There was a long pause as I summoned the courage to ask the question that had shredded my peace of mind for weeks.

"Will we ever have anything more?"

He cocked his head, searching my face. "My dear," he said. "I hardly think that's up to me."

"What do you mean?"

"You're the one with the husband and the child, not I." A shadow passed over his face, and he turned briefly away from me, staring at the floor. Then, turning back, he said, "If you were free, don't you think I would take you away with me? To Paris in September?"

I couldn't believe what I was hearing. It was the best and worst that I could hope for. I felt simultaneously saved and doomed. We both knew the words were empty, hollow, with not a chance in the world of becoming reality, but for a few moments I allowed myself the luxury, the cool, floating gossamer luxury of imagining life with Daniel in Paris.

Paris! To live, to learn, to paint, to make love, to sleep in his arms, and wake up to the sound of pigeons cooing on the rooftop and the sight of his face and the warmth of his body. To speak Maman's language— the language of my childhood. To visit the galleries, the museums, the salons. To attend lectures and concerts. To meet with other artists, to see their studios, to stay up late discussing the very latest in technique and innovation. To visit Monet at Giverny, to meet Mary Cassatt, Edgar

Degas, Paul Cezanne! Perhaps a trip to Aix-en-Provence in the spring! To walk and paint among them, perhaps be considered one of them someday!

To be woman, artist, lover.

To be fully alive.

To be.

The powerful and seductive images rolled in and out of my brain like the waves of the ocean. One would recede, and another would take its place. Brilliant hues of promise and possibilities flickered like a kaleidoscope behind my eyes.

"Angel." His voice brought me back. "Don't." His eyes burned into mine, and his expression was tender and concerned.

"Why not?" I whispered plaintively, as the momentary dream withered, crumbled, disintegrated into the reality of the impossible present.

"We're in a situation," he said solemnly. "We're in a situation. Let us enjoy the time we have together while we have it?" He took my face in his hands. "Can't you live in the moment with me, my darling? Can't you?"

Then I remembered that other story that I had heard at the sewing circle. The one that had sent me out to the porch, gasping for air. The one about the girl who had tried to kill herself over Daniel. And I thought about the approach of September, less than a month away. I realized that we had never discussed what would happen after September. Would he simply disappear from my life? Would we ever see each other again? Would he come back in the spring? How was I supposed to live without him?

More images passed before my eyes. Leaden skies, bitter cold, empty days and frozen nights, days without color or hope, nights without warmth or release. I saw myself rocking in a rocking chair, listless, lost, abandoned. Perhaps driven wild by his absence. Driven insane. Suddenly I felt the walls of the studio closing in on me as the world without grew black and stifling. I couldn't catch my breath. I felt myself shrinking into a black dot, a puff of smoke, a wisp of ash. Not an artist. Not a lover. Not a woman.

Nothing.

The panic rose and rose, engulfing me, and I covered my face with my hands, and I could see that poor young girl cutting her wrists, and then she became me. I swayed on my feet, uttering a little moan.

"What is it?" He grasped my wrists, pulling my hands away from my face. "What?"

"The girl!" I whispered, feeling shame pricking my cheeks. "What about the other girl who tried to kill herself because of you?"

"What?" he spat out incredulously. He let go of my wrists and stepped away from me, as if he couldn't believe what I was saying. "Where did you hear that?"

Shame crept across my breast and under my arms. "At the quilting bee!" I murmured.

"Goddamn them!" he roared. "Goddamn bloody gossiping bitches! What did they say? Tell me!"

His anger frightened me. I wondered if I had crossed into a dangerous place, one where I might be held prisoner. But it was too late.

"They said that you were involved with a young girl and that she tried to kill herself over you—over a love affair with you—and that her parents had to send her away—"

"Oh, for God's sake!" His voice held disgust. "And you believed it? You'll just listen to anything that anybody tells you, won't you? Why don't you use your head?"

"How could I—?" I sputtered. "What do I know? I don't know anything about you—your past, your present. Besides, you never mentioned it to me. Is it some big secret, something you've been hiding from me?"

"Christ, Evangeline!" he said, running a hand through his mass of hair in utter consternation. He took my arm, leading me to the couch. "Come over here and sit down." When we were seated, he took a deep breath. "Five years ago, after I had moved here and I began my classes, a family signed up their daughter. She was a neurotic, adolescent girl—barely fifteen years old. They thought she had talent—which she didn't—but at that time I was just starting the classes here, and I took anybody that signed up. The girl developed an insane crush on me. It was completely in her imagination. I never said or did anything to lead her on. She used to leave me ridiculous love notes after class. Then she started coming here unbidden, literally throwing herself at me. Despite my efforts to get her to see how irrationally she was behaving—that she was a child, and that I was merely a teacher hired by her parents—she refused to listen to reason. One day she showed up at the studio while I was deeply immersed in painting. I told her that I was busy and did not have time to speak with her. She became completely undone, crying and pounding on the door. Finally I let her in, and told her flatly that if she didn't behave, I could no longer have her as a student, and I would have to tell her parents why. She became quite hysterical at the thought of my speaking to her parents and the threat of my refusing to continue as her teacher. That's when she ran over to the washstand next to the studio couch, grabbed my razor, and tried to cut her wrists. I barely got to her in time. There was blood all over everything; she was screaming. Thank God I managed to stop the bleeding. Her parents were sent for. They came to get her and wound up putting her in a sanitarium for some weeks, then sending her off to Europe with a cousin. I never saw her again. Certainly no charges could be filed against me, because the young lady in question was examined by her doctors and pronounced intact."

I was silent.

He studied me. "That's it. That's exactly what happened. And, frankly, Angel, I would appreciate it if you would speak to me first instead of jumping to all these conclusions. You seem bent upon thinking ill of me."

"I'm not. But how can I speak to you when you're not there? When days go by before we're together!"

"Well, if you can't trust me by now..." He shook his head.

"I want to trust you, but I hear these things, and you're not there to reassure me, and I don't know what to think."

"Well, what kind of reassurance do you want?" he said with irritation. "I just told you the truth about that girl. And I told you the truth about the people I was with the other night. And I had to explain the presence of a model that was here last week. Jesus Christ, I'm beginning to feel that I'm on the witness stand with you all the time!"

"Don't be angry with me."

"I'm not angry," he said, but I didn't believe him. "Look." His voice sounded weary. "I don't want to make you unhappy." He reached for his shirt, pulling it on. "That's the last thing I want to do." He buttoned the shirt and lit another cigarette. Without looking at me, he said, "I'll be leaving in a few weeks." He paused, and I heard the heavy thud of my heart inside my ears. "Maybe we should just end it now."

I felt the color drain from my face, and my hands went numb.

In a tiny voice, I said, "Is that what you want?"

His face sagged, and he looked at me for a long time. "My God," he said quietly. "What do you think?"

"I don't know what to think!" I cried out.

"Good Christ, woman!" he shouted. "Why do you torment me like this!"

"I? Torment you!"

"Yes, God dammit! You look at me with those enormous sad eyes— doubting me, accusing me!"

"Because I'm tormented! I'm tormented! By thoughts of you with other women! By the hours I'm away from you! By—"

"And what about me?" he thundered. "You don't think I lie here at night, thinking of you sharing a bed with him! A life with him!" He grabbed me roughly in his arms. "The idea of him touching you! His hands in the places that I think of as only mine! Sometimes I think my head will explode with it!" He ran his hands over my body. "I wish I could feed you, and dress you, and bathe you, and watch you paint. I want to eat you and drink you and breathe you." His breath came in small gasps as he roughly pulled at my skirt and my undergarments, jamming his fingers into me. "I want to be here!" he whispered fiercely. "Here!" He fumbled with his buttons, and then he was lifting me, his hands grasping my buttocks as he splayed my legs around him. He groaned as he thrust himself deeply into me. I cried out as he began to pound away at me, biting my neck, hurting me.

"It can't be!" He whispered harshly in my ear. And again, with every thrust, "It can't be!"

"Why?" I cried, feeling him in my womb, in my stomach, in my throat. "Why?" I screamed, as we exploded together in a torrent of grief and passion. My fists pounded his back, and my face pressed into his neck and shoulders. Then we sagged against each other as he fell out of me, and we stood there, holding on because to let go would be to give up.

Finally we moved to the sofa and sank into it, still embracing. We lay there silently. Finally he spoke.

"My darling. You are the minister's wife. You have a child. If this affair were to be discovered, your life would be ruined."

"I don't care!" I said thickly, wearily.

"Of course you care."

"No! All I care about is being with you!"

He looked at me incredulously. "Are you saying that you would be willing to leave your husband and child and come with me to Paris?"

An arrow of pain slit my heart at the thought of leaving Willie. A twin arrow crossed it at the thought of giving up Daniel.

"I can't—" I started to say. Then, "Why must I have to choose between my lover and my child?"

"Because that's the way life is. But, Angel, I don't want you to even think those thoughts. Because I would never allow you to do that. I would never, never allow you to abandon your child. And certainly not for my sake. I know what it's like to be abandoned." There was bitterness in his voice. "It does not make for a happy life. You can never, never leave your son who needs and loves you. Not for me. Not for anyone. He deserves you so much more than I do."

I thought about that for a few moments. Then I said softly, "What if I brought him with me?" I turned my head to gauge Daniel's reaction.

His face tightened. "Angel, that's a crime."

"I know," I said, my thoughts tumbling over one another in a race to find a solution.

He looked incredulous. "Do you actually mean to tell me that you would risk it? And aside from the risk of getting caught, what about William? He's a decent man who has not done anything but love you and take care of you, who has been a good husband to you and a good father to your child. You would take his child away, out of the country, never to be seen again? You would do that to William and Willie? I know you. You can't mean it." He searched my face. "Can you?"

"I don't know," I whispered, fearing that he thought me heartless. I snuggled closer to him. "I just know that I want what I have with you, and I want my child."

"My darling," he said gently, "you can't have both."

"Why?" I said. "Why can't I have both?"

"Even if you were to take the child away—kidnap him—for which you could be arrested, Angel, I couldn't be a part of it. I couldn't live with myself if you separated a father from his son, and furthermore, I couldn't live with you if your child were with us. I've told you how I feel about children. I could never be a parent. Not to my own child, and certainly not to another man's child. I wouldn't know how to do it. I'm too selfish. I don't have the patience. Children need too much attention. They interfere with work and with thinking. They're needy all the time. I can't give that much of myself. I would be a terrible father. I never had one to show me how. And I'll be damned if I'll deprive your child of his. You're a wonderful mother. And I know that your husband is a wonderful father. And your son deserves nothing less than the best of both of you."

He tightened his arms around me, resting his chin on my head, and his voice caught as he said, "This will have to end. When I leave for Paris."

"Why do you even have to go to Paris?" I asked, blinking back tears.

"I go to Paris every year. I told you. I have obligations. I teach a course at the Académie Julian. I have a show in January. I have a life there."

"What about your life here?"

He was silent.

"What about me?" I twisted out of his arms and looked at him accusingly.

He returned my stare, but the blue eyes revealed nothing.

Finally he shrugged his shoulders and said, "I simply do not know."

"So you've used me," I said coldly.

"What?"

"You've used me. You've had your way with me, and now you're going to throw me away."

"Oh, Angel. Don't."

"How many other women have you had affairs with? Your summertime fling? Am I just one in a long line of students that you've seduced and abandoned? Just one more pathetic, corrupted, lovesick woman who's become a burden to you, and now you have to figure out a way to get rid of her? Very convenient how you have to leave for Paris at the end of the summer. Is there someone waiting for you there? Someone whom you'll abandon in the spring when you come back here to start the whole exercise all over? Is that what you do, Daniel?" With a stricken look, he reached for my arm, but I wrenched it away, feeling a growing rage. "Arrange your relations with women so that you can seduce them and discard them, and never have to answer for your actions? Am I to be just like the others, used up, and thrown away and left here to slit my wrists or throw myself off the quarry cliff?" My eyes burned with tears of rage, and frustration, and anguish.

"Angel—please—"

"Maybe that's what I should do! Kill myself now! Where's your razor?" I leapt up, but he held me back.

"Stop it!" he said.

"No! I will! It will be better for everyone! I'm no good to you anymore! I'm no good to my husband! No use to my child. You've ruined me for everyone. I'd be better off dead!"

"Angel, for God's sake—" He tried to restrain me with his arms.

"No! I want to die! I want to!" I was sobbing. "I'll die anyway when you go! It might as well be now. I can't live without you! I can't live without this place! I can't live without my painting! Look what you've done to me!" I cried. "I'm nothing without you! You've taken everything from me! You used me! You seduced me, and now you don't want me anymore!"

He shook me by the shoulders. "Stop it!" he boomed. "Stop it! Who seduced whom?" He released me and began to pace. "How many times did you come here, Evangeline? How many times did you show up at my door? I did everything in my power to resist you, but you kept on coming back."

"You didn't do everything in your power to resist me!" I challenged. "You came to church that Sunday!"

"I came to the church," he bellowed, "to fight for you as an artist. Evangeline, don't place the blame for this on me, because I won't carry it alone. We share responsibility. I'm an adult! You're an adult! You knew what you were getting into! So don't come here," he warned, "claiming that you were seduced and corrupted! You wanted it as much as I did! You were begging for it!"

I drew my arm back and slapped him.

The sight of my handprint on his cheek stunned me.

He barely flinched but grabbed my wrist and held it until I thought the bone would snap. He spoke right into my face.

"The first time I touched you, I almost scorched my fingers."

I tried to pull away from him, but he held on.

"So don't you say that I seduced and corrupted you as if you were a poor little virgin who had no idea what you were getting into. You knew exactly what you were getting into!"

He dropped my wrist and pointed a finger at me. "And don't you tell me that I wrecked your life. I opened up your life! I made you see the kind of artist you could be! And the kind of woman you could be! I gave you the confidence and the freedom to do the kind of work that you're doing now—and that you'll continue to do, God help you, for the rest of your life, with or without me! So let's just get it straight right now who used *whom*," he said through clenched teeth. "I made you what you are."

"Precisely! And what I am is your whore!" I shouted.

"All right! If that's the way you want to see it. You're my whore! The best piece of arse I've ever had! There! I've said it! The minister's wife is a whore! My whore! Are you happy now?"

I threw myself at him, clawing his face, beating on his chest with my fists. "You never loved me!" I shrieked.

He seized me by the elbows and held me in a vise-like grip. His face darkened, and there was a world of pain in his eyes. And out of that void came these words: "I never said I loved you."

A primal cry rose in my chest, and I crumpled where he held me, exhaustion and defeat weighing me down like sacksful of wet sand. I thought I might sink to the floor, never to rise, but some inner resolve drew me up, strengthened me, and I wrenched my arms out of his grasp. Running, running, out the door, down the steps, down the path, stumbling, falling, tripping, dragging myself up, blindly heading for my bicycle. Then I heard him coming after me, calling my name.

"Angel! Angel! Wait!" He reached me and tried to pull me away from the bicycle. Both of us were heaving with exertion, with the shock of the horrible words that could not be unspoken.

I struggled to get past him, flailing with my arms.

"Listen to me!" he said, his breath hitching, "I didn't mean it. Don't go like this. Talk to me."

I pushed my feet on the pedals and clutched the handlebars, half blinded by thick tears. The bicycle wobbled but soon gained speed, the tires spitting gravel and dust.

"Angel!" he shouted behind me. I pedaled furiously away. In the distance, his cry was a roar: "Don't leave me!"

I never looked back.

NINETEEN
CHAPTER

1996

It is much later, when Victor and I are on our second bottle of Châteauneuf-du-Pape, that we finally share our thoughts about all the bizarre events that led us to this moment in time. From that first morning, when he almost ran me down with his truck, through the eerie night of the levitating carpet, the "automatic" writing in my journal, the disappearing text from my computer, the strange feelings evoked at Aquatong Farm, my weird nightmares of the hovering phantom, and today's stunning realization that I live in Angel's very house! Chad's description of his ghostly photographs has fired the pot to a rolling boil.

Edgy, excited, and giddy with possibilities for the documentary, we re-hash, dissect, and marvel over how each happening has led to the next and the next, ultimately drawing us here to Madame Sancerre, Giverny, and the living heart of Angel and Daniel's story.

"This is nuts," I keep saying.

"Yeah, but it's good nuts!" says Victor. We laugh, clink glasses, and drink more wine.

The one topic that is tacitly avoided is the topic of *us*. Its nearness hovers in the air, mingling with the sensual aromas of garlic and oven-warm bread, Roquefort cheese and cigarette smoke, melting chocolate and ripe pears. It is its own unique story, separate and apart, I think, to unfold and be revealed in its own time.

After Chad's call interrupted our frantic grappling on the floor of the gallery, we regained enough composure to focus on shooting several of the masterpieces. The technical requirements demanded concentration and a cool head: setting up the tripod, adjusting the lights, peering into the lens, zooming in and out, tilting up and down, panning left and right. I found calm in the attention to detail. Victor, too, appeared to be relaxing into the task.

True to her word, Madame reappeared precisely one and a half hours after taking her leave. We resumed the interview, then shot some B-roll of the exterior of the house, with Madame and I strolling the gardens as we talked.

By six thirty we were on our way back to the hotel.

Now we're seated at a table nestled in the bistro's tiny garden, more than a little buzzed, as the emotional intensity of the past twenty-four hours begins dissipate.

"Do you believe in the supernatural?" I ask, watching the silhouette of a moth flutter just above the flickering blue flame of a votive candle set squarely in the center of the white linen tablecloth.

"That's like asking a man who's in Scotland if he believes in Scotland," Victor replies, arching a brow.

"Really? That's what you think, then? I mean, it's too weird, isn't it?"

He swirls his wine. It's black as pitch now in the descending darkness. Like black hemlock, I think with a slight frisson.

"There's been an element of the bizarre ever since I backed into you in the village square," he admits.

"Maybe it's just an extreme form of synchronicity," I offer. "On the other hand, maybe I should throw salt over my shoulder."

He mimes spitting between his fingers. "Ptoo! Ptoo!" he says. We laugh, clink glasses, and swill more black hemlock.

In the lobby of the small hotel, we say good night. But later, as I lie on my back, trying to deep-breathe away a red wine headache, cotton mouth, and free-floating anxiety, there's a soft knock. Instantly aroused, I stop breathing altogether for a moment, then pad to the door in anticipation, reminded of English country houses, long corridors, midnight trysts.

It's him.

This time there is no hesitation and no holding back. He slides my nightgown up over my head and eases me back onto the tangled sheets. We can't get close enough, naked enough soon enough. I open myself to him in a release of lips and tongues and fingertips. He rolls on top of me and is all over me at once. Mutual ravishment is our delight and our goal. I can't remember experiencing sex like this anywhere but in my fantasies.

Victor and I make love wildly and wordlessly until the sky turns from dark velvet to purple gray, when the pigeons begin to coo in the eaves. Then we fall sleep in each other's arms with him still inside me, and stay that way. Before drifting off, I realize that my anxiety has dissolved, my soul is at peace, my perfect bliss is at hand.

Thank you, Angel.

I experience the next forty-eight hours as a dazzling blend of sensuality and creativity fulfilled. Never before have my longings so completely dissolved in the realization that everything I need to express—as an artist and as a woman—is coming to fruition in Giverny. The atmosphere between Victor and me is charged. I can feel his eyes on me, sense his hunger. His appetite feeds mine. I'm impatient to get back to the hotel that second night; can't wait to tumble into his arms.

In the interim, there is so much more that thrills me. Madame Sancerre's memory grows sharper the more she talks. Her recollections about her grandparents, Angel and Duvall, become increasingly specific, richly detailed. We capture many of these anecdotes on tape; some are confided to me in conversations off-camera—usually when Victor is somewhere else shooting stills in the gallery or exteriors in the village. But there are some questions that she simply cannot or will not answer, especially when it comes to how Evangeline Laury, the minister's wife, metamorphosed into Angel.

I sense that she knows much more than she's willing to reveal—even now, when we seem to have forged a special bond. Though she isn't really French by birth, I attribute her reticence to Francophile reserve. Perhaps there are some family skeletons that she feels are best left in the closet. But I crave every morsel of relevant information about my subjects and am constantly on alert as to how I might draw them out of her, especially in light of the marvelous personal connection we've established.

In the past few days, her attitude toward me has softened into something maternal, protective. She often inquires about Chad, whom she refers to as "your boy." I also watch her assessing Victor. Once she said to me as Victor drove off, "It's new, isn't it, between the two of you?" Barely able to suppress a smile, I nodded.

"Be careful," she said.

My heart lurched. "Do you know something I don't know?" I asked lightly.

"He's mercurial," she replied. "An unsettling quality in a lover." Before I could ask what she meant, she held up her hand to silence me. "I believe you must know a man through four seasons before deciding if he is the one for you. There's no hurry, my dear. This relationship will manifest as it was intended. You cannot control that."

Now as we sit together under the trees, she says brightly, "I have made a decision."

Involuntarily I hold my breath, sensing that something momentous is about to happen.

"Angel's personal papers are in a safe deposit box in Paris. Her instructions were that they not be accessed until forty years after her death. Though that anniversary has passed, I have studiously avoided confronting the whole business. But now that you and I have met, I have a strong desire to share whatever there is with you. I told you I would do everything I could to help you with the documentary. If I am to be true to my word, I must go to Paris and retrieve these documents. I'll go on Monday. You'll accompany me."

My mind races. Victor and I are scheduled to fly home tomorrow. Will he be angry? Feel somehow left out, or worse, betrayed? What about Chad? He was getting antsy alone in the house. I could tell from our phone conversations that he was drinking, and I feared he'd go on a binge, take off in my car, and do God knows what. But this! This!

I speak carefully over the hammering of my heart. "Madame, dear Madame, I'm overwhelmed. And honored. Of course I'll accompany you."

"Good. I'll phone my attorney now to make sure that all the paperwork is ready for us when we arrive."

"I feel as though you're leading me to buried treasure. I can't believe you're entrusting me with such a gift!"

"Well, not entirely entrusting you. After all, the outcome of the documentary is as important to me as it is to you. If I give you access to the papers, I expect to have final approval over how you use them. That's why I'll be accompanying you back to the United States. To Bucks County. It's time that someone in the family revisited the place where the story began. Besides, I want to meet that son of yours."

∽ ∽ ∽

Madame suggests that once Victor leaves, I move out of the hotel and into her guest room for the duration of my stay. She determines that we'll fly back to the states on Tuesday and charges Suzette with the travel arrangements.

Now I have to break the news to Victor.

"You and Madame seem to have hit it off." The waiter has just set down a basket of bread on the table and poured the wine. Victor swirls his. Candlelight reflects off the crystal, making pretty ruby patterns on the inside of the glass.

"I do feel an amazing connection to her." I rest my hand on my heart. "Here."

He takes a big swallow of wine. "I don't think she likes me very much."

He senses it, then. It's disingenuous of me, but I casually ask, "Why do you say that?"

"Oh, come on. It's obvious. The Gallic snort of disapproval. Especially where you and I are concerned."

"What do you mean, 'Gallic'? She's not even French, not really, and what makes you think she even knows about us?"

"Are you kidding? We've been giving off so much heat for the past few days, it's a wonder we didn't start a fire in the gallery. She sees how I look at you, hound that I am. I'm surprised she hasn't poured a bucket of water on us."

He leans into me, his lips grazing my ear. "What do you say we skip dinner? Or have them wrap it up?" Our eyes lock. My stomach does a backflip.

"Oh, you're distracting me," I sigh, "and I have to talk to you."

"Talk to me later." His arm slips around me, his fingertips skimming my breast. With his other hand, he signals the waiter.

Back at the hotel, he makes love to me with an intensity that leaves us both trembling and spent. After, he clings to me, whispering over and over again, "You're my angel, you're my angel."

I rouse myself from the haze of afterglow to murmur, "That's funny."

"What's funny?"

"You. Calling me 'Angel.' Hello!"

He pushes himself up on his elbow. "Could we make this only about us for a minute?"

I snuggle into him. "I'm sorry. It's just, at times it's hard to separate the now from the then. Everything seems to get all mixed up. Besides, you may not think I'm such an angel, when I tell you what I have to tell you."

"Uh-oh." Now he completely disengages himself. I feel cold where his skin and mine no longer touch.

"It's not bad," I say, reaching out to stroke his arm. "It's good. In fact, it's fantastic!"

I've actually rehearsed how I would tell him about Angel's personal papers and Madame Sancerre's decision to share them. As I tiptoe over the words, I see relief and a growing excitement in his eyes. With that comes my own relief.

"Now here's the tricky part," I continue. "She's asked me to go with her to retrieve the papers in Paris on Monday."

"She wants you to stay?"

"Just until Tuesday to get the papers."

"So you're not flying back with me tomorrow?"

"No." I wait for his reaction.

"I knew she didn't like me." Now he untangles from the bedcovers and from me, walking to the table by the window and pouring a glass of wine. After taking a sip, he begins to pull foil off the plates of food we've carried back from the restaurant. He sits down and focuses on cold steak and frites.

"Victor, what does that have to do with anything? This is an unbelievable opportunity. What difference does it make who goes with her as long as we have access to the material? Besides, you yourself acknowledge that she and I have really hit it off."

"Just so she understands that you and I are full partners. She understands that, doesn't she? I don't want her pulling any power plays."

"She's not. She wants us to have these documents, but she's worried about their security. I mean, she's not going to just pull them out of a vault, stick them in a box, and Fed Ex them to us."

"Look," he says reasonably, still chewing, "I think it's great. I admit I'm pissed off that you get the first look, but she's calling the shots, and we have to go along with her. Do what you have to do, and then get on a plane." He pours more wine and hands it to me. "I don't relish the idea of being apart from you for five days."

I make room for him on the bed, and he stretches out, putting his arm around me once again.

"This thing is taking on a life of its own," he says. "Who'd have believed it?" He clinks his glass with mine. "To *The Angel Collection*. To us."

"Victor, there's more."

He pauses mid sip.

"She's coming back with me."

"Back where?"

"Back to the States. Madame Sancerre is coming home with me to Bucks County."

"Oh, no, no, no. No way."

Here I make my voice small. "She wants to oversee the doc. Be there as we put it together."

"Ahhh, shit." Now he's off the bed again and pacing. "I will not have that old bitch breathing down my neck! This is our project! We have final say!"

"Wait a minute. It was understood when she agreed to meet with us that if she decided to give us access to the paintings and the house and all of it, that she would have final approval. She made that clear from the beginning."

"She didn't say she was planning to sit on my lap in the edit booth."

"Victor! I know how you feel, but think what we're getting in return! This is huge! This is more than a documentary for the Historic Society of Milltown. We could end up selling it to PBS...or A & E...or HBO, even."

"If she starts having lawyers draw up papers, don't you dare sign anything without talking to me first. I mean it, Morgan!"

"Okay, okay."

"This is all spiraling out of control. I don't like leaving you here with her. God, and the thought of having her lord it over us at home is a fucking nightmare."

"I kind of think it could work in our favor."

He snorts.

"No, look—" The idea comes in a burst. "We can make it part of the story. She's the first one in the family to come back to Bucks County since Angel left. We can shoot her at Aquatong Farm, where Daniel's studio was, around the village, around my house, where Angel lived. It adds a fabulous human interest element. Imagine a shot of her looking over the sketches I found under the floorboards! And who knows what treasure we'll have in those papers that I'll be getting on Monday? Victor, admit it. We have hit the lottery!"

And it is true.

Angel's safe deposit box, unopened for more than forty years, yields more than I could have imagined or dared hope for. There are journals—stacks of them. Forty-three in all. Plus letters and even photographs. I'm breathless to read it all, giddy at the prospect.

By the time we return to Le Meurice Hotel in Paris with our treasures, Madame Sancerre is exhausted. She says she'll order room service and retire early so that she'll be rested for tomorrow's long flight.

I call my friend Kate. We've had no contact since my stay with her more than two months ago. By chance, she's free, and within the hour we're tucked into a café around the corner from her apartment on Rue Vavin, sipping pastis.

"Where to start?" I say, accepting the cigarette she offers.

"Start by telling me why you're here and why you didn't call to tell me you were coming!"

"Okay." I inhale deeply, gathering my thoughts. "Truthfully, I think this all began when you took me to that exhibit at the Musée d'Orsay and I fainted."

"I thought that was your fear of heights and dehydration."

"That's what I said. That's what I wanted to think at the time."

"But…?"

"I don't know. That exhibit—*The Angel Collection*—it freaked me out. And now here I am, in the middle of the weirdest, most unbelievable series of circumstances in my life! My work life and my personal life. And it all revolves around *The Angel Collection*. I am not kidding! It's insane."

The whole crazy story comes pouring out. About arriving home in Bucks County, settling into the house, meeting Victor, finding the drawings under the floorboards, the floor itself rising, the spooky cemetery next door, the little boy who died, the rumors about the minister's wife, the grant for the documentary, my rapprochement with Chad, the automatic writing, my intense and strange attraction for Victor, how crazy I am about him, how Chad resents him and vice-versa, how Chad had tracked down Madame Sancerre.

"And—this part, you are not going to believe," I say.

"I'm finding it hard to believe everything you've told me up to this point," she says, laughing. "It's like a spooky novel—but I can't put it down!"

I take a deep breath. "The minister's wife turns out to be Angel. *The* Angel. I'm living in her house. Those were her drawings I found under the floorboards. I've just spent five days in Giverny with her *stepgranddaughter*, who is Madame Sancerre—"

Kate's mouth drops open and stays that way.

"-and, I now have in my possession forty-three of Angel's journals, which have been in a safe deposit box for forty some years! Plus photos and letters and stuff!"

Kate lets out a whoop, and we both start laughing like conspirators and can't stop.

"Oh, *mon dieu*," she finally says, catching her breath, "what a documentary you're going to have!"

"I know! And Madame is actually flying back with me tomorrow to Bucks County to see my house—where Angel lived—to see the farm where Daniel Duvall painted. Of course Victor is not very happy about that, but..."

Kate and I just keep grinning at each other. "Well I guess Victor will have to deal, huh?"

"I hope," I say. "I'm so in love with that man. I just pray everything is the same when I get home."

"Why wouldn't it be?"

"I don't know. Victor is...He's kind of slippery. I don't know if it's insecurity or what. But he seems to go in and out of wanting to have a real relationship with me."

"Red flag," says Kate. "You've been there and done that."

I shake my head. "No. This is different. Everything changed when we were in Giverny. Then, he was...It was as if he fell absolutely madly in love with me. It was blissful. But then when Madame asked me to stay behind and go with her to get these journals, Victor resented it. And he's furious that she's coming back with me. Doesn't want her looking over his shoulder while we put this thing together."

"Well, that's understandable. It's your piece, not hers. We both know how messy it is editing by committee."

"Oh, I know. Plus Chad has had some weird stuff happen to him since we left. He's freaked out, and I'm worried about him. I don't want anything to screw up the little bit of progress he and I have made in our relationship. I have to be so careful not to get caught up in some kind of triangle with him and Victor."

"Well, what's more important to you? A relationship with a new man or a relationship with your son? I know how much you've suffered about Chad. You told me when you were here before that you'd give anything to have him back in your life. So you're right to be careful."

"But I've always longed to have a man in my life too. Is that wrong? Why can't I have both?"

"Hey, I'm not judging. But isn't that desire to have a man in your life what got you into trouble with your son in the first place?"

I sigh. "It's so damn complicated."

"So, okay," she says, "just be alert to the fact that you're at a fragile point in your relationship with Chad. Be careful with that. And as for your Victor, it sounds like there's potential there, but don't let your feelings for him interfere with producing the best documentary you can. Really, Morgan, with everything you have going for you on this project, it really could be your ticket to—who knows what? Don't screw it up, *ma chère*. Especially for a *man.*"

The next morning I stuff ten of the journals in my own carry-on to read on the flight to Philadelphia. The rest of the treasure goes on the plane with us in another carry-on. We are not letting any of it out of our sight.

Madame Sancerre is in first class. I settle her there, then make my way back to coach, where I am relieved to have the entire row to myself. Well before the plane lifts off the ground, I am immersed in the first of the journals, marveling at the exquisite delicate handwriting that lines the pages. As the plane rises to cruising altitude, Angel's story begins to rise off the yellowed pages and settle into in my consciousness. With no resistance at all, I feel myself disappear into her life.

The sound of the captain's voice coming over the speaker is a rude intrusion. I cover my ears, trying to shut it out, annoyed at the prospect of enduring a prolonged announcement in both French and English. Then I hear, "Cork, engine trouble," and the passengers around me begin to shift in their seats, murmuring to one another.

I unfasten my seatbelt and scoot across the two empty seats in my row.

"What's happening?" I ask the woman across from me.

"There's engine trouble. We're putting down in Cork, Ireland."

"Cork? What? Is it serious?" My stomach dips as I picture crashing into the sea, myself and the journals in a tangle of crushed metal. I tap a passing flight attendant on the arm.

"Excuse me. What exactly is wrong?"

"Don't worry, madame," he says, rather unconvincingly. "It is merely a precaution. There is a problem with the instrument panel, and we will land in Cork to have the problem fixed." He continues on his way before I can ask another question. I'm about to get up to check on Madame Sancerre in first class, but the seatbelt sign flashes on. I consider looking out the window to see if the engine is on fire, but the thought scares me so much that I pull down the shade, settle back in the seat, close my eyes, and pray to Ganesh, Buddha, Jesus, and Saint Christopher.

Forty tense minutes later, the plane sets down on the runway, accompanied by applause and cheers.

After exiting the plane and retrieving our luggage, Madame Sancerre and I make our way to the airline counter, where a few hundred other displaced passengers are lined up like cattle, trying to book new flights back to the US. There aren't any. We're told to check back with the airlines the next day. In the meantime, they hand us vouchers for hotels and meals. I'm so grateful to be alive and so grateful that the journals are safe, that the prospect of holing up in a hotel and reading all day seems like a gift. As we make our way toward the airport exit, Madame suddenly changes course, ending up at the transportation counter.

"We're hiring a car," she announces.

Twenty minutes later, our luggage safely stored in the trunk, we are comfortably ensconced in a chauffeur-driven car, heading west out of the airport toward County Kerry.

"Have you ever been to Ireland?" she asks.

"No, never," I say. As I gaze out the window, blurred edges of the dream I'd had just days ago flutter in my consciousness. I had been in Ireland, in a whitewashed house in the country, in Victorian times, weeping heavy, hot tears. The woman who held me against her pillowy breast and stroked my hair was all that separated me from salvation and utter despair.

"I'm taking you to the countryside, to Lizzie's farmhouse, if we can find it. As I told you, Lizzie was my mother's namesake and godmother. Angel absolutely adored her. In fact Angel's wonderful paintings of rural Irish farm life were painted at that farm. Even after Lizzie died, the family kept in touch with Seamus and the children. I spent many happy summers there when I was a girl." Madame's eyes seem to gaze into her own past, and for a moment she is lost in reverie. "Seamus died in 1942. The war was on then, it was difficult to maintain contact, and we all lost track of one another. But I have such marvelous memories of those summers in Ireland."

I watch as the outskirts of the city of Cork give way to the countryside, the emerald green of the fields that I've read about. The sense of comfort that settles over me is soon overtaken by a sensory alert. I feel my eyes and ears prick up, like a hunting dog frozen en pointe. I breathe in the sweet, pungent fragrance of freshly mown grass and newly plowed fields. I find myself looking out the window for landmarks, though I have no idea what these landmarks might be, since I've never been here before. I think, *Déjà vu,* but the phrase seems too trite for what I'm feeling.

Suddenly I hear myself saying, "Turn left up here."

"What?" Madame has been resting her eyes. She instantly comes alert, peering through the window, examining the passing landscape. "How do you know where we turn?"

"I don't know. I just…" *How do I know?*

"Oh, yes!" says Madame. Up here is Fiddlegreen Lane! I recognize it! Turn left, driver."

Five minutes later, past a copse of swaying maple trees and across a wee stone bridge, we see a pasture, where a herd of black and white spotted cows graze. Then there's a lane cutting between a large dairy barn and several smaller structures. A red tractor slowly and patiently plows its way across a field to our left. In front of us, a menagerie of chickens and geese struts and pecks at the dirt. Gravel crunches, and a snoozing border collie springs to its feet, barking as our car eases its way down the lane.

"There it is!" exclaims Madame.

I shade my eyes against the blinding sun, whose shards of light bounce off the whitewashed walls of the two-story farmhouse, limning it with a shimmering halo that seems to give off heat. Gradually my eyes adjust to the brightness, and windows, roof, doors, and chimneys reveal themselves. With that, the backs of my knees begin to tingle, and my hands feel numb.

"Lizzie!" I whisper, almost as if I were calling her.

Madame turns to me with a beatific smile. "Yes," she says. "We have found her."

I get out of the car with a sense of wonder, of wanting to take everything in at once. My senses feel keenly alive. It isn't just the mingling aromas of the farm: prickly hay smells and sweet-sour grass smells; pungent fertilizer and acrid dirt; feathers and fur; and perhaps a trace of fresh milk. These are familiar smells, and I breathe them in, savoring the combined taste of them on my tongue. The trees above me rustle in the seductive sway of a dance; the tractor hums in the field, a rooster crows, the border collie circles us, still barking; somewhere a child calls, "Mama." The air around me seems kinetic, vibrating. I look up at the clouds, and they're swirling, threatening clouds, moving very quickly through the sky, blocking a sun that had, moments ago, been blinding.

Madame approaches the front door and knocks.

"How can I help you?"

A thirty-something woman with a baby on her hip answers the knock and listens politely, then with increasing interest as Madame Sancerre explains her past connection to the farm. Within moments, we're sitting in the parlor, sipping tea, and shortly after that, our hostess, Janie Connelly, graciously offers to take us on a tour of the house and grounds.

As we wander from room to room, Madame keeps a running dialogue of her memories, marveling at how the outhouse and hand water pump have given way to indoor plumbing and microwaves. Upstairs she recalls the bedrooms of various family members and shows us a favorite hiding place under the attic stairs.

As Janie, with little Connor slung over her hip, starts to lead the way back down to the first floor, Madame Sancerre asks if she might use the bathroom.

Janie says, "Surely, and we'll wait for you downstairs."

As she begins to descend the steps, I say, "May we go up to the attic rooms?"

"How didja know about them?" she asks.

"I don't—I just…" I shrug.

"Oh, it's such a mess up there. I've been meaning to clean it out forever but don't seem to be getting around to it any time soon."

"Please," I say, not knowing why. "If it's not too much trouble."

"Oh, well, I suppose you're wanting to take the whole Cook's tour. All right, then."

She unlatches the door and switches on a light. "If you don't mind, I'll stay down here. It gives me the willies up there, truth be told."

The stairs are narrow and curved. I have to duck from the low ceiling and place my hands on the walls to keep my balance as I make my way up.

Janie wasn't kidding. The space is crammed with junk: boxes, clothes on overhead hangars, furniture, magazines, books, files. I don't know what's drawn me up here. I take a few steps into the room, batting cobwebs from my face, and squeeze around the boxes to a window in the eaves. The tattered remnant of an old lace curtain hangs limply from a tarnished brass rod resting diagonally across the grimy, flaked sill of the window, whose dulled panes are sooty with dust. I use the curtain to rub off a circle of dirt and peer out, down to the yard. A black-haired woman is hanging sheets on the line. As the sheets billow and flap, the woman appears and disappears among them. I have an urge to call out to her; instead, I tap on the window to get her attention, an exercise in futility, I realize as I straighten, rubbing my back.

Sidling past an old bureau piled high with newspapers, I notice a door, apparently leading into another part of the attic. I pull hard on the stubborn latch. It finally gives, and the door swings open with a groan. Dust motes silently explode, revealing more junk, more cobwebs. I trip over a rolled-up carpet and grab a nearby iron bedpost to keep from slamming to my knees. There's another window here, like the one in the adjacent room, and I gingerly make my way to it, stepping over boxes and stacks of books. The window is partially obscured by a rectangular object wrapped in a moth-eaten and faded ruby velvet drape, its folds coated with dirt and mildew. I lift a corner of the velvet, displacing a cloud of dust and a frantic scurrying mouse. Undeterred, I slowly draw back the heavy fabric, allowing it to droop to the floor. I hear myself murmur, "Oh my God."

There are two large canvases. I squat down to look more closely. They appear to be unfinished paintings. The first one seems to be a figure of a woman—a woman hanging sheets on a clothesline! Almost exactly like the scene I'd just witnessed peering out the window in the other room. My hands begin to tremble as I examine the second canvas. It's the half-painted portrait of a young woman who appears to be standing in front of a mirror, but much of it is defaced by thick swatches and smears of black. I study it more closely. A faintly sketched arm looks as if it might hold a hairbrush. Or is it an artist's brush?

Clambering to my feet, I almost lose my balance in the folds of the velvet drape. But I stumble over the boxes, the iron bedstead, and the rolled-up carpet. At the door, breathless, I lean against the jamb for support and shout at the top of my lungs: "Madame Sancerre!"

Janie Connelly has summoned her husband from the dairy barn, and the four of us are seated at the dining room table. The two unfinished paintings rest against the sides of the baby's playpen in the adjoining parlor. It's not a difficult negotiation. Michael and Janie realize that in their unfinished form, the paintings are of little market value to them and tremendous personal value to Madame, who writes a handsome check in compensation. Receipts are exchanged. Michael spends a good hour in his workshop crafting packing crates for the paintings. By mid-afternoon, we're back in the car, heading for Cork Airport, our precious cargo stored in the trunk. As we said our final good-byes, the Connelly family stood framed on the sun-dappled doorstep of the whitewashed farmhouse, waving. Michael held little Connor in his arms, and Janie lifted the baby's hand aloft in the sweetly universal gesture of bye-bye. As we reached the curve in the lane, I looked back. Michael kissed Janie on the forehead and passed Connor to her. Then he took off toward the dairy barn, adjusting his cap at a jaunty angle. Janie and Connor disappeared into the house.

Bless that family, I thought.

At the airport, I try repeatedly to call Chad. He'd not answered the phone since our brief conversation at Giverny, when he'd told me about the ghostly images on the photographs he'd taken at Aquatong Farm. I'd spoken briefly to Victor when we were diverted to Cork, but he hadn't been in contact with my wayward son either. Just as our flight is announced, my cell phone rings. It's Victor.

"You're not going to believe what happened," I crow without preamble.

"What?"

"No, I'm going to save it as a surprise!" I say. "It's completely awesome."

"Where are you?" he asks. I detect irritation in his voice.

"Still in Cork. The flight is boarding, so I can't talk long. Is something wrong?"

"You'd better get back here and tend to your errant son."

"Why? Is he okay?"

"If you consider driving your car around Doylestown with a suspended license okay."

"Oh, shit. How do you know?"

"I saw him in the parking lot of the video store. And I hate to be the bearer of even worse tidings, but it seemed to me he was stoned out of his gourd."

I am speechless, mortified.

Victor continues. "I followed him back to Milltown in my truck, just to make sure he didn't get arrested. He was supposed to come over to the farm this morning to start logging tapes, and he showed up two hours late. Still stoned, it looked to me."

I'm so disheartened by my conversation with Victor that I almost forget to ask him to reserve a suite for Madame at The 1746 House, a local bed-and-breakfast. He replies sarcastically that booking reservations is really an assistant's job, but since my son is proving to be unreliable in that capacity, he will make the call himself. Grudgingly.

I feel sick by the time I hang up with Victor. Sick to my stomach and back to square one with my son.

As the plane climbs out over the Atlantic Ocean, I make a feeble attempt to meditate away my discomfort at the prospect of a confrontation with Chad. Is he determined to self-destruct? How am I going to deal with him? Here I am, bringing Madame Sancerre, the quintessence of civilized behavior, into our home! Will I be trying to quell an embarrassing rebellion with one hand, while serving tea and brioche on the other? And I am angry with Victor, too. As if it were my fault that Chad went driving without his license. What was I supposed to do? Put him under house arrest? I know Victor thinks I'm a lousy mother. The idea mortifies me and angers me. Let him try to raise a child alone! Then he can judge me!

Chad, Victor, Madame Sancerre, the documentary. The stew of swirling emotions threatens to unnerve me completely. I dread what might await me back in Milltown when it all comes to a fiery boil.

With a sigh, I withdraw a journal from my carry-on. After pressing the recline button, adjusting the overhead light, and leaning back in the seat, I begin to read.

Birth of Elizabeth
February 25, 1896
Milltown, Pennsylvania
William patted his lips with his linen napkin, set it down on the table, and told me he would be going to Trenton next week for the convening of the Christian Conference. He asked if I would be all right alone with Clara, since her time was near.

I told him that with Dr. Mardigian down the road, we would be fine.

My relations with William are formal and distant. I only speak when spoken to, never meeting his gaze. He seems satisfied that I have resumed most of my domestic responsibilities, though I still never leave the house, relying on deliveries from the General Store and the creamery.

Clara spends most of her days resting. The swelling in her legs and ankles grows worse, and the doctor has warned that she must stay off her feet.

A light snow was falling as William set off for Trenton. It continued to fall throughout the day, burying the village under a blanket of white silence. I put the carcass from the previous night's chicken dinner in a pot of water with some parsley and an onion, and let it simmer, then added some carrots and potatoes and corn. By evening the house was filled with the comforting aroma of chicken vegetable soup, which Clara and I sipped in companionable silence, while the crackle of tiny snowflakes whipped across the windowpanes.

By the next afternoon, the snow was still falling, and the wind picked up, blowing enormous drifts across the front yard and onto the porch.

Clara shuffled out of her room as I was pouring hot water for tea. She sat down heavily.

I think I'm starting she said.

Are you having pains I said, feeling a little flutter of apprehension.

She told me they started a few hours ago. Not too bad, really.

I asked why she hadn't called me.

She said she didn't want to bother me, wanted to wait to see if they went away.

I asked how do you feel now, and she said her back hurt and the pains are coming closer together.

I told her to go back to bed, and I would summon Dr. Mardigian. How will you get up to his house she said. All this snow. It must be two feet deep. And it will be getting dark soon. There was alarm in her voice.

Don't worry, I'll get there I promised.

I settled Clara back into bed and went to the closet to find my heavy cloak and mittens. When I was bundled up, I opened the front door and tried to step out onto the porch. The drifts were up to my thighs, and the swirling snow felt like needles on my face. Very slowly, lifting my legs as high as I could, I made my way through the drifts, down what I thought to be the porch steps, and into the yard. The snow was blowing so hard that I could barely see the road. My feet were soaked and my toes frozen before I had gone ten yards. I knew it would take me at least a half hour to reach Dr. Mardigian's house in this weather, and I feared leaving Clara alone for the time it would take me to get there and back. I searched up and down the blanketed road, but it was deserted. The thick white sky seemed low enough to touch, and there was an eerie silence, and a strange acrid smell in the air. I paused, trying to shield my face from the harsh bite of the spinning snow. Snowflakes froze on my lashes, making it difficult to see in any direction.

Off in the distance, I thought I could hear sleigh bells and see the outline of a horse and sleigh slowly slogging its way up the hill. As it came closer, I recognized one of the Webster boys behind the reins. I called to him, and my own voice sounded buried in the weight of the swirling drifts.

He waved to me and approached, slowing to a halt. He leaned over the side, red-faced and out of breath.

Mrs. Laury what are you doing out in this weather, he said.

I told him I need the doctor and asked can you go to his house and tell him that Miss Shaw's baby is coming.

Ice clung to his eyebrows and lashes, and his cheeks were bluish red as he told me he's not there.

I asked him, what do you mean, he's not there.

Haven't you heard he said.

Heard what? We were both shouting over the wind.

Then he told me there's a fire. He said a real bad one in Lumberville at the mill. Lots of people burned. Dr. Mardigian's been there all afternoon. They've organized a volunteer fire brigade. Todd said he was sent to get the Reverend.

I shouted he's not here, he's in Trenton. I'm alone in the house with Miss Shaw.

He said I'm sorry, Mrs. Laury, I don't think I can help you. They're afraid the fire will spread to the houses nearby. I have to try to round up more volunteers.

My mind raced and I asked him where's your mother? Is she at home?

He shook his head. She and some of the other women from the village left a little while ago to take coffee and soup to the firefighters. I think it's going to be a long night.

I asked him will you tell your mother that I'm here alone and that the baby is coming? Will you do that?

He said I'll tell her, then he slapped the reins and the bells jingled. I have to go now, he said. I stood there in the freezing swirling snow and watched the sleigh disappear up the hill into the blizzard and into the deepening winter dusk.

Slowly I fought my way back up to the house, stumbling through the drifts, my mind as numb as my feet.

As I pushed the front door open, an animal cry slammed into the quiet of the front hall, resonating against the whispery murmur of the wind outside. I leaned back against the door, forcing it shut. I undid my cloak that was coated with snow and shook the flakes out of my damp hair, some strands of it frozen like dark icicles.

A low moan reverberated from the back of the house. Then I heard help me!

Dragging myself up the stairs on feet that were numb blocks of wood, I made my way into the safety of my bedroom and slammed the door, leaning against it. My whole body trembled with fear and cold as I threw off my wet skirt and ice-covered boots.

I could hear her in the room below me. The moans were wrenching, almost inhuman. I sat down on the bed unable to move. My hands shook as I toweled off my feet. She cried out again and again and her cries became the cries of my mother, and I was a little girl again cowering in my room covering my ears. I could once again see the blood and smell it, hear the muffled cries of my father as he alternately paced and sobbed in the library. I curled myself up into a ball and put the pillow over my head. My guilty heart thudded in the darkness.

But over its pounding I still could hear as she cried out my name. Evangeline help me. Oh, somebody help me. Up through the floorboards came her entreaties, now a piercing cry, now a long, drawn out moan. What if Sarah Webster didn't come? What if I were left here to do this thing by myself? It was unthinkable, not possible. I could not bear witness to the agony, the spilt blood. And what if it all went terribly wrong? What if the baby came out the wrong way? My mind raced. My legs had the instinct to escape...out of the house into the unblemished snow the innocent white snow unstained by human suffering. Let it bury me I prayed. Let heaven unleash the celestial purity of falling snow upon me into numb oblivion.

Beneath me as I lay in frozen cowardice I heard her crying for her mama, Mama, help me! Ohhh, please.

At long last, in the deepening shadows of a slate-blue dusk, something loosed deep inside me, very gently at first, and I stirred, rolling onto my back. My hand touched the space where my heart once was, that hollow cracked place. Beneath my palm I could almost feel a trickle of something warm and good filling the parched forgotten space. The desire to tend, to soothe, to nurture. Dare I write these words: the desire to mother. A sudden resolve swept over me followed by a deep calm. It was as if my heart's seeping wound had been seared shut and tenderly swathed with the healing balm of Gilead. As was spoken in Jeremiah 8:22, I might be the physician. I might heal the broken daughter and restore her to health.

I would.

Suddenly I was out of the bed. I pulled on a skirt and heavy jersey, pushed my feet into slippers, and raced down the stairs, through the cold dark house and back to Clara's room.

She lay on the bed, her back arched her legs splayed out. Her hair was matted on the pillow, her face soaked in the sweat of labor.

I ran to her side and said I'm here Clara it's all right.

Her eyes were like a wild animal and she clutched my arm, her nails digging into my skin. Where's the doctor she whispered. Where is he.

He'll be here I said don't worry. I reached for the bed sheet and pulled it off the bed. The sheet underneath was sopping wet. I tied the top sheet onto the bedpost and pulled the long end toward Clara. Take this I said. Whenever there's a pain pull on it. Pull on it hard. I went to the washstand and soaked a towel in the water. Then I bathed her face and neck. She moaned I can't take it I can't take it.

Yes you can I told her, it will be over soon. I'm going to boil some water. I lit the lamp by her bed and fluffed the pillows under her head. They were drenched.

I left her and ran into the kitchen, putting the kettle on to boil. I yanked open the utility closet and pulled out a sack of clean rags. Then I raced to the parlor where I kept my sewing basket and grabbed my scissors and a ball of twine, carrying them into Clara's room and setting them down on the dresser. Then I went back into the parlor and lit two lamps, bringing them back with me, and placing one on the dresser and one on the other side of the bed.

Clara twisted and writhed whimpering is the doctor here yet.

Not yet I told her, don't think about that. Just hold onto the sheet and try to rest between pains.

She was gasping, there is no rest, they keep coming.

She pulled on the sheet, arching her back, bending her legs at the knees. Her thighs trembled convulsively. Through the dark wet patch between her legs, I saw a purplish bulge, and a steady stream of blood leaked onto the sheet. My heart lurched. I knew it was the afterbirth, and I knew it was a bad sign. I grabbed a towel and pushed it under her hips.

Then she screamed it's coming, it's coming.

I leaned over her, trying to get her to focus on me. You're gong to have to push Clara I told her. When you feel a pain coming push hard.

She flung her head from side to side and let out a moan from deep in her throat.

Push I shouted. I moved down the bed to look between her legs again. The huge purplish mass was slowly oozing out of her body onto the towel. A gush of bright crimson blood followed it.

Behind that, I could see the crown of the baby's head.

Push Clara, I told her, I can see the baby's head. It's almost here.

She groaned as she drew up her head and held her breath. Her eyes squeezed shut, and her face twisted as she bore down, finally releasing her breath in a loud gasp.

The crown began to protrude, stretching the flesh around it as if it would explode into a thousand bits of skin and tissue. Blood coursed from Clara's body, streaming out and around the baby's head and the bedclothes.

I heard a tearing sound and a cry from Clara, and the head appeared. I reached for it and felt its wet, slippery, warm weight. My hands were covered in blood, and I had trouble grasping the tiny shoulders to guide the baby out. Then I realized that the cord was twisted around its fragile neck. I struggled to wedge my fingers between the cord and the neck, working the shoulders out at the same time. The rest of the baby suddenly slipped out, and I caught her in my arms placing her on Clara's stomach.

It's a girl Clara, you have a girl I told her.

A girl she whispered and she lifted her head to see the baby, then sank back down on the pillow.

The child was still and not breathing. I picked her up and reached into her mouth, trying to clear her throat with my fingers. Still she lay silent. Her skin was blue under the blood and cheesy, white substance. Quickly I turned her upside down, holding her by the heels.

Cry I said, cry little one.

Silence.

What is it said Clara weakly, raising herself on her elbows.

She's not dead is she.

Cry I commanded and slapped the tiny wrinkled bottom twice.

There was a dreadful pause, then a shuddering intake of breath and finally, a wail.

She was alive.

I turned her upright and hugged her to me, then lay her back on Clara's stomach. I went to the dresser and got my scissors, passing them back and forth over the candle several times. Then I cut through the thick slimy cord and tied the end of it with twine. I disposed of it with the afterbirth.

Then I got the kettle and poured some hot water into the washbowl. When it cooled, I gently began to sponge the baby, wiping her clean, and wrapping her in a towel. I laid her in Clara's arms.

Your daughter I said as my eyes blurred with tears. Your baby girl Clara. Clara looked at the baby, then looked at me with feverish eyes. Thank you, Evangeline thank you. Her face was very pale.

Clara I said, you've lost some blood. I'm going to put some pillows under you. We'll clean you up a little later. I helped her lift her hips, and I slid the pillows underneath, then stuffed clean rags between her legs.

After taking the kettle back into the kitchen to brew some chamomile tea, I returned to the room. Clara's eyes were closed. The baby was nestled in the crook of her arm. The rags between her legs were soaked with blood.

I said her name, Clara.

She opened her eyes. They looked huge in her face. Huge and luminous.

I offered her some tea, telling her, it'll help you get your strength back.

I helped her lift her head, and she took a few sips, then lay back down.

Would you like to nurse the baby I asked.

She nodded weakly.

I helped her arrange her nightgown and positioned the baby's head against her breast. The little mouth rooted around, then settled into a steady sucking.

Sweet said Clara, that's all, and closed her eyes again.

I changed the rags between her legs, and within minutes they too were drenched in blood.

I went to the front door and opened it. A drift of snow blew in. I tried to see across the yard to the road, but all was silent and dark except for the whisper of the wind. I closed the door and walked through the parlor. The clock on the mantle said, eight o'clock. I made myself a cup of tea and went back into Clara's room, and gently lifted the baby from her arms, and settled into a chair. Her little face was rosy and placid, and she opened her eyes and seemed to look right at me.

Well I guess you're not Willie, are you I whispered cuddling her to me. She yawned a wide lazy yawn, and I could see her tiny pink tongue. I traced the outline of her face, from her cap of fuzzy hair that came to a point at the top of her forehead, to her chubby cheeks and rounded chin. I cradled her to me.

We drifted off to sleep in the chair.

I awoke with a start.

There was a strange sound in the room. I turned to Clara. Her breathing was shallow and labored. I laid the baby on the bed and felt

Clara's forehead. It was cold and clammy. Her face was ghostly white. It was if all the color that had been in her body had been soaked up by the rags between her legs.

Clara I said Clara, can you hear me.

Slowly she opened her eyes. They were sunken.

I said her name again.

I feel strange she said, like I'm floating.

Can you take some more tea, I said.

No, no tea she whispered.

Please I said. You're very weak. You need to keep up your strength.

Her eyes seemed to focus and clear. I'm dying she said.

No, you're not I said, Dr. Mardigian will be here soon, and he'll take care of you. You'll be fine. You have to hold on.

No she said. I won't be. Where's my baby?

She's right here I said, lifting the sleeping infant and placing her next to Clara.

Isn't she beautiful I said.

Take care of her for me said Clara.

Don't talk like that I said. Don't talk like that. Your baby needs you and I need you. My tears dropped onto the baby's cheek.

I can feel myself slipping away murmured Clara.

You'll get well I said, you will if you try. Please.

No I want you to have her she said. You're such a wonderful mother.

I shook my head. No no I'm not. The tears rolled down my cheeks.

Oh, yes, yes you are. Don't blame yourself. She reached out to gently touch my face. I held her hand with my own and kissed it.

Clara, please, please try I begged.

Forgive yourself she whispered. You must forgive yourself.

I hung my head. My shoulders shook with sobs at the tragedy of it. All of it.

Forgive she breathed softly. Then her eyes closed, and she seemed to slip away. Her chest rose and fell in ragged shallow gasps, and I counted each breath until I, too, drifted off in the chair.

I awoke with a start when I felt her hand on my arm.

Evangeline she whispered.

Instantly alert, I leaned into her, searching for some sign of improvement. Her eyes seemed to be all there was of her face. Burning with fever and some kind of desperate yearning, they bored into me. Clara what can I get for you I said. Can you take some soup.

She said no.

I could smell the blood. It was as if the room were adrift in it. I was afraid to look at the rags between her legs.

And you need to forgive me she whispered.

For what? Hush now, save your strength.

No no time. Forgive. Promise. Her fingers clung to my sleeve.

Clara you're weak and confused I said, there's nothing to forgive.

Still her fingers fluttered on my arm and she whispered so good. So good to me.

And you to me I said. You took care of me.

No betrayed you she said.

How I said. How do you think you betrayed me.

He was like Jesus. To me she said.

Who I said.

Told me I was Mary Magdalene she said. To his Jesus.

I felt the skin shrink on my face.

Clara closed her eyes remembering. Washed his feet she said. Dried. With my hair, my wild hair. I felt a prickling sensation begin to creep up my arms and around my neck and face.

She opened her febrile eyes and stared at me for so long that I had to turn away from her.

Look at me she said. I turned back to her, and twin tears slid onto her chalk-white face. Promise. You forgive. Say it.

Of course I said, but my voice shook. Whatever it is. Of course I forgive you.

The baby. Is his.

I felt the floor go out from under me, and the room begin to spin. What do you mean I said.

William's daughter she whispered.

I looked at the little scrunched up face. The high brow, the widow's peak.

We sat in silence for many minutes. Then I asked her does he know that the baby is his.

She said he fears it. There was a long pause as if she needed to gather her strength for each few words. Wanted me away. From here. Afraid I would tell you. The truth. She closed her eyes and I held my own breath until I heard her breathe and saw the rapid rise and fall of her chest.

I got up from the chair and made my way out of the room. In the kitchen, I sank into a chair, and stared across the table to the window, where the snow clung in pale blue crescents on the clear glass panes.

I listened to the awful silence.

Finally I stood up. My back ached, and I rubbed it as I walked through the dining room and the parlor to the front door. I peered out. The snow had stopped. I opened the door a little way. Snow drifted in. I listened for sound, a movement. I searched up and down the road for a light. But the only light came from the glitter of a black sky sprinkled with a million tiny crystals. And a half-moon face that looked to me as if it were weeping.

When I returned to the little room behind the kitchen Clara was dead.

I named the baby Elizabeth, after Lizzie.

ờ ờ ờ

I bumble my way to first class on legs that threaten to give way.

"Madame?"

She is engrossed in her own journal reading.

"I'm sorry to disturb you, but—"

She pulls off her glasses and marks her place. "I'm reading about Angel's early days in Milltown. When she was the minister's wife. He was a very stern man. Repressive misogynist, I would say."

"I think you should switch to this journal." I proffer the one I've been reading. "It's the story of your mother's birth."

Her eyes widen. "Really? How wonderful!"

"Prepare yourself, though. It's very upsetting, tragic in fact. Angel wrote so descriptively, I felt I was there. And it also reveals who Elizabeth's father was."

"That would be my grandfather. Oh my. That was a mystery that haunted my mother her entire life. Angel would never discuss it. It was all tucked under the shroud of her past in Milltown."

"When you read this, you'll understand why."

I leave her and return to my seat, where I drift into a restless sleep and dream that my beautiful young son is drowning in a vortex of inky water. Victor swims past him, waves, then floats on his back, whistling. But instead of sound, a burst of foamy blood issues from Victor's lips, and Chad goes under.

I awaken, unsettled by the dream, and randomly pull another journal from the duffel bag. It's dated September 1895. I rifle through the yellowed pages and begin to read:

The next thing I knew, we were in the wagon, bumping down the lane that I loved. But it was dark there, and the trees rustled eerily, and the big drops of rain fell down on us. I huddled over Willie, not wanting him to get wet again.

I stared straight ahead, sometimes looking over at Daniel. His jaw was set, and he drove the horse hard, as if he were in a hurry.

I wasn't in a hurry. Except maybe to get Willie out of the rain, out of his wet clothes, and into a warm, dry bed. Maybe I would read him a story and rock him tonight.

I knew I wouldn't read him a story and rock him.

I feel a thundering in my heart. My throat goes dry, but I can't tear my eyes away. It's like marching wide-eyed into the wet, black, spindly fingers of a strangling abyss. I can't get a deep breath, but I read on:

I wanted to pretend for a while. Just until we got to the house.

So I daydreamed and even sang to him as we trundled along down Old Milltown Road.

I sang Toorah-Loorah-Loorah.

I heard Lizzie's voice as I sang. Maybe Lizzie would be waiting for me at home. Maybe Lizzie would take me in her arms and rock me and tell me it was all a bad dream.

I wanted to pretend these things for a while.

Maybe I would wake up and be in Paris. And Daniel and I would be sitting on an iron bench in the Tuileries Gardens, laughing and watching Willie sail his boat in the tranquil pool.

No. Not the pool.

The Angel Connection

Onward we rode, down River Road, up Old Milltown Road, where I could hear the rush of the creek as we rounded the bend where the waters cascaded over a little waterfall.

Across the Paunacussing bridge, where just that morning, so long ago, I had read Daniel's dear letter. Through the square, past the hotel and the General Store, up Holicong Road to the fourth house on the left.

Home.

William was on the porch. So was Clara. As we pulled into the driveway, William stood up.

Daniel jumped down from the wagon and walked a few steps up the path to meet William, who was moving slowly down the steps toward him.

I sat in the wagon holding Willie, watching the two men approach each other in the rainy blue dusk.

William spoke first. Sir, you had better explain yourself.

Reverend, there has been an accident said Daniel.

William looked over at us in the wagon, then back at Daniel. If any misfortune has come to my wife or son, I shall hold you personally responsible. William started toward the wagon. Daniel put a hand on his shoulder to stop him. Wait he said.

William spun around to face him, shaking the hand off.

Daniel spoke very distinctly. I am responsible he said. And after a pause, your son had an accident on my property this afternoon.

William backed away from him. Slowly, he turned to lock his gaze on me in the wagon, holding Willie in my arms. I could see his mind working, comprehending, recoiling. Then he let out a roar as he turned back to Daniel, lunging at him. Daniel stepped aside, and William came at him again. God damn you, God damn you he shouted.

Daniel grabbed William by the shoulders, and they struggled.

God damn you. William kept repeating it over and over. Daniel shook him by the shoulders.

Get hold of yourself, man he said. Your wife needs you. She's in shock. He called up to Clara who stood on the porch steps, her hand covering her mouth.

Get a doctor he said.

Clara came hurrying down the steps and around to my side of the wagon. She looked at me, then at Willie, and let out a cry. Oh, my God, my God.

255

Go shouted Daniel, still trying to subdue William. Clara ran down the driveway, and up the hill in the direction of Dr. Mardigian's house.

Help me get Evangeline out of the wagon and into the house said Daniel to William. William stumbled on the small patch of grass where he was standing, as if he were drunk. He rubbed his hands up and down on his temples. Daniel started toward the wagon, then turned back to William. He strode to him and once again shook him by the shoulders. For God's sake, pull yourself together I heard him say.

William weaved, blocking his eyes with his arm. Then he let Daniel guide him to us. My boy, mumbled William. Where's my boy? Where's Willie.

The two of them approached me. I was sitting very quietly, cradling Willie. William's hair was slicked down from the rain, and his face was very white, and his eyes flamed with a wild light. He didn't look at me but only at Willie. His eyes slowly made their way over the length of his little body, and there was a look of awe on his face. He reached for Willie, and I let him take my baby away from me, because my arms were so tired. And he lifted him down, and held him out in front of him, like a sacrificial offering, then he fell to his knees in the sopping mud, praying Our Father, which art in heaven. And he was crying as he did this, and I sat there listening to him, and then I looked at Daniel. His face was drawn as tight as a mask. His pale blue eyes seemed almost colorless as they burned into me with an icy heat. Our eyes locked, but there was nothing there. The air was empty between us, and all there was, was the crying drone of William's voice, and the still body of Willie, and the droplets of rain falling from the trees, and the swollen yellow face of the waxing harvest moon in a flirtatious dance with the fast-moving clouds.

The rain had stopped. A gentle breeze rustled the leaves.

Daniel reached for my hand, and I stood up. I leaned on him as he lifted me from the carriage. We stood next to William.

Reverend Laury said Daniel. Reverend Laury. He bent down to help William up. Let's take Willie into the house now.

The three of us went up the path to the porch, and it felt strange to be walking between William and Daniel, and stranger still to see Daniel standing in my parlor.

They put Willie on the kitchen table, and I thought how curious it was that just this afternoon, William and Clara and Willie and I had been passing plates of cold meat and sliced tomatoes around that table. Now it looked like an altar, and Willie was the offering.

I walked back into the parlor and sat down in the Windsor chair next to the desk. I didn't want to sit in a comfortable chair. I wanted to feel the solid hard bars of wood against my back.

I heard William's voice from the dining room. It was low, and threatening, and vibrating with emotion.

I don't want to know under what circumstances my wife and son were on your property today he said. But if you ever come near her again, I'll kill you. If you so much as set foot in this village, I'll kill you.

That won't be necessary. Daniel's voice sounded hollow, exhausted. I'm leaving for Paris on Sunday. I won't return. But I beg you to give me your word that you'll take care of her. She's very fragile. See that she gets medical attention.

William's voice was a growl. Don't you dare to presume to tell me how to deal with my wife. Get out. Get out. And may God damn you to hell for all eternity. His voice cracked, and I heard him stifle a sob.

Then Daniel appeared on the threshold between the dining room and the parlor. He paused and looked at me. There was grief on his brow, and in his eyes, and in the droop of his mouth, and the sallow color of his skin. He started to say something, but William came up behind him and shoved him hard between his shoulder blades. Daniel fell forward, sprawling on the floor.

Get out roared William, kicking him. The strength seemed to have drained out of Daniel along with his will. Applying great effort, he pushed himself off the floor and got to his feet. William shoved him toward the door. Get out. Daniel stumbled into the hall, and I heard the screen slam after him, then his footsteps on the front porch. I closed my eyes and covered my ears as William crumpled to his knees on the parlor floor, howling great heaving sobs.

And by the light of the weeping harvest moon, Daniel Duvall disappeared into the twilight down Holicong Road, into the dark shroud of the forests, into the pitch black of night and finally into nothingness.

After some minutes, William pressed himself up from the floor. He blew his nose, and wiped his eyes, then made his way heavily to the kitchen.

When he returned he was composed. He seated himself in the wing chair. Without looking at me, he said in a tight voice did anyone see you there today.

I shook my head no. Not hearing me answer he turned to me and repeated the question. I shook my head again.

Did anyone see you riding back here in the wagon with him.

I couldn't remember, but I shook my head anyway.

His eyes were very cold. I won't have scandal on top of tragedy. Do you understand.

I nodded.

He got up and went into the kitchen, and I could hear him praying The Lord is my shepherd I shall not want.

I sat there in the darkness. My body began to shake, and my teeth made a clicking noise. I wrapped my arms around myself and began to rock silently in the chair.

Then there were footsteps on the porch, and Clara came in, followed by Dr. Mardigian, carrying his little black bag.

Where is Willie he said gravely. I looked toward the dining room. Dr. Mardigian hurried past me.

Clara came over and knelt beside me.

Let me take you upstairs she said so gently.

She stood up and eased me out of the chair, then guided me up the stairs, down the hall, past Willie's bedroom, and into the room that I shared with William. I sank down on the bed.

She took my nightgown off the hook on the door and laid it down next to me, then began to help me undress.

With a shock of shame that rippled through me like a thunderbolt, I realized that I wasn't wearing my corset. I had left it on the floor of Daniel's studio. Somehow that humiliation unleashed the first rush of salt-thick tears that would swell and rise and flood into an infinite ocean of grief. I bowed my head as Clara eased my arms out of my dress. Then I crossed my arms over the sin of my naked breasts.

Clara gently slipped the nightgown over my head and removed my undergarments, my shoes, and my stockings.

She pulled back the sheet and guided me into the bed. I'll be back in a few minutes with some tea she said.

I lay back on the pillow and stared at the ceiling.

When she returned, she sat down next to me on the bed and urged me to take a few sips of chamomile tea. She held the cup to my lips, speaking softly.

We sat there for a half hour or more before Dr. Mardigian came up.

William stood in the doorway while the doctor felt my pulse, listened to my heart, and peeled back my eyelids.

He emptied some powder into a glass of water. Drink this he said, handing me the glass. It will help you sleep.

My hand shook so that some water spilled over the edge of the glass, but I drank it down.

I'm leaving several packets of this he said to Clara, it's a sedative. See that she gets it every six hours or so.

He took my hand. You've had a shock, Mrs. Laury, it's important that you rest.

Then he stood up, snapped his bag shut, and left the room. William followed him out.

Do you want me to lower the lamp asked Clara. I looked at her with alarm and shook my head.

Don't worry she said, pulling a chair over next to the bed. I won't leave you.

I could feel my eyelids growing heavy, but I didn't want to go to sleep. I wanted to stay in this day. As long as it was still today, it was the day that Willie was safe. When tomorrow came, his presence in this day would be a memory.

So I lay there, fighting to keep my eyes wide open, watching the silvery strip of moonlight shimmer across Clara's shoulder, listening to the rustle of leaves and the droplets of rain plop plop outside the window, the hoot of an owl in the distance, and closer by, the chirrup of the crickets. And I breathed in the sweet fragrant night air and felt a sense of wonder at how natural and familiar it all seemed. It was just like any other late summer night after a rainstorm. I could almost tiptoe out of bed and down the hall to Willie's room and listen to the sweet, steady, sound of his breathing.

But another sound came up through the floor under the bed where I lay. It came from the kitchen below.

It was the sound of William's shuddering sobs.

And I knew that Willie wasn't breathing sweetly and softly in his crib.

He was downstairs on the kitchen table, not breathing at all.

Early the next morning, I could hear people coming and going, speaking in hushed voices. I knew they were laying Willie out, getting him ready for the funeral.

And I could smell the food that the townspeople kept bringing. The fresh baked pies, the casseroles and meat loaves, the zucchini bread and fried chicken. I swallowed down the bile that edged up my throat.

I lay in bed all day staring out the window, listening to the front door open and close, open and close.

Clara brought me tea and toast and soup.

I wasn't hungry.

Some time after noon, she appeared in my room and sat down on the bed next to me.

The viewing will be tomorrow night she said, and the funeral is Monday morning. A friend of the Reverend's is coming up from Philadelphia to assist in the service. There was some talk that he would preach for the Reverend at Sunday service tomorrow, but the Reverend says he wants to do it himself.

She said gently what would you like him to wear. Willie. For the viewing.

I looked at her helplessly, unable to respond.

Would you like me to pick something out.

I nodded.

She patted my hand and got up. I heard her opening and closing drawers in Willie's room. A little while later, she came in carrying an armful of clothes.

His little sailor suit.

She held it up. Will this be all right.

It looked so small without him in it. So empty and limp.

I nodded. Tears as thick as phlegm rolled down my face.

You don't want to talk, do you she said with understanding.

I shook my head.

That's all right she said. She patted my hand. That's all right.

Late that night, after I heard William's footsteps on the stairs, heard him enter the spare bedroom and close the door behind him, I left the bed and tiptoed down the stairs in my bare feet. The house was absolutely still.

I stood at the door to the dining room. The furniture had been moved around, and Willie lay in a little casket on the table, surrounded by flowers, and illuminated by the candles in my mother's silver candelabra.

I walked over to him. He was dressed in his sailor suit, his honey-colored curls gleaming in the candlelight, his little hands folded on his chest, and a look of infinite sweetness on his sleeping face.

He was so still.

I touched his face and laid my cheek against his cheek, longing to feel the soft little puff of his breath.

I kissed his rosebud mouth.

No answering kiss.

I wanted to speak to him, but I couldn't.

Gone, all gone. Gone forever.

My Willie, my own and only true love.

I went into the parlor and took a pair of scissors out of my sewing basket. I walked back to the casket, and lifted a tendril of Willie's hair, and snipped it off. Then I lifted the scissors to my own hair and snipped again. I tucked my lock of hair under his folded hands. Then I replaced the scissors in the drawer and tiptoed back up the stairs, the silky golden ringlet pressed to my lips.

After the funeral, when Willie was in the ground, Clara had helped me up the stairs and into the bedroom, then gone down to the kitchen to put the kettle on for tea.

I sank down on the bed, looking at my useless hands through the gauzy black netting of my mourning veil. What would I do with these hands? I wouldn't pet my baby with them. I wouldn't caress my lover with them. I wouldn't paint with them.

William appeared at the bedroom door.

I wish to speak with you he said. He stepped into the room and closed the door. I looked at him through the veil, and it felt almost safe. It was as if he were addressing me from a faraway place, a sooty, darkly distant, lofty place.

I will be moving permanently into the spare room. From this day forward, ours will be a marriage in name only. You will fulfill your responsibilities as the minister's wife. You will put on a good face to the world. And you will obey me.

He spoke through clenched teeth. I have worked far too hard to have everything fall apart because my wife is a whore. He spat out the word. Do you think I don't know what was going on between the two of you? Do you think that I didn't see that you came back to this house carrying our dead child and that you were HALF NAKED. You killed him with your whoring and your deception and your lies. Spend the rest of your life on your knees begging for mercy, and perhaps God will forgive you.

But I never shall.

And he walked out of the room.

I liked the powders that Dr. Mardigian left for me. Because I wanted to sleep now. Now that Willie was in the ground. I liked to sink into the pillow, and close my eyes, and let the warm, lazy, floating sensation sweep over me.

And then I liked to dream. I would go back over everything that I could remember from the moment I first held him in my arms. The exquisite sensation of his fuzzy little head against my breast as we rocked together. The tender soft spot on his crown, the peaceful sucking sound as he hungrily took his nourishment from my body.

I remembered the times in the night when he would cry for me, and William would put a firm hand on my arm, saying you're spoiling him. He has to learn that he can't have what he wants when he wants it. How I would lie there, fighting tears, feeling my milk leak out, spilling onto the front of my nightgown, waiting to hear the cries turn to whimpers, then sighs, then silence. I remembered the first time he found his hands and the first time he turned over. His first words. Pa. Ma. Then Papa. Mama. Down. Night-night.

His first faltering steps. Taking him for walks in his pram around Rittenhouse Square. The time he overturned his cereal bowl, and it fell to the floor, and Lizzie on her hands and knees cleaning it up, when he overturned his silver juice cup, and the orange juice went all over her head, and she sat back on her haunches with orange juice running down her forehead, and into her eyes, and we laughed until the tears came.

I remembered how his face would light up when I entered his room in the morning. How he would take his thumb out of his mouth and smile at me through the bars of the crib. Then he would pull himself up and say happily Mama.

Picking blueberries along the Paunacussing Creek. Coasting down to the village on my bicycle with Willie in the basket.

Playing hide-and-seek between the sheets of the freshly hung wash.

Lying in bed with my eyes closed, remembering all these things, I was happy. Finally, I would sleep. A deep, dark, heavy drugged sleep as deep as a cave.

The nightmare began when I woke up. I would stir and turn over, and for the first few seconds my mind would be empty. And then like a blow to the solar plexus, reality would slam into my consciousness. And a freezing black pain would roar through my middle into my core, into my soul, continuing its plunge into a place without beginning and without end, beyond all eternity, leaving in its wake ravaged flesh and tissue, frozen blood, a seared heart, a blackened brain.

My breath would come in shallow gasps, my chest would nearly crack with the sobbing.

I slept most of the time.

Clara kept a loving vigil, bringing me trays of food, which I had no taste for. Sometimes she would simply sit with me, mending or embroidering or reading silently.

One day she said to me as she was washing my face I won't leave you, you know. I'm not going back to my family. I decided that even before. Before the accident. They said cruel things to me, awful things. As long as you need me, I'll be here to take care of you. She smiled at me. We'll take care of each other.

I took her hand that held the washing cloth and pressed it to my lips.

I could hear William coming and going, hear his footsteps on the stairs and the click of the lock as he shut himself up in the spare room each night. Sometimes, before the powder took effect, I would hear him crying.

One morning he came into my room and said do you plan to stay in bed forever.

When I didn't answer, he said this can't go on, you know. You have responsibilities.

Still I was silent. People are starting to talk about you, about how you stay cooped up in this room all day. About how you haven't spoken since Willie died. It's unseemly. I won't have it.

I turned my face away from him and looked out the window, out beyond the meadow to the woods, where the trees were beginning to turn orange and yellow and gold. The date was October 15. It would have been Willie's fourth birthday.

One day Clara came into my room, holding her hand behind her back.

I have something to cheer you she said. She handed me a letter. Immediately I recognized Lizzie's generous, childlike handwriting. Something thickened in my throat as I carefully withdrew the thin pages of tissue.

My dearest Vangie,

My voyage here was not too bad. Only two days bad weather when I stayed below. I forgot all pain and suffering when I saw Seamus standing on the dock at the quay, with his hat in one hand and a spray of roses in other. I pray you are all safe and in good health. Please write to me soon and tell me how you are faring, and give a kiss to my sweet baby Willie, and tell him his Lizzie thinks of him and his dear mother.

God Bless you.

Your Lizzie (Missus Seamus O'Connell)

I lay back in the bed, holding the letter against my heart, feeling a dull wonder at how much had changed since I kissed Lizzie good-bye at the Bull's Island train station. It awed me that she could be in Ireland thinking of Willie as alive and growing. That she could send him kisses believing that he was here to receive them. For a scant few moments, the thought comforted me, the thought that Willie still existed in Lizzie's part of the world. I wished fervently to be in Ireland with Lizzie, thinking of Willie back in Milltown, laughing and playing and eating and sleeping and doing all the things that happy little boys do. Then I thought of having to write to Lizzie to tell her the truth about my life now.

I could not.

I held the letter in my hand and slid it under the pillow, then laid my head down and let the tears pool on the cool linen, closing my eyes against the harsh autumn sunlight.

Sometimes when Clara would sit by my bed, reading or sewing, I would watch her expanding belly and wonder about the baby that was growing in there. Sometimes I pretended that it was Willie. That Willie was hiding inside Clara's body and that he would be born to me again through Clara. I often wept with happiness at the thought.

Afternoons I liked to sit in a chair by the window, watching the leaves as they drifted off the trees and floated down, down to the yard below. I would hear them crunching under William's feet as he made his way across the yard to the church. Sometimes he would turn around and look up at the window. Then I would shrink back behind the curtain. I did not want him to see me.

The doctor said I had a condition known as neurasthenia. He visited me once a week, prescribing rest, Warner's Safe Tonic Bitters, and the little packets of powder that had now become indispensable to me.

One day William came upstairs after lunch and stood in the door-way. He never came into my room anymore. He just stood there on the threshold.

He watched me silently for a minute or more, then in a low voice he said the Websters have invited us to take Thanksgiving dinner with them. He paused, waiting for a response, and asked me will you be accompanying me.

I didn't answer. There seemed to be no words inside me.

In a low voice he said Evangeline this cannot go on. We must all recover from this.

The trees were barren now. Through the window I could see the naked branches silhouetted against a pale sky.

He shifted impatiently and said dammit woman in a hissing voice, will you not speak to me? Have you gone deaf and dumb.

A squirrel scuttled across a branch and stood on its hind legs, nibbling an acorn.

Speak! he thundered. Then more quietly he said you know I can have you put away. There are places for people like you.

Clara had come up the stairs behind him, carrying my tray. She retreated as he walked past her and back down the stairs. Then she came into the room and set the tray down.

Don't worry she said. He won't do it. I won't let him.

I don't remember when the first snows drifted down. I only remember that the skies were often gray, and I liked that. The sullen ash-colored days were in keeping with my leaden limbs, my bleak mind, my silence.

Christmas came and went. From my room, I could hear the sounds of sleigh bells and caroling in the square. William spent Christmas Eve and most of Christmas Day at church.

Clara gave me a soft peach-colored angora shawl that she had knitted.

I had no gift for her.

As her time approached, Clara grew big. Her footsteps on the stairs were slow and heavy, and she was often breathless when she set my tray down next to the bed. One afternoon I noticed when she sat with me that her ankles were badly swollen.

The next morning, I rose from the bed, washed myself, pinned up my hair, dressed, and quietly made my way downstairs, holding on to the banister for support.

I entered the silent kitchen and put the kettle on to boil, stoked the fire, and laid the table for William's breakfast. When the kettle was boiling, I made a pot of tea, set out two cups, with cream and sugar, sliced some raisin bread that I found in the larder, put it all on a tray, and carried it to Clara's room. I knocked softly, then pushed the door open. Clara was sitting on the side of the bed, her enormous belly protruding from under the voluminous folds of her white nightgown. She turned. Her mouth dropped. Evangeline, Ma'am she said with wonder.

I've brought you breakfast I said, setting the tray down.

A big smile stretched her swollen features. Are you feeling better then, are you well?

I handed her a cup of steaming tea. I can't have you chasing up and down the stairs waiting on me anymore. You need your rest.

She sipped the tea gratefully, saying are you sure you're strong enough to be out of bed.

One of us has to be I said. Now it's my turn.

$$\cdot$$

Ꙩ Ꙩ Ꙩ

"It seems your son, our *assistant*, was unable to secure a hotel reservation." Victor speaks softly but with unmistakable rancor as he merges smoothly onto I-95 heading north from the airport. I feel dazed and irritable. The diary accounts of Willie's death and Angel's descent into mute grief have wedged uncomfortably between my stomach and heart. And the revelations of Clara's doomed childbirth and deathbed confession have both mesmerized and depressed me. At the same time, the discovery of Madame's true ancestry is the kind of scoop that makes the reporter in me want to crow. This abrasive mantle of conflicting emotions clings and itches and pulls at me like a sodden wetsuit. I'm experiencing an anxiety free fall, with the additional concern of exposing the minefield of my relationship with Chad to the scrutiny of the genteel Madame Sancerre. I'm in no mood for Victor's assault on my son. He may be a slacker, but he's *my slacker.*

"You don't have to be so nasty about it," I say quietly, hoping Madame can't hear from the backseat. "There must be some bed-and-breakfast or something available somewhere."

"I don't know how hard he tried. But he claims that every room within twenty-five miles of New Hope is booked. It's Strawberry Festival Week."

"What's Strawberry Festival Week?" My mind is hopping all over the place, wondering where in the hell I'll put Madame Sancerre if there truly are no rooms available.

"It's one of the most popular tourist attractions of the whole year. They come from miles around."

"Well, that's not Chad's fault," I say. "How was he supposed to know?"

Victor glares at me. "I'm not saying it's his fault. I'm just telling you…and the timing of this," he adds, sotto voce, "sucks."

"Like I had a choice."

Madame leans forward. "Did I hear you say no hotel rooms?"

Turning to reassure her, I alter my expression from a look-that-could-kill to one of bland nonchalance. "There's some festival going on. It's okay. We'll figure it out."

"Well, don't worry, my dear. I'll stay with *you*. In the Rectory. That is, if you've room for me."

Oh, sure, a maid's room off the kitchen with a bathroom you can hardly turn around in. Victor's spacious farmhouse, with all its vacant bedrooms seems highly preferable. "Oh, Madame, I don't know how comfortable that will be for you," I say, poking Victor with my elbow.

"Forget it," he mouths.

From the backseat Madame says, "Well, I guess we shall have to make do. At least until something becomes available, *non?*"

I gamely try to visualize a tidy house and a well-behaved son. Even with my imagination, the vision fails to materialize, morphing into a slob haven with Chad passed out on the sofa.

As we cruise up I-95, I call Chad's cell. No answer. I glance over at Victor. To my consternation, he seems almost pleased at the turn of events, as if he might relish the prospect of my having to introduce Madame Sancerre to the humiliating chaos that is my real life. I fold my arms and gaze out the window.

While Victor unloads the luggage, I assist Madame up the path to the house. I notice that the lawn has been freshly mowed and inhale the pungent sweet-sour fragrance.

Madame hesitates, gazing up at the house in wonder. "So this is it," she says. "This is the Rectory, where it all began."

As we climb the steps to the front porch, my palms are so sweaty that the keys slip from my hand, clattering to the floorboards. I bend to retrieve them and realize that there is music playing in the house.

"Ah, Debussy," Madame exclaims. I stand up slowly, listening in wonder to the classical strains of a Debussy piano concerto as it floats through the screen door.

"Chad?" I call uncertainly, holding the door open for Madame.

The fragrance of something sweet and fresh and lemony hangs in the air. Furniture polish?

As I step into the foyer and peer into the living room, I cannot believe what I see. The floors gleam. The mirror at the foot of the stairs shimmers. There's a huge bouquet of lilies on the coffee table. Not a newspaper or magazine is out of place.

"Hey! Mom! Welcome back!"

A clean-shaven and neatly dressed Chad rounds the corner from the direction of the kitchen. He approaches me and gives me a hug. As his arms come around me, I feel an overwhelming sense of relief. *My son! My son!*

He breaks away.

"This must be the lovely Madame Sancerre." He puts out his hand. "Welcome to Bucks County. I'm Chad, Morgan's son. The one who found you through the magic of the Internet."

Madame extends her hand, and Chad actually bends over and kisses it!

"Enchanté," he says smoothly.

I almost fall over.

Madame positively twinkles. "What charming manners you have. Your mother obviously raised you well."

Chad smiles, then turns to me. His eyes tell me he knows he's aced my homecoming. But there's more. "Mom, I thought we'd grill steaks tonight. I already made a salad and set the table outside."

He sees Victor struggling with the bags and heads out to the porch. "Hey, man, let me help you with that. You'll get a hernia."

The breath I've been holding in for what seemed like hours is released in one long, grateful and slightly skeptical sigh.

I turn to Madame Sancerre, and suddenly my welcome is sincere. "Let me show you to your room," I say, silently thanking my higher source that I'd had the sense to upgrade the little bathroom next to the bedroom off the kitchen.

As we make our way through the living room, Madame whispers to me, "Your son is charming. He is exactly as I imagined him."

I'm still processing my pride and relief at the spotless house.

I push the door open to the maid's room. "I hope you'll be comfortable here," I say. "I would put you upstairs, but there's only my office, and it's such a mess."

She looks around the little room, a pleased expression on her face. "I'm sure this will be just fine," she says. "I shall be most at home here."

Victor begs off dinner, claiming he feels a bit under the weather. I don't believe him but am just as glad. There's a tension between him and Chad that I don't feel like dealing with, and a sharp disconnect between the two of us. He mutters something about calling me later, but I doubt he will. And I know I won't call him. It's almost as if we'd left our romance behind in Giverny. That scares me, but I have too much to deal with at the moment. I accept his lukewarm kiss good-bye and concentrate on getting Madame settled.

Dinner turns out to be a lovely relaxed affair. Chad and Madame take to each other immediately. I watch my son be the charming, delightful, intelligent young man I've raised him to be and am flooded with love and pride. After our meal, the fireflies perform, shooting tiny sparks in the deepening dusk.

Later we lead Madame upstairs to my office and show her Angel's charcoal drawings and tell her the story of my finding them under the floorboards. I even tell her the bizarre account of how the carpet had risen under the drawings, of the weird sensations I'd experienced, the automatic writing, the computer screen of writings that vanished. She listens without comment.

Chad reaches for a packet of photographs on my desk.

"Remember I told you about these pictures I took at Aquatong Farm?" he says, handing me the photos. "Wait'll you see. Really freaked me out."

I extract the pictures from the envelope and examine them one by one, handing them over to Madame.

"Look," says Chad, pointing. There seem to be shadowy figures, barely decipherable, in some of the photos. "Don't they look like ghosts?"

"Chad!" I say. "You're giving me the creeps." But it is true. The shadows look like those amorphous forms you see in videos on TV shows about unexplained phenomena.

"Where were these photographs taken?" asks Madame Sancerre, studying them, one after the other.

"Oh! I forgot for a minute that you haven't seen any of this. This is Aquatong Farm where Daniel Duvall had his studio. It's where Daniel and Angel…" I hesitate. "Where they carried out their affair."

Madame presses her lips together. Her hands tremble as she peers closely at the photo she holds. "Mon Dieu," she whispers. "Of course. I recognize this place from the paintings. So many paintings. Both Angel and Duvall painted this place. Some of those paintings were dark. So very dark." I look at the photo she holds. It's of the waterwheel, the mill. She studies it for a moment, then a kind of sob escapes her. Instantly she regains her composure and says, "You must take me to this place."

The next morning I walk Madame over to the cemetery, to Willie's grave. She's silent for a long time. Then she says, "Do you realize that he would have been my mother's half-brother? I know that now, thanks to Angel's journal. The entry you showed me on the plane. And the Reverend, William Laury, his moral turpitude notwithstanding, was my grandfather! How strange life is, that I should be standing in this place, in this time, stepping into a life that I knew so little about, yet one that has everything to do with who I am and where I came from. *Incroyable*!"

As we walk back toward the house, she says, "Today you must take me to Aquatong Farm."

"Do you feel up to it?" I ask.

"It is a matter of paying my respects to the past. Yes, I am most certainly up to it."

I hesitate. "You know, Madame, seeing you at Aquatong Farm, recording your impressions, it would be an important part of the documentary. I don't want in any way to intrude on your privacy, but could we possibly, very discreetly, film you at Aquatong Farm? And get your impressions on camera?"

I hold my breath.

"I am not in the habit of opening my private moments to the world, but I made a promise to you that I would do everything I could to help you with this film, and I keep my promises. I request only that you allow me some time alone with my thoughts before you begin to film. Do you mind?"

"Of course, of course! Take as much time as you need. We'll follow your cue."

Victor had not called the previous night. I wrestle butterflies as I punch in his number, even though the call is meant to be entirely professional.

He doesn't pick up until the fifth ring.

"Did I wake you?"

"No."

"You sound weird. Like you're under water."

He groans. "I've had food poisoning or something. I've been sick all night. I think I got some bad sushi."

"You should have called me. What can I do?"

"Nothing. The worst of it's over. I'm just weak. I need to sleep. How's it going with Her Ladyship?"

"Great, actually. I'm calling because she wants to go to Aquatong Farm today. I wanted us to shoot it. Interview her over there. Get her impressions."

"Shit. Can't we do it tomorrow?"

"I guess…she wants to go today, but…" I hear a rustling of paper.

"Oh, fuck!"

"What?"

He swears again. "I'm going through my mail. Fuck me…! They're still determined to get me for jury duty."

"I thought you got out of it," I say, remembering that he got a notice a few months back.

"I thought so too. What day is this? Oh, shit, I have to report tomorrow!"

"Oh, Victor. What are we going to do? We have a deadline."

"Like they care. Maybe I'll be rejected. I'll try to sound very opinionated at the voir dire if it goes that far."

"Well, I guess…I guess since Madame is set on going over to the farm today, I'll have Chad shoot it. I mean, if that's okay with you."

"Well now, what do you think?"

"I know, but what else can we do? He knows how to shoot. He's good. I've seen his stuff."

A deep sigh. "Do what you want. I'm too sick to argue."

"I'll bring you some chicken soup later."

I was hoping that some soup and sympathy might heal the emotional rift between us. I envisioned carrying a tray up to his airy bedroom, with a rhododendron blossom in a vase and a linen napkin. I'd watch him eat the soup, enjoying every spoonful, making little sounds of satisfaction. Then I'd cuddle up next to him on his king-size bed, and he'd hold me, and everything would be the way it was before. In Giverny, back when we were lovers.

My fantasy is short-lived, however. When I announce to Chad that he'll be shooting in Victor's place, he's so excited that he insists I drive him to Victor's immediately to pick up the camera and gear. I barely have time to pull a container of homemade soup out of the freezer before we're in the car and on our way up the road.

A pale and bad-tempered Victor doesn't so much as greet us as point to his study, where he stores the camera and light box, and then he sets the frozen soup down on the kitchen table.

"Thanks," he says, "I'll have some later."

Chad appears in the kitchen, carrying the camera gear and battery pack. Victor eyes him.

"You're carrying around thirty-five thousand dollars' worth of my stuff there. I hope you know what you're doing."

Chad stares right back at him. "I know what I'm doing. Ready, Mom?"

"Uh, yeah," I say. "Take care," I say to Victor. "Feel better."

"Right," he says. "Thanks for the soup."

"You're welcome. Um, call me when you find out about the jury thing."

His wan and disheveled appearance is so pathetic that despite his horrible attitude, I'm inclined at least to kiss him on the cheek, but with Chad standing there, it feels awkward.

"Bye."

I drive slowly along the curving lane that leads to Aquatong Farm. Giant rhododendrons, weighed down with blossoms of magenta, white, pink, and orange, loom over us on either side of the road. To the left, the Paunacussing Creek rushes toward the river. The June afternoon is overcast, with patches of blue sky peeking through fast-moving cumulus clouds.

As we approach the clearing, we can hear the bleating of newborn sheep. Then suddenly there it is: the pond, the waterwheel, the barn, the house, the studio, the outbuildings. They appear to us all at once, like a painting from a book of fairytales. *Grimms Fairytales*: magical, yet foreboding, blazing with a riot of color that cleverly conceals the darkness within.

"How picturesque," says Madame.

We get out of the car, and she looks around her, taking it all in. "I feel I've walked into the paintings," she says wonderingly. "Walked into the past, into my grandmother and grandfather's lives."

"Look there," she points. "That little manger. I feel I know it. I can almost see Angel there with her little Willie. The lambs gamboling around them. Do you know the painting I'm talking about?"

I nod. "Yes, I know it well. I first saw it at the exhibit at the Musée d'Orsay. Then later in your gallery at Giverny."

And now here I stand in this magical, almost sacred space, with a history as agonized as it is exquisite. The source of the deepest pain and highest artistic inspiration. I stand with my son and with Angel's granddaughter. I should feel triumphant. But what I really feel is scared.

I have my own memories of this place. They're recent and involve both my son and my erstwhile lover. Victor first kissed me here as we stood gazing at the pond and waterwheel. I remember thinking I might pass out from the sheer *voluptuousness* of that kiss. How we both seemed to be lost in it. And then he suddenly pulled away and made that awful speech about wanting to be just friends, about how he always messes up in relationships. It was here, too, that Chad and I reconciled.

There's definitely a vibe in this place. I just can't decide if it's good or bad. Lingering thoughts of Victor and that first kiss threaten to bring me down. A primal yearning stirs in me; my stomach begins to roil, and the ends of my fingers literally ache. Now that I've experienced the sensations of being skin to skin, heart to heart with him, I want him even more. What was it that Shakespeare said? *"Why she would hang on him, as if increase of appetite had grown by what it fed on."* Is that *me*?

In Giverny our coming together had been so spontaneous, so authentic. There was not a whisper of doubt that we were lovers for life. I had never felt that kind of intensity. From the first moment, Victor and I had a connection. We seemed to recognize each other, know each other in an instant.

There had been other men, God knows. As Chad pointed out, all of them disappointments. In a moment of sudden, heart-wrenching clarity, it occurs to me that not one of them had ever really loved me. Not the "jump off a cliff, follow you to the ends of the earth, beg, borrow, or steal for you" kind of love. As adolescent as those romantic ideals may be, I actually had believed that Victor possessed the potential and the desire to fulfill them. In Giverny everything had seemed possible for us. Now, back in Milltown—and, in particular, here at Aquatong Farm, where the ghosts of Angel and Duvall linger—Victor seems to have taken on an unsettling demeanor. Oddly, Madame Sancerre had referred to him in Giverny as mercurial when she'd cryptically warned me against him. At that time, I was so caught up in our affair I could hear nothing negative about him. Now a descriptive word comes back to me, squatting like a stubborn homesteader in my mind. Victor as the archetype shape-shifter of Joseph Campbell's Hero's Journey: the ambivalent, mercurial lover who blew hot, blew cold, and blew out of my life.

My stomach lurches. If Victor hadn't insisted that his recent ailment was food poisoning, my own churning guts would have me believing I'd caught an intestinal flu from him. I gaze at the pond and the water-wheel, and my head begins to buzz. I grab the fence post to steady myself.

"Mom?"

Chad's voice brings me back.

"Could you move out of range and let me get some long shots of Madame Sancerre?" He hefts the camera onto his shoulder.

I glance at Madame to see if this meets with her approval.

"It's okay," says Chad. "I cleared it with her."

Madame nods. "It's fine," she says. "Your son and I have an understanding. He has promised not to breach my 'personal space,' as he calls it."

Her smile is genuine.

I move out of the way, following Chad as he retreats about twenty yards back from where Madame stands.

"You want to know the truth?" he mumbles as we walk. "This place still give me the willies."

"You want to know the truth?" I say. "It gives me the willies too."

He pauses behind a thick old maple tree and arranges himself and the camera between low-hanging branches, where lush green leaves obscure just enough of Madame to make the image seem unobtrusive without being voyeuristic. Then he begins to film.

She stands for a long time at the fence by the pond. Then she wanders up the lane to a gate that opens into the meadow leading to the weathered and moss-covered manger. Slowly she strolls across the grass, where lambs nurse and geese waddle. At the manger, she peers through the opening into the darkness, then turns back into the sunshine, walking past towering sycamores toward the creek. I can picture how lovely the tableau will appear on video, mentally picking the right music to underscore it. The septuagenarian, slightly stooped, yet still regal in her bearing, stepping into a past that she had only imagined. I can almost hear her voice: the slightly formal, perfectly articulated cadence, as she describes her reactions to this remarkable personal encounter with her grandparents' history.

Thoughts of Victor's ambivalence easily give way to the pulsing *qui vive* of my creative process. *At least that's dependable.*

TWENTY
CHAPTER

1996

A light rain dances on the roof, and a gentle breeze carries the sweet fragrance of an early summer shower through the screen door.

The four of us—Madame, Chad, Victor, and I—are hunkered down in the Rectory living room, sipping iced mint tea, reading. On the coffee table, Angel's journals lay in stacks, along with photographs, notes, and piles of letters tied with lavender ribbon. We've been attempting to arrange the journals in chronological order—not an easy task, as Angel often wrote only "Tuesday" or "September 3" at the top of her entries. We have set aside the photographs and letters. As eager as we are to peruse absolutely everything, it is the journals that compel our attention now. We needed to get a handle on the "who, what, when, where, how" of Angel's incredible journey.

Our detective work has a specific goal: to find the journal entry about the event that triggered her escape from her husband and her flight from Milltown. The newspaper clippings I've tracked down from the Spruance Historic Museum give an approximate date for her disappearance. It had been at the end of March in 1896. Now, for purposes of the script, to say nothing of flat-out curiosity, we need to know how it came about. Once we learn the facts, we can determine what video, stills, or even dramatization will be necessary to cover the voice-over.

Victor, thankfully, has been released as a juror. The lawyer for the defendant, a night nurse in a retirement home, who stood accused of beating an Alzheimer's patient to death, declined Victor on the grounds that he'd claimed to have had a grandparent who died of Alzheimer's. Victor later told me he'd lied about the Alzheimer's to get out of the jury duty. I didn't approve but kept it to myself. Besides, I am so happy to have him back, I would never jeopardize that by criticizing him.

But do I have him back?

The previous night, out of the blue, he'd invited all of us to dinner. Madame begged off, saying she was too tired, and Chad had plans to be picked up by some friends. They were going into New Hope to hear a new grunge band.

So it was just me who cruised up the lane to his farmhouse and parked my car in the turnaround. The late afternoon light held the tinge of a blush, and the combined fragrance of honeysuckle and clematis made me feel a little tipsy. I'd taken my time getting ready and looked damn good, if I did say so myself. I smelled good too, thanks to several dabs in strategic places from the flacon of Je Reviens I'd bought at the duty-free shop on the way home from France. I chuckled to myself, recalling Blanche's line from *A Streetcar Named Desire*: "Hello, Stanley! Well, here I am, all freshly bathed and scented, and feelin' like a brand new human being."

I felt *seductive*.

After a delicious dinner of grilled prawns, baked potatoes, and Caesar salad (my contribution) washed down with a flowery chardonnay, we began to clear the table. As I set the dishes down in the sink and turned on the water, he came up behind me and wrapped his arms around my waist.

"You smell good," he said. "What is it?"

I leaned back into him.

"It's called Je Reviens," I said. "It means, 'I will come back.'"

"Mmmm, good," he said and began to nuzzle and kiss my neck. I turned around in the circle of his arms for a long, lingering kiss. We stood there like that, kissing and breathing each other in, with the water running into the sink. Finally he reached around me and turned the water off, saying, "Let's leave this for later." Then he kissed me some more. Then there were buttons being undone, and zippers, and shirts slipping over our heads, and then he was leading me up the stairs to that airy room with the king-size bed, newly dressed in starched white sheets, where we made love to a background of hauntingly melodic wind chimes just outside the window. He was so tantalizingly slow, so tender, so devoted to pleasing me, that the shadow of our separation seemed to dissolve. Yet, oddly, my feelings of being slightly off-kilter did not. There was an aching in my throat, where a flood of "I love yous" was dammed up, poised for release, if only, *if only* he would say it first.

"Do you want something to drink?" he said. I felt the sudden, sharp absence of his warmth as he disengaged himself from the sweet damp tangle of our arms and legs.

"No thanks," I said, wanting only more of the taste of him and of us. He stood up. "I'm getting something. I'm thirsty."

I curled up, making a nest in the warmth of where he'd been lying. He pulled the sheet over me. "Don't catch cold."

Then I listened to his footsteps pad down the stairs until I couldn't hear them anymore. I closed my eyes and tried to relax into the comfort of having been physically close to him again. It was okay that he didn't say I love you.

Outside the wind chimes rang in beautiful sequential harmony, one against the other. I felt happy, I decided, and breathed into that happiness, waiting to hear his footsteps coming back up the stairs. Waiting for a talk and a cuddle and more kisses.

After about ten minutes, I began to wonder what was keeping him. After fifteen, I got out of bed and walked to the top of the stairs, listening. I heard nothing. I walked down a few steps and listened for sounds from the kitchen.

"Victor?" I called.

There was no response. I walked the rest of the way down the stairs and peered into Victor's study, where there was a light burning. He wasn't there. Then I padded into the kitchen. Our discarded clothes were strewn across the floor. Now, in the half-light, they looked like crouching animals. I stepped on his T-shirt, then bent over, picked it up, and pulled it on inside out.

"Victor?" I called tentatively, opening the back door, searching the darkness.

"Out here."

I stepped down onto the patio. The slate felt cool and hard under my feet.

"Where are you?" I saw only the winking of fireflies off in the distance. Now I felt frightened and a little foolish.

"Over here." I saw him then, across the grass beyond the patio, stretched out in a lawn chair, naked.

I walked through the damp grass to where he was. He saw me approach but didn't get up.

"I thought you were coming back upstairs," I said, hoping I didn't sound whiny.

"I just saw another shooting star!" he said excitedly, pointing. "Look at that! Did you see it?"

"No."

"Why don't you pull a chair over for yourself," he said, indicating another lawn chair on the patio.

I trudged back to the patio, grabbed the chair, and dragged it across the grass next to, but not too close, to where he was. I sat down and stretched out.

"It's so beautiful out here," he said. "Look up there. See that cluster of stars? That's the weeping Pleiades."

At that moment I couldn't care less about the weeping Pleiades. I wondered if he would have gotten so excited about a weeping Morgan. But I dutifully searched the sky, while a knot of resentment hardened in my stomach.

We reclined side-by-side, yet separately in the darkness of his backyard. A strong breeze rose upward, rustling the branches of a nearby towering oak tree. Night creatures stirred. June bugs, then an owl; frog sounds from the pond. And then to my dismay, I spied by the light of the house, dozens of bats swarming the top of the tree, darting and circling, coming too close for comfort.

"I'm going in," I said. I pulled myself up out of the lawn chair and walked back to the house. In the kitchen I slid out of his T-shirt and picked around the clothes until I found my bra, panties, slacks, shirt, and sandals. Once dressed, I leaned out the back door.

"Thanks for dinner."

"Oh, are you leaving?" he called out. He got up and came toward me across the patio to the kitchen door, where I stood feeling so mad and so stupid.

"I'll walk you to your car," he offered, coming into the kitchen. So we walked silently back through the house to the front entrance, then out to where I'd parked my car in the turnaround. "Ouch!" he grumbled, stepping gingerly over the sharp gravel in his bare feet. I reached for the door handle, but he grabbed it first, swinging the door open and bowing expansively. I wanted to smack him.

"Madame, your chariot," he said as I slid in. "Good Caesar salad," he added, shutting the door. That's all. Just, "good Caesar salad."

I started the engine, pulled around the circular drive, and headed down the lane. In the rearview mirror, he strolled back into the house, his naked backside the last thing that disappeared through his front door.

Now, as the four of us peruse the diaries, the rain begins to fall more steadily, and in the distance, thunder rumbles.

"I think I've found it!" blurts Chad, and instantly, all eyes are on him. "Listen to this." He begins to read:

Elizabeth was nestled in my arms, gently sucking on her late-night bottle. A peaceful melancholy had settled over me as I rocked her in the candlelight, which illuminated the tender familiarity of the room that once belonged to my dearest, my Willie. I breathed deeply, feeling my heartbeat slow, the tension slip from the back of my neck. For a few moments, with this child in my arms, the weight of despair was lifted, the pain of loss almost bearable, the anguish about my future postponed for one more day.

William's sharp rap on the door shattered the calm. Elizabeth's tiny body started at the sound, and she pulled away from the bottle, her face puckering.

Holding the baby close, I rose from the rocking chair and opened the door.

His expression was stern as he said I've made arrangements to take the child to the orphanage. Have it ready to go on Thursday morning. He turned to cross the hall to his room.

For the briefest moment, I was too shaken to respond. Then I said I told you I don't want her to go to an orphanage. I told you I want to raise her. It was Clara's last wish.

He stopped, and turned back to me, resolute.

And I made it clear to you that we are not raising that woman's child. There will be no more children in this house.

His words were a crippling blow. There will be I said, though my voice shook. I will honor my promise to Clara. Elizabeth will have a home. I cradled her to me as if I expected William to snatch her from my arms then and there.

He raised his finger and pointed it at me.

Have that child ready to go on Thursday morning he said in a low voice, I'll hear no more about it. He turned back toward his room, reaching for the doorknob.

Summoning my courage I quietly said the words I know she's yours William.

He froze, his hand poised on the knob, but didn't turn around.

Clara told me I said.

Slowly he faced me. His eyes glittered, and his expression was inscrutable. He said nothing.

If you take her away from me I'll tell everyone. I'll tell them that you're an adulterer. I said those words.

You'll tell? He gave a short laugh and said Really.

Yes. I'll tell them that their sainted minister fathered Clara's child.

He studied me and his expression turned to one of pity. No one would believe you he said.

They will when they see her I said. See how she grows to look more like you each day.

My dear he said you are delusional. Everyone knows that. Knows that you've been out of your mind with grief. That you locked yourself up in your room without speaking for six months. Dr. Mardigian will testify to it.

You know it's true she's yours I said, and you would cast her out, surrender her to God knows what kind of fate.

Evangeline I think you're becoming hysterical he said in that way of his. Then he moved closer to me. If you persist in this ridiculous fantasy of yours, I'll be forced to have you committed.

You wouldn't do that I whispered, an icy finger of fear tracing its way down my spine. Elizabeth began to whimper and I pressed my cheek to her face, rocking her in my arms.

He aimed his finger at me once again and said you have brought me nothing but tragedy and humiliation and heartbreak. He spit the words out. Every time I look at you I am reminded of what I've lost. Of course I would do it, if only to ease the pain of having to look at you every day of my life and see the face my son. Who has been taken from me forever, damn you.

I cowered, holding Elizabeth even tighter.

Thursday morning he said. I heard his footsteps retreat and his door slam.

I leaned against the wall, so weak-kneed so that I feared I'd drop the baby.

All night long I kept my eyes open to the dark formulating a plan.

The next morning, we met at breakfast and sat in silence. The dainty way he dipped his bread in the viscous goo of the soft boiled egg made me want to gag. Dip, crunch, dip, crunch. Crumbs of bread attached themselves to the corners of his gray lips. My fingers gripped the sides of my chair to keep from lunging at him across the table. Afterward he informed me that he was going to Doylestown and would expect lunch on his return.

As soon as he left, I threw as many of my clothes as could fit into a carpetbag, then packed my toiletry box. In another bag, I packed a supply of diapers and clothes for Elizabeth.

In the kitchen, I prepared several bottles of milk for her, grateful that the milk would not spoil so quickly in the chilly March weather.

When I was washed and dressed, I hurried up to the barn and hitched Jeremiah to the wagon, leaving Elizabeth in the crib. I loaded the bags onto the wagon and wrapped Elizabeth in a heavy blanket, placing her in a basket on the floor next to the wagon seat. I said a silent prayer of thanks that the late March day held no signs of inclement weather.

As the wagon rolled down Holicong Road into the village, I did not look back at the Rectory, but the pounding of my heart drummed unmercifully as I approached the square, fearful that somehow William would be lying in wait there or that a neighbor would waylay me. I gripped the reins hard, slapping them on the horse's back, trying to maneuver my way through the confusion of mule carts, and wagons of logs, and foot traffic. I felt several pairs of eyes on me as I steered the wagon onto Old Milltown Road, and heaved a sigh of relief as I crossed the Paunacussing Creek bridge. I resisted the images that floated through my mind: reading Daniel's letter under the bridge, picking raspberries with Willie in the field, the baptismal procession across the meadow, gliding on the bicycle with Willie's golden head bobbing in the basket in front of me.

I could barely hear the sound of the rushing creek waters over that steady thrumming of my heart, each thud charged with alarm. Constantly I turned to look over my shoulder, fearful that William might have returned early and come searching for me.

I reached River Road without incident and turned south toward Bull's Island, praying that I wouldn't have to wait long for a train.

So great was my focus on reaching the station, that I was almost past Aquatong Road before I realized it, and with that realization came a pain so great that I cried out and almost lost control of the reins. I gripped them harder and snapped them, calling out the names of the two human beings that I had loved more than life itself and that I had lost forever.

The train ride was a blur. I stared out the window, my heart lurching with the engine at every stop, my eyes scanning every passenger who waited on the platform. I was weak with relief when we hissed into the station at Trenton.

The connecting train carried us to New York. Thankfully, Elizabeth slept most of the way. It was only when we were safely inside a hansom cab, on our way to the Albemarle Hotel on Madison Square, that my insides ceased their quaking.

After registering and settling into the room, which overlooked the square, I wired my father's attorney to send money.

While I waited anxiously for a reply, I left the hotel for brief periods, making travel arrangements and shopping along the Ladies' Mile for essentials for the journey.

At midnight, on March 23, 1896, exactly one year after my arrival in Milltown, Elizabeth and I set sail for Ireland.

For a moment the room is silent. The only sound is the rain tapping on the roof. Then Victor, who is sitting next to me, says what I'm thinking: "How did she get the funds for an undertaking like that? You can bet that the minister kept a tight hold on the family purse strings."

"It wasn't easy for women to have their own money back in those days, was it?" I reply.

Once again, all four of us begin paging through the journals.

As focused as I am on the task at hand, I'm acutely aware of Victor's nearness. The solid bulk of him against my arm, my thigh, is a distraction. Even in my living room, in the presence of my son and Madame Sancerre, I crave him physically. *Doesn't he feel it too?* I wonder. *How can he not?*

For about twenty minutes, there's silence except for the turning of pages. Then Madame stirs, adjusting her glasses. "Here it is!" she announces triumphantly.

We're all instantly attentive as she reads aloud:

I had recently written to Lizzie, finally letting her know of Willie's passing and the events surrounding the birth of her namesake, Elizabeth.

Madame looks up. "Imagine. All of these references are to my own mother. Quite extraordinary."

Once more, she bends to the pages.

I knew it was unrealistic to expect a reply so soon, but I still entered the post office each morning with a feeling of anticipation. I prayed for her words of comfort, some healing balm from across the ocean that could offer a brief respite from the despair that gripped me day after bereft day.

Mr. Barnes, the postmaster, handed me a large packet of letters and told me that the mail had been backed up because of the inclement weather of the past few weeks. I thanked him and stepped outside onto the tiny porch.

Cradling Elizabeth in one arm, I scanned the letters. One in particular caught my eye. A creamy white envelope with engraving on the outside that said Durand-Ruel Galleries New York.

My hands trembled as I carefully opened the envelope and unfolded the paper. Something fluttered to the ground.

I bent over to pick it up.

It was a check, made out to me, for the sum of one hundred ninety dollars.

I interrupt the reading. "Wow. Do you think that letter is somewhere in this pile here on the coffee table?"

Chad and I move over to the coffee table, kneeling at its edge. I reach for one stack of letters; he reaches for another. Then Victor leans over and grabs another stack. Almost in tandem, we untie the delicate ribbons securing the letters and proceed to rifle through them. Chad passes half of his stack to Madame, and we all hunker down for the task at hand.

For minutes, the only sound is the swish and rustle of papers unfolding, then a subtle tap as they're set back down on the table.

Madame withdraws folded papers from a creamy envelope. She peruses the pages and lets out a tiny gasp. "Oh my," she breathes. "This must be the letter! Yes, I'm certain!" She looks up at all of us. "Listen to what it says!" She clears her throat, adjusts her glasses, and begins to read:

My Dear Madam,

I am pleased to enclose a check in the amount of one hundred ninety dollars for the sale of five of your paintings, the titles and dimensions attached herein. A commission of ten per cent has been deducted from the gross sales. The public response to your work, which was brought to our attention by Mr. Duvall, has been quite enthusiastic, and we await more paintings from you as soon as you have accomplished them. Please let me know if I may be of service to you.

Very truly yours,
Paul Durand-Ruel

The four of us exchange triumphant looks.

Once again, Madame looks up, removing her glasses. She gently sets the letter down on the table. "That name is very familiar to me," she says. "Paul Durand-Ruel was my grandparents' art dealer. He was quite well-known in Paris. I think I remember meeting him once or twice at Giverny when I was a very little girl. A dapper, distinguished-looking man with a well-trimmed beard."

"A hundred and ninety dollars," says Chad. "How much would that buy a hundred years ago? Could that be enough for her to start a new life?"

"Now—*un moment,*" says Madame, putting her glasses back on. "There's more about the money. And, oh my, there's another letter tucked in the pages." She gently holds the second letter aside as she reads. "Let me see…ah…here…"

It was as if my bruised heart had been pummeled anew. An avalanche of longing, of loss, of regret descended on me as memories of Daniel and Willie and my living, breathing paintings swirled around me, biting at me, mocking me with what might have been. I felt an overwhelming fatigue, as if the reminder of all I had lost had sucked up my life's blood, or what was left of it.

My head began to ache. I folded the check into the letter and replaced both in the envelope.

My paintings had been sold! Someone had paid money for my work! The bitter irony of it rocked me.

As I stood on the stoop of the post office, cradling another woman's child, I felt that my future had arrived too late.

I started the walk back up the hill to the house. When I arrived, I put the pile of mail down on the kitchen table and warmed a bottle for Elizabeth. After I fed her and put her down for a nap, I came downstairs again and put the kettle on for tea. While I waited for the water to boil, I sank down into a chair and rested my aching head on my arms. The kitchen was absolutely still, except for the rising hiss of the kettle on the fire. As I lay my head on the table, I ran my hand over the place where they had put Willie on that awful night. Back and forth, back and forth, slowly caressing the wood surface that had supported his little lifeless body. Tears spilled over and dropped onto my arm and onto the table.

Here Madame pauses, removing her glasses.

"This is somewhat difficult, *non?*" she says, blinking rapidly. She takes a sip of tea, clears her throat, replaces her glasses, and begins to read aloud again.

I felt too tired to wipe them away. The kettle shrieked out its whistle, and I languished there, silently weeping.

Finally annoyed by the sound, I rose and made myself a cup of tea. Then I blew my nose and sat back down again, listlessly flipping through the pile of letters that lay on the table that was only my enemy now.

There was a thick, official-looking letter addressed to me. It was from my father's attorney in Philadelphia. Here I enclose the second letter that enabled me to change my life utterly.

Once again Madame unfolds the tissue-like paper with great care and begins to read.

Dear Mrs. Laury,

I am happy to inform you that with the sale of your late father's house on Locust Street, his estate has at last been settled, and a final accounting has been made. Since you were pre-deceased by your son, William Devore Laury, his share of the bequest will revert to you. There is also a bequest of five thousand dollars to Dr. Devore's faithful family servant, Elizabeth Kerr. Does she still reside with you? If not, will you be kind enough to forward this check and the accompanying documents to her? As primary beneficiary you will receive forty-seven thousand two hundred eighty-four dollars. A copy of the last will and testament and a detailed accounting of all disbursements is enclosed herewith. As executor and trustee of your father's estate, I have opened an account in your name at the Provident Bank on Chestnut Street, where I have deposited all but the amount of the enclosed check, made out to you. If I

may be of any further assistance, or if you have any questions concerning this correspondence, please do not hesitate to contact me.
I hope this letter finds you in good health.
Very truly yours,
Andrew Beckwith, Esquire

Madame sets the second letter down next to the first one and bends over the journal once again. She reads:

'I stared at the check. One thousand dollars. I turned it over and over in my hands. There was also a check made out to Lizzie for five thousand dollars.

A sob started from somewhere deep inside, and it wrenched out of me, and I could hear myself crying, and my teacup rattled, and the table shook, and the silent kitchen shuddered with the sounds of a heart that was in pieces, shattered beyond all endurance, unbearably, inconsolably broken apart.

For a moment, we're all too moved to speak. Then Madame sighs and removes her glasses, letting the journal rest in her lap.

At that moment, a flash of lightning crackles through the living room, illuminating all of us and our surroundings in a blinding whiteness. Simultaneously, an earsplitting *boom* of thunder rattles the iced tea glasses on their coasters.

The lights flash twice, then the house goes dark.

There's a hush as the four of us wait for the electricity to come back on.

Finally Victor says, "Do you have candles?"

"Yes, in the drawer of the dining room hutch," I say. "And there's a flashlight in the kitchen on top of the refrigerator."

"Shit," I hear Chad say. "Um, sorry, Madame, but, Mom, did you unplug your computer?"

"No, why would I? I didn't know a storm was coming…" I say, trying to remember how much of the script I'd backed up on disc. "Do you think it's too late?"

"I'll go up and unplug it," says Victor.

"I'll come with you," says Chad. "Let me get the flashlight in the kitchen."

"I'll get some candles," I say. "Madame, are you all right?"

I can barely make her out in the dark living room.

"I'm fine," she says, "Don't worry about me."

Chad and Victor make their way upstairs by the light of a weak flashlight. I light a few candles in the living room.

A crack of thunder, and lightning illuminates the room again. Almost immediately I hear a thud, then Chad shouting from upstairs.

"Mom!" The urgency in his voice terrifies me. "Mom! Come quick! Call 911!"

In a panic I try to decide which would be quicker: stumbling back to the kitchen to use the wall phone, or finding my cell phone. *Where is it? In my purse? Where is my purse?*

With the balustrade as a guide, I stumble up the stairs calling out, "What? What? Chad!"

"Mom! Hurry up!"

Feeling my way along the wall, I stumble toward my office.

"What?"

By the fading light of the flashlight, I see Chad bent over Victor, who is lying on the floor, not moving.

"Oh my God!" I cry.

Chad pounds Victor's chest.

With a mouth suddenly gone dry, I manage to say, "What happened?" Chad continues to press rhythmically on Victor's chest.

"He was unplugging the power strip to the computer," he says, his voice trembling. "The thing blew or something. Sparks came out. I think he was electrocuted."

Chad stops pounding and bends again to Victor. Holding Victor's nose closed, he breathes into his mouth. When he comes up for a gulp of air, he gasps, "Did you call 911?"

I feel along my desk to the phone. Mercifully, there's a dial tone. I punch in 911, and wait. Another crash of thunder, another flash of light. It's as if I've looked too long at the sun, searing into my vision the awful specter of Chad hunched over Victor, frantically trying to breathe life into him. I kneel down next to them, feeling nothing but dread. I wonder if this is how it will end between Victor and me. I have a flash of some awful, primal sacrifice, of some terrible but necessary ritual being reenacted, and the three of us—mother, son, and lover—are at the center of it.

When Victor regains consciousness barely a minute later, I swallow an involuntary sob.

"What the—?" he mumbles as Chad rolls off him, sweating and out of breath.

"Thank God, man," whispers Chad, leaning against my desk.

"Victor," I say, trying to regain my own composure, "just lie still. The ambulance is coming."

He tries to push himself up to sitting. "Ow! God dammit! My hands!" Even by the glow of the weak flashlight, it's obvious that his hands are blistering. "Ooh, jeez!" His face distorts with pain.

Just then I see flashing red lights reflecting off the window. I peer out. A fire engine and rescue van pull into the driveway.

"You were electrocuted, man," says Chad. "I went to unplug the thing myself, and you, like, shoved me aside."

"Looks like you saved my life," says Victor, still wincing with pain.

Chad looks at me, then back at Victor. "Looks like you saved mine."

I ride in the ambulance with Victor. It's an eerie ride as the rain pounds down. Although the thunderclaps seem more distant, flashes of lightning continue, illuminating the narrow country roads, swollen gullies belching water. Jagged branches have split off trees and are strewn everywhere. Victor curses the whole way, partly out of pain and partly because he knows that his burned hands could seriously impact his ability to shoot and edit.

Back at the house, while they were settling Victor onto a gurney, one of the firefighters who'd arrived on the scene inspected the singed electrical outlet near the computer and warned me to get an electrician in there as soon as possible to check all the wiring. He said it was really old.

In the ongoing chaos I made a mental note.

It isn't until Victor disappears behind the emergency room doors and I settle into a plastic chair in the waiting room that I think about my computer and wonder if its precious contents have survived. My insides are tender from fear, as if they've been scraped out. I close my eyes against the bright halogen lights, and the whimpering of the toddler burrowing into his father's chest, and the police radio in the ambulance bay. I'll worry about the computer tomorrow.

TWENTY-ONE

C H A P T E R

1996

Chad's jaw drops. "You want to what? You've got to be kidding!"

Chad, Madame, and I are finishing lunch out on the patio when I broach the subject of Victor. I'd picked him up at the hospital earlier this morning and dropped him off at his farmhouse, promising to return later with his prescriptions and some groceries and microwavable meals. In truth though, I've been contemplating a far more chummy plan.

I rationalize that it had nothing to do with getting our derailed relationship back on track, though the memory of how he disengaged from me so coolly our last night together, has left me feeling confused, humiliated, and mad enough to not give a damn how incapacitated he is. Still, I don't see how he is going to manage on his own. He can't even dress himself, let alone prepare food, drive, or take care of simple personal hygiene. I have decided I can put my feelings aside and, for the sake of meeting the documentary deadline, bring him into my home and take care of him until the bandages come off. Now I've explained my plan to Chad and Madame.

"Where's he going to sleep?" asks Chad suspiciously, as if I'd concocted the plan as an excuse to bring Victor into my bed. Madame politely averts her gaze, folding her napkin and placing it neatly on the table.

"I thought with you, in your room, in the other twin bed," I reply casually, calling his bluff.

Silence as he makes a mental adjustment. Then, "Oh, great," he mutters, "I save the guy's life, and now I get him as a roommate."

Madame interjects. "Perhaps this is the time for me to move into a hotel. Surely there must be a vacancy now. Victor can have my little room off the kitchen."

"Oh, no, Madame," I protest, "I wouldn't think of it. You're comfortable there, or so you've said—"

"Yes, yes, I am quite comfortable, my dear, but I don't like to see Chad displaced—"

Chad jumps in. "No, Madame, I don't want you to leave because of me. I can deal."

"Besides," I reason, "I really think it will be good for all of us to be under one roof, with all the work we have to do. I intend to have Victor's editing equipment moved up to my office. Chad, you know that you're going to have to take over almost all of Victor's responsibilities. Shooting, editing."

My son brightens considerably, then says, "I haven't done that much editing, Mom. Not a big project."

"Well, that's where Victor can mentor you. I think it can all work out fine, as long as Victor agrees to it." I turn to Madame. "You must promise me that you'll stay. I can't think of bringing Victor here if that means putting you out."

Madame smiles and pats Chad's hand. "What do you say, young man? Do you really think you can put up with him in your 'space,' as you say?"

Chad drapes his arm around Madame, a gesture of familiarity that touches me. "If it means we get to keep you here, it's a sacrifice I'll gladly make," he says gallantly. Madame beams.

"Then it's arranged," she says. "Whether Victor likes it or not!"

Victor doesn't like it.

"No way. There is no way that I'm leaving here. I can manage perfectly well." He's camped out on his living room sofa, watching Chris Matthews bleat his way though *Hardball*.

"You cannot manage perfectly well. You can't even dress yourself. Or turn the water on and off!"

"I can turn the water on and off with my elbows. My teeth have come in pretty handy too. Zipping my fly is a problem."

"Oh for God's sake, Victor," I laugh. "Look at you."

His hands, encased in bandages, look like two giant panda paws. And while he insists that he can manage on his own, after the indignity of that last admission it's obvious that sooner or later he'll be forced to surrender to the inevitable.

The analogy of his hands looking like huge paws is apt, because the frustration of sudden helplessness, not to mention his temporary inability to shoot video or push edit buttons, has transformed the man into a growling saturnine bear of a human being. His mood is so dark that I almost back off.

Instead, I surprise myself by saying, "Stop being such a pain in the ass. You know this is the best plan if we're going to finish the documentary by our deadline. You're coming out of your cave and up to the Rectory if we have to anesthetize you and heave you into your truck to get you there."

"Fuck." He clicks off the television with his elbow and kicks the remote across the room. We go upstairs to his bedroom, where he grudgingly allows me to pack a bag for him, grumbling out instructions on what items are in what drawers or closet or bathroom cabinet. Within the hour he's in the front seat of my car, and a duffel bag of his personal belongings is in the back.

"So, are we sharing a bed? Is that part of the plan?"

It sounds from his tone like there's no right answer to the question.

"Absolutely not. This is a totally professional arrangement."

He lifts an eyebrow. "Where are you going to put me? On the couch with the levitating rug?"

"You can sleep in the other twin bed in Chad's room."

"You should warn him that I grind my teeth."

I want to say, "I never heard you grind your teeth when we were in France," but feel certain that now is not the time to bring up our recent *amour fou.*

This is to be a strictly professional, strictly convenient, and strictly temporary living arrangement.

"We'll move your edit equipment into my office. Chad can get some of his buddies to help transport it and set it up. It'll be good, actually, all of us in the same house. We'll get more done…be more organized. You'll see."

My computer was badly damaged. I sent the hard drive off to the manufacturer, but they warned me it was unlikely that any of the documents could be saved or retrieved. There is no time to lament the loss. We face a deadline, and there is still so much to be done. In any case, the discovery of the journals and the information they provided, have given me a whole new perspective on the story. I decide it is a blessing to have to start the script from page one. I also feel compelled to write it out in longhand. Somehow the action of putting pen to paper seems more organic, more closely attuned to my Source.

There is also the added boon of the photographs that had been unearthed along with the journals. How strange and wonderful it is to gaze on the faces of those who had so deeply impacted Angel's life in Milltown. Most of the people in the photographs had been identified in pencil on the backs of the pictures.

First there is the stern visage of the Reverend William Laury, Angel's husband and Madame's biological grandfather. She seems mesmerized by the picture, looking at it again and again, insisting she discerns a trace of her mother in the shape of the jaw, the feathering of the brows. She compares the photo with that of Clara Shaw, her mother's mother, trying to imagine the blending of those disparate genes that had created her own mother, Elizabeth. There is a picture of her too. She looks to be about three or four years old. Madame studies this photo, again and again, endeavoring to match it in her memory with the familiar face of the woman who bore her.

"You haven't spoken much about your mother, Madame," I say. "What was she like?"

Madame gazes at the photograph of the young Elizabeth. "My mother was a restless sort," she answers. "Never able to stay still, it seemed to me. Maybe it was in the genes, as they say." She raises an eyebrow. "Remember, Clara Shaw's wanderlust—running off to become a Circassian circus girl? In any case, my mother was always moving us around. Vienna, Zurich, Rome. Different schools for me, different friends. Finally, when I was about eleven, I'd had enough. I threw the most dreadful temper tantrum and threatened to run away and never come back. There was quite a scene. My mother hadn't a clue what to do with me and had no intentions of giving up her peripatetic ways. Angel and Duvall stepped in and insisted that I come to stay with them in the house at Giverny. There were other children in the village and a sweet little village school nearby. I was happy. My mother would send postcards from exotic places and breeze in for a visit from time to time, but I didn't miss her. We were never close."

"What about your father?" I ask.

"My father was her second husband, a Russian émigré called Goudonov, living in Paris at the time. They separated when I was quite young, and I never saw him again. I have a few memories of an elegant man with a pencil moustache and a strange accent. I remember he would play the opera *Prince Igor* on the Victrola and cry when it came to the 'Polivetzian Dances.'" Madame pauses. "Then she married the Italian count. Paolo Conti-Verdi. That was in Venice. They divorced after a few years. His wandering eye, I surmise."

As we peruse the photographs, there's a picture that's almost painful to look at. It's little Willie, with his angelic face, fair hair, and button shoes peeking out from under his white dress. How Angel must have loved this child. How his loss must have consumed her.

Madame immediately recognizes the picture of Lizzie—not merely from photographs she'd seen while growing up, but more importantly from Angel's paintings of the period she spent recovering in Ireland with Lizzie and Seamus in 1896. There she is: Angel's round-faced, dark-haired companion with lively eyes and the sweetest smile. There is a picture of Seamus too.

The separate photographs of Daniel Duvall and Angel are quite formally posed and benign in expression. They hold no clues to the tragic and turbulent events that would be triggered by their affair. Each time I look at one of the photographs, I feel a primal stirring, a yearning for something elusive and intangible. Although it's been a true blessing that these beings and their extraordinary story have miraculously fallen into my life, I often have the queasy feeling that it is I who am falling into theirs. Their love, their tragedy, their essence now live in my brain and my blood. It's hard to know where they leave off and I begin. I'm alternately troubled and euphoric.

*⁄ɔ *⁄ɔ *⁄ɔ

The Pennsylvania Academy of the Fine Arts is the oldest art museum and fine arts school in the country. It was here, in the ornate red brick building on Broad Street, that the young Angel, known then as Evangeline DeVore, first studied painting and drawing in a special "ladies' class." Her marriage to William Laury and their ultimate move to Milltown had put those studies to an end.

Ironically, though there's no record of their ever having encountered each other at the academy, Daniel Duvall taught classes there. It was in those classes that he first met and mingled with Mary Cassatt, Cecilia Beaux, Childe Hassam, Winslow Homer, and Thomas Eakins.

Upon our visit to the venerable museum a few days ago, we were granted access to its archives, where we found some wonderful photographs of classes from the late nineteenth century. A group of young ladies (perhaps Angel was among them, though we couldn't recognize her) posed against a backdrop of paintings, faces somber beneath tidy hairdos parted in the middle, dripping curls over the ears, their tightly corseted forms weighed down by Victorian finery. We uncovered a wonderful photo of Daniel in his shirtsleeves, lecturing to a class of about twenty young men. There were three of Daniel's early paintings in the galleries. We also shot video of the oldest classroom in the museum. It was high ceilinged and spacious, with windows overlooking the courtyard. Dozens of paint-splattered easels were stationed around the room like soldiers at attention. The mixed aromas of more than a hundred years of paint, turpentine, oil, and dust hung in the air, sharp and pungent. I inhaled deeply. It smelled good and familiar to me, and I felt at home there.

The role of cameraperson now falls exclusively to Chad, though Victor accompanies us on almost every outing. Occasionally, I allow myself a moment to admire the grace with which my son handles his new responsibility. He is sensitive to Victor's vulnerability and defers to him often, asking his advice, listening respectfully to his ideas and recommendations.

The day after our excursion to the Pennsylvania Academy of the Fine Arts, we take our camera to the Spruance Library in Doylestown, where I'd found the newspaper clippings about Angel's disappearance from Milltown. There in the archives, we uncover dozens of other local documents and clippings pertaining to Milltown in the 1890s, all carefully preserved between plastic covers. As the three of us pour over the published accounts of life in Bucks County more than a hundred years ago, Victor suddenly calls out a triumphant, "Look here!" Chad and I abandon our perusals, hurrying to peer over his shoulder. He's reading a newspaper clipping reporting the death of Reverend William Laury. It seems that the Reverend was struck down by a heart attack during an immersion baptism ceremony in 1899. He was dead before the congregants could pull him from the water. He was forty-four years of age.

Victor reads aloud from the article:

The Reverend William Laury, man of God, whose zeal and determination as the pastor of the Milltown Christian Church is credited with restoring civility and temperance to Milltown, left this life on Sunday last.

While baptizing Miss Hannah Eli of our village, Reverend Laury placed his hand on her head and called out, "I baptize thee Hannah Jane Eli in the name of the Father and the Son and the Holy Spirit!" As the young woman was immersed back into the waters of the Paunacussing Creek pond, Reverend Laury clutched his heart and fell into the water adjacent to her. Members of the congregation, led by Dr. Mardigian, attempted to revive him, but the efforts proved to be in vain. Funeral services for the esteemed minister will be held at the Milltown Christian Church on Thursday. Members of the Christian Conference, of which Reverend Laury was an active member, will gather from Philadelphia, Trenton, Newark, and Ocean Grove to attend. The service will be led by The Very Reverend Asquith Montgomery of Old Pine Street Church in Philadelphia, assisted by Reverend Whitney Longstreth of the Society Hill Christian Church. Interment will be at the cemetery of the Milltown Christian Church, next to Reverend Laury's young son, William, who died four years ago in a tragic accident.

"It's such an irony," I murmur. "He died in the baptismal pond in the middle of a baptism."

"Perfect retribution, isn't it?" says Victor.

Chad is dragging the tripod over and setting up the camera to shoot stills of the article.

With Victor's guidance on angles, framing, and pulling out or zooming in on a shot, he patiently films the various articles, photographs, posters, and documents that we've set aside for possible background and B-roll.

Despite initial resistance to the domestic situation, Chad and Victor have settled into a grudging acceptance of each other and the circumstances. Often in the morning, when I pass the bathroom on my way downstairs to make coffee, I can hear water running and masculine exchanges in there, as Chad assists Victor through his daily ablutions. Sometimes I even hear them laughing.

I've been trying to get permission from the owners of Aquatong Farm to take our camera into the outbuilding that had once been Daniel's studio. The entire farm complex is now the private residence of a wealthy former CEO, who also has homes in Lake Como, Aspen, New York, and Palm Beach. He and his wife are well aware of the historic nature of Aquatong Farm and the lure of its fairy tale-like natural beauty. They occasionally hold fund-raisers there for their various charitable causes. Although the farm is never promoted as a tourist destination, its grounds are open to the public. Word of mouth draws curious visitors, hikers, and savvy locals down the curving lane, past the rushing creek, the limestone quarry, and the giant rhododendrons, around the final bend in the road, to the bucolic setting. These visitors are always respectful, speaking in hushed voices as if in church. They park one leg up on a split rail and watch the slow turning of the waterwheel or pet a lamb that nuzzles up to the fence. Then they meander down the lane to gaze at the moss-covered manger shaded between towering sycamore trees, while geese, ducks, and chickens honk and cluck and cock-a-doodle-doo.

Aquatong's owners have been traveling in Italy for several weeks, so my request, which I'd made in person to the caretaker, has been on hold. When I call again, pleading a deadline and reminding him that the documentary is being filmed under the auspices of the Milltown Historic Society, he promises to get back to me within twenty-four hours.

I'm elated when he calls to tell me that we have permission to film inside the studio the following day.

As Chad unloads equipment from the truck, Victor and I follow the caretaker up the path to the dark brown clapboard structure that once housed the studio.

We stand behind him as he unlocks the door.

"Just go straight up the stairs," he says. "If you need me for anything, I'll be up the lane past the manger, putting in a new fence post."

We thank him, and he ambles down the stone path.

The air feels close in the stairwell as I follow Victor up. When he pauses to turn the old brass doorknob at the top of the steps, the front of my body presses lightly into his back. My mouth grazes the collar of his shirt, and I breathe in the familiar mix of soap, sweat, and testosterone. I fight the urge to slip my arms around him.

A shaft of morning light pierces the gloom, as dozens of glittering dust motes, like tiny fireflies, disperse upward toward the cathedral ceiling. We step inside, onto the polished random-width floorboards. Despite the spaciousness of the room, enhanced by two sets of French doors, I feel claustrophobic. My throat constricts. There's a silence here that seems to echo into some vortex of itself. Whether out of reverence or something more complex and mysterious, neither of us speaks. I scan the room quickly like a cornered animal looking for an escape route. A flash of the studio as it was once flashes in my mind. Images whirl in a colorful kaleidoscope: the battered old studio couch, strewn with gaily colored scarves for draping, endless tubes of paint, pots of pigment, palette knives lined up like scalpels, dozens of brushes of every size, piles of stretched clean canvases on the long work table, melting candles, steeping tea, the scent of tobacco mingling with grease and turpentine and old rags, and commingling with all of it, the thick, dizzying, aromatic, musky, unmistakable smell of sex.

All of it assaults me in a matter of seconds, then quickly dissipates into the stark reality of the nearly empty present- day space. A smattering of vibrant hues on the wall draws my attention. It's Daniel's well-used palette, encased in glass, splattered with thick colorful splotches of dried paint. Next to the palette, along the length of the wall, are several framed black-and-white photographs of life in Milltown and the surrounding area as it was one hundred years ago.

Despite the sparseness of furnishings, the room is so alive that I feel it vibrating and tilting; I sense a distant humming. My feet are rooted where I stand. Then I see the mirror leaning against the wall in the shadows. It's at least eight feet by four feet, with a gilded frame. I am drawn to it, momentarily, insanely thinking that I might walk into it and discover the secret of my own life in the abyss of its reflection. I move toward it and stand facing it, gazing into my own eyes. Silently Victor approaches and stands next to me. Wordlessly we stare into the shimmering glass. We are looking at the couple in the reflection, and strangely, in a way having nothing to do with the mirror, the couple in the reflection is looking back at us.

"I call it 'Angel,'" he said.

My breath caught. It was a nearly life-size canvas of me standing in front of the mirror, painting my self-portrait. My figure was framed against the enormous French doors, and a shaft of diffused light shone down and all around, enveloping me in a shimmering radiance. The mirrored reflection was a masterpiece, a corona of scattered light and implied form that suggested a luminous celestial being, an angel.

I felt a thrill that started somewhere in the core of me and raked down through my fingertips until they began to ache. Tears sprang from some closed-up place in my being that seemed to gush open, flooding me with oceans of released liquid longing that had been dammed up inside me since the beginning of time.

He put his hands on my shoulders, barely touching them, but I could feel each one, separately, branding me as if they would drive me to my knees, which is where I wanted to be. I wanted to worship at the altar of his genius, his raw power, and his rapturous and transcendent vision of me.

"It's how I see you," he said in a low voice. "How I've seen you since that first day."

My mouth was dry, and my heart galloped. It seemed that the studio was shrouded in a blanket of trapped heat. My limbs were weighted, and I didn't trust myself to move or stir. Although he stood directly behind me, I didn't have the strength or the courage to turn around and face him. I closed my eyes and tried to inhale, but my breath came shallow.

"Do you like it?" he whispered. Very gently, he turned me around until we were standing face-to-face. He searched my eyes. "Do you like it?" he asked again.

His face blurred as stinging tears spilled over, forming rivulets on my cheeks. With the lightest touch, he tendered them away. His fingers were warm.

"Why do you cry?" he whispered. He lifted my chin. "Why do you cry, my Angel?"

"Oh!" I said. "Oh!" And I tried to look away from him, away from those all-seeing, red-rimmed blue eyes, but he held my face in his hands, and I could smell the paint on them and the tobacco, and his breath was on my face, and I wanted to taste it all, and drink it all, and then he was kissing me, and it was as if everything mingled, and what was me was him, and what was him was me, and I held onto him to keep from falling, and there was heat everywhere—heat and energy and colors swirling, and a need to be as close as close could be—and as I fainted, I thought of Lizzie and Seamus cleaving together as they fell down, down, down into the darkness.

"Mom!"

Chad's voice comes from very far away. I am lost. Lost in Victor's arms, in his lips and tongue and taste and smell and the weight of his body pressing me into the floorboards.

"What?" I mumble, pushing myself up on my elbow, groping for a sense of where I am. Who I am.

I hear a pounding on the downstairs door, then heavy footsteps on the stairs. Victor pulls me up clumsily, his still bandaged hands hurriedly trying to stuff his shirt into his pants. I swipe my hand across my mouth and check my palm for smeared lipstick as Chad bursts into the studio, a look of sheer terror on his face.

"What?" I say, wiping my hand on my jeans. "What happened?"

"The pond!" he cries out. He's bent over, hugging his sides. "Oh, Jesus! There's a dead baby in the pond!"

In stuttering disbelief, Victor and I stumble past him, down the steps.

We race down the stone path, across the lane, and through the open gate. Chad has followed us, but now he pauses, as if frozen at the threshold leading to the pond. My heart hammers in my throat as I watch Victor steady himself at the water's edge and peer into the murky stillness.

"Where?" he says. "Where did you see something?"

Chad remains at the gate, unable or unwilling to come closer.

"Over there," he gestures weakly toward the waterwheel.

Victor studies the water. "Shit!" he says finally, leaning in more closely.

"What?" I'm beginning to tremble.

"There's something down there," he says.

"I told you," says Chad, clutching the fence post.

"Go get the caretaker," says Victor. "See if he has some kind of grappling hook."

"Well, I'll be damned," says the caretaker, carefully easing the tiny corpse to the water's edge. "I thought a fox had gotten to this little guy. He disappeared about ten days ago."

It's a lamb. A little lamb. Sopping and bloated and very dead.

While Victor and I take the tripod and the light kit from the back of the truck, Chad stays behind to help the caretaker slide the lamb into a plastic bag. The two exchange a few words, then Chad hoists the camera onto his shoulder and follows us back up the stairs to the studio.

Victor directs him to shoot the stark space at unusual angles, focusing on the mirror, the French doors, the easel and the palette. Then they set about filming the individual framed photos depicting life at the farm and surrounding village towns more than a hundred years ago. We're a somber threesome with the specter of the drowned lamb weighing us down.

I keep trying to catch Victor's eye, searching for some indication that the sudden rapturous passion in front of the mirror has rekindled our intimacy. Permanently this time. From my groin to my temples, my body is roiling with the events of the past half hour. First, the galvanizing moment at the mirror when time and thought were suspended. I can't even remember how we ended up on the floor. I don't know how his clumsy hands with their bandages managed to pull at my clothes. It was as if I had lost consciousness with the intensity of physical desire. Then the interruption of Chad's anguished cry, the pounding of his steps on the stairs. I remember blinking, then grappling to collect the scattered pieces of lust and emotion that had impelled Victor and me into each others arms, willing myself to get up, get real, and pay attention to the urgent "now" of my son's call.

Then the panicked race to the pond, while harrowing images spattered like blood across the screen of my brain. Thank God, thank God it was only a lamb, yet even the corpse of the little drowned creature set my heart to breaking.

A bit calmer now, I wonder as Chad sets the camera on the tripod and Victor adjusts the lights to film the photographs: How much did Chad see of what had happened between Victor and me? How much did he surmise? Did he notice the furtive adjustments, the flushed faces, or was he too frightened and distracted by what he'd seen in the pond? I feel a powerful mix of thwarted desire and shame. I want Victor! I want Chad! In ways that are worlds apart, of course, but the goal is the same: I want both of them in my life, loving me. Does having the love of one preclude my having the love of the other? It seems never to be completely right with both of them at the same time.

As I watch them work, I feel redundant. An unnamed anxiety bordering on panic returns to tug at me from the murky corners of the old studio. I have to move around, walk it off. I have to get out.

"I'm getting some air," I say and escape down the stairs. Outside I take big heaving gulps of oxygen and command my skittering heartbeat to regulate. I scramble down the stone path, across the lane, through the gate to the pond, and kneel on the grass along its edge, searching. As the giant waterwheel churns and groans, I listen to the cascading fall of water and stare deeply into the murky water.

Willie! Willie!

Tears come then, familiar and thick. What is happening to me? Am I losing emotional perspective because I'm too close to the story? Is Angel's tragedy becoming my own? Or do I have an atavistic sense of some other impending disaster, one that hasn't yet played out?

Eventually Chad and Victor emerge from the studio. I watch from the grass as they load the gear in the truck. Then I hear Chad say, "See you later," and he heads down the lane on foot.

I jump up and run after him.

"Chad? Where are you going?" *Are you punishing me again? Are you running away?*

He looks back at the pond. "The old guy was just going to throw the lamb in the trash, like garbage. I told him if he waited a little, I'd dig the grave so we could give it a burial. It was so little and helpless. To drown like that. Seems like the least I could do. We're going to put it over behind the manger."

"Okay. Should we wait?"

"No. I'll walk home."

He shows up a few hours later, dirt streaked and smelling of sweat and overturned earth. His eyes are bleary and bloodshot. *Tears or dope?* I wonder.

"I'm going to take a shower," he says, heading past me up the stairs.

"Are you okay?" I say to my son's back.

No reply. "Chad?"

Without stopping, he says, "At least he got a decent burial."

I wait at the foot of the stairs, looking after him until I hear the bathroom door close and the shower running. Then I go out to the front porch and sit on the top step, staring out at the yard, where yellow heads of dandelions are beginning their annual June sprout. Victor and Madame have driven into Doylestown for groceries, and I find myself looking up and down Holicong Road, anxious for their return. I need to gauge Victor's mood, measure the level of his withdrawal. Emotions churn in me. Why am I always so worried about what everybody else is thinking or feeling? I stomp across the lawn and squat down, yanking out a half dozen dandelions, as if the lawn were my psyche and the weeds my unwanted thoughts.

Out of nowhere, deadline panic replaces self-scrutiny. On impulse, I head across the yard, past the church, and into the cemetery, where the late afternoon sun casts an elongated steeple-shaped shadow over the rows of gravestones.

I walk the perimeter that parallels the road, then head up the rise, past the weathered sloping markers that date to the Civil War and, behind them, as far back as the Revolution, which had been fought not far from here, in the fields near Washington's Crossing and Trenton. On some stones, the carving is barely discernible. A faded date here, a vanishing name there.

Crossing the rise, I find myself standing at the foot of the obelisk that marks the final resting places of the Reverend William Laury and little Willie. The overbearing, hypocritical preacher, so cruel and menacing in Angel's journals, seems pathetic now that we've discovered he'd died of a heart attack while baptizing in the Paunacussing Creek pond.

My gaze shifts to the relief carving over Willie's name. A little lamb nestled at the foot of a cross. I shiver at the recent memory of the bloated lamb being pulled from the pond. How Chad had been certain he'd seen a baby in the murky waters. The quote on the grave takes on an eerie new meaning. "Beloved Lamb of God. Out of our arms into His."

The Lamb of God.
The lamb in the pond.
Willie.
Chad.
I sink to my knees and pray for the first time in years.
Oh, Lord, protect my dear little boys.

ʓ ʓ ʓ

On Saturday, thoughts of the documentary are temporarily laid aside as we join the other villagers in the celebration of Milltown Day, the annual Historic Society fundraiser that transforms our little town square into a village carnival. Volunteers began arriving at dawn, clutching doughnuts and mugs of steaming coffee, compliments of the General Store, which opened extra early for the festivities.

Then they set to work sweeping the square, unloading pickup trucks and SUVs, carting boxes, hanging banners, arranging white elephant sale items, setting up the cotton candy and popcorn machines, arguing over the grid for the placement of booths, and lugging bags stuffed with "Moo Poo," the eagerly awaited natural fertilizer mucked up and sold only once a year at this event by the Milltown Garden Club.

Then the vendors arrived: jewelry makers, tinsmiths, fine artists, a book antiquarian, a weaver, a woodworker, the village historian, the official Milltown souvenir and village artifact booth, the local historic home researcher, and a number of chefs competitively cooking up delectables from local restaurants.

As I stood brushing my teeth and gazing out the bathroom window, my breath caught. A magnificent blue heron swept across the backyard, lighting momentarily on a branch of the maple tree. Dew still shimmered on the grass, and a shard of sunlight bounced off the heron's silvery blue wing. *An auspicious beginning to this glorious June day*, I told myself.

I am eager to experience my very first Milltown Day. The night before, Madame and I had baked cookies for the highly competitive cookie tasting contest, using her favorite French recipe for macaroons. Chad had volunteered to help put up the booths and even dug out his guitar, hoping to sit in with the bluegrass band that is scheduled to play in the afternoon. We are, all four of us, in a festive mood as we traipse down to the square to pitch in wherever we are needed.

Victor is an old hand at Milltown Day. For years he's been the master of ceremonies for the Pet Parade. It is the highlight of the day's events: a hilarious spectacle of dogs, cats, guinea pigs, hens, rabbits, birds, donkeys, reptiles, and all manner of domestic and farm animals, many in costume, led through the square by their proud owners to the judge's podium, a kind of platform set up in the side yard of the Milltown Inn. As each pet is led, yanked, pulled, prodded, or carried up the platform steps, a panel of judges takes notes and confers in hushed tones, while the nervous owners encourage their pets to perform a trick, or at least be on their best behavior. Victor, his bandaged hands notwithstanding, easily keeps the crowd laughing with his commentary on the pet performances. Even Madame is seduced by his stage presence.

"He's very good," she murmurs to me. "A natural comedian."

Something settles in me as I watch him ad-lib and play to the audience. Regardless of his so-called shape-shifting ways, his mercurial emotions, his mysterious withdrawals, I love him. I love the way he makes me laugh and makes me think; I love his creativity and his curiosity. I love the solid bulk of him and how when he holds me, he really *holds* me. I love his melodious voice and his profile and the way he sometimes bursts into song, and his confidence in the kitchen, and the graceful way he's surrendered his role as cameraman and editor to Chad, mentoring him with patience and all the creative guidance he can offer.

As if he can sense my thoughts, Victor looks my way. Our eyes meet, and I give him a big smile and nod my approval.

The best aspect of the Pet Parade is that every contestant takes home a ribbon, which means there are never any losers in the competition. Today, Victor and the judges come up with awards categories for even the most uncooperative or snarly pet. For example, "prize for most uncooperative and snarly pet." Afterward, the kids' faces positively glow with pride as they pose for pictures with their blue ribbon pets.

When the parade wraps up, the bluegrass band starts playing in front of the General Store, with Chad on guitar. Madame finds a chair in the shade, and I wander from booth to booth, stopping at the official Historic Society tent to buy a canvas shopping bag with the phrase, "Milltown Pennsylvania, 1833–1996" stenciled on its side.

A few steps away is a roomy makeshift tent bearing a calligraphied sign that says, "M. Dilton, Book Antiquarian." In the murky shadows, protected from the scorching afternoon sun, are four long tables stacked with dozens of old volumes and periodicals. Several cartons of books poke out from under the counter. The cartons are labeled, "Novels," "Poetry," "Civil War," "Local history," "Religious." I squat down and begin to go through the carton marked, "Religious." There are several prayer missals, hymnals, and a few Bibles. I pull out one of the Bibles. It has a plain black textured cover, embossed with a faded gold cross. The spine is cracked slightly, and I hold the Bible gingerly as I open it to the first page. There's an inscription in a flowery hand. I have to read it three times before it sinks in, and when it does, I gasp and sit down with a painful thud on the macadam of the square. This is what it says:

To Clara Shaw on the occasion of her forthcoming baptism. From Reverend William Laury, Pastor, Milltown Christian Church. June 11, 1895.

My jaw drops, and I look around for Madame, for Victor, for Chad—someone to tell! Then, a second jolt raises the hackles on my perspiring neck as I reread the date in the inscription: June 11. Today's date! My hands tremble as I finger the delicate ribbon marker buried deep in the crease of one of the tissue-thin pages. The Bible falls open to the marked place. A folded piece of paper is tucked deep into the groove between the pages. I withdraw it oh so carefully and attempt to open it without tearing the delicate folds. It appears to be a recipe of some kind. The list of ingredients is written in pencil, barely discernible.

Begin by boiling in a quart of water, one tablespoon kliptsweet and one tablespoon pennyroyal. Let it boil for fifteen minutes. Add a cup of quinine, and continue boiling for five minutes. Remove from fire and add one-eighth teaspoon iron sulfate.

Take a handful of human hair, and snip it into small pieces. When swallowed, these will bring on stomach contractions. Pour the mixture in a cup, and allow to cool slightly. Stir the hair into the mixture. When it is cool, drink down whole mixture at once. All will be over in a few hours.

"What, may I ask, are you doing?" Victor stares down at me with a bemused look. "Morgan?"

"He had no right," I say. "He had no right to reject the child you bore him!"

"What? Who? What are you talking about?"

Then it was as if he yanked me out of a conversation I was having with myself. Feeling caught up in a sticky web of confusion, I can only blink. I realize how ridiculous I must look, splayed on the ground next to the booth, with the Bible open in my lap, mumbling nonsense as people step around me.

He extends his bandaged his hand. "Shall I help you up? Grab my wrist."

Holding the Bible and recipe carefully, I let him haul me to my feet.

"Are you okay?"

"You are not going to believe what I found."

I hand him the Bible and the paper, brushing off the seat of my jeans. "Be careful with it," I say. "Read the inscription."

He opens the Bible to the first page. His eyes widen. "Holy shit," he breathes. "Holy H. Shit. Clara fucking Shaw." Then he grins. "You're a magnet for things pertaining to our project, you know that? It's incredible. You found it here in this booth?"

I nod. "And that piece of paper? It was tucked between the pages. It's apparently an old recipe for inducing abortion."

"How do you know?"

"I just know," I reply, feeling cryptic even to myself.

He gazes at the paper with fascination. "What the heck is kliptsweet?"

"I have no idea. Some herb, probably. We'll have to look it up."

Victor gazes at the Bible in fascination. "I can't believe this belonged to Clara. And an abortion recipe hidden in Exodus Twenty! Do you think we should tell Madame that her mother almost went down the hole in the outhouse?"

I pay twelve dollars for the Bible. The dealer carefully wraps it in newspaper, and I gently slip it into my new canvas bag.

As hard as it will be to keep the secret, I decide after buying the Bible that I'll save it to give to Madame for her birthday, which is coming up in a few weeks. Her grandmother's Bible! Despite the implications of the crude recipe, the Bible itself is symbolic of the tapestry of intertwined life stories that have brought us all together in this moment.

After Victor and another volunteer leave to pick up some more items for the white elephant sale, I wander back over to where the band plays. Chad looks flushed and happy twanging away to "Bad Moon Rising." Madame claps along, as proud as if she were my son's grandmother. For a wistful moment, I fancy that it's true.

On the porch of the inn, the owner and chef, Todd, is selling his county-wide famous crab cakes as fast as he can sauté them on the makeshift grill. I buy two and stroll over to Madame, offering her one of them. As we nibble, she notices a sign posted at the door that says, "Psychic Readings." She looks at me and her eyebrows shoot up.

"What do you think?" she asks. "Perhaps today is an auspicious day to have our fortunes told, no?"

More auspicious than you can imagine.

I follow her into the cool darkness of the inn's foyer, where we hear low voices coming from the smaller of the two dining rooms on the right. We peek in and see a woman in gypsy costume, with wild, frizzy, coppery hair, sitting at a table opposite Dorothy Ivey, the president of the Historic Society. The woman speaks softly as she turns tarot cards. I step into the room. Dorothy turns around, looking annoyed at the interruption.

"It will be about ten minutes," says the psychic.

"Thank you," I say. "We'll wait in the hall."

Madame and I perch on stools in the empty bar.

"I had my fortune told once," she says. "I was eighteen and visiting New York for the first time. There was a place on, I think, Forty-Second Street, near the library. It was up the stairs, called the Gypsy Tea Room. I've never forgotten what she told me. She said, 'You will find your true love across the sea. You will love him at first sight and never love like that again.'"

"Did that happen?" I ask. "We've never talked about your personal life, your marriage. I'm assuming there was a Monsieur Sancerre. Do you mind my asking?"

Madame fingers the slender gold band on the third finger of her left hand. "I had one true love. My husband Guillaume. And I did find him across the sea, because of course, I was in New York when the gypsy read my tea leaves. And then I went back across the sea to France, where I first saw Guillaume at an exhibit at the gallery Jeu de Paume. He was alone and devastatingly beautiful. I calibrated my own movements so that we would be admiring the same picture at the same time. I let him notice me. Then I dropped my glove. On purpose, of course!" Madame giggles at the memory. "He swooped it up, and as he handed it back to me, he said, 'Mademoiselle, would that I might be that glove, to caress that gentle hand.' I was a goner, as they say. Guillaume Henri Sancerre." She grows pensive. "Angel met him, just before she passed on. She approved! We were married in 1953 in Paris. A small ceremony with just our friends, because neither Guillaume nor I had any family left to speak of. We were mad about each other, absolutely mad. He was like Belmondo! And like Belmondo, he was an actor. I'm not sure how talented he was or how far he would have gone." Here, Madame's speech slows, and her face grows somber. "He had a streak of the daredevil in him." She shrugs. "He was killed in a motorcycle accident just nine months after our marriage." She pauses, turning the ring. "After that, there were other men, some very elegant and very eligible, but I never found anyone who could measure up to the memory of my beautiful young husband."

"I'm so sorry."

She pats my hand. "But that gypsy in New York, she did tell me something else that I've always wondered about. She said I would be a patron of the arts, of one artist in particular. She told me that I would save the creative life of an artist. Well, Angel certainly did not need my help, at least not creatively. Her career was very well-established by the time I was born."

She studies me with a bemused expression and raises an elegant finger, pointing it directly at me. "Perhaps *you* are my artist!" she exclaims. "Perhaps it is you that I shall save!"

TWENTY-TWO
CHAPTER

1895

The smell of turf and fish and salt water seemed to cling to each droplet of mist as the ship slowly eked its way into the quay at Cork harbor. Water slapped against the hull, and gulls squawked and dipped around the deck, as strong-armed men threw ropes over the pilings and lowered the gangplank to dry land.

After disembarking, I found a cab to take Elizabeth and me to the Royal Victoria Hotel, which had been recommended to me by a couple I had met on the journey over to Cork from Liverpool.

When we were settled in our room at the hotel and Elizabeth had fallen asleep, I went downstairs to the front desk, where I inquired about hiring a trap to take us to County Kerry the following morning.

The astonishing emerald green of the countryside was a breathtaking contrast to the somber gray waters of the Atlantic Ocean, which had been my dreary overcast companion for the past ten days. I pulled the carriage blanket closer around Elizabeth and me and inhaled the aroma of freshly cut turf and grass, and marveled at the sight of clusters of yellow daffodils that dotted the stretches of green on either side of the gently winding road. *Spring must come early to Ireland*, I thought.

My mind wandered as I cradled the sleeping Elizabeth against the bouncing carriage. I tried to imagine the look on Lizzie's face when I appeared unannounced on her doorstep. All I had thought about on the lonely journey from America was the sweet healing balm of her embrace and the comforting lilt of her familiar dear voice. She would take care of me as she had done since I was a child. She would help me through this maze of sorrow and loss. I would tell her everything, and she would understand. Together we would remember Willie, and weep. I knew that if there was any solace in the world to be found, it was here, in Lizzie's land, in Lizzie's home, and in Lizzie's protective, capable arms.

Each time we crested a hill, I craned my neck in anticipation, hoping that beyond the meadows where dairy cows grazed, the next whitewashed cottage or house or barn would belong to Lizzie and Seamus and that my bitter, lonely journey would at last be over. The sun shone high, winking through billowing clouds, when the trap crossed a tiny stone bridge and wound its way alongside a pasture, past a barn, and down a narrow lane toward a two-story whitewashed stone house. As we approached, I could see a clothesline in the backyard and a row of snow-white sheets dancing a jig in the breeze. The figure of a woman bent over a laundry basket, while nearby two little girls chased each other in and out of the washing, and a spotted puppy playfully nipped at their heels.

The woman looked up as the trap approached. Then she straightened, shading her eyes with her hand. As the carriage pulled up to the front of the house and stopped, I pushed off the blanket and stood up, with a sleepy Elizabeth nestling against my breast.

Lizzie moved very slowly across the yard. Suddenly, she put her hand to her heart, and her mouth fell open. She lifted her skirt and began to run. The driver opened the door for me, and I stepped down from the carriage, my limbs trembling, my throat squeezed shut so that I could hardly breathe. I stood there gulping the beautiful sight of her running to me with arms outstretched, and my relief was so great that all of the strength ran out of me. I couldn't move, only stand there mute, as she gathered me in her arms, crying, "Oh, Vangie, oh, Jesus, Mary, and Joseph, oh sweet Jesus in heaven, my God, child, how did you get here? Oh, I thought I was seein' a ghost. Oh, is it really you? Is it a baby you've got there? Oh, Lord, help me, I think I must be dreamin'. Dear Lord, dear Lord, bless me."

And as I stood there, feeling the solid warm flesh of her embrace and hearing her sobs laced with prayers of thanks, I closed my eyes and fell against her, knowing that at last, here was someone to whom I could tender the raw fragments of my bleeding heart.

"How did you get here?" she murmured. "And this darlin' baby? It can't be yours, can it? What brought you, Vangie? What's happened?" She drew back, holding me by the shoulders and studying my face. "You're a wraith, you are. Dear Lord, child, is it some disease that's got hold o' ya?"

I shook my head and closed my eyes briefly, too exhausted to explain it all. "Later," I whispered.

She held me close again and patted my back. "You'll tell me when you're ready. For now, let's get you and this baby in the house, get some food into you. And let you rest."

I was safe.

The house was spacious, with two spare rooms in the attic. The hired girl was immediately dispatched upstairs to throw open the windows, admitting fresh air. Clean linens and towels appeared, and a pine cradle was dusted off for Elizabeth. The two little girls, Molly and Katy, eagerly vied for the privilege of tending to her. They chattered and cooed over her like miniature mothers, and under Lizzie's watchful eye, they took turns feeding her and rocking her.

At dusk, Seamus and young Seamus came in from the fields and greeted me as if I were a long-lost member of the family.

Seamus was a strapping man, with ginger hair and pale green eyes. He had a quick smile and an easy, good-natured way about him. I liked him instantly. His son was as Lizzie had described him, a gentle, shy, sweet young boy of ten, well-mannered and handsome like his father.

During supper, Molly and Katy peppered me with questions about America, and afterward, we all sat in the parlor, while the girls played musical duets on the upright organ, and Seamus Jr. did his schoolwork. Lizzie positively glowed in the presence of her little family, and the looks that she and Seamus exchanged were so filled with love that I had to turn away.

By eight o'clock I could feel my eyelids growing heavy. Lizzie accompanied me upstairs, and we tucked Elizabeth in the cradle while elsewhere in the farmhouse Seamus supervised the nightly rituals of the older children.

I slid under the sweet-smelling sheets and lay back on the pillow. Lizzie settled down on the bed beside me, clasping my hand.

We sat there in the silence, smiling at one another.

"When is your baby due?" I said, for it was impossible to ignore her swollen belly.

"Just a few months' time, now," she said, her eyes glowing.

"You're happy, aren't you?" I said, knowing the answer.

She nodded beatifically. Then she caressed my hair and studied my face. "We'll talk tomorrow," she said. "You'll tell me everything after you've had a rest."

I closed my eyes and heard her blow out the candle. I felt the mattress rise as she got up, and that is the last thing I remember until I woke up twenty-one hours later.

Lizzie was setting a tray down on the table next to the bed.

"Elizabeth?" I asked, rubbing my eyes and sitting up.

"Oh, she's fine, don't you worry. The girls an' me are takin' good care of her. And a sweet little thing she is. I been checkin' on you for hours. Thought you might go through another night without so much as a bite of soup." She handed me a cup of broth. It smelled delicious. "So I brung you some broth just to keep up your strength. Are you feelin' like gettin' up for dinner?"

I sipped the steaming broth and felt its heat all the way to my stomach. "If you don't mind," I said, "I think I'd like to sleep a little longer. As long as you're sure Elizabeth is all right."

Lizzie smiled and fluffed my pillow. "Don't you worry about that baby," she said. "You just get your rest."

"She's named after you, you know," I said. "Your namesake."

Lizzie smiled. "I suspected as much," she said. "It's flattered, I am."

"I hope she grows up to be just like you."

"Oh, go on, now," pooh-poohed Lizzie, with a self-conscious flush.

"I mean it." And I felt my eyes closing once again.

I didn't stir until noon the next day.

Enormous white clouds tumbled across the sky, and soft breezes made delicate waves on the grassy meadow as Lizzie and I strolled along a little rock-walled footpath. It followed a winding brook that edged a grazing pasture on the north side of the farm. The air was damp but exhilarating, and I could feel the cobwebs of my long sleep gradually unraveling, unloosing the words that had been backed up inside me for so long, for want of a sympathetic ear.

As we took turns carrying Elizabeth, I began to relate the events of the past several months, studiously avoiding any mention of Willie's death or the circumstances surrounding it. I began by telling Lizzie about Clara, how she had come into my life shortly after Lizzie's departure, how she had cared for me throughout the sad, bleak, lost months of autumn and early winter. I related the frightening and ultimately tragic circumstances of Elizabeth's birth and Clara's deathbed confession that William was the father of the baby. I told her how Clara had asked me to take care of Elizabeth and how William had insisted she be put in an orphanage and had threatened to have me committed if I resisted him.

Then I told her about the same-day arrival of the check from the Durand-Ruel gallery and the thick envelope from my father's attorney and how they became the means of my escape.

Ultimately we came to a grouping of large, slate-colored boulders overlooking the silver lake, and we sat down to rest.

"And Lizzie, there's something else. Papa left you some money. A good amount. Five thousand dollars."

Her eyes grew wide, and she put a hand up to her cheek. "No," she said. "Surely—oh, dear Lord, you're...you wouldn't be jokin' about such a thing?"

I shook my head, smiling, shifting Elizabeth over my shoulder. "I have the check with me. I'll give it to you as soon as we get back to the house."

She looked out across the meadow, and I could almost see the dreams spinning in her head. "Oh my, oh my, oh my," she kept repeating. "Wait until I tell my Seamus that now we can put a new roof on the cowshed and maybe even buy some more cows. Oh, won't he be proud an' his wife is a rich lady!"

We both giggled, and I felt a deep pleasure in her delight. Then she grew serious and said, "Your father was a good man, God rest his soul, but he never got over losin' your mother. You paid a dear price for that. From the time I first met you, you were tryin' for a love from him that his poor broken heart wouldn't allow him to give. It hurt me to watch."

I was silent as I remembered the pain in my father's eyes when he looked at me and the way he stiffened when I leaned over his chair to kiss him good night.

"We'd better be startin' back," said Lizzie, getting up and reaching to take Elizabeth from me. "The children will be comin' home from school, and I like to be there to greet them."

We meandered back along the footpath. Neither of us had mentioned Willie, and yet his unspoken fate hung in the air between us, like a thick wet shroud, heavy and dark and suffocating.

Spring crept across County Kerry in an ever-expanding carpet of variegated shades of green, yellow, and white. Every day there was a new bud, or a new blossom, or a new flower. Lizzie and I took many walks together, sometimes with the children, if they weren't in school, sometimes just the two of us while the hired girl looked after Elizabeth.

One afternoon, as we sat on the rocks, letting the sun warm our backs, she said, "I think it's time you talked about it, Vangie."

I took a deep breath and looked off into the distance, where the brook cascaded into the lake. The placid water glistened in a series of silvery ribbons, and its beauty hurt my eyes.

"You can't keep it inside forever. I see it like a poison layin' waste to you. Lance the poison, Vangie. Let it out before it eats you alive."

I swallowed, feeling the slow, dull thud of my heart, the sluggish, tired pounding of blood that was thick with shame and culpability.

I looked down at my hands, twisted together, and wondered at how long it had been since they had caressed my own sweet baby's silken head, or traced the planes of Daniel's cheekbones, or held a paintbrush.

Useless hands. Even Elizabeth's care and tending had been virtually relinquished to Lizzie and the little girls.

I slowly shook my head back and forth, back and forth.

Lizzie sat patiently on the rock next to me, waiting.

"It seems that it all began, somehow, on the day you left. I was driving back from Bull's Island, and I felt hopeless, in a way I hadn't felt since I couldn't remember when. There was an emptiness inside me, a feeling that I had lost my only friend in the world, the only one who understood me, who really knew me. William had been so preoccupied with the baptism and all of his other responsibilities. It seemed that I barely existed for him. And I needed—"

Here I stopped, searching for the words, for I couldn't remember what it was that I thought I needed that day.

I shrugged my shoulders. "I guess I needed a friend. Somehow, I found myself at Aquatong Farm, looking for…for him, and he wasn't there, but then I came upon him as I was leaving. He set Willie up on his horse, and we talked for just a few minutes, really, and I told him about you—that I had just put you on the train—and he was very kind. He understood. And then he asked me if I could possibly come back to the farm for lessons, and I said it wasn't possible, and he told me that I had a God-given talent, and that I shouldn't waste it, and that if there was ever a way that I could manage to come back for a lesson, that he would be happy to teach me. That was all, really. Willie and I left. I really didn't think I'd see him again. I…I had no intention of ever seeing him again. I believed that whatever had passed between us was over."

I stole a glance at Lizzie. Her gaze was steady, her expression grave. I looked back out toward the lake.

"In truth," I said, "it was just beginning."

And so I told her, in a dull monotone, how after Clara had come to live with us, she had encouraged me to paint again, to paint a portrait of Willie for William, and how I had gone to Aquatong Farm to retrieve my paint box, and how on that day, I had been swept irrevocably into an affair with Daniel.

Occasionally, as I related the events leading up to that last, awful day, the day that Willie died, I paused, focusing on a circling rook or a wisp of cloud. Then, finally, haltingly, I told her about how I had gone to the farm after receiving Daniel's letter begging me for reconciliation. How I had taken Willie because Clara had gone visiting her cousins with William. How Daniel had begged me to run away with him and sworn to be a father to Willie. How we had left Willie alone on the swing. How he had disappeared in a few minutes' time.

How.

The tears flowed then, thick, salty rivers of them, and Lizzie cried, too, as I described the long, dark ride home, and how they laid Willie on the kitchen table, and William's wild-eyed agony, and the sight of Daniel sprawled on the floor, with William's foot in his back, and the sound of William's sobs as Daniel lurched out the door and out of my life.

Many minutes passed as we sat together in the sun, weeping. Finally, we rose and began to walk slowly back up the lane, arm in arm, and it seemed to me, through the blur of my tears, that our two shadows blended into one and that the burden of misery I carried would no longer be borne alone.

∝ ∝ ∝

Lizzie and I had spent the morning putting down seeds in the vegetable garden behind the house. Lizzie's time was approaching, yet she managed to get up and down with the grace of a young girl, and I said a silent prayer that the impending birth would go smoothly. From time to time, as we moved along the freshly turned furrows, dropping seeds, she looked over at me with a mischievous expression, as if she were holding a great secret, yet when I asked her what was wrong, she declared that there was nothing, nothing at all.

We returned to the house just before lunch, when Seamus would be coming back from the dairy. Elizabeth lay sleeping peacefully in the buggy.

I went upstairs to my room to wash my face and hands.

As I closed the door and walked to the washstand, my eyes were drawn to something on the bed. A rectangular wooden box.

I sat down on the bed and ran my hand over the smooth grain. Then, almost trancelike, I unlatched the twin clasps that held the box shut.

I lifted the lid. Paints. Tubes and tubes of fresh new paints. Brushes. A palette. A gleaming palette knife. I looked up. Against the wall, near the window, an easel. Next to it on the floor, a sketchbook, several fresh canvases.

I slammed down the cover of the paint box and stood up, jamming my shaking hand into my mouth. My eyes darted around the room as if looking for an escape. I felt my body give way to a convulsive trembling.

At that moment, there was a slight knock on the door, and Lizzie poked her head in, smiling triumphantly, her eyes twinkling.

"So you found it, then?" she said with satisfaction.

I stared at her, wide-eyed.

"I thought it was time enough you'd been away from your paints," she said, coming into the room.

I couldn't speak.

She sat down on the bed and opened the box. "It's the best you can buy. All the way from London. My, look at all the pretty colors." She lifted one of the tubes of paint out of the box.

I cowered in the corner as one by one, she admired the colors.

Yellow ochre. The color of Willie's hair. Cerulean blue. The color of Daniel's eyes. French blue. The color of the pond. Alizarin crimson. The color of Clara's blood. Ivory black.

The color of my soul.

I slowly made my way to the bed and grasped the tube of ivory black, slowly twisting it open. I squeezed the tube from the middle, watching as a slug of sleek black paint wormed from the opening. I touched the finger of my right hand to the paint and squeezed a mess of it onto my palm. Then I lifted my hand to my face and began to smear the black paint across my cheeks, and on my forehead, and over my nose and mouth. The acrid perfume of familiar smells dizzied me, made a swirling sensation in my brain. I felt I would swoon.

Lizzie's smile turned to horror.

"Dear Lord, girl, what're you doin'?"

She tried to take the paint tube out of my hand. I grabbed it away, squeezing thick black paint onto the front of my dress, ripping the bodice down, sliming black across my breasts.

"Vangie, darlin', don't," said Lizzie. She struggled to seize the paint away from me. I lunged for one of the canvases, dragging the black paint across its snowy surface in the outline of the devil. Then with my sticky black hands, I defiled another canvas.

One after the other, I threw the canvases across the room and with both hands, began to rub the black paint all over my face and hair, and arms, and body.

Lizzie stood up, grabbing me by the shoulders. "Stop it! Stop it right now!"

I flung my arm out, pushing her away. "No!" I screamed. "No!"

I snatched the palette out of the box and jumped up from the bed, smashing the thin, fine wood against the corner of the washstand, smashing and smashing, hearing the wood crack and hearing my voice shrieking, "I killed him! I killed him! I killed him!"

Lizzie tried to put her arms around me, to restrain me, but I shoved her away, and she fell against the bed, protecting her swollen belly with both her hands. I could feel the shards of splintered wood cutting into my hand, and I flung the pieces against the wall, then pushed the water pitcher and the basin off the washstand, onto the floor, where they shattered.

"Vangie, please! Stop!"

"No!" I screamed. "I killed him! I! I!" I pounded both my sticky black fists against my breasts.

I reached for the lace curtains at the window and jerked them down from the rod, twisting and tearing them, first with my hands, then with my teeth, until I shredded them, heard them ripping apart. Lizzie pushed herself up off the bed and tried to seize my arms again, but I lunged past her to the paint box and pulled out the palette knife, holding it high in the air.

"God damn you!" I screamed at her. "Why do you torture me? I killed him! My lust killed him! My vanity killed him! My so-called *artistry* killed him! He died for my sins! He died because of me!" With that I brought the palette knife down and slashed it across the inside of my wrist.

Lizzie grabbed for it, and we struggled. "Stop it, Vangie! For God's sake, stop it!"

A rivulet of blood trickled from a small cut on my wrist and ran down my arm under my sleeve. "No," I cried, trying to wrest the knife away from her. "No! I want to die! Let me die."

"You're not goin' to die! You're not! Give me the knife! Give. It. To me!" I felt her tug it out of my hand, and I felt my knees buckle, and I sank to the floor, with my blackened face in my sticky blackened hands, and I began to keen, rocking back and forth on my knees.

I felt her sink to her knees next to me, felt her wrap a handkerchief around my wrist and pull it tight, felt her put her arms around me, rocking with me, heard her crooning words, and felt her lips against my wet, sticky face.

"Oh, there, there, darlin'. Oh, there, there. Shhhh. All right. All's right now. There, there." She crooned and rocked me, all the time whispering words I don't even remember, but after a time, my wails became moans, and my moans became whimpers, and finally, finally I relaxed in her arms, silent and spent.

She caressed my hair. "Oh, my girl, my little girl. Forgive yourself now. Forgive yourself. God forgives you, I'm sure of it, and I forgive you, and your little angel boy in heaven forgives you. It's over, Vangie. God love you, it's over, and he's with the saints and angels now, and sweet Jesus is lookin' after him, and little Willie loves you from where he is, and he's watchin' over you. He'll always be in your heart, as you loved him, as you'll always love him, and you have to take that love and let it heal you, darlin'. Forgive yourself, and let it heal you. Let the love heal you."

For many minutes, there was no other sound but the shuddering gasps of my sobs as they slowly subsided. There was a stinging throb in my wrist, but the palette knife had been too dull to cause any real damage. My head felt as if it were stuffed with cotton, and the smell of the paint on my skin made me dizzy once more. Though this time I gladly surrendered. And throughout my limbs, the blood popped and tingled as it coursed freely out of its pent-up dark places, returning me at last to the land of the living.

Then, through the open window came the lusty, reproachful cry of a hungry baby.

Elizabeth.

In the weeks that followed, the tender fragments of my grieving heart seemed to yearn toward each other. I could physically feel the first tentative buds of renewal take root and begin to swell, filling me with hope and a sense of purpose. I could feel Lizzie's eyes on me, witnessing my gradual recovery. I remember the first time she caught me humming softly to myself as I lit the fire under the kettle for tea. Our eyes met and held. Then I could feel a smile, a real genuine smile, beginning somewhere down around my knees and working its way up through my whole body, until it swelled into my mouth, splitting it wide, stretching across my lips, my cheeks, until my jaw ached. And so I began to heal.

Lizzie's son was born just after sunrise on a misty June morning. He came swiftly and easily, and she named him David Edward O'Connell, after my father.

I hired a nanny from the village to help look after the babies, and when David was two months old, I convinced a reluctant Lizzie to accompany me on a trip into Cork, where we stayed at the Royal Victoria Hotel.

For three days we made the rounds of shops and restaurants, indulging in rich meals, and sweets piled high with whipped cream and chocolate.

We ordered dresses from the dressmaker, made stops at the bonnet shop, the glove shop, and the stay-maker. Then we bought presents: a silver-headed walking stick for Seamus, a revolving globe for young Seamus, baby dolls and ribbons for Molly and Katy, and a handsome new pram for Elizabeth and David.

Back in our room at the Royal Victoria, exhausted and flushed with excitement over our purchases, we ordered room service and drank a whole bottle of champagne in celebration of our successful shopping excursion.

On the morning of our departure, while the driver was piling our packages and bags in the trap, I told Lizzie that I had one more errand to complete and would return in a few minutes.

I had noticed a shop around the corner from the hotel, and I quickly made my last purchases there.

When I settled in the carriage next to Lizzie, I shyly unwrapped my packages and showed her the shiny new palette, sketchbook, and gleaming fat tube of ivory black paint. Her eyes filled up, and we were both smiling as the driver snapped the reins and eased the trap out onto the thoroughfare for the journey home.

Like a patient recovering from a long illness, I began with small steps: simple sketches and still lifes. Gradually I moved to landscapes, the shaded greens of the undulating countryside, the lazily grazing cows in the meadow, the placid silvery blue waters of the pond. I would rise early to capture the morning light and carry my paints and easel down the lane and across the fields, where I would lose myself in peaceful concentration until lunchtime, when I would wander back to the house.

Afternoons, Lizzie and I would take longs walks with the children or sit in the garden, tending our babies. I would read; she would knit.

On Sundays, the whole family piled into a carriage and went calling on Lizzie's mother and father, who lived on a tiny farm on the other side of Killarney. There would always be a crowd of brothers and sisters and cousins and aunts and uncles coming and going, a noisy, robust group, who lifted the babies up in the air, and teased Lizzie and Seamus, and exchanged village gossip as if they were revealing the secrets of the Holy Grail.

The birth of their little son seemed to bring Lizzie and Seamus even closer. I watched how they greeted each other when he and young Seamus came in from the fields or from milking, how she listened for the sound of his whistle, and how her face brightened as he appeared at the back door, his shirt stained through with sweat, his boots covered with mud.

"Don't you be trackin' that mud on my floor, Seamus O'Connell, nor you, young Seamus," she'd warn. And big Seamus would lean over, grinning at his son, and they would pull off their boots, grunting and grumbling.

Big Seamus would often say, "I hear ya', woman. Ya don't have to wake up the dead."

Then Lizzie would pull the towel from the hook and walk outside to where they stood, and young Seamus would hang back as his father and Lizzie strolled to the well, leaning toward each other, talking in low voices. Lizzie would watch as big Seamus stripped off his shirt and splashed himself with water. Then she would dry him off with a towel, and sometimes he would playfully slap her on the bottom, and she would push his hand away and frown, cocking her head toward young Seamus, who stood in the shadow of the porch, pretending not to watch.

When they all came back into the house, Seamus would greet me and Elizabeth and kiss Katy and Molly, then say, "Where's my new son?" And he would lift little David out of the cradle, high into the air, and swing him around and around.

I began to sketch these scenes of happy family life. Night after night, when the house was finally quiet, I would fill in the sketches, make additional studies, plan my paintings.

They came out in a torrent of color and expression: Lizzie and Seamus at the well, young Seamus shyly waiting his turn in the shadow of the porch, Katy and Molly playing little mother with the babies, Seamus swinging David in the air, the family at supper, bowing their heads for grace. Scenes of rural Irish domesticity.

On the anniversary of Willie's death, I sat in my room, surrounded by the canvases of love and joy and family life and healing.

I stayed there all day, looking at the paintings, and letting my thoughts dissolve from the scenes before me to the scenes of the life that I had lost.

That night, I wrote a letter to Paul Durand-Ruel in Paris, telling him that I had completed several paintings and would like to submit them to his gallery.

TWENTY-THREE

CHAPTER

1996

Madame's session with the psychic lasts fifteen minutes.

"Well?" I ask, when she reappears.

She rolls her eyes. "What a character!" she whispers. "She calls herself 'Minerva.'"

"What did she tell you?" I whisper back.

"She told me I'm going to get a letter, calling me to make a journey. My decision about whether to go or stay will have tragic implications. She kept referring to my 'daughter.'" Madame laughs. "On the one hand, it made no sense at all, but on the other hand, it gave me a frisson." She shivers, then waves her hand in the air, as if to dismiss it all. "I'm going to head back to the house. It's time for my nap." Then, with a wink, "Have fun!"

I enter the dining room and take a seat across the table from the psychic. I place the bag with the Bible on the table next to me.

She's colorful all right. She appears to be in her fifties, but her hair is a wild bird's nest of orange frizz, most likely from a bottle. She has shimmery copper-colored eye shadow and false eyelashes. Her cheeks are bronzed, and her lips are outlined in brown pencil. The lipstick is pearled tangerine.

"I'm Minerva," she says. "And you are?"

"I'm Morgan."

She begins to scribble on a yellow tablet. Her pen moves quickly all over the page. I can't tell what she's writing.

"Morgan. Ah, this is the name of a famous Celtic tribe. A tribe of powerful women. Is your ancestry Welsh?"

"On my mother's side, yes. It was her maiden name."

"You have strong intuitive powers from your Morgan heritage," she says. "Are you aware of that?"

"I guess so," I say.

"I ask twenty dollars for the first fifteen minutes." She smiles, revealing a mouthful of bad teeth.

I pass a twenty-dollar bill across the table, and she stops scribbling long enough to pocket it.

Pulling her chair closer to the table, she eyes the canvas bag and says, "Let's take that bag off the table so we have a clear plane for the exchange of energy."

I reach for the bag, and suddenly she puts her hand on top of mine.

"Wait," she says.

I pause, feeling the heat from her hand.

"This bag. It contains something very important."

Well, you're the psychic, I think.

"It's an old book I bought outside at the fair," I volunteer. "A Bible."

"Can I see it? It's putting out powerful energy."

As I withdraw the Bible and carefully unwrap it, Minerva moves the yellow writing tablet aside.

"Do you mind?" she says. She places her hand on the Bible and closes her eyes. I wait, feeling simultaneously curious, skeptical, and uneasy.

With her eyes still closed, she says, "I feel suffering. Suffering and betrayal around this Bible. It was not used for its highest spiritual purpose."

I keep quiet as she opens her eyes and opens the Bible. She reads the inscription.

"Oh, the church up the road," she says, nodding. "You know, there's something dark about that church and the house next to it. I always bless myself when I go by."

"I live there," I blurt out.

She lifts her gaze. The eyes behind the heavy makeup seem clear and keenly aware.

"How long? How long have you lived there?"

"Not long. Five months or so."

Damn, I think! I keep giving her information!

I determine to stop talking.

Looking at me intently, she says, "Be careful. You're a conduit for old energies. The house, the church, the cemetery. Some of these energies are negative. The more you pursue them, the more power you give them. Like the tarot or the Ouija."

I think about the documentary and all the events leading up to it, but try to keep a poker face.

She opens the Bible to the pages marked by the ribbon, where the abortion recipe is tucked in the folds. She carefully withdraws it.

I watch her read the faded instructions.

Once again she raises her eyes to mine. The spots of rouge seem almost clown-like against skin that has suddenly drained of color.

"Where did you say you found this Bible?"

"At the antique book dealer's. In the square."

She studies the recipe, sighs, and shakes her head. "It didn't always work, you know. Sometimes all it brought on was more fear. More tragedy."

For some reason, my attempt to remain Sphinx-like gives way to a sudden urge to confide in this woman.

"The owner of the Bible, Clara Shaw, did end up having a baby. She died in childbirth. I know because I'm making a documentary, and she's part of the history. That's why this Bible was such a great find for me today."

Her pallor changes beneath the heavy makeup. She presses her lips together. I detect a slight tremor in her hand.

"It's a long story," I say, feeling apologetic.

Suddenly she shakes the colorful Indian shawl off her shoulders. "It's so warm in here." She reaches for a bottle of water next to her chair and takes a long drink, leaving a worm of lipstick around the rim. My own mouth is dry, and I wish I'd brought a water bottle of my own.

Minerva puts down the bottle, readjusts herself in the chair, and stretches her hands across the table. "Give me your hands," she says. "Cold," she remarks as her palms settle against mine. In contrast, her hands feel very hot. "Let's close our eyes."

My heart begins a slight thrumming. It feels loud in the expanse of the quiet dining room. Despite its size, the atmosphere here feels close, claustrophobic. My own hands start to sweat. We're silent for maybe two minutes, when I feel her hands twitch. She moans slightly. It sounds like "uunnh." My eyes pop open. I see that her forehead glistens with sweat, and her lavishly applied foundation seems to have melted and settled in the creases around her eyes and mouth.

"Are you all right?" I ask.

She hunches over the table, withdrawing her hands.

"I feel…I'm sorry, hon, I…my insides are boiling…I think I need to take a break." She fumbles in her pocket. "Here's your twenty back…I can't take money for this reading."

With some effort she pushes her chair away from the table.

"Can I help you?" I ask, standing up. "Is there some place you can lie down?" I think crazily that I should take her up to my house.

"I think I can make it," she says, holding her stomach. "I just live upstairs."

"Upstairs here at the inn?" I say.

She nods.

"Well, let me help you," I say, putting the Bible back into the canvas bag and pulling the bag over my shoulder. She leans into me as I guide her into the hall and toward the staircase. She seems to age with every step as we slowly climb to the second floor of the old inn.

"It's at the end of the hall," she says with some effort. "You're so good to help me like this."

The old floorboards groan as we make our way down the corridor, passing four apartments as we go. I have a flash of the inn as it might have been a hundred years ago, when it was a brothel, when Clara Shaw had lived here. I almost tell Minerva that the woman whose Bible she'd just handled had lived here at the inn, also, but it seems irrelevant in light of her discomfort.

"Here we are, hon." She pulls out a key and unlocks the door. Sunlight floods the room, which seems to consist of a combination bedroom-parlor, with a Pullman kitchen behind a room divider. The walls are draped with scarves. There's an altar with crystals, statuettes, candles, and other artifacts. I catch a glimpse of dozens of occult books stacked in a case near the altar.

She sighs, steps out of her sandals, and sinks down onto the bed. Then she curls into a fetal position, hugging her middle.

"What can I do?" I say. "Shall I call a doctor?"

"No," she whispers. "It will pass. The pain will be over soon."

"Are you sure?" I ask. "Shouldn't I call someone?"

"There's no one to call. I'll be all right. You can go now."

She seems so small and vulnerable curled up there on the bed.

"Let me sit with you awhile," I say. "Please. I want to make sure you're all right."

"Aren't you nice," she murmurs. She closes her eyes. Outside the window I can hear the music of the bluegrass band and the din of voices in the square.

I sit down in a wooden rocker across from the bed and study Minerva's face in repose. The eye shadow and rouge and tangerine lipstick appear neon-like against the pale canvas of her aging face. It looks like a face that has lived hard. I spot a bottle of gin on the counter in the little kitchen and wonder if she has a problem with alcohol.

Within minutes she begins to snore softly. I lean back in the rocker and gaze at the book titles stacked next to the bed. Astrology, occult, tarot, witchcraft. I see a framed photo on the wall and stand up to look at it. It's an old black-and-white picture of the inn. It looks to have been taken around the turn of the century. There are a few horses tied up at the hitching post. A young woman with wild hair stands on the porch, languorously leaning against a pillar and shielding her eyes from the sun.

"I was dreaming."

Minerva's voice startles me.

"How do you feel?" I ask.

"Still a little woozy," she says. She pats the bed. "Sit down for a minute. I have to tell you something."

I sit down next to her. She reaches for my hand. "You're a good girl," she says. "But I have to warn you. The temptation is very strong. Almost irresistible, I know. This is the way with affairs of the heart. But if you give in to it, there will be terrible tragedy. I saw it in my dream. That house. Darkness and rain, and something terrible."

She closes her eyes against the images, leaving me shaken and downright spooked.

"What do you mean? Minerva? What kind of tragedy?"

For a moment it looks as if she's fallen asleep again, leaving me to freak out on my own. Then her eyes open. She smiles at me and stretches as if waking from a pleasant nap.

"Oh, my gosh, hon, are you still here? How long was I asleep?"

I don't know how to answer. "About ten minutes, I think. How are you feeling?"

She pushes herself up. "Much better," she says. "The pain's all gone."

She swings her deeply veined legs over the side of the bed and squeezes bunioned feet into her sandals.

"If you want to, we can go back downstairs and finish your reading. No charge."

"Oh, that's okay," I say, "I really have to get back."

The room feels stultifying, and I need air. A combination of old grease from the little kitchen, stale incense from the altar, and a dusky body odor that emanates from Minerva, makes me queasy. I suddenly crave the upbeat bustling of the crowd in the square. I want to cheer Chad and sing along as he plays with the band. Most of all, I want Victor.

TWENTY-FOUR

1996

We work around the clock the following week, making last-minute script changes, choosing music, and laying down video and sound tracks. Madame proves particularly helpful in the selection of music. Her knowledge extends from the great classical composers, to Irish and French songs from the early twentieth century. She scours the computer, downloading songs for our approval. By the end of the week, we have thirty-five minutes of the documentary, and we're optimistic about how it is coming together.

On Friday I drive Victor to the Medical Center at Doylestown Hospital, where the doctor removes his bandages. Although the skin on his burned hands has regenerated and healed, Victor's fingers are stiff and sore. And though he was given a regimen of exercises, including squeezing a rubber ball, it will be a while before he regains the dexterity necessary for pushing the edit buttons. He'll continue to oversee Chad.

Still, he's exhilarated to be free of the cumbersome bandages and the dependence they represented. He insists that we celebrate over lunch.

We drive up old Route 202 to New Hope and decide to eat at The Landing, a charming restaurant situated right on the banks of the Delaware River. We're lucky enough to secure an outside table under a bright yellow umbrella. Victor orders a bottle of Frascati, and for a few minutes, we sip our wine and enjoy the view. Ducks quack and squabble on the shore just beneath us, sunlight makes dancing patterns across the lazy river current, and on the opposite banks, swans drift gracefully in the shadow of the New Hope-Lambertville Bridge. The wine is crisp and light, the mood is buoyant, and I feel a surge of such happiness.

"What are you thinking?" Victor asks.

"Oh, just that I feel happy today," I say.

"I'm feeling rather sanguine myself," he says, in that funny formal way he has of speaking.

We clink glasses.

"It's been a long haul," he says. I wait for him to offer some kind of thanks for my having been such a good caregiver over the past weeks.

Instead he picks up the menu and begins to study it. "What looks good?" he says.

Later that afternoon, Victor packs his belongings and drives down the road to his farmhouse to resume the bachelor life that had been disrupted by the injury to his hands. He plans to take the weekend to address the mound of paperwork, unpaid bills, overgrown lawns, weed-choked gardens, and general household maintenance that has been neglected during his stay at the Rectory. That evening, Chad goes off with friends, and as Madame and I dine alone on the patio, I feel an acute absence of male energy, as if something tangible and life-giving has been drained from the air around us. I drink too much wine and wait for Victor to call. He doesn't, and I fall asleep feeling utterly abandoned.

The next day, Madame and I make an outing to the local nursery to buy tomato plants. We spend the afternoon planting and fertilizing. At one point she turns to me and says, "I am sorry that I won't be here to harvest our crop." It hasn't occurred to me that our time together will soon come to an end. When the documentary is finished, she'll return to Giverny.

"Me too," I say, resting back on my haunches. "I'm going to miss you so much." And it's true.

On Sunday I take her to the Golden Nugget Flea Market on Route 29 outside of Lambertville. There she buys me an exquisite set of eight antique demitasse cups and saucers, charmingly mismatched.

"A going away present," she says.

We stroll up and down the aisles of booths, pausing here and there. While she's distracted looking through old linens, I buy a set of framed prints by the local artist, Charles Hargens, depicting scenes from Milltown, including one of the Rectory. These will be my farewell gift to Madame Sancerre.

Later, we order fresh orange juice and bacon and egg sandwiches at the open-air diner on the premises, carrying them on a tray to a picnic table in the shade.

As we sit munching, Madame suddenly says, "I think I've misjudged Victor."

I sit up straight, stopping mid chew. "Why do you say that?"

"I've watched him with Chad these past weeks. What a wonderful mentor he's been. And I like the way he handled himself after his hands were burned. It must have been very frustrating for him, to hand over such responsibility. But he did it gracefully. I like him. He's a good man. Also very talented. Temperamental, but then, aren't all artists? How is it between the two of you?"

I feel myself flush a little. "I'm not sure," I say slowly. "I feel as if I'm always mentally plucking petals off a daisy: he loves me…he loves me not…he loves me."

"I told you he was mercurial back in Giverny…remember?"

I nod. "I wasn't listening then. I was so caught up in the drama of meeting you, discovering the amazing coincidences about Angel, the paintings, the potential for our project. It was so intense that Victor and I just sort of fell, drowning into each other. I don't know how else to put it." I pause. "Then when we came back, he seemed to withdraw. I don't know if it was tension between him and Chad or the pressure of the documentary. Or, just what you said about him at Giverny—that he's mercurial. As if that's an excuse."

"Men! They blame us, but it is they who never make it easy. I think he does love you. But perfection in love is ephemeral under the most ideal circumstances. Remember what I told you: you must know a man through all four seasons before you can determine if he is the right one."

"I've barely known Victor for one season. And yet it's as if I can't remember a time when I didn't love him. As if he's always existed in my heart and my senses. But so often, I have no idea who he really is."

When Victor bursts through the door Monday morning, singing, "Oh, What a Beautiful Mornin'," I feel a mix of relief at the sight of him, and resentment that he hasn't phoned all weekend. But he's so buoyant, helping himself to a cup of coffee as if he'd never left, that when he pecks me on the cheek, saying mockingly, "Honey, I'm home," all my anger dissipates.

Chad slouches at the kitchen table, reading the sports section. Victor gives the paper a whack. "So, sweetie," he croons in a falsetto voice, "did you miss me?"

Without looking up, Chad says, "You mean the snoring part or the farting part?"

In a lightning motion, Victor has one arm around Chad's neck and the other, despite the stiffness of his hands, attempting to raze his scalp with a noogie. Chad easily slips out of his grasp, and the two chase each other out into the back yard, laughing, as the screen door slams behind them.

In the final draft of the script, I've written a segment depicting the reunion of Daniel and Angel at the École des Beaux-Artes in Paris. At that time, a few years after Willie's death, Angel had traveled from Ireland, where she'd been living and painting, to attend a gallery exhibit of her own work in Paris. At the opening, much of the gossip centered around a current exhibition of Daniel Duvall's paintings. It was called

The Angel Collection and was said to be a series of paintings featuring a woman and child.

Angel anguished over whether her fragile, still wounded psyche could withstand the sight of *The Angel Collection*, but after a restless night's sleep, she'd gathered her courage and made a solitary pilgrimage to the École Des Beaux-Artes. Not far from the entrance, on the Quai Malaquais, in a heart-stopping juxtaposition of fates, she encountered Daniel Duvall. They had a brief, awkward, painful exchange, then went their separate ways.

Angel proceeded on to the exhibit hall, where she came face-to-face with the tangible evidence of Daniel's love for her and his torment over the loss of Willie.

Moments later, Daniel was suddenly by her side, and with the paintings of *The Angel Collection* as silent witnesses, an emotional reconciliation followed.

Since I had experience as a voice-over artist, we all agreed that I would play Angel in the scenes lifted directly from her journals. Victor had a wonderful speaking voice and had actually cut some scratch sound tracks back in the days when he was shooting sports for the network, so in the interests of saving money, we had decided that he would play Daniel.

Chad and Victor had jerry-rigged a recording booth in the closet of the guest room, where the editing equipment was set up.

Now, on the appointed morning, as Chad and Victor fiddle with wires and switches and microphones, I'm jittery and keep going over and over the script, suddenly insecure about casting myself as Angel. Chad oversees the soundboard while Madame, as script supervisor, takes a seat next to him. It's hot and unusually humid for June, and as Victor and I squeeze into the tiny closet, with its Styrofoamed sound-proof walls, it feels airless. Our bodies are standing pressed together, clutching scripts in front of the microphone. We both start to perspire almost immediately. Despite the pressure and focus of the job at hand, the close quarters enliven my senses. I feel the press of Victor's arm against mine, inhale the familiar, heady aroma of his skin, his hair. I'm even aware of breathing his breath as the oxygen in the tiny space closes in on us. We put on our headphones and practice sound levels until Chad calls out that he is ready to record.

Then the tape is rolling, and Chad says, "This is take one of Beaux-Artes voice-over. Whenever you're ready."

I count down, "Three, two…" a pause, and then, holding the papers as steadily as I can, I begin to read.

"*I felt very small as I entered the enormous chamber of the* cour vitrée *and passed under the soaring glass and metal skylight that hovered two stories above the hall like a transparent skeletal canopy.*

"*The steady click of my heels echoed on the marble floor and floated up past the double tiers of columned arches that bordered the vast room. A pleasant buzzing had begun in my head, and I felt detached, outside of myself, as if I were watching the straight-backed woman in the rust-colored cloak as she approached the exhibit called* The Angel Collection.*"*

At this point in the journal, now the script I am reading, Angel had suddenly changed her perspective from first person to that of observer. She was watching herself. It was as if the intensity of the experience required emotional distance. I understood that and tried to create a dream-like quality to my reading.

"*I watched her enter the small gallery and pause at the door, taking in the life-sized painting on the opposite wall. I saw her eyes widen and her pupils dilate in awe at the shimmering portrait of herself as she stood reflected in the huge gilt mirror of Daniel's studio, painting her own self-portrait. It was the painting that Daniel had called, 'Angel'— the luminescent rendering of a woman, half mortal, half celestial being, that symbolized the beginning of their affair.*"

A wave of heat rises from my groin, up to the roots of my hair. It was that same gilt mirror that had galvanized Victor and me in Daniel Duvall's studio. I remember the madness that swept over us, how we sank to the floor, our hands all over each other; how Chad came running up the stairs, so frantic about what he thought he saw in the pond. I force myself to concentrate on the words before me.

"*I watched the woman as her eyes briefly swept the room. There were at least a dozen paintings. The colors leapt up at her, swirled around her. They were the colors of buttery sunlight, verdant greens, creamy flesh, silvery-blue waters, violet shadows, crimson berries. The woman took a few steps forward, studying herself in the painting called, 'Angel Rising,' as she emerged naked from the tranquil pool, her dark hair matted with water and cascading over her shoulders, her arms stretched out above her head, her chin tilted up, exultant. There were three other nudes. One, kneeling on the grass next to the pool, holding a cluster of wild strawberries, mouth opened like a baby bird, poised to bite into the succulently sharlet—shucculent—*

"I'm sorry," I say, stopping. "Could I pick that up?"

"No problem," replies Chad through the headset. "We're still rolling."

My eyes race over the copy, mentally rehearsing the words that had caught me: succulently scarlet. My face feels scarlet. It's unlike me to stumble during a reading. I begin again.

"Poised to bite into the succulently scarlet heart-shaped berries."

I relax a little, having gotten through the sentence.

"Another of the nude from a distance, her long, languorous limbs stretched out on the blanket, the curve of her hip a blend of blush and shadowy gray-blues. Her head rested on her arm, and the remains of a picnic lay half on the blanket and half on the grass.

"The woman moved slowly along the gallery walls, taking in every detail of every painting with eyes that revealed nothing and a face that reflected nothing.

"Then she stopped, and her hand moved to her chest. The painting was on the opposite wall, and it was large, life-size. Big enough to walk into. The woman slowly moved toward it and put her hand out, as if to touch it. And she did touch it. She touched the face of the little boy in the painting, the little boy with the coppery curls, who reclined in his mother's arms, as they leaned against the manger in the sun-drenched field."

A drop of sweat trickles its way over my eyebrow and lid, into my eye, stinging, and suddenly I'm blinded. Both my eyes blur with tears, and despite blinking rapidly, I can't see to read the words on the paper.

"I'm sorry," I say. "I have to stop again."

"What's the matter?" murmurs Victor.

"Are you okay, Mom?"

"Can you open the door?" I say to Victor. "I need some air."

Victor pushes the door open, and I climb past him. Madame looks up at me with concern. Chad seems mildly irritated.

"Bathroom break," I announce.

I hurry across the hall and close the door behind me. I turn on the water, let it run cold, and splash my face several times. A gentle breeze flows in the lone window, and as I dry my face and sink down on the toilet, I shut my eyes and let the waft of air sweep over me. Suddenly, I'm doubled over with cramps, and it feels as though the bottom half of my body is exploding away from me. More sweat pops out on my face. It's a different kind of sweat. A cold sweat. For several minutes, I huddle there, crippled. A sudden, vivid sense memory of my first encounter with *The Angel Collection* at The Musée d'Orsay springs to mind. How I'd felt dizzy, nauseated. How I'd fainted. I take deep breaths and lower my head between my knees, until the lightheadedness subsides.

My legs are rubbery as I splash water on my face again. I drink a glass of water and let the cool crystal rest against my forehead for a moment. Then I dry my face again and make my wobbly way back across the hall.

Three pairs of eyes stare at me, assessing.

"You're so pale, my dear," says Madame. "Are you feeling well?"

"I don't know," I answer. "I think I might have a touch of virus."

I turn back toward the booth. "Let's go again," I say.

Victor and I resume our places, don the headphones, and wait.

"Rolling, Beaux Artes voice-over, take two," says Chad.

There's a knot in my throat. *Jesus Christ*, I think to myself, *I hope I don't* throw up.

I begin to read.

"The little boy was looking up at his mama's face, and his hand caressed her cheek as she smiled down on him. It was a painting of joy and possibility and well-being, and the woman laid her cheek against the canvas, and closed her eyes, and uttered just the whisper of something—a sigh, maybe, or a little moan. It was as if she wanted to climb into the painting, to climb into it and be frozen in it, frozen in the sunlight, and trapped in the happiness, and captured in the sheer solace of it. It was called, 'Angel in Paradise.'"

A wave of nausea undulates from my stomach, up to the back of my throat. I stumble over the words.

"Cut!" I say, feeling terribly unprofessional. I turn to Victor and mumble, "I'm sorry."

"What's going on?" he says.

"I just need to get out of here for another minute." I pull off the headphones, and he pushes the door open. I practically fall across him in my scramble to escape. Madame and Chad look on with concern as I drop into a chair.

"Mom?" says Chad.

"I don't know what's the matter with me," I say. "Maybe the flu coming on. Could we take ten minutes? I'm just going to lie down to see if it passes."

"Of course, of course. Go on," says Madame. "We'll all take a break."

I make my way to my bedroom and gratefully stretch out on the cool white duvet. Closing my eyes, I will the nausea away as Angel's images and emotions swirl in my brain.

"Mom?"

I open my eyes. Chad stands uncertainly at the door. "Are you okay?"

I pat the bed. "Hi, sweetie. I'm sorry to gum up the works."

He sits down gingerly. "No, I know it's not like you. Can I get you something?"

I gaze at his beautiful face, his brow lined with concern. So very different from the hostile, accusing young man who had come so reluctantly to live with me a few short months ago.

"I love you, son," I say, my eyes welling up. "I love you so much. You know I never ever meant to hurt you. I would rather die than hurt you."

"I know that, Mom. That's all behind us."

"You have to believe me. If I'd known what would happen, I never would have done it. Never!"

"Mom, you didn't do anything. It's okay."

"You should have come first! You always should have come first! I'm sorry. Oh, so sorry!"

Then it's as if the floodgates burst open. I begin to sob without restraint. The tears pour out.

"I can't lose you!" I cry, "I can't lose you!"

"Mom! Mom, come on, it's okay. You're okay. We're okay."

He puts his arms around me, and I hold onto him, sensing a dark cavity of immeasurable loss, of never-ending loss, of love that could never be retrieved, not in this lifetime or the next.

I cry until his shirt is soaking wet, and he holds onto me all through it, saying, "Shhh, it's okay, it's okay, Mom."

Finally, I grow quiet. The terrible thoughts begin to retreat. I feel my limbs relaxing. I blow my nose, splash water on my face, and brush my hair. Then Chad and I return to the editing room, where Madame and Victor are waiting.

"Okay," I say. Let's go again."

Victor and I resume our places in the tiny closet. He draws the door shut, and I await Chad's cue.

"We're rolling. Voice-over for Beaux-Artes, take three."

I continue.

"She leaned against it for several minutes, with her cheek against the cool, hard, bumpy surface of the canvas. Finally she pulled back, and her eyes were shimmering now, as she blinked twice and moved on to a series of portraits of Willie. Willie chasing a rooster, and Willie squatting down to pick a violet, and Willie and her bumping down the lane on the bicycle.

"The woman's steps slowed now, and her shoulders folded in slightly, like trembling feathered wings.

"She stood in front of the last painting. Unlike the others, this one was dark and sinister, with menacing skies and swirling, violent waters. The only touch of color was a red ball in the lower left-hand corner.

"It was the pond.

"It was called, 'Paradise Lost.'

"The woman put her hand up to her mouth and seemed to sway on her feet for a moment, then she backed away, letting out a sharp cry. With trembling fingers, she drew out her handkerchief and pressed it against her lips, trying to swallow the bile that threatened to spew out onto the marble floor.

"And then she felt a hand on her shoulder, and without thought, she sank back, allowing familiar strong arms to encircle her. A sigh of a thousand years passed her lips as she gratefully closed her eyes and turned, reaching out and holding on to all that was left of her life.

"They stood clinging and shuddering, as their separate sorrows merged and roiled and erupted together in a cataclysm of emotion, sacred and terrible in its power.

"Half words, moans, utterances, spilled out on top of each other. Little rivers of unshed tears blended and blinded, making way for more cleansing rivers. And still they stood, locked together in loss and shame, riveted to the moment that both had feared and sought throughout the endless loneliness of their separation."

It is finally Victor's turn at the microphone. *"I can't—"*

I say, *"I heard him murmur."*

"I can't—" Victor reads.

"And slowly I drew back my head, and through swollen eyes, looked on that one dear face contorted with anguish, gazed at those crystalline eyes bleary with tears."

Victor is crying. Tears course down his face. I try to keep my eyes on the page, but I feel his body trembling, can literally smell the salt of his tears. I want to reach for him, to hold him in my arms, but we both continue with the script.

"I can't bring him back!" reads Victor. *"If I could trade my life for his, I would, but I can't bring him back!"* Victor speaks the lines with emotion that pierces my heart.

Then I speak again.

"I leaned my cheek against his, feeling the warm sticky wetness.

"'Shhh,' I said softly, gently caressing his hair. 'Shhh, now. It's all right. Shhh.'

"And I led him over to a bench, and we sank down onto it, and I held him and rocked him like a baby. And he cried like a baby as we rested there together, and in front of us, looking out at us, my other baby, my Willie laughed in my arms as we lay on the grass beside the manger at Aquatong Farm, forever joined and forever sundered by the love of Daniel Duvall."

It is over. Victor's script slides from his hands, and I let go of mine as we turn into each other's arms and embrace fiercely in the tiny closed space, both of us weeping without shame.

"Hey, you guys coming out of there?"

Suddenly the door is flung open, and Chad stands there. "That was amazing. Mom, what a recovery. I knew you could do it. You two were awesome together. Wait'll you hear the playback!"

Behind Chad I can see Madame wiping her eyes.

Victor and I quickly disengage and step out of the booth. I'm shaky, but I feel cleansed somehow. That "after-a-spring-rain" cleanliness that coats the world with a sheen of radiance. I feel almost disembodied, lightened with grace and gratitude.

Madame comes to me. "My dear," she says, her eyes glistening, "I am so moved. You made me feel—" Here she turns to include Victor. "Both of you made me feel that Angel and Daniel were here in the room with us. It was extraordinary."

"Holy Christ!" says Victor, grabbing a tissue. "I need a drink!" He looks at me. "I think I know what they mean by Method acting. What the hell happened in there? You made me feel like we were inhabiting those people! Or they were inhabiting us! Look, I've still got goose bumps!" He holds out his arm, and sure enough, it's covered with tiny bumps.

Despite the emotion of the past several minutes, he looks jubilant, triumphant.

I think at this moment we all know that the documentary is going to exceed our expectations.

TWENTY-FIVE

C H A P T E R

1996

On Saturday, August 23, Victor and Chad insert the final credits into the documentary.

THE ANGEL COLLECTION
A film by Morgan Reed and Victor Cenzo
Executive Producer: Anne-Claire Goudonov Sancerre
Producers: Morgan Reed, Victor Cenzo, Chad Reed
Written by Morgan Reed
Directed by Victor Cenzo
Cinematographers/Editors: Victor Cenzo, Chad Reed

347

I readily agreed when Victor insisted that Chad share equal credit with us. Chad had proved himself as a professional. His talent and perseverance had contributed greatly to the project, which was scheduled for its premiere screening for the entire Historic Society membership the following night at The Milltown Inn. I was particularly proud that Chad had taken back our family name.

This Saturday has extra special significance. It's Madame's birthday, and she's hosting a celebratory dinner for the four of us at the La Bonne Auberge, an elegant French restaurant in New Hope. While Victor went home to shower and change, Chad burned the master DVD, carefully placing it in its plastic case, marked, simply, MASTER.

As I slipped into a turquoise sundress, my mirror told me that I looked marvelous, and gratitude settled over me, like a cherished fragrance.

We're a triumphant group that gathers on the patio this summer evening, heady with accomplishment and camaraderie. The air is balmy, but not too hot. The combined fragrances of freshly mown grass, honeysuckle, and even a trace of the flourishing tomato plants drifts across the yard like an intoxicating happiness cocktail.

Victor arrives at seven, looking sexy and handsome in a beautiful white linen shirt and beige linen trousers. He brings a chilled bottle of Dom Pérignon, and we fill an ice bucket, take champagne glasses down from the cabinet, and carry it all outside.

Madame positively glows as she emerges from the house, elegantly coiffed and dressed in a beautifully cut raspberry silk suit.

When my son steps outside, being careful not to slam the screen door, I can't move from where I stand. He's wearing a blue shirt that matches his eyes. His hair is carefully slicked back, still damp from the shower. The grizzled stubble is gone, revealing his beautiful face and strong jaw. As he approaches me, kissing my cheek, we exchange a look that holds nothing but love and mutual respect, and in that moment I know that his past grievances are at rest. We're on a new course. I hug him tightly.

"I love you," I whisper.

"I love you too," he replies.

When the four of us are assembled, Victor pours the champagne and raises his glass.

"To *The Angel Collection*," he says.

"To *The Angel Collection*," we all echo, clinking glasses. I sip and let the fizzing bubbles dance on my tongue.
This is happiness.

At La Bonne Auberge, our table is situated next to a stone wall banked with wisteria. In the purple dusk, votive candles flicker, their light bouncing off the crystal glasses. Just inside the French doors, a pianist plays jazz classics. Madame whispers to the sommelier, and within moments, he reappears bearing an expensive bottle of Chateau Margaux for her approval. The evening is launched.

When the wine has been poured, we each present our gifts to Madame. Victor gives her a set of coasters from the Michener museum. Each one depicts a scene of local pastoral beauty. Chad hands her a pink baseball cap inscribed with "Milltown Historic Society." She laughs with pleasure. "A perfect memento from Milltown!" she exclaims. "I shall wear it when I'm gardening at Giverny!"

I had wrapped the Clara Shaw Bible in tissue and placed it in a pretty gift bag. When it's my turn, I present it to her. Chad, Victor, and I exchange looks as we wait for her reaction. As she gently unwraps the tissue and lifts out the worn Bible, she seems merely curious. But when she turns the first page and reads the inscription to Clara Shaw, the Bible's significance registers. Her jaw drops. She looks up at me, and her eyes are glistening.

"Oh! My dear! How did you ever—?" Her chin begins to tremble, and for a moment I worry that culmination of the week's events, in all their intensity, have been too much for her. But she wipes her eyes and gives me a big hug, thanking me again and again, and turning the Bible over in her hands as if it were a miracle. I gladly relate every detail of how I found the Bible at the book antiquarian's booth on Milltown Day. When I finish my story, she says, "This is the most extraordinary gift I have ever received." Then, indicating the baseball hat and the coasters, she says, "Thank you, all of you."

We raise our glasses. "Happy Birthday," we chime.

"And what a happy one it is," she agrees. "Une vrai Bonne Anniversaire! Merci, merci beaucoup!"

The conversation, laughter, and mutual accolades pass back and forth. We're heady with the relief and satisfaction of a job very well done. Madame keeps ordering more wine, and, somewhere between the entrée and the salad, I notice that Chad has begun slurring his words.

After the waiter takes our dessert order, Chad pushes back his chair and announces that he's going out to the parking lot for a smoke. The three of us watch him make his unsteady way across the patio and around the stone wall into the darkness.

Despite the amount of wine I've consumed, I feel a rush of anxiety and embarrassment.

"I'm afraid I have to apologize for my son," I say to Madame. "He seems to have gotten carried away with all this fabulous wine."

Madame responds graciously. "Oh, I think he's not the first young man to test his own limits. Shall I cancel the champagne I've ordered for our dessert?"

"That's probably a good idea," I say. "Thank you."

Victor pushes back his chair. "I'm going to the men's room. I'll tell the waiter about the champagne. And I'll check on Chad, too."

"Thanks," I say. Then I whisper, "And don't be too long. We have a cake coming!"

Some minutes later, Victor escorts a flushed Chad back to the table just as the birthday cake arrives in a dazzle of sparklers and candles. Other diners join in as we sing "Happy Birthday," and then everyone applauds. A beaming Madame tilts her head in a kind of bow, then extinguishes all the candles in one breath.

It's nearing eleven when we pull into the driveway of the Rectory. Victor half carries Chad into the house and up the stairs, while Madame and I say our good nights. Outside her little room off the kitchen, we embrace each other for a long time.

"Thank you so much for tonight," I say. "It was so wonderful. All of us celebrating together. I'm sorry about Chad. I'm going to have a word with him tomorrow."

"I expect he might have a bit of a headache in the morning, poor boy," Madame says. "As far as this evening, and this whole time together—it is I who thanks you. You and Victor and Chad. You've all become like my family."

"I feel the same way," I tell her.

"It's going to be difficult saying good-bye to you." In a motherly gesture, she pinches my cheek. "You must promise me that you'll look after yourself. Make that man do right by you!"

"I will," I say.

"And I expect you to come and visit me in Giverny often. You must consider it your second home."

"We will. I promise," I say.

"Good night, then, my dear, dear girl. Thank you for bringing Angel back to life." She kisses me on both cheeks, the French way.

I squeeze both her hands. "Good night, dear Madame Sancerre, and happy birthday."

I walk back into the living room just as Victor comes down the stairs. "How is he?" I ask.

"I held his head while he puked his guts up. He's going to have a hell of a hangover. I came down to get him some aspirin and a glass of ice water."

"I feel like going up there and pouring the ice water on his head."

"Oh, don't be too hard on him. He was just letting off steam. And, hey, it was great wine."

"Oh, come on, Victor. He doesn't deserve a pass on this. I can't believe he pulled such a stunt, tonight of all nights. I was so embarrassed in front of Madame. I thought he'd straightened himself out. Now I don't know what to think. Is he an alcoholic?"

"Morgan, you're overreacting. Let him sleep it off, and talk to him in the morning. Or if you want me to, I'll talk to him. We'll talk to him together. For now, let me handle it." He heads for the kitchen. I follow.

"I'm going to take this up to him and get him settled," he says, running the cold water and reaching into the cabinet for a glass.

I pull out the bottle of aspirin and hand it to him.

"Meet me out on the patio," he says. "I want to talk to you."

I fill a big glass of water for myself and carry it outside. As I pull a chaise lounge onto the grass, I gaze up at Chad's window and see a light blink on. Then I see Victor's shadow move across the room. I feel a sense of relief that he's handling this and not me.

I sink down onto the chaise and listen to the swaying rustle of the trees. A breeze rises, and the fragrance of the air is pungent, sensual even. Above, the stars close in, like a net of crystals descending onto the sleeping earth. I wrap my arms around myself and wonder what it is that Victor wants to say.

The Pond

TWENTY-SIX
CHAPTER

1895

"Mama, get up."

My eyelids felt thick and swollen, my limbs like deadweights.

"Mama?"

With great effort, I opened my eyes and looked at him. His lower lip stuck out in a little pout, and his round ocean-gray eyes were clouded over with concern.

"Mama doesn't feel well, Willie. I need to stay in bed today."

"But you stayed in bed yesterday, Mama. I don't want you to be sick."

I closed my eyes against the sight of him, and the sunlight, and the pain that throbbed in my head and my breast, and in my soul.

"I'm sorry, sweetheart," I said thickly.

"Will you get up tomorrow?" he asked, laying his head on the pillow next to me.

"Maybe," I said. "Maybe tomorrow." I caressed his face and felt the tears trickle out of the corners of my eyes and into my hair.

"Don't cry, Mama." His eyes filled up.

I wiped my face. "I'm not crying, honey," I said. "Only a wee bit. Why don't you ask Clara to take you to pick blueberries today? Then she can make a nice blueberry cobbler. Wouldn't you like that?"

"And Papa would like it, too," he said. "Papa likes blueberry cobbler."

"Yes, he does," I said. "Papa likes blueberry cobbler, too. And he'll be home for dinner tonight, and won't that be a nice surprise for him?"

"Will you eat dinner with us tonight?"

"Maybe I will. Maybe if you let me rest now, I'll feel well enough to get up for dinner tonight. You give me a get well kiss, and go back down to Clara."

He kissed me on my cheek with a big smacking sound and ran out of the room, calling, "Clara! Mama said we should go pick blueberries for a cobbler for Papa and me."

As soon as he was out of sight, I turned on my back and put my hands over my face as the sobs pushed up out of my chest, into my throat, shaking the bed.

I felt like a figure in a Hieronymus Bosch painting, trapped in a dead woman's body. Half animal, half human, torturing my sinful soul from within.

All I wanted was sleep, but it wouldn't come. I had lain awake all night, every night, then pleaded illness during the day, barely able to lift my head from the pillow.

William had been very patient with me, concerned that I might be coming down with some grave illness.

I wished that I would.

I wanted to be overtaken by some rare and fatal disease, one that I could sink into, drifting through the endless days and nights of my future in a morphine-induced coma. I didn't want to move or speak or think.

I didn't want to be.

I never said I loved you.

Another wave of humiliation engulfed me. How could I have been so mistaken about his feelings for me? How could something that felt so real, so true, so powerful, be anything other than love? Had I been so caught up in my own feelings that I misinterpreted his? If what Daniel and I had experienced together wasn't love, then what was love, after all?

I was a fool. An ignorant fool. An adulteress.

A whore.

And still the demons darted about inside me, mocking me, pulling at my insides, stirring my loins until I almost cried out with craving. I wanted to stuff myself with something, anything, to stop the drawing, aching pull between my legs, in my core. The void down there seemed enormous, unfillable. It amazed me that just days ago, when he had been inside me, it all felt so snug, so tight, so compact and warm.

Now, something ugly and useless. A gaping maw.

I hated myself.

And still I loved him.

It was guilt and guilt alone that heaved me out of my bed, forced me to wash my face, put on a robe, and appear at the dinner table.

"If you're not better by tomorrow, I'm getting Dr. Mardigian over here," said William, setting down his coffee cup. "I don't like your pallor."

"I'll be better tomorrow," I lied. "But, if you don't mind, I think I'll go back up now."

William stood up and came over to me, pulling out my chair and gently helping me to my feet.

"I'll take you up," he said.

"Night-night, Mama," said Willie. His mouth was smeared with blueberries.

"Good night, sweetheart," I said, feeling too weak to walk over to kiss him.

William guided me up the stairs and into bed. I lay back on the pillow as he tucked the covers around me and sat down on the bed.

He put his hand on my forehead. "You don't have a fever," he said. "That's a relief."

"I will be better tomorrow," I said. "Really."

"Well, if you're not, I'm fetching the doctor before I leave for Frenchtown." He leaned down and kissed my forehead. "I've been neglecting you, haven't I?" he said tenderly.

"No, of course not," I said, avoiding his loving gaze. "I know how important your work is. It's all right."

He stared at me thoughtfully. "Maybe you should start dabbling in your painting again. I know how much you enjoy it."

Crickets chirruped outside the window, and somewhere in the distance a dog barked.

There was a bitter taste in my mouth as I said in a small voice, "I don't know if I enjoy it as much as I used to." My chin wobbled, and I turned away from him to hide the tears. "But, thank you," I whispered.

The next morning, to avoid a doctor's visit, I left my bed, dressed, and walked with Willie down the road to the village.

"Good morning, Mrs. Laury! So nice to see you out and about." It was Jonathan Paist, the choirmaster. He bent down to pinch Willie's cheek. "How's the little man?" Then, straightening, he said, "Beautiful morning, isn't it?" I nodded, forcing a smile.

"It surely is," I said.

As I made the round of errands, I felt like a stick figure, all stiff arms and legs, no roundness of flesh, no animated expression.

At home I resumed my schedule, helping Clara with the chores, passing through the days and nights and nights and days. Numbness alternating with pain and back to numbness.

Like a miser counting and recounting her money, I went over everything he said the last time we were together, searching for nuggets of proof that he really cared. Then I would come back to his final words:

I never said I loved you.

A week passed. Two weeks. I watched the hours and days drip by as from a distance. I was in them, but I was not involved in them. I lived through them, but I wasn't really alive.

He would be leaving for Paris soon. Maybe he was already gone. Maybe he left early because there was another woman waiting for him there. Maybe he was in her arms right now. Maybe he was telling her about me, about how silly and foolish I was. Maybe they were laughing at me. I stared at my reflection in the mirror, the red-rimmed eyes, the sunken cheeks. My ears pounded with the sound of their laughter: his deep and rumbling, hers high-pitched and mocking. I watched in fascination as my hands gripped my skull, wrapping and weaving my lank hair tightly around my knuckles, pressing it all against my ears.

"Mama?"

Willie stood at the bedroom door. I turned quickly, realizing as I did so that clumps of hair lay limply in my hands.

Then his letter came.

I awoke that morning with the same leaden weight in my breast, my nightgown sticking to me, my hair damp.

The kitchen was already stifling when I arrived downstairs. William and Clara were seated at the kitchen table. Willie was nibbling on a piece of bread.

William looked up. "Ah, Evangeline, I was just telling Clara that I have a little surprise for her."

I looked at Clara. She seemed pale.

"What is it?" I said, pouring myself a cup of coffee.

William looked inordinately pleased. Relieved, even.

"I've been to visit her cousins in Wycombe. I've had a long conversation with them about Clara. We've discussed her situation, and they've agreed to meet with her today. I believe that if I can get everyone to sit down face-to-face, we can work out an arrangement that will benefit Clara. All of us." He smiled. "I think they're willing to forgive and forget. I venture to predict that they may be willing to take her in after the... after her confinement. Offer her a home for herself and the child."

"Oh," I said. "Oh." I turned to Clara and searched her face. "That's good. Isn't it, Clara?"

She shrugged and nodded. "I guess so. Yes, if that's what you and the Reverend want."

"Well," said William expansively, "it's the best thing for you and the child, Clara. You have to think of your future. Of course you'll want to be with family. Everyone wants to be with family at times like this. We've been your... your interim family, but soon it will be time to move on."

Clara bowed her head, nodding silently.

"So I'm taking Clara to call on her relatives this afternoon. Right after lunch." He rose. "I've some calls to make in the village and some paper work that needs attention at the church. I'll be back for lunch, and then we'll set out." He kissed me, and kissed Willie, and said, "I'll see you all later." Then he disappeared out the back door.

I came out of the General Store and carried my parcels over to my bicycle. I was about to set the packages down in the basket, when I saw a flash of white. I reached into the basket and pulled out an envelope.

Written on it was one word: "Angel."

My heart began to pound as I looked around, expecting to see him. Then I feared that someone might be watching me. I stuffed the envelope in my pocket and got on the bicycle, pedaling a little way down Milltown Road to the bridge over the Paunacussing Creek. I leaned the bicycle against the stone wall and walked down the grassy slope to the underside of the bridge, where I would be hidden from passing traffic.

Clusters of gnats swarmed around me as I pressed my hand against the letter in my pocket, wanting to savor the moment, wanting to feel the outline of it against my body, wanting to allow myself the first release, the first glimmer of hope that I'd felt in almost three weeks. I was weak with the relief of it. For that moment I didn't even care what the letter said. All that mattered was that it was from him. That he was still in my world and still thinking of me as I had been thinking of him.

I pulled the letter from my pocket. The stationery was thick and cream colored. On the return flap, the initials "DD" were engraved in an elaborate script. I pressed the envelope to my lips and breathed deeply, trying to inhale the essence of him through the paper.

With trembling fingers, I pulled back the flap and withdrew the folded paper within.

My dearest Angel,
Without you there is no light by which to see, no air by which to breathe. I must meet with you before my departure for Paris. I beseech you to come to me this afternoon. Please, my love, receive this letter with a merciful heart.
Your Daniel

I stifled a sob and sank to the grassy bank next to the creek. Trickling water echoed under the hollow arch of the little bridge. Heart pounding,

I read the words again, and tears blinded me as my eyes rested on the words, "my love."

"Oh! And you are my love!" I sobbed, kissing the words, laughing and crying, and holding the precious paper in trembling fingers, as if it were a wounded butterfly. I wanted to clamber up the slope on my hands and knees and run down the road toward the river, toward Aquatong Farm. I wanted to sprout wings and fly there, afraid that if I allowed one more second to pass, this miracle would evaporate, he would change his mind, all hope would be lost. My mind began to race as I remembered that Clara would be leaving with William directly after lunch to visit her relatives near Wycombe. There was no one to stay with Willie.

I rose to my feet, putting the letter back in my pocket. I would take him with me. He could play outside while Daniel and I talked.

My arms and legs were like rags as I pedaled through the village square. The bicycle swerved, and I nearly lost my balance several times.

I arrived back at the house just as William was walking across the yard from the church. He waved to me. I parked the bicycle against the side of the house and lifted my packages from the basket, trying to gain control of my breathing before he reached me. In momentary panic, I fancied he could see through the fabric of my dress into my pocket, that he would take one look at me, and say, "What is it that you're hiding in your pocket?"

Instead, he approached with a broad smile, saying, "You're looking particularly glowing and healthy today. You've actually got some color back in your cheeks!"

And he kissed me lightly.

"I was thinking," he said, as we walked across the back porch and into the kitchen, "that I'll make some ice cream this weekend. Maybe Sunday afternoon, after services. Willie's just about old enough to help me turn the handle, and he'll certainly enjoy licking off the dasher. Won't you, young fellow?" He swept Willie up in his arms.

"Won't I what, Papa?" said Willie, grinning.

"Won't you like licking the dasher when we make ice cream!"

Willie's eyes widened. "Can we make ice cream?" he said, clapping his hands together.

"Yes, we can! Can't we, Mama?" William turned to me.

"Yes, yes, of course," I mumbled, smiling dumbly.

359

"We're two big strong men, and we've got the muscles to turn that handle around and around." He squeezed Willie. "Show me your muscle," he said.

Willie raised his arms, bending them at the elbows and making fists. William made a show out of feeling the muscles. "Yessir. I think you're strong enough to make ice cream."

"Lunch is ready," said Clara, setting plates of cold meat and sliced tomatoes on the table. I noticed that she had taken extra care with her hair and was wearing her Sunday dress, the sides and waist having been let out to accommodate her expanding middle. She seemed distracted and on edge, barely acknowledging the ice cream conversation and Willie's obvious excitement.

The four of us sat down to eat, but Clara barely touched her food, and my stomach was in such turmoil that I knew I would be sick if I swallowed one bite. My arms felt mechanical and rigid as I made a sandwich for Willie. I watched each piece of food on William's plate as he scooped it onto his fork and raised it to his lips. I concentrated on how long it took him to chew each bite, and silently cursed him when he took a second helping.

The clock in the dining room chimed once for the half hour, and I prayed that Clara and William would be out of the house by one o'clock so that I could rush upstairs to wash my face, and brush my hair, and dab lavender cologne on my neck and wrists, and between my breasts. I felt myself growing moist at the thought of preparing myself to see Daniel. Involuntarily I shifted in the chair, squeezing my thighs together as the familiar craving snaked its way between my legs. Then I remembered that Willie would be with me. There would be no way that Daniel and I could make love. And after all this time! How would we keep our hands to ourselves? *Well, we would have to*, I told myself. Besides, after today, after we made our plans, there would be all the time in the world to make love. The rest of our lives.

I looked at William. He was ruffling Willie's hair and laughing at something Willie had said. My throat constricted. He was a good man. A decent man.

It was better not to think about it.

Finally, blessedly, lunch was over. After a brief washing up, William helped Clara into the carriage, and they rolled down the lane, out onto Holicong Road, and up the hill.

I flew upstairs, hastily performed my toilette, grabbed Willie by the hand, led him outside and across the porch, lifted him into the basket, mounted my bicycle, and careened out of the lane, down to the village square, over the creek bridge, and onto Old Milltown Road.

A crowing rooster heralded our arrival into the clearing. The tinkle of bells drew Willie's attention to the cluster of lambs grazing by the fence with their mothers. I was amazed at how much they'd grown in just a few weeks.

"Look, Mama!" shouted Willie, pointing to the lambs and trying to stand up in the basket.

"Wait," I said. "Wait until we stop, and I'll lift you out, and we can go look at them."

I leaned the bicycle against the fence, searching for Daniel as I did so. He was nowhere in sight.

I lifted Willie down and, taking his hand, walked a little way down the length of the fence. The sheep were padlocked in one area adjacent to the smaller meadow that surrounded the cottage and the water-wheel and the pond. Ducks and geese floated gracefully across the still waters, flipping their feathery tails and quacking contentedly. Willie put his hand through the fence to touch the recently shorn fleece of a ewe. Then he moved down the fence until we were standing facing the pond.

"Quack, quack," he called. "See the duckies, Mama?"

"I see them," I said, enjoying his pleasure and looking back up toward the studio.

"How can they walk on the water, Mama?"

"They're not walking. They're swimming," I said.

"Are they baptie, Mama?"

"No," I said. "They're just swimming. Just duckies swimming to stay cool on this hot summer day."

"Can I baptie like Papa? In the water?"

"When you get big, you can baptize," I said, then thought of William and was overcome with guilt.

"Angel!"

His voice exploded through me, and I turned around. He was standing on the balcony. He waved to me and disappeared through the French doors. Leaving Willie at the fence, I hurried across the lane and up the slope.

The door to the studio was flung open, and he came through it, bigger and more powerful than I remembered him. My heart stopped, and we looked at each other, each frozen to the spot.

Slowly, he came toward me, his face a study in exhaustion and relief. I noted with tenderness that he looked as if he hadn't slept in days. He had several days' growth of beard, and the crystal blue eyes were bloodshot and red rimmed. I wanted to cradle him like a baby.

We stood face-to-face, gazing, searching.

"I was afraid you wouldn't come," he said finally.

"You knew I'd come," I said. His eyes traveled over my shoulder toward the fence.

"I brought Willie," I said. "Clara had to go off with William."

"I'm glad you brought him," he said. Then he took my arm. "I'd like to go down and say hello."

We strolled across the lane to where Willie stood, his face pressed against the fence, watching the ducks.

"Willie, this is Mr. Duvall. You remember him."

Daniel squatted down on his haunches next to Willie. "Hello, Willie," he said gently. "What do you think of that waterwheel?"

"What's the waterwheel?" said Willie, looking Daniel over.

Daniel pointed. "It's that big wheel over there. See it? It picks the water up, and spins it around, and makes it come down the other side."

Willie looked to where Daniel was pointing. "Well, how does it work, anyway?" he said.

"Would you like to get a closer look?" said Daniel, standing up.

"Yes," said Willie.

"Well, I'll show you. Come on." Daniel lifted the latch on the gate that opened into the meadow. I followed as he took Willie's hand and led him around the pond to the side of the cottage mill, where the huge moss-covered wheel creaked and turned, lifting the water and dropping it in a cascade on the other side.

Daniel knelt down again. "You see, this is like a big wheel, the biggest wheel you've ever seen. And as it turns in the water, it moves the water, and picks it up, and spins it around, and that creates a force in the water, a power that can make things go. Can make machines go."

"Really?" said Willie.

"Really," said Daniel.

"My Papa can make baptie in the water," said Willie solemnly.

Daniel looked at him, and a shadow darkened his face. "I know he can."

"And when I grow up, I can baptie, too."

Daniel looked up at me, and our eyes met.

"I'll bet you can," said Daniel, standing up. "Would you like to feed the ducks?"

Willie looked up at him and smiled, squinting in the sun. "I would like to feed the ducks," he said.

Daniel walked onto the porch of the mill cottage and scooped a container of feed out of a burlap bag. He came back down to us and handed the container to Willie. "Now you must feed them very slowly, just a few bits at a time. Make it last as long as you can."

"Stand back from the water, Willie," I said.

"Throw it way out on the water," said Daniel. "As far as you can." He showed Willie how to throw it, then took me by the elbow, and led me over to the fence, a few yards away.

He smoothed back my hair, and ran his hand over my face. We stood inches apart, looking into each other's eyes.

"I was such a fool," he said. "Such a heartless, thoughtless, stupid fool."

I bowed my head, not speaking. He put his hand under my chin and lifted my face to his.

"Can you ever, ever forgive me?" His eyes looked ancient and tired and infinitely sad. I wanted to pour a cool liquid balm of healing love into them.

I swallowed. "I thought you didn't care, that you never cared. You said—"

"I know what I said." He looked back over his shoulder at Willie, then moved closer to me. He bit his lip, looking down at the ground, then off into the distance, then back at me. He took a deep breath. "The day that my mother left was like any other day," he said. "She kissed me good-bye as she always did before she went off to the mill, then stopped at the door, and turned around, and came back to me. She knelt down, and put her arms around me. 'I love you, Danny,' she said to me. And

I'd never heard her say that to me before. And then she said, 'Tell me you love me. Say, "I love you, Mother." Say it.' And I said it. I said, 'I love you, Mother.' And she cried, and hugged me, and walked out the door. And that was the last time I ever saw her. And from that moment to this, I have never said 'I love you' to another living being." His voice cracked, and his eyes filled up. They burned into me as he said, "I love you."

"I love you," I whispered, raising my hand to his cheek. He closed his eyes, as if in pain, and covered my hand with his, turning my palm to his lips. Our foreheads touched, and he whispered, "I can't live without you. Whatever it takes, whatever we have to do. Don't leave me."

I held him as we rocked and swayed together.

"Come with me," he said. "Bring Willie. I swear to God I'll try to be a good father to him. I want you both."

I drew back and searched his face.

"I mean it," he said. "Come with me to Paris. I can arrange it. We can leave on Sunday."

My insides expanded with a surge of pure joy.

He kissed me then. And in that kiss all the pain and passion and hope and fear melded, merged, and fused us together for the past and the future and all eternity.

"Come upstairs with me," he whispered. "Come upstairs with me. I need you."

I looked over his shoulder at Willie, still throwing feed to the ducks.

"But, Willie?" I looked back at Daniel questioningly.

"We'll put him in the yard with the swing. There's a ball in there. He can play by himself for a few minutes." He looked at me, questioning. "Can't he?" he said, trying to draw a smile out of me.

My mind was spinning with elation and desire and a sense of unreality.

I turned to Willie. "Willie," I called. "Finish feeding the ducks, and you can play on the swing for a little while."

Willie shook the last bits of seed from his hand and threw down the container. He ran over to us.

"Where's the swing?" he said.

"It's over there," said Daniel, pointing across the lane. "In the yard. Come along, I'll show you."

Willie ran ahead, through the open gate and across the lane. Daniel and I strolled after him, arm in arm. Just before we got to the gate, he pulled me to him and kissed me again, backing me up to the fence. "How I've wanted you. Missed you."

"Come on, Mama!" called Willie.

My knees were weak. I was drowning with desire. I had the fleeting thought that it was all right if Willie saw me being affectionate with Daniel now. Now that we were all three going to be together.

"I'm coming," I called. Breathlessly, I pushed Daniel away. "Wait," I whispered, "Wait until we get upstairs." In a daze, I followed him through the gate and across the lane, where Willie waited. Daniel lifted the rope that held the gate, and we walked into the yard and over to the towering oak tree where the swing hung.

"Can you climb up here?" he said to Willie. The swing was low, and Willie had no trouble arranging his bottom on the wooden seat. Daniel pushed him a few times, and said, "I need to talk to your Mama for a few minutes. Up there." He pointed toward the studio.

Willie, still swinging, looked dubious.

"I'll be right up there, honey. Just for a minute. If you need me, you just call, and I'll hear you."

Daniel reached down and picked up a red ball that lay in the grass. "And here's a ball that you can play with." He tossed it over toward Willie. It rolled on the dirt under Willie's feet, and he laughed as he swayed back and forth on the swing, his chubby hands clutching the ropes, his head straining up toward the top of the tree.

"I'll be right back," I said. "I love you."

I'll be right back. I love you.

Daniel and I left Willie swinging in the yard, and hurried up the slope and climbed the stairs to the studio. When we reached the top, he slammed the door behind us and pulled me to him. Our fingers shook as we unbuttoned the rest of my bodice together. He tugged at my chemise until my breasts were bare. He moaned as he took them in his mouth, one after the other. Frantically, he unlaced my corset, and I felt myself loosed and deliciously free. His hands lifted my skirt, and he sank to his knees. I bent forward, clutching his head with both my hands, shuddering with the thrill of it, the feel of him lapping me up. He pulled me down to the floor, and I lay back, making little cries of pleasure. The room began to spin, and I arched my back in delicious agony. Then he drew back, and before I could feel his absence, he plunged himself into me, crying out as he began to move smoothly, rhythmically, magically, burning himself into my core, filling me, feeding me, saving me.

We exploded together in a dazzling eruption of color and thunder and molten heat.

And then I was drowning, drowning in the feel of him, and the taste of him, and the smell of him.

I was drowning in the love of him.

We lay there together, trembling and sweating and breathless.

Eventually I gently pulled myself away, saying, "I have to check on Willie."

He playfully pulled me back down. I laughed, disentangling myself. "Later," I said, kissing his nose.

I stood up and walked, naked, to the French doors and looked out.

"Willie!" I called.

There was no answer.

"Willie?"

My eyes searched the length of the yard. The swing was still, and there was no sign of him.

"Willie!" I called again, leaning over the balcony and straining to see up and down the lane. My bicycle lay against the fence where I had left it.

The red ball lay against the fence post beside the bicycle.

"Willie!" I screamed, running back into the studio. Daniel was buttoning his trousers. I threw on my knickers and stepped into my dress, tripping over the hem.

"What?" he said. "What's the matter?"

I flung open the door and pounded down the stairs. "I can't see him!" I called over my shoulder. "Willie!" I screamed as I threw open the outside door and ran down the path. Daniel raced past me out into the lane. He looked up and down, then saw the ball and ran over to the fence.

The gate to the pond was open.

I stood at the foot of the path, unable to make my legs move.

Daniel raced through the gate and dove into the pond.

"Oh, my God, no," I whimpered. "Oh, my God, please, no."

Daniel burst out of the water, gasping, then disappeared again.

"No, no, no, no, no, Willie, please God, no."

There was no way I could breathe while Daniel was underwater. No way I could stand while Daniel was underwater. I staggered toward the open gate. He came up again and went under again, the ripples making tiny waves in a circle around him.

Then I realized from someplace far away that I didn't want him to come up again. As long as he stayed underwater, everything was fine. Willie was somewhere other than at the bottom of the pond. He was down the lane, chasing the rooster, or hiding in the little manger, or picking flowers down by the creek. He could be anywhere on this clear, hot, sunny afternoon. This happy day of sapphire-blue skies and puffy white clouds, and crowing roosters, and floating ducks, and tinkling lamb bells, and swaying swings, and promises of a future filled with light and love. This day when my life stretched before me like a magic carpet. This day when my love, my own true love, pledged his heart to me forever.

But Willie is my own true love.

My only true love.

From some distant place I watched as Daniel dragged himself out of the pond, gasping and heaving.

In his arms, something.

Something very small and limp and lifeless.

My own true love.

He laid him down on the grass and knelt over him, pushing down on his little body, trying to breathe his breath into him. I wanted to breathe my breath into him, but I had no breath, and I was glad that Daniel was there, breathing his breath into him. Because Daniel's breath was my own. And Willie's breath was mine, too. He came out of me, and that made my breath his. But I didn't have any breath for him right now, and that's why he would need Daniel's, and that was all right.

I watched Daniel lean over him, my hand on the fence post. Just outside the gate.

He would move soon, I knew. He would breathe Daniel's breath and then take his own breath, and stir, and move, and sit up, and look over at me, and smile, and say, "Mama!" And I would smile back at the round ocean blue of his eyes. And then he would say, "When I grow up, I'm going to baptie like Papa." And I would walk over to him and lift him in my arms, oh, he was getting so heavy! And I would hug him and say, "Yes, when you're a big boy, you can baptize like Papa, or maybe be a great painter like Mr. Duvall. You can be anything you want to be." And I would swing him around and bury my face in his neck, and we would go around and around and around and around until we were dizzy and we fell on the ground together in a heap, laughing and looking up at the sky.

My head buzzed, and it was only me looking up at the sky. The pretty puffy white clouds floating and drifting. So clean against the heavenly blue.

Daniel hovered over me, blocking the clouds, a huge, dark presence. "The clouds," I said. "I can't see the clouds. I can't see heaven."

"He's gone, Angel." He dripped water on me, or maybe it was tears, but it didn't matter because I couldn't see heaven.

He lifted my head and cradled me in his arms. I heard sobbing sounds, and I didn't know where they came from, but I could feel Daniel's cold, wet body shuddering as he rocked me back and forth in his arms.

But then I had to get up to go to my baby, my own true love, and I twisted myself out of Daniel's arms, but he was all wet anyway, and I didn't want him against me, so I stood up, and walked over to where my baby lay on the grass, so still, so still.

And I very gently scooped him up in my arms, and he was wet, too, very wet, and his flat curls smelled like pond water, and his skin was cool, and his eyes were not quite closed, and I could almost see the sweet ocean blue of them. And his lips were a beautiful shade of purple blue and just the slightest bit apart. I could see his little tongue and the rows of perfect white teeth. And I pressed my lips on his. They were cold. So I pressed my cheek against his. And it was cold. And I took his hand between my hands, and rubbed and rubbed. And, oh, that little hand was limp in mine.

And then his head rolled back against the crook of my arm, and he was suddenly so heavy! So heavy that I had to lay him down on the ground, and lie down next to him, and take him into my arms that way, and in that way, we could both look up and try to see past the clouds to heaven.

We stayed like that for a long time, looking at heaven.

At some point Daniel came over to where we were, and he lay down beside us and put his arms around us, and we lay there. Daniel's voice came to me from far away. His arms were still around me, that much I knew. And my arms were still around Willie. But the sky was no longer blue. It was gray and angry, and heavy drops of rain were beginning to fall on us.

"Angel." It was the gentlest voice I had ever heard. "We're going to take Willie home now."

TWENTY-SEVEN
C H A P T E R

1996

I hear the screen door close quietly, and then Victor drags a chaise lounge onto the grass next to me. Before he sits down, he leans over and kisses me gently on the lips. "Need anything?" he asks.

"Mm-mmm," I say, shaking my head.

The lawn chair creaks as he stretches out on it.

"How is he?" I ask.

Victor chuckles. "He kept saying, 'I love you, man. You're like a dad to me.'"

"He did? That's kind of sweet."

"Yeah, let's see how he feels about in the morning when I give him a father-to-son lecture."

"Thanks for taking over."

"Happy to do it," he says, reaching for my hand. "Part of what I wanted to talk to you about, actually."

"What do you mean?"

He sits upright and swings his legs over the chair, moving closer to me. "Morgan, I know I'm no prize. I'm moody and I tend to retreat just when I should be advancing. But I want you to know these last months have been life altering for me. When we decided to do the documentary together, I have to admit, I thought you were smart and attractive, and entertained the possibility that a dalliance might be part of the project. But then it veered off into this…crazy…intense…series of impossible coincidences…and then we were in France, and the insanity at Giverny, with seeing the paintings…and my own emotions terrified me…I didn't recognize myself. And that kid of yours…" He nods toward the upstairs window. "He was such a challenge. It was as if I was jousting with him for your attention. Everything was this…this male dance. He was such a pain in my ass."

Victor leans back into the chair as he continues.

"But gradually everything changed. The way he literally saved my life when I was electrocuted…the way he took care of me when we shared the room…his respect and capacity to learn. What I'm saying is, you have a great kid there. Despite what happened tonight, he's a great kid, and this may sound nuts, but I feel as close to him as if he were my own son."

"Victor, I don't know what to say—"

"Don't say anything. This is my speech. No matter what happens with the documentary, I've gotten something out of it that I never thought I'd have. A family."

I cannot believe what I'm hearing, yet I know he means every word. He sits back up again then, and I sit up too. Our knees touch, and he places his hands on my shoulders.

"Morgan, I don't want to let that go, ever. I love you. I'm in love with you. I think I've felt that way all along, but I never was able to process it, because so many crazy things kept happening. The intensity of it was more than I could handle sometimes. I didn't trust the feelings. So I backed off."

He looks at me so earnestly, as if trying to gauge my reaction.

"Am I making any sense here? Am I completely off base?"

I can't articulate the surge of happiness that I feel. I just shake my head, and say, "No, no…You're not off base."

"This is corny as hell. You'll probably laugh at me, but I feel we're kindred spirits. In you I think I've found my soul mate. Now, please, say you love me, so I know I haven't made a complete jackass out of myself."

I put my arms around him, drawing in the welcome, familiar male smell of him, feeling his solid shoulders, the thickness of his arms. "I love you! Oh, I love you! Of course I do!"

"Do you think we could be a family? I'm talking, official. Living together, seeing each other through death, the whole nine yards. I'll even marry you, if that's what you want."

"I don't care," I say, holding onto him. "As long as you love me, I don't care how it plays out."

He kisses me then, and we tumble out of the chairs, onto the grass, the soft, sweet-smelling lush bed of grass, where we make love, solemnly at first, almost reverently. Then with increasing intensity and passion. How many "I love you's" are exchanged I can't say, but at last, Victor covers us with our discarded clothes, and we drift to sleep in each other's arms on the dampening grass.

In my dream, we were at a barbecue. Chad and Victor were cooking on the grill, like they had the first night they met. I knelt down in the garden and picked a huge ripe tomato, but when I pulled it off the vine, it burst in my hand, and my hand was covered in blood. I walked to the grill to tell Chad and Victor what had happened, and when I looked over Victor's shoulder, I saw what they were barbecuing.

"What is it?" I said.

"It's the lamb," said Chad. "The lamb from the bottom of the pond."

I sit up like a shot, with my heart thudding in my chest. My throat is parched, and there's an acrid smell in the air. I twist myself away from Victor and catch an odd reflection of undulating light on the roof of the barn. I stand and turn toward the house. Thick black smoke is swirling from Chad's window, blackening the white clapboards of the house. I shriek.

"Chad! Oh, my God! Chad! Victor!"

Victor is instantly awake and realizes what was happening.

"You get Madame out!" he says. "I'll get Chad."

He pulls on his pants and takes off at a run toward the front of the house. "Call 911!" he shouts over his shoulder.

I pull his shirt around me and scramble into the kitchen, banging on Madame's door.

"Madame! Madame! Wake up! There's a fire!"

I push her door open just as she sits up in bed, looking dazed.

I grab her robe at the foot of the bed and wrap her in it while I help her up. She seems too confused to speak as I herd her out the back door.

"Get away from the house!" I say. "Get far away. I'm calling 911."

The kitchen is very hot. I can literally feel the fire above me. I reach for the phone and just as quickly drop it. It's too hot to touch. I frantically try to remember where I've left my cell phone. I race back outside and around to the front of the house, where Madame cowers on the lawn, gazing up at the flames, now shooting through the roof on the north side of the house, which includes Chad's room and the editing room.

"Go next door and call 911!" I shout to her. I clamber up to the porch and pull open the screen door. There's smoke everywhere. I try to see up the stairs, frantic for the sight of Victor and Chad.

"Victor!" I scream. "Victor!"

Through the black smoke, I hear coughing, then Victor's voice at the top of the stairs. "I've got him!"

"Oh, God!" I cry, "Oh thank God. Is he all right?" Through watering, burning eyes, I see Victor and Chad emerging from the smoke, Victor carrying an unconscious Chad down the stairs, past me, and out of the house. He staggers halfway down the lawn and lays Chad on the grass. I kneel down next to him.

Somewhere in the distance I hear the wail of sirens.

"He needs oxygen," says Victor, panting from exertion. "But I think he'll be okay."

He leans over, out of breath, and presses his hands against his knees, coughing deep, rasping coughs.

"Give me the shirt," he says, reaching for the shirt I'd wrapped around me. Too stunned to protest, I comply and sit naked on the grass, watching him race around the house to where the hose is connected. He douses the shirt with water, and before I realize what's happening, he runs back up the steps to the porch. I jump up and run after him.

"What are you doing?" I shout.

"I'm going back in. For the doc!" He holds the wet shirt up to his face.

"What?" I grab his arm. "No! You can't go in there!"

"It's our story!" he shouts, yanking his arm away. "I'm saving it!"

"Victor, No!" I scream. But he pushes past me and into the house. I see his form rise up the stairs like a phantom disappearing into hell.

At that moment, the swirling lights of the fire engines commingle with the light of the fire, and I'm suddenly surrounded by people in yellow helmets and heavy coats. Someone wraps a blanket around my naked shoulders.

"My son!" I shout, crying and trembling. "He needs oxygen!"

"We're taking care of it, ma'am. You just come on over here out of the way." It's a woman, a young girl, really, no more than twenty. She wears a helmet and all the firefighting regalia.

She leads me down the lawn to where an EMT team works on Chad. They've placed an oxygen mask over his face. His eyes are open, and he's stirring. My knees almost give out with relief. But then I turn back toward the house, shouting to whomever will listen, "Victor went back in! He went upstairs!"

"Someone else is in the house?" says the young girl.

"Yes! He went upstairs to get the DVD! Somebody! Help him! He went to the bedroom in the back on the left!"

There are shouts then, and a team of firefighters descends on the house. One group raises a ladder along one side, all the way up to the roof. The other team, armed with axes, heads into the house through the front door. A third team runs toward the back.

"Please help him!" I scream. "Please, somebody help him!" My throat is raw, my eyes riveted on the front door, willing Victor to appear.

Just then, I hear a "vrooom" like thunder, and a huge explosion erupts through the roof on the north side.

I watch as billows of brilliant orange flames rumble and lick their way toward heaven. A massive balloon of sparks follows, propelled upward like a thousand glittering stars soaring toward home. I follow one dazzling ember until it disappears and dissolves into the darkness.

Victor is gone.

Epilogue

After the funeral, I went back to Giverny with Madame. Chad came too.

We could have stayed at Victor's farm, I guess, but it would have been too painful.

In the meantime, there was so much to do before we left. At Victor's house, Madame and I found his beat-up leather address book. He'd mentioned a sister who lived in Charleston, and I found her number and called her. She and her husband arrived the next day and made arrangements for Victor's burial. When I suggested that we put him in the Milltown cemetery, they agreed. It's not as if he had any connection to Charleston. They hired a lawyer to deal with the property, with Victor's estate. How odd and cold those words sound: Victor's "estate." But that's all it was now.

So Chad and I went to Giverny with Madame, and after a few weeks, Chad took off on his own to travel around Europe. I hated to see him go but believed it was best for him. He needed to grieve in his own way. I couldn't expect him to hang around me forever. I was such a mess.

Madame was a patient, gentle, encouraging friend. She listened to me when others might have grown tired of hearing the same lament over and over. She made me tea, and handed me tissues, and took me on long walks, and fed me rich, comforting meals. My friend Kate came out to visit often, and sometimes I returned to Paris with her to spend a few days here and there. The change of scene didn't help much.

By the end of November, I was obligated to go back to Milltown to check on the progress of the Rectory. The reconstruction was almost complete, and I had to decide whether to sell the house or continue to live there. Luckily, by then Chad had returned from his backpacking sojourn, and we flew back to the States together.

Before I left Giverny, Madame sat me down and shared with me the terms of her will. After her death, she intended to have part of the house and the studio of paintings turned into a museum. She was appointing me conservator and hoped that I would consider being the curator of the museum, which would mean that I would have to live there permanently. She also told me she was bequeathing a painting to me, the one called, "Angel," and to Chad, the one of Willie and Angel playing near the manger. Moved to tears, I thanked her profusely but told her I wasn't in any shape to even contemplate her demise, and though I was flattered, it was far too soon to make a decision about one day moving to Giverny.

I had to brace myself to drive down Holicong Road into the village of Milltown, even with Chad beside me. We were both emotional as we turned into the driveway of the Rectory, each with our own memories of that awful night. Chad wore his guilt like a hair shirt. The fire had begun with a cigarette that he'd lit, then dropped to the floor when he passed out. The faulty electrical wiring in the edit room, the one I'd been warned about, had then triggered an inferno.

The reconstruction on the house was almost finished. The outside was freshly painted. It was as if nothing had happened here.

Chad stationed himself on the front lawn, shivering in the cold, with his hands in his pockets, just staring up at the refurbished second floor.

I wandered around to the back, pausing at the lilac bush, Angel's beloved lilac bush, now bereft of blossoms. It stood just beneath the second floor window. I looked up at that window, with its sturdy new frames, the new panes of glass shiny in the afternoon sun. I leaned into the thicket of green leaves, closing my eyes, trying to conjure the lost fragrance of masses of swollen lavender blossoms, of the days and nights of magical mystical May, the season of possibilities. Gone now, all of it.

As I drew away, a flash of sunlight glinted off something wedged in the base of the bush. I knelt down and pushed the lower branches of the undergrowth aside. I reached my hand deep into the cluster of roots. There was something there. I pulled it out.

It was the DVD Master of the documentary. Victor must have tossed it out the window before he died. Though its plastic case was melted in one corner, the DVD had been protected from the elements. It was pristine.

With the addition of a few graphics, we dedicated the documentary to Victor.

Then, with the permission of the Historic Society, which was thrilled that the documentary existed, we entered *The Angel Collection* in several film festivals, where it garnered excellent reviews.

Eventually it sold to a major cable network. Last week it aired. Chad and his new girlfriend, Amelia, the young firefighter, watched it with me. When the credits rolled, we drank a champagne toast to Victor. Or rather, Amelia and I drank champagne. Chad toasted with iced coffee.

I don't sleep well. But on the exceptional nights when sleep does come, it comes swiftly and deeply. I find myself cartwheeling down, down into the purple velvet edge of time, where I am finally at peace, resting in the arms of my beloved. Together we tumble deeper, gathering speed as we roll, tightly enmeshed, a tangle of arms and legs, spiraling into the inky depths, melded whiteness cocooned in black, sighing and climaxing in an awesome and awful shudder as we drift silently toward a bottomless eternity. Then in a contentment so vast, so complete and so perfect, I once again see his face, the face I've carried with me since time's beginning, the face of my beloved:

Daniel!

Author's note:

The entry below was written four days before Angel's death.

Giverny

March 23, 1952

I am painting my self-portrait. An exercise in masochisme, non? The somber reflection that gazes back at me from the mirror is my judge and jury. But I do not flinch, though I am well beyond that euphemistic "Une femme d'un certain âge." The truth is all I have left of my past.

Maybe they'll put this final canvas in a museum with the others. Next to his. That would please me very much.

My knuckles are so swollen with arthritis that I must hold the brush tentatively. But my strokes are confident. I keep a kettle of water on a hot plate next to me, and when the stiffness sets in, I wrap my fingers around the warmth of it for a few minutes and then return to the canvas and the mirror, the canvas and the mirror. My life is splashed all over my face like a maquillage that has been left on long after the party has ended. Its passion and betrayal, scandal and triumph have dried and caked and settled into furrows and creases, lines and shadows. And the exquisite loss that bleeds my heart to this day is there behind the hollows of my eyes. So here I am, painting my story, and vanity be damned. I am trying, despite this stiffness on my hands, to be brutally honest and precise in how I portray myself. As I was when I wrote down the words. All those years of furtive scribbling, silent screaming spattered across hundreds of pages. The journals now safely locked away deep in a vault, their dark secrets not to be revealed until it no longer matters to any living person, how it all happened and why.

Now that I'm forced to sit each day and relive the story as it is revealed in this old lady's face, it seems like just that: a story that somebody made up.

I smell spring tonight, damp and prescient. I am breathing it in through the open shutters.

Anne-Claire came yesterday for dinner and to spend the night. We had a lovely visit, but she left after lunch to return to Paris and a heavy date with her new lover called Guillaume, about whom she's positively giddy. Ah, to be young and in love, with no imaginable ending other than "happily ever after."

I confess that as I watched her little Renault turn out of the drive, spraying gravel, I felt the fullness of my love for her clogging my throat and blurring my eyes. "Au revoir," I whispered. "Au revoir, sweet girl."

Now, looking up past the leafy tips of the poplars at river's edge, I can see a piece of midnight sky embracing my two special stars. They twinkle and dance so brightly tonight, as if to taunt me: "When will you join us?"

I think it will be soon.

Acknowledgments

The first version of *The Angel Connection* (then it was titled the *Angel Collection*) was birthed in 1996. I read chunks of it to my writing group, founded by the late beloved dramatist JP Miller, author of *Days of Wine and Roses*. JP's Thursday evening classes in an old barn in Solebury Township fired and inspired me. Special thanks to Charlene Chapman, Steve Skolits, Patrick Gallagher, Loriann Fell, and Sue Dershin.

On our daily walks to the river and back, my friend Anne Carney was a great listener. Brenda Meredith answered questions about Ireland. Ned Harrington shared his trove of local village history. For a deeper sense of the history of the Pennsylvania Impressionists, I turned to the Spruance Library and James A. Michener Art Museum in Doylestown, and The Pennsylvania Academy of the Fine Arts in Philadelphia. I thank Anne Dorrian, Judy Donohue, Gale Egoville, Susie Pevaroff, and Saundra Yizzi, who were early readers.

After my move to Los Angeles, the theme of reincarnation boldly asserted itself into the original story, and the characters of Morgan, Chad, Victor, and Madame Sancerre emerged. A Rubik's Cube of reinvention ensued, with weekly critiques from my Los Angeles writing group: Mara Squar, Edwina Anderson, Michael Okin, and Alice Spring. I remain especially grateful for Mara's superb editing skills and steadfast belief in my story.

My sons, Bill Wheeler and Tom Wheeler, have provided professional guidance along the way. I marvel at their individual writing achievements and take pride in the fact that their talents are exceeded only by their integrity. In short, they are good men.

Finally, thank you to the tiny village where my muse lives and breathes; to the Paunacussing Creek and the Delaware River; to the weeping ridges and impenetrable forests; to the narrow meandering roads overhung with trees that utterly seduced me; to the ancient voices that whispered through the mist, *Follow this path. It will lead you to us.*

Judith Anne Barton
Los Angeles, 2012

24026104R00212

Made in the USA
Lexington, KY
02 July 2013